SIDE EFFECTS

Science is toil and hard work—except when it verges on miracle. When Larry O'Shawnessy Chao managed to harness the giant Ring of Charon, orbiting Pluto's only moon, to control a field of over one million gravities, he felt a touch of the miraculous . . .

Until the autocratic director of Pluto's Gravitics Research Lab tried to deny and suppress Larry's discovery, tried to keep the world from hearing of the miracle that would change everything.

In a secret experiment, Larry and a colleague conspired to leak the discovery to scientists around the Solar System. Their success was unprecedented.

But no one knew of the entity hidden in Earth's Moon, waiting for a signal—a signal tripped by Larry's innocent gravity-wave demonstration.

No one knew that signal would then tell the aliens it was time to vanish the Earth!

THE RING OF CHARON
First Book of the Hunted Earth

D1007689

ROGER MacBRIDE ALLEN

THE RING OF CHARON

THE FIRST BOOK OF THE
HUNTED EARTH

A TOM DOHERTY ASSOCIATES BOOK
NEW YORK

THE RING OF CHARON

Copyright © 1990 by Roger MacBride Allen

A Tor Book
Published by Tom Doherty Associates, Inc.
49 West 24th St.
New York, NY 10010

Cover art by Boris Vallejo

ISBN: 0-812-53014-4

First edition: December 1990

Printed in the United States of America

0 9 8 7 6 5 4 3 2 1

To Charles Sheffield—
friend, colleague, and the sanest man in this business

Acknowledgments

I would like to offer my thanks to a number of people who have been tremendously helpful on this book.

Thanks first of all to Charles Sheffield, to whom this book is dedicated. He read and critiqued *The Ring of Charon*, but it goes far past that. He deserves a lot more than a book dedication for all his kindnesses to me over the years. He is a good man, and a good friend. Read his books.

To Debbie Notkin, my editor, who rode herd on me and did that tricky thing editors must do: she forced me to be faithful to my own vision of the book, without imposing her own. She got the book focused and moving.

To my father, Thomas B. Allen, who zeroed in on the cuts that needed to be made, substantially improving the book you hold in your hands. Read his books too.

To practically everyone at Tor Books—Ellie Lang, Patrick Nielsen Hayden, Heather Wood, and Tom Doherty. They did more than publish this book. They got behind it.

And finally, thanks to the others who read over this book and kept me honest—my mother Scottie Allen, and my friend Rachel Russell.

One last thing. This book is subtitled *The First Book of the Hunted Earth*, and yes, there will be others. But this book, and the next, and all the books I have ever written or will ever write *stand alone*. You'll never pick up a book of mine and not be able to understand it without reading 37 other titles. That's a promise.

Roger MacBride Allen
April, 1990
Washington, D.C.

"Why, sometimes I've believed as many as six impossible things before breakfast."

—White Queen in *Through the Looking-Glass*
by Lewis Carroll

Table of Contents

Dramatis Personae

Note: a glossary of terms used in **The Ring of Charon** *can be found at the end of the book.*

Jansen Alter. A Martian geologist.

Sondra Berghoff. Young gravitics scientist at the Gravitics Research Station, Pluto.

Wolf Bernhardt. Night shift duty scientist at the Jet Propulsion Laboratory, later head of the U.N. Directorate of Spatial Investigation (DSI).

Larry O'Shawnessy Chao. Junior researcher at the Gravitics Research Station, Pluto.

Chelated Noisemaker Extreme, also know as *Frank Barlow.* Naked Purple radio technician.

Lucian Dreyfuss. Technician at the Moon's Orbital Traffic Control Center.

Gerald MacDougal, husband to Marcia MacDougal. Born-again Canadian exobiologist.

Marcia MacDougal, wife to Gerald MacDougal. Planetary engineer on Venus Initial Station for Operational Research (VISOR). Escaped from Naked Purple Movement in Tycho Purple Penal as a teenager.

Hiram McGillicutty. Dyspeptic staff physicist at VISOR.

Ohio Template Windbag. Maximum Windbag, or leader, of the Naked Purple Habitat (NaPurHab).

Dr. Simon Raphael. Elderly and embittered director of the Gravitics Research Station, Pluto.

Mercer Sanchez. A Martian geologist.

Dianne Steiger. Pilot of the cargo tug *Pack Rat*. Later, captain of the *Terra Nova*.

Tyrone Vespasian. Director of the Moon's Orbital Traffic Control Center.

Dr. Jane Webling. Science Director, Gravitics Research Station, Pluto.

Coyote Westlake. Solo asteroid miner, owner of the mining ship *Vegas Girl*.

Part One

CHAPTER ONE

—◇—

The End

ONE MILLION GRAVITIES, AND CLIMBING. LARRY O'SHAW-nessy Chao grinned victoriously and leaned back in his seat to watch the show. They hadn't shut the Ring down, not yet. Maybe *this* would change some minds. *One million ten thousand gravities. One million twenty. One million twenty-five. One million thirty.* Leveling off there. Larry frowned, reached forward and twitched the vernier gain up just a trifle, working more by feel and intuition than by calculation.

It was lonely, deathly quiet in the half darkness of Control Room One of the Gravitics Research Station. But then all this world of Pluto was silence. Larry ignored the stillness, the gnawing hunger in his stomach, the bleariness in his eyes. Food and sleep could come later.

The numbers on the readout stuttered downward for a moment, then began their upward climb once again. *One million fifty, sixty, seventy, eighty, ninety—*

One million one hundred thousand gravities. Eleven

3

hundred thousand times more powerful than Earth-normal gravity. Larry looked at the number gleaming on the control panel: *1,100,000.*

He glanced up, as if he could see through the ceiling of the control room, through the station's pressure dome, through the cold of space to the massive Ring hanging in the sky. The Ring was where the action was, not here in this control room. He was merely poking at switches and dials. It was out *there*, on the Ring orbiting Pluto's moon Charon, thousands of kilometers overhead, that the work was being done.

A feeling of triumph washed over him. He had used that Ring, and done this. Granted, he was working in a volume only a few microns across, and the thing wasn't stable, but what the hell. Generating a field this powerful put the whole team back on track. Now even Dr. Raphael would have to admit they were well on the way to generating Virtual Black Holes, to spinning wormholes and stepping through them.

More immediately, a viable VBH would be impressive enough to solve a hell of a lot of budget problems. Maybe even enough to make Raphael happy. Larry, though, had a hard time even imagining the director as anything but distant, cold, stiffly angry. Larry's father had been like that. There was no pleasing him, no effort that could be great enough to win his approval.

But all things were possible—*if* Larry could achieve a Virtual Black Hole. Even with this 1.1 million field, that was still a long way off. Field size and stability were still major headaches. Even as he watched, the numbers on the gravity meter flickered and then abruptly dropped to zero. The microscopic field had gone unstable and collapsed.

Larry shook his head and sighed. There went yet another massless gravity field, evaporating spontaneously. But damn it, this one had reached 1.1 million gees and had lasted all of thirty seconds. Those were breakthrough numbers, miracle numbers, no matter how much work was still left to do.

Too bad the rest of the staff was asleep. That was the trouble with getting an inspiration at 0100 hours: no witnesses, no one to celebrate with, no one to be inspired by this success and dream up the next screwball idea. But then he barely knew anyone on the staff. Even after five months here, and with such a glorious reason for doing it, he couldn't think of anyone he would dare wake up at this hour. Lonely place to be, low man on the totem pole.

Never mind. Tomorrow would be time enough. And maybe this little run would earn him enough attention so he could get to know some people. Larry stood up, stretched and made sure all the logging instruments had recorded the figures and the procedures. He ordered the computer system to prep a hard-copy report for the next day's science staff meeting, and then powered the system down.

The Observer felt something.

Brief, far-off, tantalizing. Weak, fleeting. But unquestionably, the feeling was there. For the first time in uncounted years, it felt the touch it had awaited.

The Observer did not sense with vision, and the energy was not light, but the Observer's sensations were analogous to vision. It had been in standby, in watchkeeping mode, for a long time. The something it felt was, to it, a brilliant pinpoint in the darkness, a bright but distant beacon. It correctly interpreted this to mean the source was a small, intensely powerful point of energy at great distance.

The Observer became excited. This was the signal it had waited for for so long.

And yet not precisely the signal. Not powerful enough, not well directed enough. The Observer backed down, calmed itself.

It longed to respond, to do the thing it had been bred and built to do, but the signal stimulus was not strong enough. It was under the rigid control of what, for lack of a better term, might be called its instincts, or perhaps its programming—and it had no discretion whatsoever in choosing to respond or not. It had to respond to pre- cisely the right stimulus, and not to any other.

A quiver of emotion played over it as it struggled against its inborn restraints.

But now was not the time. Not yet.

At least, not the time for action. But certainly the time to awaken, and watch more closely. Perhaps the moment for action was close.

It directed its senses toward the source of the power, and settled in to watch carefully.

Ten minutes after the run was over, Larry was out in the corridor, bone weary and feeling very much alone. The excitement of a new idea, the thrill of the chase, was starting to fade away, now that the idea had worked. Larry always felt a letdown after a victory.

Perhaps that was because even his greatest victories were hard to explain. In the world of subatomic physics, the challenges were so obscure, the solutions so tiny and intricate, that it was almost impossible for Larry to dis- cuss them with anyone outside the field. For that matter, Larry was working so far out on the edge of theory he had trouble talking shop with most people in the field.

The price you pay for genius, he thought to himself

with a silent, self-deprecating laugh. Larry was twenty-five, and starting to feel a bit long in the tooth for a boy wonder. He looked younger than his age, and the Chinese half of his ancestry showed in his face far more than the Irish half. He was a short, slender, delicate-looking young man. His skin was pale, his straight black hair cut short, his almond eyes wide and expressive. He was one of the few people aboard the station who occasionally chose to wear the standard-issue coveralls instead of his own clothes. The gray coveralls were a bit too large for him, and made him seem younger and smaller than he was. His fondness at other times for Hawaiian shirts didn't help him seem more mature. It never occurred to Larry that his appearance helped make others underestimate him.

He planted his slippered feet carefully on the Velcro carpet and started walking. Pluto's gravity, only four percent of Earth's, was tricky when you were tired. The Gravitics Research Station would be an ideal place to put artificial gravity to use, if such a fairy-tale technology were ever possible.

Fat chance of that—but the popular press had latched on to the everyday use of artificial gravity as one of the reasons for funding the station in the first place. There had been all sorts of imaginative "artist's conceptions" put about, of a research station floating on Jupiter's surface, hovering on antigravity, of full-gravity space habitats that did not have to spin. Those were at best far-off dreams, at worst spectacular bits of nonsense that made everyone look foolish as it became obvious they were all impossible.

The researchers still hadn't learned to generate a stable point-source gravity field yet. How could they hope to float a shielded one-gee field in Jupiter's atmosphere?

Nonsensical though the idea might be, Larry would have welcomed an artificial gee field under his feet just then. He was thoroughly sick of shoes with Velcro. Four-percent gravity was a nuisance, combining the worst features of zero gee and full gravity, without the merits of either. In zero gee you couldn't fall down; in a decent gee field, your feet stayed under you. Neither was true here.

Larry felt a wave of exhaustion sweep through him. He was suddenly much aware that it was three-thirty in the morning and he was billions of kilometers from home. Unbidden, the image of his hometown street back in Scranton, Pennsylvania, popped into his head. A vague depression sank down on him.

It was when he was deep in the problem that he felt happy. Solutions meant the game was over. It was like the math problems back at school. From grade school, to high school, to college and grad school, math had been his special love. Algebra, trig, calculus, and beyond. Larry had gobbled them all up. The first time he demonstrated a proof, or calculated a function, it was fun, challenging. Puzzlement would give way to understanding and triumph. But afterwards—afterwards the problems were dead to him, static, unchanging. He *knew* how they worked. From then on, working on that whole *type* of problem was anticlimactic, redundant. It was as if he were condemned to reading the same mystery novel over and over again, when he already knew the ending.

While the rest of his classmates would struggle through example after example, practicing their skills, he would be bored, rattling through the second problem, and the third, and hundredth, at record speed, while the other kids dragged behind.

Only when the professor deemed it time to move on to the next kind of problem could Larry experience even a new, brief moment of excitement.

Postgrad school and the field of high-energy physics had given him a new freedom, a place where all the problems were new, not only to him, but to everyone. There was no longer the slightly mocking knowledge that the answers were there to be found in the back of the book. But still, when he cracked the problem at hand, the letdown came.

Larry was not an introspective person, and even spotting such an obvious pattern in his behavior was an accomplishment for him. But before anyone got sent to Pluto, the psychiatrists worked hard to make that person more aware of how the mind worked. Put a bit less formally, they made damn sure that you didn't drive yourself crazy on Pluto. People kept a close eye on sanity on Pluto, watching it the way a man in his pressure suit kept an eye on his air supply.

A tiny leak in the suit could be fatal, and just so with the human mind on Pluto. One tiny weakness, one microscopic break in the armor between you and the cold and the dark, was all it took to leave good men and women watching helplessly as their own sanity dribbled away, evaporating out into the frozen wastes.

Sanity was a scarce commodity on Pluto, easily used up, carefully rationed. The oppressive sense of isolation—of being trapped in this remote place, locked away with 120 other edgy souls, with no escape possible—that was what gnawed at reason.

Not just the grimness of the planet but the knowledge that there was no way home, for months or years at a time, drew nightmares close to so many souls here.

True, there was the supply ship from home every six months. But when it departed, the denizens of the station were stranded for another half year. There was one, count it, one, ship capable of reaching the Inner System stationed at Pluto. The *Nenya* could, at need, bear the entire station staff home, but it would be a long and grueling flight of many months. Alternatively, she could gun for Earth and get there in sixteen days—but with a maximum of only five people aboard, which meant everyone else would be utterly stranded while she was gone. So far, the *Nenya* was insurance no one had used.

She could also function as an auxiliary control station for the Ring. But without the anchor of Pluto's mass to provide calibration, the *Nenya*'s Ring Control Room was not capable of the sort of fine measurement the station could get. The *Nenya*'s real value was psychological. She represented a way home, knowledge that it was possible to get back to Earth.

The Gravitics Research Station was the only human-habitable place for a billion kilometers in any direction, and every waking moment of their lives, everyone at the station was aware of that fact.

In the silence of the Plutonian night, Larry could imagine that the planet itself resented the presence of humans. Life, light, warmth, activity weren't welcome here, in this land of unliving cold. Larry shivered at the mere thought of the frigid desolation outside the station.

Without making any conscious decision to go there, he found himself walking toward the observation dome. He needed to get a look outside, a look at the sky.

The darkness, the emptiness, the coldness that surrounded the windowless station preyed on all their minds. The station designer had known all that, and had made sure the station was brightly lit and painted in cheery colors. But the designers had also known it was important for the staff to be able to look on the empty landscape, the barren skyscape; perhaps more importantly, the station staff needed to be able to look toward the distant Sun, needed to use the small telescope in the observation dome to spot the Earth, needed to be able to prove to themselves that light and life and the warm, busy, lively homeworld were still there.

And so is all the weirdness, Larry reminded himself. All the raucous, angry pressure groups, unsure of what they were for, but certain of what they were against. They were a big part of his memory of MIT, and they had frightened him. And scared him worse when they had showed up back home in Pennsylvania. But then, they frightened a lot of people. And in the wake of the half-imaginary Knowledge Crash, the rad groups were spreading.

Larry made his way down the darkened access tunnel to the dome building. The route was long, and he had to find his way there by touch. The way to the dome was deliberately left in darkness, so that a person's eyes would have the length of time it took to pass through the tunnel to adapt to the gloomy darkness of the Plutonian surface.

At last he stepped out into the large, domed room. It was a big place, big enough for the entire staff to crowd in for important meetings.

Larry stepped to the edge of the room and looked through the transparent dome at the world around him.

In stillness, in silence, the sad gray landscape of Pluto was laid out before him, dimly seen by the faintness of starlight.

Virtually all of the land he could see would have been liquid or gas, back on Earth. Pluto's surface was made of frozen gases—methane, nitrogen, and traces of a few other light elements. All the surface features were low and rounded, all color subdued. To the west, a slumped-over line of yellowish ammonia-ice hills had somehow thrust its way up out of the interior.

Elsewhere on Pluto, a thin, bright frosting of frozen methane blanketed the land. Only at perihelion, a hundred years from now, would the distant Sun be close enough to sublimate some of the methane back out into a gas.

But here, on this plain, the methane snow was cooked away by waste heat from the station, exposing the dismal grayish brown landscape below. Here, water ice, carbon compounds, veins of ammonia ice, and a certain amount of plain old rock made up the jumbled surface of Pluto, just as they made up the interior. No one yet had developed a theory that satisfactorily explained how Pluto had come to be made that way, or accounted for the presence of Pluto's moon, Charon.

Larry stared out across the frozen land. The insulation of the transparent dome was not perfect. He felt a distinct chill. Ice crystals formed on the inside of the dome as he exhaled.

Not all the landscape was natural. Close to the horizon, the jagged, shattered remains of the first and second attempts to land a station lay exposed to the stars. Larry knew the tiny graveyard was there as well, even if it was carefully hidden, out of sight of the dome.

The design psychologists had protested vehemently against building again in view of the first two disastrous attempts, but there had been no real choice in the matter. Both of the earlier stations had collapsed to the ground and shattered, like red-hot marbles dropped into ice water. But cleaning up the wreckage would have been prohibitively expensive and dangerous—and perhaps not possible at all.

This small valley was the only geothermically stable site in direct line of sight with the Ring. Here was an upthrust belt of rock that, unlike the water-ice and methane, could support the weight of the station without danger of melting. Even with the best possible insulation and laser-radiative cooling, the station's external skin temperature was a hundred degrees Kelvin. That was cold enough to kill a human in seconds, freeze the blood in the veins—but flame hot compared to the surrounding surface, hot enough to boil away the very hills.

This was the only site where the underlayer of rock was close enough to the surface to serve as a structural support. Anywhere else, the heat of the station would have melted the complex straight through the surface.

If this station held together long enough to sink, Larry reminded himself, staring at the sad wreckage on the horizon. *The first two didn't.*

But this station had been here fifteen years. So far, the third try had been the charm.

So far.

Larry tore his eyes away from the wreckage strewn about the landscape and glanced toward the telescope. It was a thirty-centimeter reflector, with a tracking system that kept it locked on the tiny blue marble of Earth whenever the planet was above the local horizon. You could bring up the image on any video monitor in the station, but nearly everyone felt the need to come here on occasion, bend over the eyepiece, and *see* the homeworld with his or her own eyes.

There was something reassuring about seeing Earth direct, without any electronic amplification, without any chance of looking at a tape or a simulation, to see for certain that Earth, and all it represented, was truly there, not a mad dream spun to make Pluto endurable.

Larry leaned over and took a look. The telescope was set on low magnification at the moment. There she was, a tiny dot of blue, the bright spark of Earth's Moon too small to form a disk. Larry stepped away from the telescope after only a moment. He was looking for something else in the sky tonight. He needed to see the Ring. The mighty Ring of Charon.

Pluto does not travel the outer marches of the Solar System by himself. The frozen satellite Charon bears the god of the Underworld company. Charon, with an average diameter of about 1,250 kilometers, is, in proportion to the planet it circles, larger than any other satellite. It rides a very close orbit around Pluto, circling the ninth planet every 6.4 days.

The rotation of both satellite and world are tidally locked: just as Earth's Moon always shows the same face to Earth, so Charon always shows the same face to Pluto. The difference is that Pluto's rotation is likewise affected, its rotation synchronized to match its satellite's orbit. Viewed from Charon, Pluto does not seem to rotate, but presents one unchanging hemisphere.

Thus, from those points on the surface where Charon is visible at all, Charon hangs motionless in Pluto's sky. The satellite is so close to the planet that it sits below the horizon from more than half the planet's surface.

None of that mattered to Larry. He did not even notice the dark shadow of Charon brooding there, blotting out the stars. He had eyes for only one object in that sky.

Encircling Charon was the Ring, its running lights gleaming in the dark sky, a diadem of jewels set about Pluto's moon. Sixteen hundred kilometers in diameter, the largest object ever built by humans, it girdled the tiny world of Charon.

Larry felt the wonder of it all steal over him again. It was a remarkable piece of engineering, no matter how much it cost. It was the reason so much time and treasure, so much effort, so many lives had been spent landing the Gravitics Research Station on Pluto and making it operational. Compared to the cost of the Ring, the cost of placing the station on Pluto was pocket change. An orbital facility would have been cheaper, but the need for precise measurement forced them to operate the Ring from a planetary surface, a stabilized reference point.

The Ring was face-on to Pluto, showing a perfect circle around the gloom-dark gray of Charon, a gleaming band of gold about a gloomy, lumpen world, a world so small and light that it had never completely formed into a sphere. Indeed, its tidal lock with Pluto had distorted its shape, warping it into an egg-shaped thing, with one long end pointed at Pluto.

The Ring was the largest particle accelerator ever built—all but certainly the largest that ever *would* be built. Designed to probe the tiniest, most subtle intersections of matter and energy, it was so large and powerful that it had to be built *here*, on the borderlands of the Solar System. It was around Charon not only to escape the disturbing influence of the Sun's radiation and the strong, interwoven gravity fields of the Inner System, but also to prevent its interfering with the inner worlds: it was capable of achieving enormous energies.

And, as Larry had proven once again tonight, it was capable of generating and manipulating the force of gravity.

No other machine ever built was capable of that. The ability to manipulate gravity should have been enough to keep the research station going. Basic research could be done here that would be impossible anywhere else.

But try convincing the funding people back at the U.N. Astrophysical Foundation. They were too focused on the pie-in-the-sky dreams of near-term gravity control.

Larry blamed Dr. Simon Raphael for that. When he had been appointed director, back when Larry was in elementary school, Raphael had made some pretty rash promises. Most of those damned artist's conceptions were based on Raphael's predictions of what would be possible once the research team on Pluto was able to solve the secret of gravity. Raphael had all but guaranteed a workable artificial gravity system—and now both he and the funding board were beginning to see that it wasn't going to happen.

Up until tonight, the Ring of Charon hadn't been able to maintain a gravity field of more than one gee, and even that was only ten meters across. Worse, the fields collapsed in milliseconds.

If, the U.N. Astrophysical Foundation asked, it took a piece of hardware 1,600 kilometers across to generate a puny, unstable gravity source a few meters across, and if even that giant generator was so delicate it had to be as far out from the Sun as Pluto in order to work at all, then what possible use could artificial gravity be? What conceivable purpose could gravity waves serve when they had to come from Pluto?

And Raphael wanted to go home. Everyone knew that. Larry Chao was very much afraid that the good doctor had figured out that the quickest way to do that was to shut the damn place down.

One million one hundred thousand gravities, sustained for thirty seconds. Larry stared harder at the Ring over-head and felt a thrill of pride. He had tweaked that mon-ster's tail, and forced that much power from it. Surely there could be no stronger argument in favor of stay-ing on.

The Gravitics Research Station was not at its best in the morning. Perhaps it was some holdover from the long-lost days when astronomers were Earthbound and forced to work at night.

Whatever the reason, mornings were not a pretty sight at the station. Maybe that was why Raphael scheduled science staff meetings for 0900. Maybe he enjoyed the sight of twenty or so science staff members grumbling and squinting in the morning. The hundred administra-tive, maintenance and technical staff workers were no doubt glad to miss them.

Dr. Simon Raphael sighed wearily as he pushed open the door to the conference room and sat down at the head of the table for this last full staff meeting. He echoed the chorus of greetings from the staff without really hearing them. He spread his papers out in front of him, relief and regret playing over him.

Strange, to be thinking in *lasts* already. The *last* meeting, the *last* experimental schedule to prepare, and then the *last* science summary report to prepare. Then time to pack up and download, power down and close up. Time to go home. Soon it would all be over and done with.

His hands clenched themselves into fists, and he forced them to relax, open out. Slowly, carefully, he lay his open hands palm down on the table. The voices fell silent around the table as the others waited for him to begin, but he ignored them. A few bold souls returned to their conversations. Low voices filled the room again. Raphael tried to stare a hole through a memo that sat on the table before him, a piece of paper full of words he didn't care about.

There was something dull and angry deep inside him, a sullen *thing* sitting on his soul. A sullen something that had grown there, all but unnoticed, as the years had played themselves out.

It was hate: he knew that. Hatred and anger for all of it. For the station that might as well have been a prison, for the pointless chase after gravity control, for the waste of so much of his life in this fruitless quest, for his own failure. Hatred for the funding board that was forcing him to quit, anger at the people here around this table who were fool enough to have faith in him. Hatred for the damned frozen planet and the damned Ring that had sucked the life out of him and wrecked his career.

And hatred for the Knowledge Crash. If you could hate something that might not even have happened. That was perhaps the surpassing irony: no one was ever quite sure if the Knowledge Crash had even taken place. Some argued that the very state of being uncertain whether or not the Crash had occurred proved that it had.

Briefly put, the K-Crash theory was that Earth had reached the point where additional education, improved (but more expensive) technology, more and better information, and faster communications had *negative* value.

If, the theory went on, there had not been a Knowledge Crash, the state of the world information economy would be orderly enough to confirm the fact that it hadn't happened. That chaos and uncertainty held such sway therefore demonstrated that the appropriate information wasn't being handled properly. QED, the Crash was real.

An economic collapse had come, that much was certain. Now that the economy was a mess, learned economists were pointing quite precisely at this point in the graph, or that part of the table, or that stage in the actuarial tables to explain why. Everyone could predict it, now that it had happened, and there were as many theories as predictions. The Knowledge Crash was merely the most popular idea.

But correct or not, the K-Crash theory was as good an explanation as any for what had happened to the Earth's economy. Certainly there had to be some reason for the global downturn. Just as certainly, there had been a great deal of knowledge, coming in from many sources, headed toward a lot of people, for a long time.

The cultural radicals—the Naked Purples, the Final Clan, all of them—were supposed to be a direct offshoot of the same info-neurosis that had ultimately caused the Crash. There were whole communities who rejected the overinformed lifestyle of Earth and reached for something else—anything else—so long as it was different. Raphael did not approve of the rads. But he could easily believe they were pushed over the edge by societal neuroses.

The mental institutions of Earth were full of info-neurotics, people who had simply become overwhelmed by all they needed to know. Information psychosis was an officially recognized—and highly prevalent—mental disorder. Living in the modern world simply took more knowledge than some people were capable of absorbing. The age-old coping mechanisms of denial, withdrawal, phobic reaction and regression expressed themselves in response to brand-new mental crises.

Granted, therefore, that too much data could give a person a nervous breakdown. Could the same thing have happened to the whole planet?

The time needed for the training required to do the average technical job was sucking up the time that should have gone to doing the job. There were cases, far too many of them, of workers going straight from training program to retirement, with never a day of productive labor in between. Such cases were extreme, but for many professions, the initial training period was substantially longer than the period of productive labor—and the need for periodic retraining only made the situation worse.

Not merely the time, but the expense required for all that training was incredible. No matter how it was subsidized or reapportioned or provided via scholarship or grant program, the education was expensive, a substantial drain on the Gross Planetary Product.

Bloated with information, choked with the needs of a world-girdling bureaucracy required to track information and put it to use, strangled by the data security nets that kept knowledge out of the wrong hands, lost in the endless maze of storing and accessing all the data required merely to keep things on an even keel, Earth's economy had simply ground to a halt. The world was so busy learning how to work that it never got the chance to do the work. The planet was losing so much time gathering vital data that it didn't have a chance to put the data to use. Earth's economy was writhing in agony. Both the planet generally, and the U.N. Astrophysical Foundation specifically, could scarcely afford necessities. They certainly could not afford luxuries—especially ones that could only add to the knowledge burden. Such as the Ring of Charon.

His heart pounding, Raphael's vision blurred for a moment, and he glared unseeingly at the paper clenched in his fist. Anger. Hatred. For the Crash, for the Board, for the Ring, for the staff—

And for himself, of course. Hatred for himself.

Marooned out here all these years, with but the rarest and briefest of pilgrimages home, trapped all that time on this rotting iceball, with that damned Ring staring down at him, the satellite Charon framed inside it, the dark blind pupil of a sightless eye, pinning him to the spot in its unblinking gaze, a relentless reminder of his failure.

The project, the station, the Ring had failed to crack the problem he had staked his reputation on. Practical gravity control was flat-out impossible. That fact he was sure of. He had certainly paid enough for that knowledge. Paid for it with his life's work.

He forced himself to be calm and looked around the table at the people. He knew that he should think of them as *his* people; he had tried for a long time to do so. But *they* were the ones that he, Raphael, had failed. *They* were the source of his guilt, and he hated them for it. For in his chase after artificial gravity, he had dragged their lives down with his.

They were the ones most harmed by his failure. The last transport ship had arrived and immediately departed for home five months before, delivering the newest recruits and taking home a lucky few. Raphael remembered few things as clearly as the faces of the stay-behinds, watching the transport head for home, leaving them behind, stranded on Pluto until the next ship came, a few wistful glances skyward at the *Nenya*'s parking orbit.

Now they would all be going home.

Going home marked as failures, on a four-month journey that would offer them little more than time to brood.

Another wave of anger washed over him, and he called the meeting to order. "Ladies and gentlemen, if we could please get started," he said. There was something that bespoke patience above and beyond the call of duty in his gravelly voice, as if he had been sitting there waiting for order for far longer than was proper. The people around the table, chastened, stopped their low conversations.

Sondra Berghoff leaned back in her seat and watched the man go to work. Raphael-watching was something of a hobby for her. She knew what was coming, or at least she had made a fairly shrewd guess. She was interested in seeing how Raphael would handle it, how he would play the room. The man was a past master of emotional blackmail, a prize manipulator—there was no question about that.

"I propose to dispense with the normal meeting procedures today, if that is acceptable to you all," Raphael said, pausing just a bit too briefly for anyone to have a chance to object. "I have a rather significant announcement to make, which I believe ought to take precedence over other matters. As per the lasergram I received from Earth this morning, I must now direct you to commence shutdown of this facility."

There was a moment of stunned silence, and then a buzz of voices raised in protest. Sondra sighed. She had expected it, but she wasn't happy about it. Dr. Raphael started speaking, a calculated half beat early once again, before someone had the chance to collect his or her wits enough to speak up. "If I *could* continue," he went on, with a warning edge to his voice. "As you all know, shutdown has been a serious possibility for some time, and I have pursued every means of preventing it. But economic problems back home—and I might add the distraction caused by certain political movements in the Earth-Moon system—are simply too much for us to overcome. The funding board feels that the massive expense of this station is not justified by the quantity or quality of your work—of *our* work." He corrected himself with great magnanimity, a gently pained expression on his face. Sondra read the meaning easily. *As your leader, I must of course willingly associate myself with your work, however inadequate it might be. Such are the trials of leadership.* Everyone in the room understood *that* subtext. "The people back home simply expected too much. Unrealistic promises were made." Two or three people shifted uncomfortably in their seats, and angry scowls clouded more than one face.

Sondra herself had a bit of trouble resisting the temptation to lean across the table and punch him. *Just who made those promises, Sunshine?* she thought.

Raphael scanned the faces about the table and continued. "Of course this is unfair, and shortsighted of the board. We have done great things, and when the history of science in this century is written, the Ring will figure prominently." Nice little blind side there, Sondra decided. *Blame the funding board, blame the staff, but don't blame yourself, Raffy,* she thought.

Obviously, Raphael wanted to keep them off balance, avoid substantive debate and open discussion while being careful to maintain the appearance of those things. "We can all be proud of what we did here." Sondra noticed that Raphael was already talking about the station in the past tense. It was over already. "Some had the dream of conquering gravity, bending it to our will as electricity, fission, fusion have been put to use. But that was not to be."

It wasn't you who tried to sell that dream, no not at all. Sondra was growing weary of the charade. No doubt whipsawing people was a reflex for him, automatic, unconscious by now. Still, at some level or another, Raphael had to know what he was doing. He must know he wasn't fighting fair with that kind of buck-passing crack.

Sondra glanced around the room. Men and women bright enough to run a particle accelerator the size of a small planet likewise had to be at least somewhat aware that they were being manipulated, even as they let it happen. Surely Raphael had figured out that they knew, and surely most members of the staff had figured out that Raphael *knew* they knew, and so on and on in a weary spiral.

Possession of that knowledge did not seem to bother Raphael. Why should it? The staff members always folded, always allowed Raphael to manipulate them. Dr. Simon Raphael had been running this station by such means from day one, and it had always worked. No doubt it had worked equally well at every other operation he had ever managed. Raphael had had decades of practice bullying and manipulating.

But the questions remained: why did these people put up with it? Perhaps some calculated that cooperation was easier than battling slippery insinuations. Others had learned the hard way that going along was simpler than arguing with an unreasonable request made in a wounded tone, or disputing an impossible order dressed up to sound like the voice of long-suffering reason.

Probably most of them simply responded with the guilt-stricken impulse of a small boy accused of unspecified sins by his parents. There is something in human nature that *wants* authority to be just. It is easier to discover imagined faults in yourself rather than accept real flaws in the people that you count on, the people you have to trust. How many children find ways to blame themselves for their parents' divorce? But very few parents deliberately try to induce that guilt as a means of control—the way Raphael did.

"We must accept the fact that we have come to a dead end. Therefore," Raphael went on, "the time has come to retreat as gracefully as possible, and move on to other things."

But a new voice spoke up. "Ah, sir, perhaps not. I think I might have found an approach." Sondra looked around in surprise, and spotted the speaker at the far end of the table. That new kid, Larry Chao.

Every head in the room swiveled around to find the person who had dared to speak out. Dr. Raphael's eyes bulged out of his head, and his face went pale with anger.

"Well, that is, I haven't solved everything, but I ran an experiment last night—and well, maybe . . ." The poor kid felt the eyes on him. He was visibly running out of steam, deathly embarrassed. "I just thought that maybe my results might be good enough to impress the board, let us keep going . . ." Larry's voice faded away altogether, and he stared helplessly at Raphael.

"Chao, isn't it?" Raphael asked in the angry tones of a schoolmaster interrupted by a naughty little boy. "I am not aware of any experiment scheduled for last night."

"It . . . it wasn't *scheduled*, sir," Larry said. "It was just an idea that came to me in the middle of the night. I tried it and it worked."

"Are you aware, Chao, of the regulations regarding unauthorized use of the station's equipment? No? I thought not. You will provide me with a complete list of equipment and materials used, and the precise length of time you operated that equipment. The costs of your experiment will be calculated at the standard basis, and the total amount will be deducted from your next pay deposit. If the amount is higher than your pay—and I won't be surprised if it is—appropriate arrangements will be made to garnishee your pay for as long as is required."

Larry's face flushed and he gestured helplessly. "But sir, the results! It's *got* to be enough to convince them."

"I seriously doubt that a funding board that has decided to shut this facility down as an economy move will be persuaded to change its mind because a junior researcher saw fit to waste even more money. That will be quite enough from you, *Mr.* Chao."

Catch that real subtle point, Larry? Sondra thought. *You're still a mere* mister. *Don't you know no one is capable of actual thought unless they have at least one doctorate?*

Raphael looked around the table with a ferocious expression on his face. "Unless someone else has an equally vital contribution to make, I think we must now proceed to the logistics of the shutdown. I intend to launch the evacuation ship no later than one month from today. I propose that all department heads report back in three days, having in the meantime set the work priorities. We are instructed by the board to leave the station, the Ring, and all our facilities in standby mode. We are to 'mothball' the station, as the lasergram puts it, in the hopes that it might be reoccupied and reactivated at some future date. As there is a great deal to do, and very little time, I propose that we close this meeting now and set about planning the task ahead." Raphael hesitated a moment, as if there were the slightest chance of anyone disagreeing. "Very well, then. Department heads will meet here at 0900 hours, three days from now, with preliminary shutdown schedules prepared."

The meeting broke up, but Sondra Berghoff kept her seat, and watched the people go, all of them moving carefully in the low gravity.

None of them had spoken up.

With the whole project about to crash down about their ears, none of them had so much as lodged a protest. What, exactly, did they have to lose, if the station was lost anyway? And what sort of madness was it to ignore the Chao kid? Sure, it was a long shot, but what harm could possibly come from listening?

Probably Chao's improvements wouldn't be enough. At a guess, Chao had managed to force some minor increase in gee-force generation, to two or three gravities, or held the field together for something more than the current record of ten seconds. Well, if he had, that would be a real accomplishment and bully for him. It wouldn't be enough to change any minds, but why couldn't anyone speak up, and at least demand that he be heard?

Sondra drummed her fingers on the table. Just to pull an example out of the air, why hadn't she spoken up herself?

CHAPTER TWO

Bills to Pay

GONE. THE BRIGHT BEACON IN THE DARK WAS GONE AF-
*ter only the briefest moment. The Observer strained itself
to find the signal again, but it was not there.*

*How could it be gone? A pang of sorrow, of loneliness,
washed over it. Abandoned. Abandoned again after such
a long time. It struggled to calm itself, and resume its
aeons-long sleep.*

*But there was a small part of itself that would not
allow complete rest. A small part of it watched still.*

And hoped.

✧ ✧ ✧

Sondra stood in front of her mirror. There she was,
for what it was worth. Pudgy figure, chubby face, red
hair a mass of tight curls. She was dressed in her usual
style: a rumpled shirt of indeterminate color, shapeless
sweatpants, and Velcro-bottom slippers. But she wasn't

27

at the mirror to check her appearance. The point here was to try an age-old test. Most people meant it figuratively, but her family had made it literal. She tried to look herself in the eye.

And failed.

She remembered the first time that had happened, when she had fibbed about dipping into the cookie jar at age five. Her father had marched her into the bathroom, stood her on the sink, and forced her to look in the mirror as she repeated her childish lie. She hadn't been able to do it then, and she couldn't do it now. Of course this time she hadn't *lied*. But she failed to do right—and that came to the same thing.

She turned and left her cabin, determined to make it up.

Five minutes later, she tapped at the door to Larry's room, more than a little embarrassed, and quite unsure what she was there for. She had a guilty conscience, and Sondra had been brought up to believe in doing something about feeling guilty. Any action, any gesture to make amends, however pointless, was better than letting guilt feelings fester.

She should have spoken up at the meeting, and she hadn't. She had to do something to fix that, even if she didn't know what that something might be.

"Come in," a muffled voice said through the thin door. She pushed the door open and stepped into the little compartment. Larry was sitting up on the bed, a portable notepack computer in his lap. He looked up in surprise. "Uh, hello, Dr. Berghoff."

"Hello, Larry."

He tossed the notepack to one side of the bed and stood up, not quite sure how to make his guest welcome.

"Um, let me pull a chair out for you." He reached behind her and yanked a fold-out seat from the wall. Larry sat back down on the narrow single bed, and Sondra sat down opposite him. She had always thought of him as young, a wide-eyed kid. Probably that was true, even if it wasn't fair. Sondra herself was twenty-six, and Larry couldn't be more than a year or two younger. Sondra had unconsciously pegged him at about seventeen or so. That was patently impossible, now that she thought about it.

The station was the province of highly specialized researchers. High-energy physics was full of whiz kids— but not even a whiz kid could make it here earlier than twenty-four. It would take a certifiable genius, the sort who skipped every other grade all through his schooling, even to get here that young. Sondra herself had been the youngest-ever fellow at the station when she had arrived here two years ago. With a start, she realized Larry was just about the same age she had been at arrival.

Had she been this much of an innocent then?

She looked more closely at him. Certainly there was something about his face that made him look more youthful than he was. His wide, solemn eyes, his jet black hair trimmed in the station's standard amateur bowl-over-the-head style, his smooth, unlined skin, the oversized coveralls added to the appearance of extreme youth. Sondra was willing to bet he didn't need to shave more than once a week.

But there was more to it than that. Life had not yet put a line upon his face, or touched his expression, his eyes, his soul. There was no hint of incident, of tragedy, of pain's lessons or sorrow's teachings in his eyes.

She had no idea where he was from. He had a strong American accent to Sondra's ear, for whatever that was worth. Was he born there, or did he merely learn English from an American tutor? So much she didn't know.

And he was one of only 120 people within a billion

kilometers of here! One of only twenty scientists who sat around that science staff table at the damned weekly meetings. How could she have lived in such a small community for so long and know so little about one of the people in it? Sondra thought for a moment about some of the other people at the station, and was stunned to realize she could not put names to several of the faces.

She had once been such a people person. Pluto had turned her into a sour recluse, even as it poisoned Raphael. But it didn't seem to have touched Larry Chao at all. She looked at him and wondered what to say.

"I'm just trying to work up my usage figures for the Ring," Larry said, trying to find something to fill up the silence. His voice sounded most unhappy. "It looks like I spent the planetary debt last night. I don't know what the hell to do."

"I'll bet. Can I see your figures?" Sondra asked, grateful that Larry had given her something to talk about.

Larry shrugged. "Sure, I guess. I can't get in any deeper than I am now."

Sondra wrinkled her brow and looked at him oddly. "What do you mean by that?"

"Well, the director sent you, didn't he? To check on me?"

Sondra opened her mouth in surprise, shut it and had to start over again before she was able to speak. "Send *me*? Raphael sending *me*? The only place he'd tell *me* to go is outside without a heater or a suit."

It was Larry's turn to look surprised. "I thought you were one of his favorites. You always sit so close to him at the meetings."

Sondra grinned wickedly. "There are always plenty of seats at that end. Besides, if I sit close I can keep an eye on him. I've sort of made a hobby out of watching how he handles things."

"He sure as hell handled me," Larry said mournfully.

"Now I don't know what I'm going to do. I'll never be able to pay this back. It's more than I'll earn in my whole life. Hell, I still haven't paid back all my loans to MIT."

"Let me see how bad it is," Sondra said gently. Larry handed the notepack over to Sondra. She took one look at the figures and gasped. "Five million BritPounds! How the hell could you possibly run up that high a tab? That's more than the monthly budget for the whole station."

Larry nodded miserably. "I know. It's all down there."

Sondra paged through the cost estimate and started to feel a little better. This guy might be a genius at what he did, but he obviously didn't know from cost estimating. His price figures were astronomically high, even for an honest cost report—though Sondra did not intend Raphael to get an honest report. "This can't be right. You've got yourself down for six full hours of Ring time."

"That's how long I was at it last night. Ring time is most of the cost. I checked the accounting records in the main computer. Ring time is billed at seven hundred thousand pounds an hour."

"First off, that's the figure we use when we bill to an external experimenter. Let me check the rate for staff experimenters." Sondra worked the controls on the notepack, powered up the radio link to query the main station computers, and pulled down the answer. "Thought so. Inside work is billed out at five hundred thousand. Besides, even that's an artificial rate set up for accounting purposes. It's got nothing to do with actual costs."

"Great. That knocks one-point-two million off my tab," Larry said. He flopped back on the bed and sighed. "I should be able to scrape up the other four-point-eight million from somewhere. Ha ha. Big laugh."

Sondra looked up from her figures with a smile. The joke wasn't funny, but the attempt to make it was promising. "Secondly," she said, "you billed yourself for power and materials when those are supposed to be covered by the hourly rate. It's not a big chunk, but we can subtract that out too. Third, six hours isn't how long you were running the Ring, it's how long you were in the control room, according to the logging report on the instruments. You couldn't possibly have been operating the Ring for that six hours straight. You'd have gone through a month's power allocation. I bet ninety-five percent of that time was in computer time and setting up the experiment, right?"

"Yeah, I guess so."

"Okay, how long was the Ring itself powered up, actually taken out of standby mode and cooking?"

Larry thought for a second. "Seven, maybe eight minutes. I'd have to check the experiment log file."

"We'll check it in a second, but let's assume we're talking eight minutes. At the internal experimenter's rate of five hundred thousand pounds an hour, that comes to sixty-six thousand, six hundred sixty-six BritPounds."

"That's still two years' pay for me!" Larry protested.

"So we fudge together a ten-year garnisheeing plan and submit that," Sondra said. "You pay the first month's installment like a good little boy—and by the second month the whole Institute shuts down. If the station shuts down, how can it dock your pay—especially when it isn't paying you anymore? And while we're at it, we arrange to have it paid off in Israeli shekels. That's the convertible currency with the highest inflation rate right now. The debt will lose half its value in a year."

Larry thought about it for a moment and frowned. "It doesn't sound exactly honest to me."

Sondra muttered a curse under her breath. "It's bad enough that Raphael wants to penalize you for showing initiative and being inspired. Why the hell do you have to cooperate with him when he does it?"

"But he's got a point. I wasn't authorized to run the test. I didn't get it scheduled."

People want authority to be just, Sondra thought. "Three–quarters of the experiments here aren't scheduled. That rule is on the books to prevent people from doing side jobs for commercial labs. We're supposed to be working in the public interest and our data is public domain. Without a rule to cover moonlighting, private companies could hit a researcher up for secret experiment runs. The rule wasn't meant to punish you for thinking, and Raphael is wrong to use it against you. We couldn't get anywhere complaining directly to him, so we have to find backdoor ways around the rule. Give me a chance and I bet I can whittle the charges down even further."

Larry thought for a minute. "Hell, there's no way I'm going to be able to pay anything more anyway. All right. I'll do it your way."

"Great. Glad to hear it." Sondra set the notepack to one side. "The real reason I came in was to apologize for not sticking up for you today. Let me fudge the figures for you, just to make it up."

"Why should you have done anything today? You barely know me."

"Yeah, but by this time, I *should* know you. The old-timer is supposed to show the new kid around. Besides, every one of us around that table should have spoken up, and none of us did. We're all too browbeaten by Raphael."

Larry sat up again. "That much I can believe. He reminds of my Uncle Tal. Tal always managed to find a way to let me know I wasn't sufficiently grateful to my parents. Nothing I did was ever enough. I don't know how many times I wanted to face up to him, but I never worked up the nerve. And Dr. Raphael is a *hundred* times worse."

Sondra felt a twinge of guilt, a legitimate one this time. Much as she hated to admit it, there was a part of her that admired Raphael's cussedness, that felt some sympathy for him. "Don't be too hard on him. He hasn't had it easy. He's spent practically his whole life being an old man in a young person's game. It took him a few extra years to get his doctorate for some reason. He fell behind the current theories and research, and never really got caught up. That was twenty-five years ago. He's lived all that time watching boy and girl wonders like us make all the big strides.

"Imagine what a whole life like that would be—always a little bit behind the curve, forever condemned to be a bright man in a field where the average worker is a genius. No wonder he gets frustrated." She paused, and shrugged. "Even so, he shouldn't take it out on the rest of us."

"And we shouldn't let him get away with it," Larry said with surprising firmness. "If we didn't cooperate, he couldn't push us around."

"I've been telling myself that for a long time," Sondra agreed. "But if we're going to close up shop in a month, it's a little late to stage a revolt."

A shy, tentative smile played over Larry's face. "There's still my results. They might be worth something."

Sondra smiled indulgently. It would take miracle numbers to do any good. Mere refinement, another tweakup in performance wouldn't help. But she wasn't going to say that to Larry. What good could it do to dash all his hopes? "Yeah, you're right. They might be something."

"Wanna see them?" Larry asked eagerly. He bounded off the bed without waiting for an answer, shot over Sondra's head and caromed off the ceiling, much to her startlement. He made a perfect landing in front of his desk and wrapped his legs around the chair legs. Obviously he had practiced a lot moving in Pluto's weak gravity. He dug through the papers clipped to the desktop, and pulled a single sheet out of the thick sheaf. "This is the summary," he said. "I've got a preliminary detail report, but the computer is still doing some number crunching."

Sondra took the paper without looking at it. "Why so long to run the calculations?" she asked.

Larry shrugged. "I didn't have a chance to start it running until after the meeting, and it's a complicated problem that'll suck up a lot of processing time. Too big for a remote terminal. I've got the Ring control computer slipstreaming pieces of my job in between legitimate work, in small enough hunks that it won't get flagged on the accounting system. I don't want Raphael nailing me for sucking up computer time too." He grinned shyly.

Sondra laughed. "You're learning," she said, and glanced casually at the summary sheet. Then she blinked, and looked at it again, more carefully. She had to read it twice more before she was certain she had read the numbers correctly. They couldn't be right. They *couldn't* be. "This has got to be wrong," she objected. "You can't have gotten that kind of gee field. Even if we knew how to do it, we don't have the power to generate even one percent that much force."

"The numbers are right," Larry said. "And I didn't generate that gravity force—I focused and *amplified* an existing gravity field. Charon's gravity field."

Sondra looked at him. His voice was calm, steady. There was nothing defensive in his tone, and he looked her straight in the eye. He believed in the figures. She looked at the page again and checked the time stamp on the experiment. Hours before Raphael had dropped his bombshell. No, Larry could not have faked the numbers in some sort of mad attempt to cancel the closing with a spectacular success. Besides, these numbers were ˜*too* spectacular. They were too good for anyone to try to fake them. No one would believe it. They had to be real.

She realized that she had been staring blankly at the summary sheet. She put it down and took a good hard look at Larry. He was not the sort to make a good liar. If he had been trying to put something over, he would have blushed and stammered, his eyes would have shifted away from hers. Either the data were right, or Larry had made a spectacular error.

He believed. But no one else would.

"Has Raphael seen this?" she asked, tapping a finger on the sum sheet.

"I haven't worked up the nerve to send the data to his terminal yet. I was going to present it at the meeting, but I didn't," Larry admitted unhappily.

"Damn it." If Larry had sent them in before the meeting, they would have had at least some credibility. "Send it right now. Not just to his terminal. Copy to every researcher on the station. Now."

"But—"

"But me no buts, Larry. When they see those figures coming after the shutdown announcement, everyone will assume you cooked them up to cancel the shutdown. If we release them now, at least there'll be the argument that you wouldn't have had the time to fabricate the figures. The longer you wait the weaker that argument will get."

"But those figures are *right*," Larry objected. "They're not faked."

"I know that, and you know that—but who else will buy it? These figures are five hundred thousand times larger than they ought to be. Use Occam's razor. What's the simplest explanation—a perfectly timed breakthrough, or a fraud?"

Larry thought for a moment, then grabbed his notepack and typed in a series of commands. For a long moment, there was no sound in the little room but the low chuckle of the keyboard. Sondra stared intently at Larry, and she realized that her heart was racing, that sweat had broken out on her forehead.

I'm scared, she told herself, wondering what in the world there was to be frightened of.

And then the answer came to her. She was scared of the power Larry had found. He had stabilized it across a microscopic volume, and only for a few seconds. But inside that tiny time and space, he had produced a gravity field a thousand times more powerful than the Sun's. He had produced force great enough to crush whole worlds.

Surely *that* should be enough to frighten anyone.

I'm coming home, Jessie. Home. Simon Raphael set down his old-fashioned pen and felt his eyes mist over for a moment. The foolish tears of an old man. But that didn't matter. No need to be ashamed. That was the whole point of the journal, of course. To let his emotions out in private, where they could do no harm. To tell everything to the one woman he had ever loved.

There were times, many of them, when he questioned the wisdom, indeed the sanity, of writing his journal down in the form of letters to his dead wife. But sanity was in short supply on Pluto. Best not to spend his hoarded supply on private thoughts. Best to have it in reserve for his dealings with the others.

The final notice came by lasergram last night, he wrote. *Soon, soon now, I will walk again under an open blue sky. Soon, once again, I shall visit you.* Her grave was a lovely place, nestled into the side of a quiet hillside, looking down on the green fields of Shenandoah Valley, looking out over the cool uplands of the Blue Ridge Mountains. *I will leave this place and come home to you.*

He set down his pen, sighed, and closed his eyes. He imagined that he could smell the cool forest air wafted over the valley. It was incredible to him that others would chose to stay *here*. Fantastic that they would struggle to find *reasons* to stay. Even make them up. Perhaps this boy Chao seriously thought he had discovered something worthwhile. Perhaps it was not deliberate fraud.

Too bad. The moment was past for wasting time on harebrained theories.

Raphael *knew* Chao was wrong. Chao could not have found anything, for there was nothing to find. Gravity research was a dead end. That, when all was said and done, was Simon Raphael's reason for giving up.

He smiled, a wan and thin creasing of his lips, and took up his pen again. *I feel no regret in leaving here*, he wrote. *I have done all I could, tried as hard as I might. Now there is nothing left but to remember what W. C. Fields said.* Jessie had always loved the ancient comedy films, even if Raphael himself had not. *"If at first you don't succeed, try, try again. Then give up. No sense being a damn fool about it."*

CHAPTER THREE

◇

From Pawn to Player

THE OBSERVER'S SLUMBERS, HERETOFORE MEASURED IN *unbroken millennia, were now irrevocably disturbed. Rest, sleep were not to be. That small ray of hope would not be stilled. The Observer stirred restlessly, unable to ignore any longer the tantalizing energies it felt.*

Something *was happening in the depths of space. Now that it had been awakened by the not-quite-correct signal, its sensitivity was increased. It could detect many faint twitches and whispers emanating from the far reaches of the Solar System, from a source moving slowly in a distant orbit.*

It formed a first theory, though the process by which it did so could not precisely be called thinking. *Rather, it was a memory search, an attempt to match new input against the results of previous experience.*

It examined its heritage memory, calling forth not only its own lengthy, if somewhat uneventful, experience, but the recollections of all its forebears. It found a circum-

stance that came close to matching the present one, in the life of a distant ancestor. Perhaps the results of that ancient event could provide an explanation for the current odd situation.

With something like a pang of disappointment, it played back the outcome of the old event. If that precedent was a guide, then this flurry of gravity signals was nothing more than one of its own group malfunctioning, erroneously radiating random gravity signals.

To set its conclusions in two human analogs, each useful and neither entirely accurate, it conjectured that an alternate phenotype of its own genotype had taken ill. Or else that a distant subsystem, another component of the same machine of which it was a part, had broken down.

Was perhaps one of its own breed orbiting in that space? It consulted its memory store and found the scans relating to that part of the sky.

It had expected to find a small, asteroid-sized body reported as orbiting there, another subtype of its breed placed in orbit. To its utter shock, it instead discovered records of a natural body, a frozen planet, accompanied by an outsized moon.

A planetary body emitting modulated gravity waves? That could not be. This was outside not only its own experience, but beyond any circumstance any of its kind had ever reported. Its denial of the situation went beyond any human ability to gainsay a set of facts. In the Observer's universe, if it had not happened before, it was physically impossible for it to happen now.

The anomaly must be investigated. It focused its senses as precisely as possible, examining the target planet.

Further shock. Insupportable. The planet's satellite now sported a ring, quite unrecorded in memory store. A ring flickering intermittently with every sort of energy.

A ring that might have been the Observer's own twin.

Larry sat outside Raphael's office, sweating bullets. The "invitation" to meet with the station head immediately had come a half hour ago, but Raphael seemed to want his rebellious underling to cool his heels for a while before being granted an audience.

Larry knitted his fingers together nervously. He had known what he was doing when he ran his million-gee experiment. That was physics, natural law, controlled and understandable. Once inspiration hit, once he could see the answer and set up the run properly—then of course it would work. It was inevitable. His experiment could no more help working than the Sun could help coming up in the morning.

But the human commotion his experiment had set off—that he did not understand at all. Four hours after his summary report had hit the station's datanet, the whole station was turned upside down.

He had used the Ring to unleash fantastic power, but that power was under control. Pull the plug and it would stop. Not so with this uproar. This controversy was a genie he could not stuff back in the bottle.

Everyone in the station was excited, or infuriated, or both. They were taking sides, all of them, and no one was shy about expressing his or her feelings, right to Larry's face. He was a hero. He was a liar. He was a genius. He was a fool. The Nobel Prize wasn't good enough. They ought to make Tycho a prison again, because a life term anywhere else wasn't bad enough. Larry found himself as alarmed by the adulation as by the excoriation.

The whole station was stampeding, running roughshod over normal procedure in the excitement. Larry's own complete analysis of his experimental results was still running whenever it could grab processing time, but it got pushed off the main computer's job queue altogether as researchers with higher access rights barged into the system on priority status to try their own simulations.

Raphael himself sanctioned a computer simulation by two of the senior scientists. Larry wasn't a bit surprised to learn that Raphael's sim had "proven" Larry's results were impossible. A rival simulation by a cadre of more junior scientists (with Sondra conspicuous by her presence) demonstrated the Chao Effect was real. (Larry himself wasn't exactly sure who had named it that, but he suspected Sondra.)

Larry didn't quite dare say anything, but from what he could see, both computer runs were based on incorrect assumptions.

But the excitement went deeper than a need to see whose figures were right. Lines were being drawn. People were being required to take sides—and not just on the objective question of whether Larry was right or wrong. Other issues were getting entangled. Were you for or against Raphael? Were you for or against closing the station? Are you on our side or theirs? In a matter of hours, the results of a scientific experiment had become politicized, had crystallized all the complex, swirling antagonisms and personality conflicts, all the morale problems at the station into one simple question: *Do you believe?* A question of science was reduced to a judgment of one's faith, a choice between orthodoxy or heresy.

At which point, Larry told himself, it ceased to be science at all. Very little of this had anything to do with the quest for knowledge.

The intercom box clicked on and Raphael's voice said, "Come in," in peremptory tones. Larry stood up, a bit uncertainly. The man had not even checked to see if Larry was waiting. He glanced up, looking for a camera. If there was one, it was concealed. Or was the point of the exercise to show Larry how confident Raphael was that his commands would be followed? Raphael's word was law, and therefore Larry would be there.

It occurred to Larry that if he *hadn't* been there, Raphael would have lost nothing by his little power play, for there would be no one there to hear it. Larry was half-tempted to just sit there and see what Raphael would do. But that wouldn't be good strategy.

He stood, opened the door, and walked into Raphael's office.

Raphael sat behind his desk, seemingly engrossed by some sort of report on his computer screen. He did not glance up or acknowledge Larry in any way. Larry stopped in front of the man's desk, and hesitated for a moment.

But Larry had had enough. If Raphael was going to turn this into a game, then Larry would rather be a player than a pawn. With a slightly theatric sigh, he sat down and pulled out his own notepack. There was some work he could be getting on with. Or at least pretend to get on with.

He opened up the little computer, switched it on, and called up a work file. His face was calm, his heart pounding. The gesture was eloquent, brazen, impudent. Larry had never done anything in his life even remotely as contemptuous of a superior. His father would have said his mother's Irish temper was making a rare appearance, and maybe that wasn't far wrong.

There was a moment, a half moment, in which Raphael could have gotten the upper hand by looking up from his work and leveling his visitor with a withering comment.

But the moment passed, and the director continued at his desk pretending to read his files, while Larry sat in the visitor's chair, pretending to be engrossed in his work.

With each passing second, it was becoming more and more impossible for Raphael to play the scene as he had planned.

Larry thought Raphael was taking quick sidelong glances at him, but he didn't dare look up from his notepack's screen to be sure. He began to wonder how the old man would recoup. At last Raphael stood, carrying a book, and walked over to his bookshelf. He put the book on the shelf. No doubt the book didn't belong on the shelf, but at least the gesture broke the stalemate. He turned back to his desk and then sat on its corner, a remarkably informal pose for Raphael. It did not pass Larry's notice that it placed Raphael in the position of looking down on Larry. "Mr. Chao?" he asked in a calm, if steely, voice.

Larry closed his notepack and looked up to see Raphael glaring balefully down at him.

The older man nodded, stood, and returned to sit down at his own desk. Now that he had Larry's attention he could sit wherever he pleased. "I see no reason to waste time with pleasantries or delicate words," Raphael began. "You have disrupted this station and its work for the last twenty-four hours. I cannot permit any further disruption. We have performed the computer simulation needed to confirm the fraudulent nature of your so-called experiment, and that should satisfy whatever duty we might have had to examine your absurd claims.

"I see no need to waste any further staff time or effort chasing this chimera, to say nothing of Ring time or other access to experimental facilities. I have ordered that all further work on testing your claim, no matter who performs it, be canceled immediately, so that this station can return to its proper work. I might add that I do not yet know who the appropriate legal and professional authorities are in cases of fraud such as this, but I intend to find out and report your actions to them."

Larry opened his mouth and tried to speak. But there were no words. His boss, his own boss, was calling him a liar to his face and threatening to turn him in for the high crime of making a breakthrough.

At last he found his voice again. "You want this station

to return to its proper work?" Larry asked. "What's that? Getting ready for shutdown?" Larry shook his head in bewilderment. "Why is it easier to think that one of the staff you yourself hired is a liar and a cheat, rather than to accept that I might have *discovered* something? Did you even *look* at the data, the real data and not your simulations?"

Raphael smiled contemptuously. "The only thing you have discovered, Mr. Chao, is how to end your career. Our simulation was quite sufficient to confirm your results were flatly impossible. There was not anything like the power required available to the system."

"I've seen your simulation equations," Larry replied in a hard-edged voice. He stood up and leaned over Raphael's desk. "They don't even attempt to account for the effects of amplifying and focusing outside gravity fields. Of *course* that power wasn't available from *inside* the Ring's power system—it came from the outside, from tapping Charon's gravity field! I grabbed a piece of Charon's gravity and compressed it in one locus. The gravity equations are still balanced. That was the whole *point* of the test. You might as well run a simulation of a radio receiver without accounting for a radio signal. Obviously it can't work without something to work *on*. The results of my test run will stand up. It's *your* work that's flawed, Doctor."

Larry stared down into the blazing fury of the old man's eyes, and then turned and left the director's office without another word, without looking back for Raphael's reaction. Anger, real anger, cold hard *adult* anger gripped him, for the first time in his life.

He realized he was angry not at Raphael's baseless accusations, but angry at the man's stupidity, his rigidity.

It was the man's assault against *truth*, against the discoveries they had all been sent here to make, that infuriated Larry. Larry had the computer records, the numbers, the readings that could prove he was right. But all those would be cold comfort back on Earth, billions of kilometers away from the Ring. Cold comfort when the Ring was mothballed for a generation, and there was no other facility available that could possibly follow up on the results.

That was what angered Larry—the blind and needless *waste*, the opportunity being thrown away.

If Larry's test results were accepted and confirmed, it would be impossible to shut down the Ring. Even with the recession back on Earth, the funding board would *have* to come up with some sort of operating budget. Maybe even the Settlements on Mars and the outer satellites would finally contribute. Hell, that was too timid a thought. *Everyone* would throw money at the Ring, in the hope of sharing in the fruits of the research. What might not be possible if artificial gravity were real? Whole new avenues of research would open up on every side, now that the initial problem had been cracked. A lifetime of work, of exciting new challenges and discoveries, would lie open in front of Larry.

And all that stood between him and that bright future was one cranky old man's bruised ego. It was not to be tolerated.

He had a strong impulse to find Sondra and ask her what he should do. But letting her call the shots would be as bad as letting Raphael roll over him. He would have to decide for himself. Once he had chosen a course of action he could ask her advice, her guidance, as to how to do it. But Larry knew he would have to decide what to do for himself, if he was going to go on respecting himself.

Without realizing where he was headed, he found himself back at the door of his own cabin. He shoved open the door, went in, and locked the door behind him. He needed some calm and quiet time alone. Time to think. Time to play the damned games, all of them.

Larry needed another experiment, a rush experiment

not only to get some science done, but for career reasons, publicity reasons. Something that might make a big
enough splash to prevent the shutdown.

Failing that, he had his own career to think of. The
million-gee Ring run was spectacular, but it would be as
discounted by the U.N. Astrophysics Foundation on Earth
as it was here. Earth would listen to Raphael over Larry.

If things broke the wrong way, if Raphael did manage
to cause trouble, Larry could not afford to have that one
unreplicated run be his only claim to fame. He needed
something further to publish, something he could bring
home to Earth and base further research on. Hell, he
needed an experiment that would get him a *job*. He
scowled unhappily. Politics.

Acting the good pure little scientist, interested only in
the Truth, would ensure that his discovery would be
thrown away. Only by getting bogged down in politics
and gamesmanship could he truly serve Truth. This situation called for scheming, not naive idealism.

*Everyone gets caught justifying the means to their ends
sometimes,* Larry told himself, a bit uncomfortably.

Okay, then. He had a goal and a fallback goal: saving
the station and/or his career. Now how to go about reaching one of both of those?

He needed to know the state of play. Had all the tests
of his results had been canceled? He had a hard time
believing that the entire research staff would meekly go
along with the cease-work order. On the other hand,
Raphael undoubtedly expected some of the staff to try to
circumvent the ruling. So anyone trying for a test would
have to disguise the run as something else.

Larry used his notepack computer to check the Ring
experiment schedule. It was certainly much heavier than
usual, with experiments scheduled around the clock. Of
course, that could be explained by the planned closing,
and people rushing to get their runs made before the

shutdown came—but perhaps some of that scheduled time was actually intended to test Larry's theory.

People working on the Chao Effect would have the sense to hide their work from Raphael. And a lot of people might well be doing that very thing. But who?

There was only one name he could be sure of. One of those covert experimenters was going to be, had to be, Sondra Berghoff. Maybe there would be other malcontents willing to do more than mouth off, actually willing to wade in and break some rules. But Sondra was the only one Larry knew who would take the chances involved.

Larry worked over the experiment roster, looking for experiments in which Sondra was involved.

There were three, only one of which listed her as primary researcher. That was likewise the only one of the three that had been scheduled after Larry had shown her his test results. He rejected it as too obvious. Raphael would certainly monitor that experiment closely. Besides, it wasn't due to be run for another week. He couldn't afford to wait that long.

One of the others seemed perfect. It had been scheduled weeks ago, and was supposed to run on the graveyard shift, 0200 GMT tonight. Sondra was listed as the technical operator, not an experimenter.

Better still, Larry noted that Dr. Jane Webling was the primary investigator. Webling, nominally the science chief of the station, was getting on in years, to put it charitably. Probably she would go to bed before the experiment ran, and simply check with her "assistant" the next morning. In all likelihood, therefore, Sondra would be on the board by herself.

So. If Sondra were going to pull something, that would be her moment. Okay, but what was the purpose of the run? Larry checked the title of the experiment: "Test of a Revised Procedure for Gravitic Collimation." *Just the sort of pompous name people learned to hang on a test when Raphael was running things*, Larry thought.

Gravitic collimation. He had seen an earlier paper by Webling on the subject—in fact, he had gotten a few ideas from it. Webling had been working for some time on developing a focused beam of gravity waves—a "graser." Like light, gravity was usually radiated in all directions from its source. But, like light, it could be manipulated, focused down into a one-dimensional beam. Larry's own techniques of gravity focusing relied on similar techniques.

A laser was a perfectly collimated light beam. Webling's graser project sought to develop a focused beam of gravity, albeit of microscopic power, and beam it at detectors on the other planets. *Strange thought*, Larry told himself, *since gravity could be defined as a curve in space. A beam of curved space.*

Actually, the basic technique produced *two* beams, pointed one hundred eighty degrees apart from each other— one aimed at the target, the other outgoing in exactly the opposite direction. Webling's greatest success was in creating a "push-pull" beam by warping the outgoing beam around, changing its direction of travel without affecting its direction of attraction. In effect, the outgoing beam signal became a repulser. Merged with the targeted beam, it had exactly zero net attractive power, because the two beams canceled each other out. The beam should be detectable, but effectively powerless.

But suppose, Larry thought, he boosted the power rating a bit? Say, by a factor of one million? It still would be self-canceling, and thus not have any effect on the target worlds—but it would sure prove Larry was on to something. Hell, it would melt the readouts right off the gravity detectors.

That should get them some off-planet attention.

CHAPTER FOUR

———————◇———————

The Finger on the Button

THE OBSERVER DID NOT UNDERSTAND THE STRANGE RING *at the edge of the Solar System. The ring should have been perfectly familiar, its actions as familiar as the Observer's own. Yet the stranger seemed to break every law, every control that should have been burned into its very being.*

Why did it behave so strangely? Why did it orbit a frozen, useless world at the very borderlands of this system? Why did it not hide itself? Why, indeed, did it ra-diate wasted, dissipated power, advertising its presence? Hourly, the stranger permitted cumulative leakage greater than what the Observer had allowed in the last million years.

And in spite of the leakage, the stranger radiated use-lessly small amounts of effective gravity power. Why did it do so with such clumsiness, such inefficiency?

So many things were quite unlike a proper ring. Only

in its shape, size, and attempt to use gravity did the stranger truly resemble the Observer.

But the obvious conclusion that this was a new thing, unknown to the Observer's heritage memory, never occurred to the Observer.

The Observer was congenitally incapable of asking the rather obvious question, Where did it come from? *It knew, beyond any possibility of contradiction, that there was only one possible ultimate source for a gravity ring.*

The Observer knew, to a certainty, that the mystery ring was at least in some degree akin to the Observer itself.

That was the error that wrecked its entire edifice of logic.

It assumed that this alien structure was of its own kind. But then why was the mystery ring so strange? Why were its procedures, its behavior so wildly unknown?

The answer was suddenly clear, brought up from some ancient memory of a forebear lost to time.

The alien was a massively modified derivative model, a mutant. Built by a related or ancestral sphere system long, long ago.

That was the Observer's second error.

On this was based its third error, which would, in time, send its entire universe reeling, and threaten a way of being millions of years old.

But for it, disaster was yet far off.

Earth was not as lucky.

"Well, Dr. Berghoff, it's a pity we could only arrange such a late-night experiment time, but I think you have matters well in hand," Dr. Webling said. "It should be a fairly straightforward experiment run. Quite routine. I think I might as well head on off to bed. I'll be looking forward to seeing your results in the morning. I suppose

we won't have the last return signals from Earth until
after lunchtime.''

"Yes, ma'am," Sondra said distractedly. She had her
mind on other things than pleasantries.

"Treat yourself to that extra cup of coffee tonight,"
Webling said playfully. "You'll need it. Good night,
then, Dr. Berghoff.''

"Good night, Dr. Webling."

Dr. Webling cautiously eased her way out of the lab,
as if she were afraid of a fall. A lot of the older scientists
never did master the tricks of moving in low gravity.

Sondra watched the door close behind Webling and
breathed a sigh of relief. She had thought the old girl would
never get moving. She stood up and locked the door behind
Webling. Sondra definitely did not want to be disturbed.

She glanced up at the main control display. Just four
hours until the scheduled start of Webling's experiment.
Damn! Barely time to scrap the preliminary setup for
Webling's run and reset the center's controls to replicate
Larry Chao's results. And there was no slack time in the
system tonight, either. The other three control rooms
were full and busy. Control Room One was running a
test now, and Two and Three were waiting their turns to
get command of the Ring. Sondra's, Control Room Four,
got its shot at the ring only after Three was done—and
there was an experimenter already signed up for the 0300
slot in Control Room One.

Once she got command of the Ring, she would have
an hour to make her run. No time to correct mistakes if
she got it wrong.

Of course Webling would discover the change and see
to it that Raphael handed Sondra her head the next morning, but that couldn't be helped. Nor would it matter.
After all, the station was shutting down. What could they
do? Fire her?

This experiment run might well be her only chance to replicate Larry's results. That was important.

Maybe others would try to duplicate his run, but this was her only shot at it. She couldn't trust the cowering sheep-scientists of this place to take the risk of pursuing this line of inquiry.

Even if she had known for certain of other runs, she still would have had to know for herself that it really worked, that the million gees were really out there waiting to be controlled. That could happen only if she set the run herself, trusting no one else to get it right.

She sat down and started to adjust the controls, reprogramming the system to Larry's specs. Larry's notes were thorough and complete, but it was a highly complex setup. She almost immediately found herself getting wrapped up in the job. Working down there at the level of controls, of meters and dials, she began to *understand* Larry's thinking. She had never been strong on theory—but hardware was something she could deal with.

She was so focused on the job she jumped nearly into the ceiling when the door chime sounded. Earth reflexes could be downright hazardous under such light gravity.

She punched the intercom switch. "Who . . . who is it?" she asked, trying to keep her voice steady. She glanced quickly at the control panel and allowed herself a reassuring thought. It would take an expert to tell she was cross-setting the system. Everything was fine. Nothing to worry about.

"It's me, Larry," a muffled voice replied. He was talking through the door rather than using the intercom. Was he afraid of Raphael bugging the place?

Sondra let her breath out, not even realizing that she had been holding it. The feeling of genuine relief that swept over her told Sondra how much she had been kidding herself a moment before. She stood up and unlocked the door.

Sondra knew she should not have been surprised that Larry had shown up. He had a brain, after all. He could look at a schedule sheet and know she'd be here. And she had offered herself as an ally—even if he had not immediately accepted the offer.

Larry stepped into the room and looked around thoughtfully. Sondra stepped back from him, more than a bit taken aback by his manner. There was something more determined, harder edged, more self-assured about him than there had been a few hours ago.

Larry went to the front of the control panel and glanced over the settings. "You're halfway through dumping Webling's run settings," he announced. It was not a question.

"Ah, well, yes," Sondra said, awkwardly fidgeting her hands. Well, here was the expert.

"Well, we've got to put it back," Larry said.

"But I need to confirm your results," Sondra protested. "That's a hell of a lot more important than the graser right now."

"Where are the gravity-wave detectors you'll be sending to?" Larry asked.

There was something in his tone of voice that told her she had better give a direct answer. "Ah, Titan, Ganymede, VISOR—that's the big Venus orbital station—and the Jet Propulsion Laboratory on Earth. Ten minutes of pulse sending to each. A millisecond pulse every second."

"How powerful?" Larry asked.

"Well, power is one thing we're trying to measure. We start with a spherical one-gee field one kilometer across here, which we can hold stable for about a millisecond. By the time we concentrate it, collimate and pulse it, we've lost most of the power. The wave front spreads as well, weakening the field strength. We'd be happy to end up delivering maybe a ten-millionth of a gee at the other end, but we don't know what we'll get.

"In fact the job tonight is to find out what we *can*

deliver at the other end. The beam isn't all that well collimated and there's a hell of a lot of leakage. In theory we should be sending a perfect column of parallel gravity waves. In practice, we're sending a conical beam, narrow at this end but broadening rapidly as it moves out. And the gee waves aren't exactly parallel either. We're *guessing* that we can deliver a ten-millionth gee, but we'd settle for anything within a factor of ten of that.''

''And they can detect gravity pulses that small?''

''We send to those stations because they have the best detectors, the same type we use. The Titan and Ganymede stations are studying the interactions of the gravity fields of Saturn and Jupiter's satellite families. The Venus station is mapping the gravity field there, trying to use the Solar tidal effect to deduce the planet's internal structure. And JPL is where they designed the sensors they're all using. Their detection gear is good, and they use a range of sensitivities. One at low end, a middle range, and a heavy-duty job,'' Sondra concluded.

''Could they measure, say, a millisecond *one-tenth* push-pull gee burst? Something like that, a million times more powerful that what they're used to getting from us?''

Suddenly Sondra understood. ''You want to amplify the gee field with your process and *then* beam it to them!''

Larry grinned wickedly. ''That'll make them sit up and take notice, won't it?''

Sondra thought for a moment, and the more she thought, the more she liked the idea. By its very nature, the experiment would attract attention to Larry's amplification effect. Attention, hell! It would blow the doors off gravity detectors all over the System. Every gravity researcher between here and the Sun would be certain to hear about it within hours, and all of them would be clamoring for more information, more verification.

That was Larry's idea, obviously, to get the news of

the Chao Effect off Pluto, spread out as far and wide as possible.

"It ought to work, Larry," she said. "No doubt about it, it ought to work. *If* we can set up the Ring to amplify the gravity field, modulate it, and collimate the gravity waves."

"That side of it I know we can do. I'm just worried about their seeing it at the other end and being able to measure it."

"Don't worry about it. All of those labs run their detectors twenty-four hours a day, recording their reading constantly. The detectors are built to operate and record automatically, to prevent a sloppy operator from missing something. If we can send it, they'll see it."

"Then let's give them something to see," Larry said, sitting down at the controls.

Long before the Ring of Charon was first powered up, astrophysics had ceased to be a strictly observational science. Active experiments, involving massive energies, were common. Not only at the Ring, but at facilities large and small across the System, powerful forces were being explored.

Unfortunately, there were also many observatories, on Earth and in space, designed to detect incredibly weak signals from millions of light-years away. Too much input could destroy them easily. The high-energy experimenters had it beaten into their heads that they must give broad notification of their plans, offering plenty of time to shut down delicate gear. Failure to do so risked destroying some colleague's delicate detection gear halfway across the Solar System.

There was another, more complex reason for thorough warnings of experiments. Back in the old days, when all the observatories were on Earth, or within the orbit of the Moon, it was always possible to call on the phone with late-breaking news, so as to get a second observation of the phenomenon in question. Coordinating observations between two or more observatories was at least reasonably straightforward. Even in cases where the observation had to be synchronized to the nanosecond, there was no great problem when the two points were tiny fractions of a light-second apart. However, the speed of light had changed the forms of etiquette: phones and easy synchronization were out of the question once there were observatories orbiting every planet from Mercury to Saturn. A wave of light energy that passed Saturn might not cross Earth's path for four hours. A two-way contact, query and reply, would take eight hours.

Communications workers invented the event radius to handle this sort of problem, and the astronomers eagerly took it up.

Consider how electromagnetic signals move. All of them move at the speed of light, and unless manipulated by a focusing device, all types of electromagnetic radiation (for example, lightwaves or radio signals) radiate out from a given point on the surface of a sphere that is expanding at the speed of light. Think of a dot drawn on the surface of an inflating balloon. The dot, representing a signal, moves outward, riding the skin of the balloon as it expands.

The distance between that dot and the center of the balloon, between the surface of the radiative sphere and the center of radiation, is an event radius.

No data about a given event can be received until the dot, the information, passes through the observer as the information sphere expands at the speed of light. Event radii can be measured in conventional linear measures, but it is generally more convenient to refer to them in light-time. Thus, Earth's distance from the sun, one hundred fifty million kilometers, is an event radius of about eight light-minutes. If the Sun blew up, Earth would not know it for eight minutes.

But knowing the light-time distance was not the only problem. At times the situation grew even more frustrating as the movement and gravity wells of the planets themselves introduced slight redshifting problems and microscopic time-dilation effects. More than once, careers were saved or wrecked by the discovery of an error in compensating for those effects.

Webling had sent out a standard notice of her planned experiment hours before. Larry and Sondra knew they had to send out advance warning of their modifications of the experiment, but they were nervous about doing it. Yet without the warning, they would infuriate any number of other experimenters. Not a good idea for an experiment that was half public relations.

Sondra drafted the notice to JPL:

> ALERT TO JPL GRAVITY LAB: THIS WILL SERVE AS NOTICE OF A MODIFIED COLLIMATED GRAVITY-WAVE PROCEDURE. TIMES OF TRANSMISSION TO YOU AND OTHER SENSOR LABS UNCHANGED, BUT NEW TECHNIQUE SHOULD PERMIT 10 TO SIXTH INCREASE IN POWER TRANSMISSION. PLEASE RIG FOR MORE POWERFUL INPUT AND ADVISE AFFECTED LABS.

They sent similar messages to the other participating labs, warning them of the high-power pulse on the way, requesting relay to other facilities that might be affected.

It seemed more than a bit foolhardy to be doing a secret experiment while providing a general warning that it was about to happen. The speed of light came to their rescue. Sondra was careful to send the alerts through the station's automated signal system, without any human intervention. Many eyes on many worlds would read their messages, but no one on Pluto would know what was up until queries and replies came back from those labs. And by then, of course, it would be far too late to stop the experiment.

Figuring in speed-of-light delays, there would be nearly an eight-hour lag between the send-off of the warning to the closest lab on Saturn, and the earliest possible response back to Pluto.

That should serve as protection enough, so long as no one at the base noticed what they were up to in real time. To avoid that problem, Sondra and Larry agreed to stay as close as possible to Webling's original experiment design, in the hope of avoiding premature attention.

Given the difficulties of aiming the untested graser system, Webling had designed the original run to hit the closest, easiest target first and work out to longer range from there. The positions of the planets dictated that Saturn be the first target. Sondra used the original aiming data as she set up the run.

It was a complicated job. She glanced again at the chronometer when she was halfway through it. Three hours until this control room had its shot at the Ring. She sighed and went back to the complex job of resetting the controls.

With a beep and a flashing green light, the control panel announced that the Ring was ready for the graser run.

With ten minutes to spare, the myriad magnets, coolant pumps, mass drivers, particle accelerators and other components of the Ring system were configured to form a Chao Effect–amplified gravity well, to modulate and to collimate the gravity waves from it, and to fire tight pulses of collimated gravity power toward Titan.

Or at least, Sondra thought they were ready. She took

another look at the control system. This was definitely a wild setup. No wonder the station's old fogies hadn't been able to believe it.

The countdown clock came on and started marking the passage of time. Eight minutes left.

Larry sighed and rubbed his weary eyes. Now it came down to one last set of checks to make, and one last button to push.

One last button.

They could have programmed those last checks on the automatic sequencer as well, even told the computer to start the actual firing of the system. If the experiment had been dependent on split-second timing, they would have.

But timing wasn't that vital here. Besides, letting the computer do the work would not have been *right*. This was a human moment, the triumph both of human ingenuity over a technical and scientific problem, and of human cussedness over damn-fool rules. It was a way to proclaim a breakthrough to all humanity—and, equally important to Larry, it was a way to thumb his nose at Raphael. No computer could be programmed to do that properly.

Seven minutes left.

Still, there was something about the moment that surpassed even Larry's deep-seated need to defy the director. It was dawning on Larry that this wasn't just an experiment, not just an attention-getting device for saving their careers. This was history. No one had ever attempted such a thing. This was gravity control on a grand scale. Crude, limited—yes. But this one moment could change everyone's lives.

Six minutes.

Just how ready was he to change the course of history? Larry licked his dry lips and glanced nervously over at Sondra. She nodded once, without looking up from her readouts. Everything was ready. In nervous silence, the last few minutes slid away to seconds. And then it came to the time itself.

For a brief moment, a frightened voice in Larry's head told him no, told him not to do this thing. He ignored the voice of fear, of caution, and stabbed the button down.

Thousands of kilometers over his head, the Ring activated the gravity containment, and then pulsed the first waves of gravity power toward Saturn. Larry pulled his finger from the button and looked around blankly, feeling the moment to be a bit anticlimactic. There should have been some dramatic effect there in the lab to make them know it had happened. *Maybe I should have programmed the lights to dim or something,* he told himself sarcastically.

Of course, nothing happened in the control room. The action was far away overhead, at the axis, the focal point, of the Ring of Charon.

But by now, the action was rushing its way down toward Saturn. The first pulse was already millions of kilometers along its way.

From here on, the automatics did take over. The sequencer fired again. The second millisecond pulse leapt from the Ring. And the third, the fourth. It was too late to bring it back. Far too late. There was nothing they could do but press on. They would catch hell no matter what they did now.

The Observer had no concept of free choice. All that it did, or thought, or decided, it was compelled to do, each stimulus producing the appropriate response. There would not be, could not be, any situation not provided for. In its memory and experience, going back far beyond its own creation, all was supposed to be categorized, un-

derstood, known. There should have been nothing new under this or any other star.

It could not fear the unknown, because such a concept was beyond it. To it, the unknown was inconceivable.

Thus, it struggled to force new phenomena into old categories—for example, choosing to see the alien ring as a mutation, a modification of its own form.

Having reached this flawed identification, it accessed the concept of change and mutation as recorded in its memory store. It explored the possible forms change might take, and the results of those changes. As best it could tell, the alien fit within the possible parameters. That was enough data to satisfy the Observer.

It only remained to determine what its distant cousin was doing. But then, the answer arrived, full-blown and complete, from its heritage memory store.

It was a relay. It was echoing a message from home, announcing that it was time. Perhaps the normal means of contact had failed, and this new ring had sailed between the stars to bring its message.

Of course. What else could it be? The Observer searched the length and breadth of its memory, and did not find an alternative answer.

To one of the Observer's kind, memory was all. Finding no other answer in its memory proved there was no other answer.

It was a way of being that had always worked.

Jupiter was next, or rather Ganymede. Larry told himself he must remember not to treat the inhabited satellites as mere appendages of the planets. The residents of the gas-giant satellite settlements were always annoyed by that sort of thing. After all, no one referred to the Moon as being part of Earth. Titan, Ganymede and the other inhabited satellites were worlds in their own right. Larry knew he had best bear that in mind—if things worked out the way they might, he would have a lot of contact with the gravity experts on Titan and Ganymede.

Yeah, those are vital points right now, Larry thought sarcastically. He was finding other things to worry about, trying to avoid the big picture. He had caught himself doing that all night, again and again. He was unable to face the meaning, the consequences of what he was doing. He did not want to be in charge of changing the world. The hell with it. Larry plunged in the start button again. The beam regenerated itself and leapt toward Jupiter's satellite.

At least, they hoped it was heading toward Ganymede. Though Sondra had run graser experiments before, they were at a ten-millionth of this power. She was finding the collimated gravity beam difficult to control even with computer-automated assistance and Larry to backstop her.

And, be it confessed, she too was more than a bit nervous about dealing with such massive amounts of power. Even with all the signal loss and fade-outs of their crude directionalizing system, they were still pulsing bursts of three hundred thousand gravities out from a point source—albeit a point source smaller than an amoeba, a point source that went unstable after a few seconds. A million kilometers from the Pluto-Charon system, the pulse had lost half its power, and lost half again in another million.

By the time it reached even the closest of its targets, the beam had lost virtually all its power, was reduced to a one-millisecond tenth-gee wisp of nothing. And since it was phased with the repulser beam, the net gravitational energy directed at a target was exactly zero. The beam pushed exactly as hard as it pulled. It was physically impossible for the beam to be anything but harmless. Besides, each beam firing only lasted a millisecond and acted on the entire target body as a whole. The beam was a push-pull type, she told herself again. The push-pull couldn't fail, not without the entire system failing utterly. It was impossible for this beam to hurt anyone or anything.

But such reassurances weren't enough to keep her from getting nervous. "How's it going, Larry?" she asked for what seemed like the hundredth time.

"Still fine," Larry replied, more than a bit distracted himself. The amplified gravity source still collapsed every thirty seconds or so, and Larry had to regenerate the point source. The strain was getting to him. He had hoped to automate the process, but he had rapidly discovered that he barely had time to look up from his primary controls before the source would go unstable again.

It wasn't until halfway through the Jupiter run that he had the time to set up the automation system. He instructed the computer to look over his shoulder, figuratively speaking, and watch the regeneration procedure he used.

After the seventh or eighth time, the computer had "learned" the regen procedure in most of its permutations and was able to take over the job itself. Larry breathed a sigh of relief and leaned back in his chair. They were on their way.

He wondered what their reactions would be—especially what the Jet Propulsion Laboratory would think.

The speed of light was the limiting factor now. Gravity waves moved at lightspeed, just like any other kind of radiation. At the moment, Pluto, Saturn, and Jupiter were all roughly lined up one side of the Sun, with Venus and Earth on the other sides of their orbits, only a few degrees away from the Sun. Of the planets in question, Saturn was currently the closest to Pluto, and Earth the furthest away.

Larry frowned and scribbled a quick diagram on a scratch

pad to help him keep it all straight. After a few brief calculations, he added the round-trip-signal time in hours for each planet.

planet position	Earth	Venus	Sun	Jupiter	Saturn	Pluto
station	JPL	VISOR		Ganymede	Titan	GRS
round trip signal time in hours from Pluto	11.2	11.1	—	9.4	8.27	0

Those were round-trip-signal times. So Titan Station, orbiting Saturn, would receive its dose of gravity waves in just over four hours. Even if Titan signaled back to Pluto immediately when the gravity waves arrived, it would still take more than four more hours for Pluto to get the word.

It worked out to over eleven hours between firing the beam at Earth and getting a reply back from JPL.

JPL was the key to it all. JPL had run the first deep-space probe 450 years before, and from that time to this, it had retained it preeminence in the field of deep-space research. JPL was the big time. It was the field leader on Earth, and that made it the leader, period. JPL was big enough to lean on the U.N. Astrophysics Foundation. And the UNAF was the one with the checkbook.

Six billion kilometers to Earth. Twelve billion, round-trip.

One hell of a long way to go for funding, Larry thought.

A timer beeped. That was the end of the Ganymede beam sequence. Time to retarget again, point the beam at Venus. Larry flexed his fingers and watched his board as Sondra laid in the new targeting data.

"All set, Larry," she said.

Larry nodded and pressed the button again. Venus. There were dreams of terraforming the planet—indeed, that idea was VISOR's reason for being there in the first place.

Now *there* was a project that could benefit from artificial gravity on a large scale. Orbit a Virtual Black Hole around the planet and let it suck away ninety percent of the atmosphere. Use lateral-pull gravity control to speed up the planet's spin. Pipe dreams. Wonderful pipe dreams.

Those were for tomorrow. Right now a millisecond burst of a tenth gee was victory enough. By now the computer had the hang of the graser control. It likewise seemed to be handling the point-source regeneration without much need for guidance. The ten minutes targeted on Venus passed quickly.

Earth was next. Earth. Not just JPL, but half the major science centers in the system were still there.

Larry watched eagerly as Sondra set up the revised targeting data. Thirty seconds ahead of time, she nodded at him. The new coordinates were locked in. Over their heads, the Ring had adjusted itself, in effect setting up a lens to focus the point source at Earth, the home planet.

Larry grinned eagerly and pressed home the fire button.

Eleven hours, he thought. *Five and a half for the beam to get there, and another five and a half for us to hear the results. Then we'll know what Earth thinks of this little surprise.*

Eleven hours.

With a whimper, not a bang, with a three-in-the-morning sense of anticlimax, the run ended. It was over, but it hadn't started yet. Larry turned to Sondra and smiled. "Ready for the excitement tomorrow?"

She shook her head and stretched, struggling to stifle a yawn. "I haven't really thought about it yet. But all hell is going to break loose when Raphael sees what we've done.''

Larry winced. ''Yeah. That's going to be the tough part. If he hates me now, tomorrow he'll want to throw me out the nearest hatch without a suit.''

Sondra looked at Larry's face, watching the expressions play over it. Fear, apprehension—guilt. *Like a son who knows he's about to disappoint his father again.*

She thought for a moment, and then spoke in a gentle voice. ''I think it might be best if I do the talking with Raphael.''

Larry looked up at her, surprised. ''No,'' he said. ''This is between me and him.''

''No it isn't,'' Sondra said, ''and that's just the point.'' She patted the control console, waved her hand to indicate the whole station. ''This is science *and* politics. It's not just two people having a private argument. And if we treat it that way, as if you two having a spat was the only issue, we're going to lose what really matters. We'll lose our focus on what you and I have *done* tonight.''

He closed his eyes and leaned back. A boy, no, a man, trying to clear his mind, think when his brain was soaked with exhaustion. ''Okay. Okay. I see what you're saying. But you remind me of another question. And not just what buttons we've pushed. For the whole future: what, exactly, *have* we done tonight? I mean, *gravity control.*'' Larry opened his eyes, and leaned forward. Even at the end of this sleepless night, Sondra could feel the excitement in him, feel it catching at her.

''Think to the future,'' he said. ''And think about what we've set loose.''

CHAPTER FIVE

Results

CERTAINTY. THE STRANGE SIGNAL CAME FROM A RELAY, *a mutant or modified relay, distantly related to the Observer's own line and design. Normal contact had collapsed. The relay had traveled here across the depths of normal space, searching for an Observer, to tell it the time had come to Link.*

Certainty. It was a mere hypothesis, and a badly flawed one at that. Any number of observations contradicted the Observer's explanation. But the Observer was sure it was the answer, the solution.

It barely mattered that the Observer was utterly wrong. For it could not ignore a stimulus, no matter what its source. No matter what conclusion it reached, it would respond to the stimulus of powerful modulated gravity waves.

And now the alien Ring, the spurious relay, was sending massive amounts of power, obviously directed at the other worlds in this star system, beaming power first at one, then another. Even though the beam was not directed at the Observer, the beam leaked atrociously. Furthermore, the gravity patterns of the target worlds refracted the beam in subtle but distinct ways. Thus the Observer detected the beams and their targets easily.

The Observer considered the targeting pattern and projected it inward: the alien was scanning in toward the Inner System, one world after another.

The alien Ring was searching for something.

And that something could only be the Observer. It would find the Observer, stimulate it—force the Observer to act, to reveal itself, to perform the task it had been waiting to perform for millions of years.

The Observer knew it would have no choice but to respond, react to that beam if it struck this place.

Something like excitement, like fear, coursed through it.

Seismographs all over the Moon recorded its spasm of feeling.

But it wanted to believe. It wanted to respond. It was lonely, eager to renew contact with the outside Universe, eager to begin a new phase of its own existence. It began to prepare for the beam, activating subsystems that had long been dormant. It drew down power from its reserves, determined to be ready the moment the beam touched.

Wolf Bernhardt breathed in the cool California air and told himself it was right that there was a Berliner involved. Berlin was the ancestral home of physics, after all. All this grand work would never have happened if not for the great minds that had labored in that city so long ago.

And it required at least a quick, agile mind to respond

to this situation quickly. He had listened to the pre-experiment broadcast from Pluto, and that had been enough. Others would have hesitated, he congratulated himself. Not *Herr Doktor* Bernhardt.

The first word that the effect was real, that powerful, controllable artificial gravity had been detected had arrived only a quarter hour ago, from Titan Station. Wolf checked his watch. He had to go on the air in another five minutes. Plenty of time. Lucky indeed that his quarters were close to the main control station.

· He smoothed his shirt down and examined himself in the bathroom mirror. *Herr Doktor* Wolf Bernhardt, age thirty, ambitious and determined, looked back out at him, blue eyes gleaming, blond hair combed back off the high forehead, angular jaw jutted just slightly forward. His suit immaculate, the fabric a pale powder blue that set off his slightly ruddy complexion. His smooth skin glowed with health and the warmth of the shower he had just had. He ran a hand over his jaw. Yes, perfectly shaved. No one could suspect he had been in rumpled clothing dozing by the duty-scientist panel fifteen minutes ago. Now he was ready for the world.

He looked again at the mirror. Yes, it was a face appropriate to history. It was 1:25 in the morning, local time, but he was fresh, sharp. And that was important. Tonight, now, he would be talking to only the scientists on Pluto, with perhaps a relay to the other off-planet stations. But tomorrow, and the next day, and the next, Earth would see the recordings of those messages over the newsnets. And the reporters—they would need a spokesman to talk to, someone who could answer their questions from here, not from the other side of an event radius light-hours across.

And he, Wolf Bernhardt, would be there, ready to talk, all the figures and results at his fingertips.

Quite literally at his fingertips—for he would be relying on the computer to educate him on the topic of gravity research. He would need to work the databases hard to get up to speed quickly.

But he would be there, he would learn, he would be ready. This was the moment he had waited for. His moment in the sun.

He turned and left his room, hurrying a bit, as if fame and history were impatient for him to arrive.

Sondra stumbled through the cafeteria the next morning. After a bare four hours' sleep, her thought processes were not as sharp as they should have been. She looked around the room and spotted Webling, indecently awake and cheerful, tucking into her fruit salad.

Webling, Sondra thought. *With the damage already done, maybe now was the time to turn a potential enemy around. Time to admit what we've done*, Sondra thought. Webling was a woman of sudden enthusiasms. If Sondra could get her excited about the amplified graser *before* word leaked out, then perhaps she would help blunt any attack Raphael might make. The next step, Sondra decided, was to suck Webling into the game.

She collected her own breakfast and a large cup of coffee, then shuffled wearily over to the older scientist's table, struggling to calculate the time dynamics in her head. Titan's initial response message ought to arrive back at Pluto in about twenty minutes. Larry was probably already in the observatory bubble, the traditional place to await messages from the Inner System.

The main comm board was patched through to the bubble, so that any public message that arrived at the station would automatically be echoed there. The early-morning shift in the computer center would have seen the overnight science and experimentation reports already.

Those reports were supposed to be strictly confidential, but the computer team was a noted den of gossips, masters of hinting at things they could not say directly. The rumors were probably flying already, at least in the station's lower echelons, if not in the circles where Webling and Raphael were likely to hear anything. Sondra thought she noticed a face or two turned toward her, and wondered if it was just her imagination.

Of course, the moment the Titan message came in, rumor would turn into fact and all hell would break loose. Everyone would know what Larry and she had done. After that, it would be too late to turn Webling around.

The trick was to tell Webling about the revised experiment, and get her excited about the probable results, before the message came—and before Raphael found out.

Anyway, it was worth a try. Sondra walked over to the table where the older woman was sitting. "Good morning, Dr. Webling!" she said, with as much false cheeriness as she could manage.

"Why, good morning, Sondra. I didn't expect to see you up and about so early," Webling replied in her slightly reedy voice. "How did the experiment run go last night?"

"Very well. Very well indeed," Sondra said. "But I'm afraid I have a confession to make about it."

Webling, whose closest attention had been focused on a slice of grapefruit, looked up sharply at Sondra. "Go on," she said in a careful voice.

Sondra bit her lip and started talking, hoping that Larry would understand the need to downplay his part in the experiment just now. The truth needed a few coarse adjustments. "I got a little inspired last night. I made an *adjustment* to the graser settings. Nothing that would affect the primary experiment goals, of course. Even so, I suppose I should have awakened you before I made the adjustment. It's just that the idea came to me so suddenly that there was barely time to set it up as it was. And with Ring time suddenly so limited, I didn't want to take the risk of losing the run altogether. And it *seems* as if your experiment was a dazzling success." She made a show of checking her watch and seeing what time it was. "We ought to be getting the first response back from Titan soon."

"Why a 'dazzling' success?" Webling asked. "It was a fairly routine experiment run." She checked the time herself. "And why expect such an immediate response? If we get a message now, they would have had to have sent it the moment they received our graser beam. Why would they be so eager?"

"Because if our—*my*—figures were right, then Titan should have received a series of one-millisecond push-pull gravity-wave pulses, sent from here at a strength of one-tenth gee."

Webling's eyes widened. "One-*tenth* gee . . ."

Sondra stood up from the table and Webling got up as well, automatically following the younger woman's lead. "I left a record of your experiment's output figures in the observation dome, Dr. Webling. Perhaps you'd be interested in seeing them while we wait to see what Titan has to say?"

The beam was moving again.

First directed at the sixth planet, then shifted toward the fifth, now sweeping over the second planet. Soon now, soon, it would sweep this way, toward the third world, and the Observer and its hiding place.

Close. The moment was close. After all the endless millennia, the wait was down to mere minutes, seconds.

The Observer all but quivered with anticipation.

When Larry walked into the dome, he instantly noticed two things: one, a much larger number of people
than usual "just happened" to be eating breakfast there,
instead of in the cafeteria, and many were lingering over
their coffee; and two, a murmur of conversation sprang
up when he walked in—though no one had the nerve to
go up and talk to him. When Sondra and Webling walked
into the dome soon after, the murmur rose to a veritable
buzz of excitement. Obviously, news traveled fast through
the station, and rumor even faster. True to form, the
computer center had leaked like a sieve when the Webling experiment had come through. Someone down there
had seen and understood the significance of the readings—and that someone had a wagging tongue.

Sondra crossed the room and sat down at the table
across from Larry, Webling beside her. "Larry," she
said with forced casualness, "tell Dr. Webling about that
experiment modification we worked up."

Webling stared hard at Larry and blinked once or
twice. "You!" she said. "You're the one who faked the
gravity-field results!"

Sondra winced. Ouch. Off on the wrong foot. "No,
Dr. Webling," she said gently. "He's the one they've
accused of faking the results. But that doesn't make the
figures less true. Go ahead, Larry. Tell the doctor how
you did it. Convince her that it really happened."

Larry swallowed hard and pulled out his notepack
computer. "Well," he said doubtfully, "the main idea
was to use the Ring's gravity power to focus and amplify
an existing gravity field."

Webling's eyes widened. "Amplify an existing field.
How on earth did you . . ." Her voice trailed off as she

looked at the math that was already on Larry's notepack screen.

Within half a minute, the old woman and the young man were completely immersed in a complex mathematical argument, rattling off hideously convoluted formulas into the notepack's voiceport.

Sondra tried to follow their arguments on the pack's tiny screen, knowing that she was supposed to understand gravitic calculation and notation—but these two were just going too fast for her. Every time she thought she caught the sense of their discussion, they rocketed off onto a new topic before she had the chance to digest the last point.

Her attention wandered and she happened to glance up. Someone must have made a whole series of intercom calls. Virtually the entire station staff was there, and not just the scientists. The tech and admin and maintenance people were all there too. By now no one was even pretending to have a good reason for being there. They were simply an audience waiting for the show to begin.

If they were waiting for Raphael to show, they didn't have long to wait. Not more than ten minutes after Sondra and Webling arrived, Raphael burst in.

He stalked up to Larry, leaned over him, and glared malevolently down at him. "I should like to know the meaning of this," he said, obviously struggling to keep his voice calm.

Larry and Webling both looked up in surprise. "Meaning of what?" Larry asked, his voice nervous and subdued.

"Don't play me for the fool," the director snapped. He waved an experiment procedure form at Larry. "This is the standard report generated by the operations computer after every experiment run, showing how the equipment was configured and used. It describes the work done by these two"—he gestured in annoyance at

Webling and Sondra—"last night. This absurd 'modification' to Webling's intended experiment stands out like a sore thumb. This was *your* work. You have acted in direct and deliberate contravention of my orders!" he sputtered. "You have completely violated my every instruction. Every dollar, every cent expended by this ridiculous 'experiment' is coming out of your pay. Every cent."

Larry stole a sidelong glance at Sondra. Now was the time for their plan from the night. Last night, he hadn't much liked the idea of hiding behind Sondra's skirts, no matter how sensible it was. Now, Sondra's taking over was fine with him. Raphael practically had smoke coming out of his ears. Anyone who wanted to deal with him was welcome to the job. Larry glanced at Webling, and saw the sweat starting to pop out on her forehead, too. She wasn't going to be much use as protective cover. No, if anyone was going to handle the director, it would have to be Sondra.

"Violated orders? But that's just not so, Dr. Raphael," Sondra cut in smoothly, dredging up a low, winsome, southern-belle accent from somewhere. Larry dimly recalled that she was from the American South, but he had certainly never heard that tone of voice from her. "I'm sure there must be some *slight* misunderstanding." Larry glanced around. Sondra was obviously playing to the crowd, using the public audience as a screen against Raphael's anger.

"Mr. Chao here was simply *assisting* Dr. Webling and myself in our graser system tests. I suppose he *did* help us augment our signal power, but I can't see how that constitutes violating orders. For that matter, I don't see how you could issue him orders as to what to work on in the first place. You *are* the administrative director, but that doesn't give you any control over research operations. Mr. Chao is a full research fellow.

"Last time I checked the station's charter, research fellows have complete access to the Station's facilities. In fact, according to the station charter, the administrator is specifically *excluded* from authorizing experiments. That's supposed to be up to the chief scientist, Dr. Webling."

From the look on Webling's face, it was apparent that even *she* had forgotten she was chief scientist. Raphael had gathered all the de facto power to himself so long ago that no one remembered the official de jure arrangements. Sondra saw Raphael's quick glance toward Webling. That brief, nervous look told her she had won. She had found a vulnerable spot in Raphael's armor. A bully who breaks the rules cannot use the rules to bully. "Unless, of course, I have it wrong. What, exactly, is your authority for controlling Mr. Chao's work? Has Dr. Webling ceded the power of her office to you?"

Raphael opened his mouth and shut it without speaking. Before he could come up with anything more cogent, Webling chimed in. "I most certainly did *not* cede my authority—not to Dr. Raphael or to anyone else. But that does not excuse *your* impertinence, Dr. Berghoff." Webling turned and addressed Raphael. "But that to one side, Simon, right protocol or wrong, young Mr. Chao seems to have his *numbers* right. It would be criminal to reject such a promising claim out of hand over some breach of scientific *etiquette*. The first response from Titan should arrive at any moment. It seems to me that we are about to receive either a confirmation or a refutation of these theories. Shouldn't *that* be the basis for our reaction to Mr. Chao's work?"

Sandbagged, Sondra thought gleefully. *The old goat just got blown out of the water by his closest ally, in front of the entire staff.* Larry seemed about to say something, but she kicked him under the table. This was no time to let Raphael off the hook. Let him squirm.

But Sondra didn't get to see Raphael's reaction. A low beeping began, a sound that seemed to come from everywhere all at once. It took Sondra a moment to realize it was her notepack, alerting her that a message was incoming for her. Larry's pack was beeping too—and so were Webling's and Raphael's.

Titan! She pulled her pack out of its belt pouch and punched in the *Read Message* command.

The screen cleared and displayed the text of the message. Even as she read to herself, Webling stood and read it aloud to the entire staff.

"FROM: TISTAT COMMCENT PERSONAL AND IMMEDIATE.

"TO: RAPHAEL, WEBLING, BERGHOFF, CHAO.

"MESSAGE READS: TITAN STATION, SAKHAROV PHYSICS INSTITUTE SENDING FOR PLUTO, GRAVITICS RESEARCH STATION. WARMEST CONGRATULATIONS TO RAPHAEL AND ENTIRE TEAM. INCREDIBLE! GRAV METERS HERE RECORDED INDISPUTABLE RECEPTION OF PULSED, MODULATED GRAVITY WAVES OF REMARKABLE POWER AS PER YOUR PREEXPERIMENT TRANSMISSION. WE ARE HONORED TO BE FIRST TO CONGRATULATE YOUR LAB FOR THIS GREAT ACHIEVEMENT. WE ARE PROCESSING INITIAL DETAILED ANALYSIS AND WILL TRANSMIT SAME TO YOU AT EARLIEST CONVENIENCE. THIS IS A BREAKTHROUGH OF THE FIRST IMPORTANCE. WE TOAST YOU HERE WITH THE TRUE STOLI VODKA. WELL DONE, SIMON. PROUD REGARDS, M. K. POPOLOV, DIRECTOR. MESSAGE CONCLUDES."

A burst of applause followed, and a dozen people reached in to shake hands with Larry. Sondra could not keep a wry smile from her face. *Well done, Simon,* indeed. Director Popolov had assumed that Dr. Simon Raphael had been responsible for doing the experiment, rather than busy attempting to squelch it. Never mind. She could see the growing knot of people swarming over Larry. They could see where the real credit lay. And there would be no keeping the true word from spreading.

Well done, Simon. Sondra looked up to where Raphael had been and discovered he wasn't there anymore. She looked toward the door just in time to see him ducking through it, escaping his humiliation while the attention was off him. For a moment, for a brief moment, she found it in herself to feel sorry for the man.

But then the crowd jostled her, and swept her into the swirl of people surrounding Larry.

Shy, blushing, smiling, Larry accepted the congratulations of his colleagues, even those who had not believed him only hours before. There was a general clamor for information of all kinds. Everyone seemed to have a notepack out, trying to link into Larry's files in the central computer. They all found the files in question had privacy blocks on them. The computer commlink system actually shut down for a minute, overwhelmed by too many people asking for a look at too many files and datasets. Larry used his own notepack to remove the blocks from every file he controlled.

The whole business was too much for him. Pride, excitement, his usual awkwardness in public situations, worry over what Raphael would do next—all of those feelings and a half dozen more besides were jumbled up inside him—and were forced to take a backseat to the endless questions from Webling and the other staff scientists. There wasn't time for anything but the moment itself, the event.

Someone—Larry thought it was Hernandez, the microgravity expert, but he wasn't sure—was shoving a notepack in his face, asking him to explain a flowchart display. Larry offered up a mental shrug, took the pack, and started trying to make sense of the graph. Maybe if he cooperated, they would all calm down sooner.

But his answer only prompted another question from someone else, started another argument. There were too many possibilities, too many theories. There wasn't room in the dome for it all.

In part because the observation dome was getting too crowded, and in part because it was easier to explain things in front of the switches and dials and screens, the throng seemed to migrate from the observation dome to the primary Ring control room. Afterwards, Larry had no recollection of actually going there.

There was something about the buttons and dials and instruments of the control room that made people remember their professionalism. Voices got lower, and people actually waited for each other to finish talking.

The room was small, and there were too many people in it. The environmental system couldn't keep up, and the air grew hot and stuffy. Nobody seemed to notice or care. If anything, the closeness of the room added to the intensity of the moment. People got sharper, more focused, and started acting more like rational scientists. Larry found himself perched on the back of a chair, running an impromptu seminar.

But just when the situation seemed to be calmed down again, the next message came in, from Ganymede station. If anything, it was more effusive than Titan's signal. Then Titan checked in again, with a more complete report, and their enthusiasm seemed to have doubled, if such a thing were possible.

When Ganymede made its complete report, they had a real set of numbers to work with for the first time. They knew the power of the gravity beam when it had left Pluto-Charon, and now they had measurements, from two locations, of its power, intensity, wave shape and frequency at arrival—in effect giving them hard data on how the beam had been affected as it moved through space.

The data not only confirmed that Larry's gravity beam was real, it also told volumes about the nature of gravity itself—and about how it interacted with the fabric of space-time, about the matter and the gravity fields it passed through and near, how it affected and was affected by the velocity of the objects it encountered. Hernandez was able to prove that gravity was subject to Doppler effects. That was no great surprise; theory had predicted it. But for the first time the matter was settled, confirmed, and not a mere assumption.

There was a lesson in there, and somewhere in the middle of the tumult that day, Larry spotted it: Before you can fully understand a force of nature, you must be able to manipulate it. Never before had scientists been able to fiddle with gravity, in effect turn it on and off to see what would happen. Now they could, and the floodgates were open. In that first four hours they learned more about gravity than all of humanity had learned in all history.

And they had some power to play with, too. That helped. Science always needed more power than nature conveniently provided. How far would humans have gotten in the study of magnetism if all they had been allowed to work with was Earth's natural magnetic fields, and the occasional lodestone?

Size for size, nature's force generators were not very strong or efficient. It takes a whole thunderstorm to produce lightning, something as huge as Earth to create a natural one-gee field, a mass the size of the Sun to start fusion. Now humans could match all those power levels, or at least come close, using much smaller devices.

It was not a time for contemplation. Still the messages came, from Ganymede and Titan, informing that VISOR and JPL had been advised. Events were happening too rapidly, over too great a span of distance.

Larry imagined the radio and laser signals that must be crisscrossing the Inner System, chasing each other, sending new information that was old by the time it arrived. By now, as word was arriving at Pluto from Titan, saying that Titan had advised Earth—by now Earth had already received the gravity beam.

JPL would send a message as soon as someone there knew what was up. That was the signal to watch for. Larry watched the clocks and calculated the signal delay a dozen times over. Twenty minutes before a return signal from Earth could possibly arrive, he stood up and stretched. ''Look,'' he said, ''there's a lot more to cover, but we should be hearing from JPL soon, and I want to be in the dome when the message comes.''

With a renewed gabble of voices, the entire group migrated back to the dome. After all, everyone else wanted to see the message arrive as well. This discovery was going to save *their* jobs as well. Larry managed to duck away long enough to sneak back to his quarters, grab his toilet kit, go to the head and freshen up a bit. This was his second day more or less without sleep. If he couldn't have rest, he could at least have a two-minute shower and a shave.

By the time he arrived at the dome, a few minutes before Earth was due to check in, the show had already begun. The lights had been dimmed in the dome, and the stars gleamed forth overhead. Charon and the mighty wheel of the Ring dominated the sky.

Larry could not look up at that sight without being inspired. That tool, that device, one of the mightiest generators ever made, and *he* had put it to use, commanded it toward a breakthrough.

Larry moved carefully into the darkened room, waited for his eyes to adjust, and looked around. The comm staff had been at work, rigging a series of large view screens at one side of the dome and rearranging the chairs to face the screens. One screen showed a countdown clock, displaying the time remaining until the receipt-of-beam signal could arrive from Earth. The second display was clicking through screen after screen of results and reports already derived from the experiment, with data from Titan, Ganymede and VISOR.

Larry realized that he must have missed the Venusian signal while he was in the shower. The third screen showed the dome telescope's view of the Earth-Moon system, the two planets glowing like fat stars in the firmament. But it was the fourth screen that surprised Larry. It showed a handsome young man, nattily dressed, talking into the camera. An ID line across the bottom said he was Wolf Bernhardt, the spokesman for JPL, talking on a live feed. Given the expense and difficulty of punching a television signal through to Pluto, that in itself told Larry that the folks back home were taking him seriously.

Larry ducked his way into the rows and found an empty seat next to Sondra. "You haven't missed much," she told him in a stage whisper that had to carry halfway across the room. "Right now this guy is talking about the results from Venus."

Larry nodded vaguely and glanced at the countdown clock. Three minutes to go. There was a slight stir from the other side of the dome. Larry glanced over and saw Dr. Simon Raphael coming in. Raphael paused at the doorway and looked around. Their eyes locked for a moment.

Larry's heart sank, just the way it had back in grade school when the principal's gimlet eyes bored into him. Justly or unjustly, fairly or not, Larry the child and Larry the adult both knew what that look meant. He was in trouble. Again. Still. Forever. Raphael was going to find some way of punishing him.

Larry thought again of Raphael's threat to take "every cent" of the experiment's cost out of his pay. That look told Larry that the threat was still good. Raphael would find some way of making it stick. And making it hurt. If not for punishment, then for revenge.

Raphael broke eye contact and moved into the room, sidling along the far wall, to watch the action from as far away as possible.

Larry breathed a sigh of relief. Raphael was not going to cause a scene just now. This moment, here and now, would belong to Larry. That was something.

The beam shifted off the second planet, focusing on the third. Inevitably, the Observer was caught in the spill-over. The gravity beam passed through the solid mass of the Moon like light through glass. But if the Moon was transparent to gravity waves, the Observer was not. Lurking far beneath the Moon's surface, a huge torus girdling the satellite's core, the Observer shuddered as the beam played over it.

And that was the signal, the alert, the command it had been born and built to receive.

It responded as reflexively as a human jerking away from an electric shock, as instinctively as a lover at the moment of climax. There was no possibility of controlling the response. The beam set off an incredibly rapid chain of events far outside the control of what served as higher consciousness for the Observer.

Power long stored was drawn in, channeled, focused. But not enough power for the job at hand, merely enough to bring the Link up to full power. The Observer felt a surge of irrepressible pleasure as half-forgotten power

*poured through the new-born hole in space. The long-
dormant Link bloomed back to life.*

*Power. Now it had the power. An overwhelming sense
of potency, of potential, of* mission *and* purpose *coursed
through its being. Now. Now was the time for its destiny.
Now it could turn its attentions toward Earth.*

*The Observer drew massive, surging power through
the Link and* grabbed.

Larry turned his attention back to the countdown clock
and realized with a start that there were only a few seconds left. He started listening to the announcer. "We
have received further confirmation of a powerful signal
from Venus. The beam moved off Venus ninety seconds
ago in real time, and we are awaiting it here. We are
standing by for scheduled reception of your beam at
Earth." There was a rustle of anticipation in the room.
This was it, not only for Larry, not only for the experiment, but for the whole station.

If JPL was suitably impressed, the U.N. Astrophysics
Foundation would be impressed. And if the UNAF was
impressed, there was no way they could shut down the
Gravitics Research Station. At least that was what Larry
hoped.

The announcer looked away from the camera toward
a timer display on his desk. "Twenty seconds now," he
said, obviously relishing the moment.

Larry swallowed hard and leaned forward in his seat.
Silly to be nervous, silly to be excited. He *knew* it had
worked. But the seconds were sliding away.

"T minus five, four, three, two, one, zero. We are
getting the first—"

The commlink from JPL went dead.

In the middle of view screen three, Earth flashed out of existence.

The Moon hung in the telescope view.

Alone.

Larry sat there, watching the monitor screen in frozen horror. The comm people were already jumping up, checking their gear. "It's everything," one of them said. "All commlinks with Earth just went dead."

"That's crazy. Check back at central."

Everything. Larry sat, motionless, his heart pounding. They would search for an answer, a malfunction in their gear.

But Larry *knew.* No evidence, no explanation, but he *knew.* Somehow, impossibly, the beam, the harmless gravity-wave beam, so weakened at that range it could not have squashed a fly or mussed a child's hair—

Somehow it had vaporized the Earth.

Eyes began to turn toward Larry. Eyes that were no longer friendly, or excited. *Yes,* he thought, *they'll all be willing to admit it was my experiment now.*

Eyes bored into his head. One pair of eyes in particular. Raphael, behind him, seething with terror and rage. Larry could feel the director's malevolent stare drilling into the back of his skull.

Two thoughts echoed in his head, one incredible, the other simply insane.

Larry Chao had destroyed the Earth.

And somehow, Simon Raphael was going to see to it that it came out of Larry's pay.

Part Two

CHAPTER SIX

$\diamond$

The Amber of Time

GERALD MACDOUGAL REACHED OUT AND SLAPPED THE alarm buzzer. Two in the morning. Vancouver, British Columbia, was a lovely city, but it had a major flaw: it was in the wrong time zone. Like the Moon and the domed Settlements and virtually all the other space installations, VISOR worked on Universal Time. Greenwich Mean Time as they insisted on calling it here.

Two A.M. here. That was ten in the morning on VISOR, ignoring the speed-of-light delays. Ten A.M., Tuesdays and Saturdays, were Marcia's assigned slots for sending view messages home. If she even got that much chance. She had sent a twenty-word-text message the night before warning about watching some gravity experiment from Pluto, just after 1000 UT. Right on top of her sending time slot.

Gerald stretched and yawned. Venus was about ninety degrees from conjunction at the moment, which worked out to a ten-minute speed-of-light delay, plus a split second or two while the Earth-orbiting comsat picked it up and relayed it around to his receiver. He had time to wake up a bit before Marcia's weekly message came in. He could have let his comm system pick it up and could have played it back later, of course, but he preferred to see the view message immediately, the moment it came down. That way he would *know* what Marcia had been doing and saying ten short minutes before. It was the one time when that was possible. God, he missed her.

He stood up, walked to the window, and looked down at the splendid city laid out before him. His hometown. Aside from the time zone, there was no place on Earth he'd rather be. And, as far as his work was concerned, no place on Earth was where he ought to be. Gerald was a big man, tall, muscular and tough, with curly brown hair and a solid jaw. He got restless waiting, and was too often forced to convince himself that patience was a virtue.

Back to space soon, he promised himself, not quite believing it. There was still hope. To Venus, and VISOR, and his wife and his work.

Strictly speaking, the primary subject of Gerald MacDougal's work did not exist. One of his career goals was to wipe out anything that resembled it.

Gerald was an exobiologist, a student of life off the planet Earth. The flaw, of course, was that there *wasn't* any life beyond Earth. Except, of course, such Earth-evolved life that continued to evolve even off planet. Every human being, every plant, every animal brought along to the Settlements carried microscopic life-forms by the billions.

Anywhere humans went, viruses, bacteria, and other microbes, disease-causing and benign, traveled as well. Normal medical practice was enough to keep most of the nasties at bay inside the sealed colonies—but some microbes escaped the domes, tunnels, ships and habitats to the outside environments. Virtually all of them died the moment they left the controlled environment. But a few survived. And of those survivors, a *very* few managed to reproduce, and evolve, often at a ferocious rate.

Earth-derived microbes lurked in the soil around Martian cities, living off dome leakages of air, moisture and organics; lived inside the rock of mining asteroids, dining on a witches' brew diet of complex hydrocarbons; lived as mildew–like patches in airlocks all over the Solar System, absorbing air, moisture and bits of organic matter whenever the locks were pressurized, encysting when they went into vacuum.

Even to Gerald, who should have been used to such things by now, the tenacity of life in such circumstances was incredible. It was proof to Gerald that there was a God. No random sequence of events could have produced living things capable of such feats. Evolution existed, yes; Gerald was no creationist. But there was a divine hand guiding evolution.

A divine hand that worked in mysterious and sometimes horrifying ways. For a few, a terrifying few, of the outsider organisms came back *inside* the domes and the spacecraft. Most such Returnees were wiped out by the drastically different environment, but some readapted to life back inside. That was when terror struck. Hardened by their generations outside air, light and pressure, some Returnee organisms bred hellaciously back inside, carrying in their genes the ability to digest unlikely things. Plastics, metal, resin compounds, semiorganic superconductors. And some of them, ancestors of disease organisms, retained the ability to infect the human body.

There were microorganisms that could cause disease in humans and also eat through pressure suits and air domes from the inside. Or dissolve the superconducting wires of power grids. Or jam valves in fusion systems.

From a human perspective, the Returnees were a

nightmare. But God, Gerald had long since decided, did *not* have a human perspective. The Good Lord wanted all life, everywhere, to have a chance. Humans and microbes were equally His children, equally miraculous. He wanted all His children to have a chance at life, from the most high unto the least. If some individuals of one species had to die so another species might survive, was that not the way of all Nature? Why should humanity be exempt?

He did not see any contradiction between admiring the dogged survival skills of the Returnees and cold-bloodedly seeking to destroy them. The wolf lives at the expense of the deer, and the buck may kill the wolf to defend his herd. Neither is right or wrong. Even the lamb lives at the expense of the foliage it crops—and many a thorn will stab at a lamb unwary enough to dine on the wrong plant. All that lives must draw life from others, and must defend itself against the assault of other species. So too with humanity.

Gerald's goal was to wipe out all off-planet microscopic life outside the human-made environments. He knew he could never achieve his goal, and this knowledge gave him a certain strange comfort. But it was not enough. The destruction of life, however needful, did not fulfill Gerald.

He wanted to *create* life, be God's tool in the work of making a whole new world full of life—but now that dream was fading. The circumstances were so frustrating.

The terraforming of Venus was technically possible. No one questioned that any longer.

Gerald's work would have played a part in it, too. The Isolated Exobiology Facility would have been an ideal source of terraforming microbes. The simplest of gene engineering would have produced microbes to break down the noxious atmosphere, to fix nitrogen to soil, to remove carbon dioxide and produce water, to convert the acid-leached rocks to soil.

But the era of grand projects, of great visions, was fading before it had gotten properly under way. The *Terra Nova* starship project had been canceled, and now the word was that the Ring of Charon was being shut down. What hope could there be for a plan to rebuild a world? More than likely, the microbes stored at Gerald's Isolated Exobiology Facility would never get their chance to seed Venus.

He looked up from the valley, into the late-night sky. Venus would not rise for hours yet, but he knew it was there. And Marcia was there, aboard VISOR as it circled that hell-hot world. He had spent much of the last year preparing to join her there—but now the two of them were forced to face the likelihood that it would be Marcia returning here, as humanity retreated from the challenge of Venus.

The comm center bleeped, and Gerald rushed over to it, sat down and powered up the screen. The countdown clock appeared, ticked down to zero, and then was replaced by Marcia's dark exquisite face.

"Hello, Gerald," she said, her voice warm and loving. "Thank heavens I got through—we just got word of a big experiment that we'll need all our transmission bandwidth for. There was supposed to be a ten o'clock cutoff on personal messages, but Lonny knew I was scheduled and stretched the rules for me. He'll keep me on as long as he can, but I might get cut off abruptly. Nothing to worry about—they just need this vision channel. Lonny's sending a text message from me on a sideband right now. It tells what the experiment is so I don't waste view time talking about it. Sorry, but the text message isn't much—just a data dump on what we've been told about the experiment. I haven't had time to write a real letter. I'm working on one. I should be able to send it tonight.''

The printer bin buzzed and a thin sheaf of papers dropped into it. Gerald ignored the document, reached out a hand and touched the screen. These few moments with her image were all he had, and now even this contact was being rationed. Never again, he decided. Once he got there, or she came here, never again would they be separated.

''There isn't much excitement beyond this experiment run,'' Marcia's image said. ''McGillicutty's driving us all even madder than usual, but I suppose I should be used to that by now. The work is going well—though we're all watching the news and hoping we're not in it.'' There was a muffled voice from off camera, and Marcia glanced away. ''Oh damn!'' she said, cursing with the sincerity of someone who didn't do it often. ''Lonny says I've got ten seconds. I love you, Gerald. I can't wait for your next message to me. Finish up all your business and get here. I love you. Good-bye—''

The screen cut off, and Gerald felt a lump in his throat. There was only so much of this separation that he could take. Thank God it would be over soon, one way or the other.

Aboard VISOR, Marcia MacDougal forced a smile, thanked Lonny, and hurried out into the corridor. But where to go? she wondered. She felt lost, empty. Gerald gone, the project dying. What did it matter? To the wardroom, she decided, almost at random. Maybe there would be people there, someone to talk to, someone to take her mind away from loneliness.

She went into the corridor and walked the short distance. But the wardroom was empty. McGillicutty must have pulled everyone in to help observe the gravity experiment. No doubt she'd get drafted herself, sooner or later.

Finding herself alone, Marcia MacDougal made the best of it. She stepped over to the wardroom's big observation port, and looked down at the planet's glaring cloud tops.

She was a striking woman, seeming taller than she really was by virtue of her determined character. She had clear, flawless skin the color of dark mahogany, and her face was round and expressive. Her eyes were dark brown, bright and clear; eyes that seemed to see everything. But there was nothing at all to see out the observation window.

To the naked eye, dayside Venus was blindingly bright, a featureless wall of cloud. She could have fixed that: the observation windows could be controlled, the contrast, brightness, and spectrum manipulated. With the right settings, pattern and order appeared in the cloud tops.

But right now, to Marcia, a blank, staring, featureless globe seemed most appropriate. The light was so bright that nothing could be seen. So much information was coming in that nothing could be understood. The metaphors seemed apt to the era of the Knowledge Crash. And VISOR seemed likely to be the next Crash victim.

Venus Initial Station for Operational Research—VISOR—had been meant to be the stuff that dreams were made of. The headquarters for the creation of a brave new world—a new Venus, cooled, watered, made new with life.

No one knew exactly how it was to be done, how a world would be brought to life. That was what VISOR was for—to find the answers. There had been some wild ideas: VISOR dropping huge probes and seeder ships onto the planet, manhandling ice-bearing asteroids and monstrous atmosphere skimmers into place. Huge sunshades orbiting the planet, floating chemical factories built under enormous dirigibles and set loose in the upper atmosphere.

Some of the more wild-eyed miners in the Asteroid Belt had their own ideas. They had quite seriously offered to blow up the planet Mercury with a fearsome device named the Core Cracker. With a second asteroid belt close to Sun, they would really get some use out of solar power. Venus didn't really have much to do with the idea, but the Belt Community crowd had tried to sell its plans to VISOR, pointing out the Mercury Belt would be an ideal place to build those massive sunshades or rotation-enhancement impact bodies.

There were other schemes, not quite so mad, and VISOR would have tried some or all of them. At the present time, of course, no one had the faintest idea how to do any of those things. And that was the whole point. VISOR was built to last for centuries, built to grow, change, evolve. The station designers expected that it would have to handle technologies whose inventors were not yet born.

VISOR. The last two words in the acronym were the key. *Operational Research.* Before Venus could be remade, the scientists and engineers had to learn how the task could be done. A lot could be resolved with computer models and small-scale simulations, but when dealing with a massive planetary environment, those techniques simply weren't enough. The engineers and scientists needed a whole planet to play with, a whole planet to make mistakes on. Terraforming required on-the-job training.

Couldn't the United Nations see that? Couldn't they see how vital the station was? How disastrous a shutdown, or even a temporary mothballing, would be? Venus was a task for decades, generations. It could not be done in fits and starts.

Suddenly the intercom hooted at her. A high-pitched slightly peevish voice that Marcia had learned to dread spoke. "MacDougal! Get on up to Main Control!" McGillicutty's voice said. "I need you to monitor some low-end radio for me."

Marcia shut her eyes and counted to ten before turning away from the window and heading up to the lab. She was willing to bet that even her husband's patience would be worn thin by Hiram McGillicutty. She'd have to try the experiment, once Gerald got here.

Hiram McGillicutty was the staff physicist of the Venus Initial Station for Operational Research. Most days, that job made Mcgillicutty as useful as a parachute on a fish.

No one disputed that VISOR *needed* a physicist, but only in the sense that a small town needed a fire department. You had to have one around, just in case something unexpected happened.

McGillicutty did not think much of his colleagues on the station. Mere engineers. Give them the numbers to plug into the equations, and they were perfectly happy. Never mind what the numbers meant, or how they were derived. Ninety-nine times out of a hundred, they not only would not *need* to know how the numbers came to be there, they would positively resent your wasting their time with such petty details.

Hiram McGillicutty imagined himself as accepting his lot philosophically—though no one else on the station would ever describe his attitude in such terms. Most of them would come up with *arrogant*, or *self-absorbed*.

But today was different. Today this was *his* station, thanks to those bad boys on Pluto. McGillicutty chuckled under his breath, shook his shaggy head, and bared his snaggled teeth in a rueful grin. He had seen the prelim data from Ganymede and Titan. What a *stunt* the gravity boys were pulling!

He checked the sequencer clock and worked out the speed-of-light delay. According to the experiment plan Pluto had transmitted, the gravity beam should have started targeting Venus just over five and a half hours ago. So if the experiment was indeed running on schedule, the gravity beam should be arriving any—

"Jesus jumping Christ willya lookit that!" he cried. Hiram McGillicutty was of an excitable sort, but for once he would seem to be entitled. The gravity-wave meter, a piece of incredibly delicate hardware that had rarely given off so much as a quiver, was now spiking high, slamming into the high end of the scale. McGillicutty adjusted the graphic display scale by a factor of a hundred.

Marcia MacDougal shook her head in wonderment. It was real. After hundreds of years as a minor curiosity— a sideshow in the world of high-energy physics—gravitic research was suddenly coming alive, right before her very eyes.

"It's a gravity beam," someone said. "Shouldn't we feel heavier, or lighter, or something? I don't feel a thing."

"How powerful is that beam?" one of the biologists asked, a bit nervously. "It's not going to start pulling us toward Pluto, is it?"

"It doesn't work that way," McGillicutty explained testily. "What they've managed to do—somehow, God only knows how—is use a phase relation to make half the wave repulse instead of attract. The effect cancels itself out overall. And the beam is damn weak before it gets here."

McGillicutty licked his lips greedily. "*God* I'd love to know how they do it. But if they've figured out how to manipulate gravity fields that well, they *can't* be more than a few steps from true gravity control—if they could fiddle the harmonics somehow and establish a standing wave front—they could create whatever gravity field they wanted.''

"That's the sort of little 'if' that takes another hundred years to crack,'' Marcia said. "I'd bet gravity waves are just a parlor trick for a long, long time.''

"Maybe,'' McGillicutty said. "But as parlor tricks go, this is a pretty major one. Gravity waves ought to provide a whole new way of looking at the Universe. Matter should be practically transparent to gee waves! Tune the waves right, and we ought to be able to use them to see right *through* the Sun and the planets, look down into them as deep as we want. Put a gee-wave sender on one side of Venus, and a detector on the other, and we'd be able to examine its internal structure in real time. Like radar. There are big times ahead. Big times.''

"For the gravity crowd,'' Chenlaw said mournfully. "The research pie is getting mighty small. So what do you think will happen to our funding if this Ring gets sexy and starts gobbling up all the money? What we have to do is come up with a way to get involved in gravity if we want to see a dime.''

Marcia glanced up at the sequence clock. "Eight more minutes here. Then they switch the beam to Earth.'' She watched her displays, and wondered what the new world would be like.

McGillicutty was also glad when the beam shifted off Venus.

Oh, those ten minutes when the beam had been directed at them, at VISOR, those were blissful, fantastic. But they were almost too much. The signal was so powerful it threatened to overwhelm his instruments. But now he could direct his gear at a remote target, at Earth. No one had ever done this sort of sensing before. It was an entirely different challenge, an entirely different opportunity.

You needed some *range* before you gained any perspective. Besides, there were all the secondary effects you could only observe at range. How did the gee waves warp radio? Lightwaves? In theory, modulated gravity waves should alternately blueshift and redshift electromagnetic radiation. Would that really happen? And what effect would the beam have on existing and interacting gravity sources? Would there be induced resonance waves in the Earth-Moon system's gravity patterns?

McGillicutty wanted to know it all. That in itself was nothing new—he spent his entire life, every waking minute, wanting to know all the answers. What was different about today was that he was getting the chance to find out.

Still, he would have to move fast to get it. The gravity-wave beam had shifted off Venus only a few minutes ago. He had only about five minutes to reorient the station's sensors toward Earth and reconfigure them for distant sensing. Fortunately, the rest of the staff was there to assist him on the job.

He checked the main control board one more time. A few of the instruments still weren't in position. ''Marcia, swivel in that damn boom antenna. We'll need the twenty-one-centimeter band on this job. I want to see if there's any ripple in the neutral hydrogen band.''

''Yes sir, boss. Right away boss. You bet, boss,'' Marcia growled as she activated the antenna system. Personally, she could not imagine a more useless task than watching the twenty-one-centimeter band. It seemed to her that twenty-one centimeters *never* showed anything.

McGillicutty wanted to see if the gravity wave would distort space-time enough to show a ripple in the carrier.

So what, either way? She watched as the indicator showed the antenna directing itself at Earth. She switched her monitor to oscilloscope mode. Yep, there it was. Twenty-one centimeters was showing a virtually flat carrier wave, as usual. She powered up the audio gain and was rewarded with a faint hiss. "Ready to go, boss," she said, "and I'm *real* excited about it."

"Good," McGillicutty said, completely missing the sarcasm. "Chenlaw, what's with the microwave receiver? I need it now, not next week!"

"For God's sake, Hiram, give me more than thirty seconds."

"Why?" McGillicutty asked. "It shouldn't take anywhere near *that* long to swing it around twenty degrees."

"I have to swing it around the other way, through three hundred forty degrees, or point it straight at the power generators as it slews around," Chenlaw replied through clenched teeth. "Do you want it blown out when it gets into position?"

But McGillicutty wasn't even listening anymore. He was on the intercom to one of the other labs, chattering on about neutrino backscatter. Chenlaw turned and shook her head at Marcia. Marcia shrugged back. What could you do? The man was utterly impossible.

"Okay, boys and girls," McGillicutty said in a loud, cheerful voice, patently unaware how many of his co-workers wanted to strangle him. He checked his chronometers. "Earth should be under the beam already, and has been for seven minutes. The event radius is moving toward us. Stand by to receive results data in three minutes—mark! All instruments and recorders should be operating now to establish pre-event background levels."

McGillicutty managed to shut up long enough to check his own control board. "Two minutes," he announced at last.

Under the beam for seven minutes. Marcia suddenly

found herself thinking of her husband, Gerald MacDougal, back on Earth, back home in the lab in Vancouver. Even at the speed of light, he was ten long minutes away. But it wasn't numbers and seconds. It was that Gerald was in the past, his reality cut off from hers by the wall of time. No matter what he did, no matter what happened to him, she could not possibly know about it until the sluggish lightwaves crossed the void between the worlds.

He could die in the midst of sending her a live message and she would not know it for ten minutes.

If, for Marcia, Gerald was trapped in her past, then she was trapped in his past. Each in the other's past. There was something deeply disturbing about that, as if both of them were frozen in place, like some insect trapped in Precambrian tree sap, imprisoned as the sap fossilized into crystal perfection, leaving its victim perfectly preserved, trapped in the amber of time.

"Twenty seconds," McGillicutty announced. This weird pulsation and manipulation of gravity was not something she understood. She was more than a little afraid of it, to tell the truth. Somehow, it smacked of magic, of voodoo and mystery. How could there be a beam made of gravity waves? It even sounded like a non-sense phrase, a cheese made of xylophones, a cloud made of steel.

She blinked and forced herself to concentrate on the display screen. "Ten seconds." Nine minutes and fifty seconds ago, the beam had struck her husband's world, but that stroke of time would not pass through her frame of experience for another ten seconds, nine seconds, eight seconds—she fiddled with her tuning controls, sharpening the image—four, three, two, one, zero—

Her screen display went wild, and her terminal speaker was suddenly overwhelmed by a powerful screeching roar of noise. She cut off the audio and stared in astonishment at the oscilloscope trace on the screen. *Something* was producing a powerful and complex signal out there. There almost seemed to be a pattern to it, as if it were repeating over and over again.

It took her a moment to look up and realize that the rest of the people in the lab were more surprised than she was. Even McGillicutty seemed to be in shock. It took her significantly longer to realize that the squeal on the twenty-one-centimeter band was all that was left of Earth.

With a bump and a clunk, the *Pack Rat* undocked herself from the Moonside cargo port of the Naked Purple Habitat. Dianne Steiger glanced at the chronometer: 1001 GMT, just after ten in the morning, departure right on schedule, though it didn't come soon enough for her. If there were weirder places than NaPurHab in the Solar System, she didn't want to know about them. The *Rat* backed off with a cough from her control jets, engaged her gyros and came about to a new heading. The big bright ball of Earth swung into view through the starboard port.

With folded hands, Dianne Steiger sat at the control panel and watched the proceedings.

The massive, somehow scruffy bulk of NaPurHab loomed large in her forward port. NaPurHab flew a looping figure-eight orbit that shuttled back and forth around Earth and Moon. Right now the hab was headed down into the Earthside portion of its orbit. That was where the *Rat* got off, fired engines to circularize her orbit and get on course for her next port of call. Dianne keyed the comm panel and called NaPurHab comm and traffic. "NaPurHab, this is Foxtrot Tango thirty-four, call signal *Pack Rat*, departing for deadhead run to High New York

Habitat. On auto departure, now sending departure vector data on side channel. Please acknowledge.''

''We copy you, *Pack Rat*. Departure plan received, recorded and approved. Slide on in to HNY easy. Milk the fatcats until they moo or meow. See you next time.'' Chelated Noisemaker Extreme, also know as Frank Barlow, was a decent sort, even if he drifted into the stilted Naked Purple lingo now and again.

''Thanks, Frank,'' Dianne replied. ''I'm looking forward to it.'' Not exactly true, of course, but what the hell. On her job description, Dianne Steiger was called a pilot-astronaut. But she knew better. Dianne was a backup system. The robots, the automatics, the artificial intelligence routines—they were the astronauts. They did all the work. She was here because this freight run flew close to inhabited areas in the crowded regions of Earth orbit, and because the astronaut union was still fairly strong, if in decline.

Union rules and safety regs required a pilot aboard in case the incredibly unlikely occurred and the automatics packed up while leaving the manual controls functional. Nice theory, except that virtually every mishap that could incapacitate the autos would wreck the *Rat* past all possibility of controlling her ever again, by any means. But regulations were regulations.

Even the few tasks left to Dianne could just as easily have been done by machines. But it was deemed wise to give the pilots at least something to do, even if the computer could have controlled that circuit, and a servo could have sealed that hatch. A pilot left completely inactive, her reflexes completely dulled by boredom, was not likely to be of much use in an emergency. Or so went the theory. Dianne felt pretty dulled down, even so.

Flying spaceships was supposed to be romantic, exciting, dangerous and challenging. Dianne had gone through eight years of training and ended up running a glorified delivery service.

She was thirty-three years old, but looked older. Her hair was long and brown, half-gone to gray. At the moment she had it bound up in a tight braid coiled on top of her head. When she let it down, it was as wiry as a bottle brush. Her face was lined and lean, and her eyes were wide and bright. People who didn't know her assumed at first sight that she hadn't eaten in a week, Her face took expressions to their extremes. Her slightest smile lit up a room, her least frown was frightening.

She sorely missed her cigarettes aboard ship. Someday they'd build a ship with an air system rated to handle tobacco smoke. She made up for it on the ground, though. She was a chain-smoker between flights, her fingers stained yellow with nicotine. She was small and slight of build, but surprisingly strong, with a bone-crushing handshake and a hard, muscular body built over her slender frame. Her appearance, her body, had helped her get a job. The shipping companies like their pilots small and quick.

She had, quite literally, set her sights a lot higher than flying an orbital shuttle. She had been a candidate for the starship project, before they scrapped it. She'd been one test away from acceptance as a cold-sleep reserve pilot aboard the *Terra Nova*. She was to have been the third-wave pilot, thawed out when the first-wave pilot retired and the second-wave pilot took command. When the second-wave pilot died or retired—then *she* would have been the commander of a starship.

Then the whole starship project had been canceled, victim of the Knowledge Crash recession that had hit Earth and the rest of the Solar System. It was an era of retreat, surrender, drawing back from the frontiers to safety. So now the nearly completed *Terra Nova* rode in low Earth orbit, mothballed.

The recession hadn't offered much to ex–starship pilots. There weren't any openings on the passenger lines, or even on the cargo ships moving between the major planets. And so Dianne was reduced to humping freight back and forth between NaPurHab, the low-Earth-orbit stations, and the dirtside spaceports. And she was lucky to get even this job. All the other *Terra Nova* pilots had out-emigrated long ago, looking for work in the Settlement worlds. But pilot jobs were lean out there, too.

She almost didn't care about that. She was thinking of quitting astronautics altogether, picking one of the Settlement worlds or a habitat and getting the hell out. It wouldn't be exploring new star systems, true, but at least it would be a frontier, of sorts.

She didn't understand the people on the Earth or the Moon anymore. The crazies were taking over. The evidence was right in front of her. She looked intently at the huge habitat floating in the darkness. The Purps had come off Earth, taken over this place and the old Tycho Penal Colony—and the United Nations actually recognized the Purps as a legitimate government.

Dianne had her mind made up. If she could not have the stars, she wanted to get out to *somewhere*, to a place, a world, that would at least be new to her. But could she live in a habitat, a tin can in the middle of space? To one of the Settlement worlds, then. Mars, or Titan, maybe. Perhaps the Asteroid Belt. If she could even get that far in the middle of a recession.

Dianne Steiger checked the *Pack Rat*'s main panel again and sighed. All was well. Far too well. Nothing for her to do. Transorbital burn in ten minutes. The *Rat* knew that with far greater accuracy than she did.

The ship lit engines and made the transorbital burn with perfect precision, shut down, and left Dianne to continue stewing in her juices. *Not much longer,* she told herself. *Not much longer at all.*

Chelated Noisemaker Extreme glanced up at his external monitor. Good-bye to the *Pack Rat*. There she was, a small dot of light ten degrees across the sky from the gleaming bulk of a nearly full Moon, a skyful of familiar old stars glowing warm and bright between them. He glanced down and checked his Moonside comm board. All green. All comm channels to the Moon operational. He'd have to do something about that, or catch hell from his boss.

But not just yet. The view was too pretty. The *Pack Rat*'s acquisition strobes blinked on and off, giving Frank an easy visual sighting. Good for Dianne. A lot of the astros didn't bother with ac-lights anymore, especially the ones who flew into Purple space. He sighed and shook his head. There was something wrong with a world where so many people worked so hard to do the absolute minimum. Not as if the Purps were much help.

Chelated did a lot of the traffic control duty, but he was mainly a radio tech, responsible for keeping the Naked Purple Habitat more or less in contact with the outside universe. That "more or less" was a key part of his job description. If things got too bad, he had to struggle to bring them up to spec. If, on the other hand, communications got too *good*, it was his job to degrade them. And he was, of course, expected to randomize the situation at times. Keeping things off an even keel was an important part of the Purple philosophy.

Even if the duties of the job were a bit strange, Chelated—known as Frank Barlow in his pre-Purple life—was skilled in his profession. That was what made him a Noisemaker *Extreme*—and earned him a bit of suspicion from the more purist Purples. who disapproved of any ability.

But that didn't matter. Chelated (or Frank, as he still secretly thought of himself) loved radio, electronics, and communications gear for themselves. In the post–K-Crash world, there were few positions for a man of his skill. He had come to the Naked Purple Habitat simply because there was no other place he could get a chance to practice his craft. He saw it as a bonus that he was allowed—even required—to try all the crazy things the other comm centers never permitted.

Still, he found the place a bit disturbing. But then, he would have been worried about himself if he ever got used to these people.

He felt the need to talk to someone and keyed the radio link open again. "Hey Dianne, you still on the feed?"

"Still here, Frank," her voice said from the overhead speaker. "What's up?" Chelated was about to reply, but the view through the monitor caught his eye again.

Some sort of flash of light overwhelmed the camera for a moment before it recovered. A chance reflection of the Sun off some polished surface, no doubt. The image came back at once. But there was something wrong. Chelated frowned and looked harder.

No, it was okay. Dianne's ship was still there, against the broad background of stars. *Stars?* That was nuts. The Moon should be behind the *Pack Rat*. An alarm began to bleat, and he checked the system. The Earthside links were okay, but all the Moonside commlinks were out. Every last one of them.

Frank looked to the external view again. A numbing horror began to take hold of his gut.

The sky was all wrong. The Moon wasn't there anymore.

And those weren't the right stars, either.

CHAPTER SEVEN

—————◇—————

Shock Waves

LUCIAN DREYFUSS WAS ONE OF THE FEW PERMANENT Lunar residents who actually witnessed Earth's disappearance.

Mostly, it was the tourists who saw it happen. At any given moment, there were thousands of tourists up on the surface, in suits or in the view-domes, seeing the Lunar sights, such as they were. The locals never went topside.

Lucian worked as a space traffic controller in his regular job, and shepherded tourists on the side when money was tight—as it usually was with Lucian. At least it was a view-dome tour today. Dealing with a gaggle of tourist in shirtsleeves, oohing and ahhing at the gray landscape from inside a bubble dome, was infinitely preferable to riding herd on a bunch of neophytes bounding about the surface, all of them merrily trying to kill themselves by finding the flaws in supposedly idiot-proofed pressure suits.

Not even the Sun could hurt them here. Outside the dome, a large occulting disk on a specially built tracking arm followed the Sun around the sky, putting itself between the dome and the Sun at all times, thus keeping the Sun's disk safely hidden from the dome's interior. Outside the dome, the Moonscape was brilliantly lit: the dome itself was in permanent shadow. Lights glowed around the edge of the dome floor, providing just enough illumination to keep the *turistas* from tripping over each other.

But dome or surface, morning tours were always a bit much for Lucian. He was a night owl, used to the night shift at Orbital Traffic Control—and the night life at the casinos. He glanced at his watch. Just before 1000, Universal Time. Of course, this crowd was fresh off the ship. Most of these grounders were probably still on their local times. God only knew what time of day it was for them.

Lucian was on the short side with a wiry, athletic build. He put in a lot of time in the gym, determined to fight off the typical Conner's tendency toward pudginess. His face was narrow and pale, with a reddish brown crew cut. His eyes were slate gray, penetrating, serious, passionate.

He looked out over the landscape. At the moment, his eyes showed nothing more impassioned than boredom. Maybe the landscape *was* awesome, but the natives—the Conners, as they called themselves—had seen it all before. None of them bothered to go up to the surface without a good reason. After all, the Lunar surface didn't change much. Or at all. The tourists never seemed to understand that attitude.

Lucian spotted a somewhat overfed matron looking around the dome, giving every person a once-over, no doubt cataloguing each by accent and clothing. She frowned, spotted Lucian, and came over to him. A Mrs.

Chester, he remembered. He knew what she was going to ask even before she opened her mouth.

"Tell me, Mr. Dreyfuss," she asked. "Why do so few *natives* came up to look at any of the sights? I've been on tour here for a week now, and the only locals I've seen aboveground have been the tour guides. The vistas are so *lovely*. Why don't you all come to look at them?"

" 'You only have to see the rocks once,' " Lucian replied in a tired voice. He didn't bother telling her that that bit of folk wisdom had the power of a proverb among the Conners. People said it to explain that something once new was getting stale, old, was something you didn't need anymore.

Lucian currently felt all of those things. *He* certainly didn't need to see the rocks again. His mind was on other things. On how long until he could bring the tour group back, on how much of the spiel he still had to give, on how many more herds of groundlings he would have to drag around to clear his casino debt.

He glanced at his watch. That was time enough to let them wander the dome, ogling on their own. Lucian clapped his hands together and stepped up onto a low dais built into the dome's floor. "All right, folks, all right. Gather around, if you please. I'll be pointing out several of the landmarks visible from here. First and foremost of these is of course the Earth, directly over my head."

As if they were all attached to the same swivel control, the sea of heads surrounding Lucian all pivoted upward at once. A forest of arms sprouted up as the groundlings pointed out home to each other. Lucian had given up wondering why they did that. Did any of them seriously think their friends were incapable of finding Earth in the sky?

Lucian looked up himself to see what sort of real estate and weather were visible at the moment. Earth was in waning half-phase, the terminator just about to reach the coast of North America, with clear weather over most of the daylight quadrant. Good. That put Africa front and center. A nice, well-known, easy-to-recognize piece of geography plainly visible with no damn cloud cover hiding it. Much preferable to when the Pacific was socked in and he was reduced to showing where Hawaii would be if it were big enough to see and the clouds weren't there. He tried to pump a little enthusiasm into his voice, just for the form's sake.

"As you can see, the Sun is just rising over the coast of North and South America, and there's clear weather over most of the Atlantic. Can anyone spot the coast of Africa?"

The murmur of voices swept toward a crescendo as the groundlings eagerly pointed out the perfectly obvious to each other. Next step. He could explain how the South American coast matched up with Africa. He looked up at the Earth and began.

"Very good. Now, if you look toward the dark side of the planet, you can just see—"

He saw it. He saw it happen. One moment the Earth was there, and then, suddenly, in a weird, twisted flash of blue light, it wasn't. He blinked, unbelieving.

The Earth wasn't there anymore.

Around him, the tourist voices rose again, a bit uncertainly. "Is it an eclipse?" one of them asked.

"Hey, sonny, is this some kind of joke?"

"Did the polarizers switch on in the wrong place?"

"No, dummy, this dome isn't polarized. It's got that Sun-blocking gizmo on the control arm outside."

"It must be a power failure. All the lights on Earth went out."

"Yeah, right, including the *Sun*?"

"Hey, mister, you ever seen anything like this before?"

"Young man, what in *heaven*'s name is going on?" Mrs. Chester demanded in an imperious voice, as if Lucian were responsible for preventing disasters.

Lucian ignored the welter of voices and stared at the impossible sky, his mind racing for an explanation. What in the name of God could create the illusion of a *planet* vanishing? He dreamed up a half dozen theories. A black dust cloud wandering through the Solar System, a bad prank by some grad students on one of the space habitats, flinging a king-size occulting disk in front of Earth, a sudden weird flaw in the dome's glass that filtered out Earth-colored light. But none of his ideas made sense, or were even physically possible.

Then if there were no way to make it *seem* the Earth was gone, then it had to be that—

Lucian never had the chance to complete the terrifying thought. The first moonquake hit.

The Moon's entire existence had been shaped by the tidal stresses imposed by Earth's massive gravity well. Internal stresses in the Moon's crust, stresses that had existed before the first trilobite ever swam Earth's seas, were suddenly no longer there. With the strain patterns of a billion years suddenly relieved, the Moon's crust *snapped,* like a rubber band let go after being stretched out. The first of the shock waves smashed into the surface, sending everyone in the dome sprawling.

Lucian, standing on the low tour-guide dais, was flung into the air, tumbling end over end in the Moon's leisurely gravity.

It was the quake that convinced Lucian of the impossible truth. The sudden, appalling shock of the very ground beneath his feet, flinging him about, made the disaster real. He slammed into the floor of the dome and clung to it, digging his fingers into the rubber matting.

Suddenly his mind was clear. A legend spoke to him, and told him what to do.

"Accept the situation, think and act," his father's voice whispered to him. His father, Bernard Dreyfuss, hero of the SubBubble Three disaster. A thousand—ten thousand more would have died, if Bernard Dreyfuss had not kept his head. "Most people *panic* when they are in danger. Not our family." That was family lore, the family *law*, Lucian told himself. "We *think* in a crisis, boy," his father had told him. "That's why we survive. When the terrible, the frightening, the incredible happens, accept it and *act* while the others are still in shock. It's in your blood to do it. Trust that and *act*."

He looked up in the sky. All his life, all the centuries humanity had lived on the Moon, all the endless millions of years before that, the Earth had hung in that *one* spot in the Lunar sky, the one unmoving object among the wheeling Sun and stars. It had hung *there*, always.

And it *wasn't* there now. Damn it, *accept* that. No one was going to believe it, but accept it. *It had happened.* How? How had it been wrecked? Had it exploded?

Stop it. *Accept the incredible.* The *how* of it didn't matter just now. The ground below his feet rattled again, and he heard a little girl whimper in fear. It refocused his mind. He could do nothing for the people of Earth, but the loss of the planet had consequences here, now.

And he had responsibilities. For starters, the people in this dome. He did not even notice that he had stopped thinking of them as tourists and groundlings.

They needed help. If the ground danced again, and the dome cracked this time . . . He had to get them safely down below, down into the panicked ant heap the city must be by now.

It struck him that down below they wouldn't know about Earth yet.

Earth. Dear God, *Earth*. He looked again at the frightened people all around him. *Earth* people. They needed help. Help in getting below to safety, help in avoiding panic.

Keeping their minds off whatever had just happened to their world was vital. Focus them on the immediate danger. Don't let *them* have time to think.

Lucian stood up carefully, adopting the cautious, wide-legged stance of a man expecting the ground to give way. "Everyone, please listen carefully." He must have gotten some sort of tone of authority into his voice; they all quieted down and turned to him. *Calm them. Downplay the situation.* "You are in no immediate danger, but safety regulations require the evacuation of these domes after even a minor tremor." There was nothing remotely "minor" about the temblor they had just experienced, but Lucian was perfectly willing to minimize the danger if it calmed these people and got them the hell out of here.

"Please form a single-file line and move in an orderly fashion back down the entrance ramp." *Warn them of the turmoil below.* "Please bear in mind that everyone under us in the city felt that tremor too, so things might be a little chaotic down there."

Fine, that will keep them from being shocked—but won't they get completely freaked if they see the goddamn natives *in an uproar? Panic is contagious. How to keep them from catching it—or causing it? Of course. Appeal to their pride.* "The people below will be scared, and *we're* scared—but let's not let other people's fear panic us. Show them tourists can handle a crisis just as well as Conners. Now let's move, *quickly.*"

He jumped down and made his way through the crowd to the exit ramp. He started ushering the people down, and found himself pleasantly surprised at how cooperative they all were. He spotted a young woman who looked levelheaded toward the head of the line and took her by the arm. What was her name? Deborah, that was it. "Listen, Deborah," he said. "We'll need to keep the whole crowd together until we get back to the hotel. Hold them at the entrance to the main concourse while I take up the rear.''

If we get that far. Lucian knew full well what a quake could do to the underground tunnel-and-dome system that made up Central City. A collapse, a major pressure breach, a jammed lock, and they would be trapped. He thrust the thought from his mind. *Just get them down below.*

He never even noticed he had managed to make himself forget the main problem:

Earth was gone.

Dianne Steiger flinched back from the madness. The sky flared up in a field of unseeable whiteness that swept toward and over her and then vanished, taking the sky with it. Her ship lurched drunkenly and pinwheeled wildly—tumbling, pitching, yawing, tumbling end over end. Fighting the errant controls, she managed to stabilize the *Rat* on one, two, three axes. Stable again. She stared in shock at what was, and what was not. The stars and the slender crescent Moon beyond had been swallowed up in that whiteness that was there and then gone. Stars, but not the stars of Earth, sprawled across the sky once again. Only Earth and the ugly bulk of NaPurHab, now several kilometers distant, remained of the familiar Universe.

Until the blue-whiteness snapped into being and lunged toward her once more

But no, it was not whiteness, but *nothingness*. For a split second, her eyes decided it was utter black, but that was wrong too. There was not even *black* to see. Unless it *was* a blinding white, or a fog leaping for her mind through the viewport. Whatever it was, it flashed over the ship once again. This time her ship held attitude. The

Universe, or at least *a* universe, snapped into existence in front of her. Again, it was not a sky she had ever seen. No Moon, no High New York, none of the familiar constellations.

At least there were stars and a proper sky. She checked her stern cameras. Below and behind her, the fat crescent of dayside Earth was suddenly night, barely visible but for the gleaming of starlight. Was the *Sun* gone? Before she had time to wonder how such a thing could be, the new sky vanished into a new world of that black/white nothingness. An unseen fist slapped at her ship and the *Pack Rat* fell off its axes again, tumbling madly. Even as she brought the nose steady, yet another new sky appeared. And the whiteness, and the mad tumbling. Then a true sky. And then it happened again, the whole nightmare cycle.

Again.

And again.

And again.

The sky outside the ship thundered in silence, exploding, vanishing, destroying itself, renewing itself over and over. Dianne's hindbrain told her such violence should have been deafening, should have made a noise that would rattle the ship apart—but the cold vacuum of space kept all sound at bay, and the nightmare outside her ship was reeling past in utter quiet.

But no, the quiet was not that absolute. With every pulse from *nothingness* to sky, with every pulse back again to the solidity of the tangible Universe, she thought she heard and felt a low rippling *boom* shudder through the ship, almost too low to hear.

That gave her hope that she had gone mad. For there could be no sound in space. Could there? But was she in any normal version of space?

She realized belatedly that every alarm on the *Pack Rat*'s control board was lit up and screaming. Dianne dared not move her hands from the control yoke long enough to shut them off. Outside the viewport was an insane pinwheel of white, red and blue-white stars. No, not stars: *suns*, close enough for their disks to be visible, close enough to be blindingly bright. She checked the rear monitor to see Earth in strange colors, lit by the light of stars it had never been meant to see.

Acting more by instinct than logic, Dianne fired the *Pack Rat*'s nose jets to back away from the churning madness of the sky, a few hundred meters back toward the imagined safety of Earth.

Damn it! There was something seriously wrong with the nose jets. They seemed to have been badly damaged in the first jolt, and tended to tumble her toward portside. Dianne held on and leaned into the port jets, and managed to back off in a more or less straight line. Her nose yawed over a bit, but this time she let the *Rat* have its head, let her tumble a bit. She might need her reaction gas later. The wall of white appeared again. With the *Pack Rat*'s nose looking to one side when it appeared, this time she saw the *edge* of the nothingness, a knife-sharp boundary between the nothing and normal space. It suddenly struck her that perhaps the nothingness was stationary, and it was she herself that was moving, falling into a series of holes in space that opened before her.

Herself, and NaPurHab, and the *Earth,* falling into the holes. HolyJesusChrist. The *Earth.*

A new hole yawned wide. New stars snapped back into being on the other side. And then another hole appeared before them. On the other side of this one, Earth, the hab and the *Pack Rat* hovered *under* an impossible hell-red plane, a throbbing scarlet landscape stretching overhead to infinity in all directions. Regular markings that resembled lines of latitude and longitude scored the surface. Dianne could *feel* the star heat burning on her face. But this could be no star. Its surface was not gaseous and moving, but distinct, solid, concrete.

But then a new hole opened and that vision vanished as well.

Dianne held the control yoke in a death grip and prayed that she was going insane. Her own personal madness was far preferable to a *universe* that could indulge in such lunacy.

The sky was falling. Gerald MacDougal lay faceup on the ground, his hands clawed into the earth, hanging on for dear life, watching it coming down.

The sky was blue, noonday bright, in the middle of the night. And not true daylight, but a deep blue skycolor he had never seen before. How could that possibly be?

A disk of white/not-white appeared in the sky and swelled outward over the clean blue Vancouver sky, stretching out in all directions until all the world was blotted out. Bigger and closer it came, sweeping all before it, coming closer, closer—and then it passed *through* him, leaving darkness where daylight had been. Stars that were strangers to Earth shone down in a night that should not have been, casting a cold light that sent a shiver through Gerald's heart.

The ground trembled again. *Earthquake.* Gerald shut his eyes and prayed. He had spent some time in Mexico and had developed a good set of earthquake reflexes there. It had been the first ground tremor, rather than the strange shifts in light, that had awakened him and sent him outside in the first place.

Again the sky fell, the cloud of nothing swelling out, sweeping down. The hole in the sky swallowed Gerald, swallowed the land he was on, and left behind still another skyworld. From horizon to horizon, it turned to fire, a hell-red glow, brightest in the north. The lush and lovely greensward of Vancouver looked as if it had been dipped in blood.

In that moment Gerald knew that this was Judgment Day. God, in His Infinite Wisdom, had decreed the long-awaited End of Days foretold for thousands of years. Here was the Rapture, the Shout, the Trump of Doom. He closed his eyes again and prayed, prayed *hard*. For who could be sure of Salvation? He thought of his wife, Marcia, far away on that station orbiting Venus, and a small part of him smiled. In Heaven, families long divided would be reunited. He prayed for her, too, and found some comfort there. An unbeliever, but a good woman, a kind and loving woman who followed her heart and used her God-given talents. How could a just Lord deny *her* Paradise?

If any of them survived this Judgment. Fear rattled his faith.

By a sheer act of will, he forced his eyelids open. Still praying, still praising the Lord with all his heart, he watched. He was determined to witness the End of all things. Few indeed would be privileged to see such a sight. He was to be a Witness of Doom. He did not wish to annoy the Lord by refusing to see the sight set before him.

But, all things being equal, to witness such events was an honor he would gladly forgo.

Wolf Bernhardt, astronomer, sat inside on the floor in the dark, with no thought for the sky. He picked himself up off the floor, moving carefully in the sudden darkness. The lights had gone out right in the middle of the first quake. He knew, already, that the quake and the gravity wave could not be a coincidence. He had no proof, no evidence whatsoever—but he *knew*. Somehow, the gravity beam had disturbed the San Andreas Fault—and the San Andreas practically ran through the parking lot of JPL. No wonder the temblor had been so violent.

But how could the microscopic power of a gravity wave jolt something as massive as a planetary fault system? It didn't make sense. But the seismologists hadn't predicted a quake, either. The Californians at JPL were forever boasting to visiting scientists that the seismo-predictions hadn't been wrong once in the last fifty years.

Until today.

But how could a gravity beam do this? There *had* to be more to it. The gravitics people out on Pluto had discovered something far greater than they had imagined.

The lights came back on, and Wolf got back into his chair. The autocamera came back to life and swiveled back to focus in on him. "Hello again to you on Pluto," he said. "You may have set something off down here. There was a quake here in California, though we can't know what caused it."

More of the reserve power system was coming back on-line. He looked up at the communications status board and noticed that the comm line from Pluto had dropped out. *Damn it!* All the comm lines had dropped, and all the backups. "Pluto, it looks as though we have lost incoming contact with you. I will keep transmitting in the hope that you can receive me." He glanced at another set of meters, displaying the readouts from the gravity-wave sensors.

And then he *stared* at the readouts. Impossible. Flat-out impossible. The Ring of Charon was supposed to be sending a steady pulsing signal from a single direction. The meters were showing a chaos of gravity signals of all strengths coming from all directions. Then, even as he watched, all of the readouts went dead at once. A warning bar appeared across the screen:

SYSTEM OVERLOADED,
SAFETY CIRCUIT BREAKERS INTERRUPTING SYSTEM.

A strange little *thud* quivered past his feet, shaking the whole building. An aftershock? It didn't quite feel like one. Too sharp, too abrupt and focused. It seemed to come from the direction of the gravity sensor lab, in a building a few hundred meters away. A new warning bar appeared:

SYSTEM FAILURE.
CATASTROPHIC FAILURE OF ALL GRAV SENSORS

God in His Heaven, what else could go wrong? "Pluto, we are getting some definitely weird results down here. I think that quake might have damaged the gear. Stand by. I will keep this message beam active while I check the situation."

Wolf stood up and shook his head. So much for dreams of glory. Duty required that he check the system. But the experiment had failed, somehow. No one was going to get famous off this one.

He headed for the gravity lab, while the message system valiantly tried to send a blank carrier beam to a planet that wasn't there anymore.

Wolf found a fair-sized crater where the gravity lab should have been, and fires still burning in the rubble.

Lucian breathed a sigh of relief as the airlock swung open. He had wondered if it had been a bad idea to head down into the depths during a quake—but now the move was vindicated. He didn't mention it to any of the tourists, but the blinking yellow panel on the lock indicator meant that there was an air leak somewhere in the observation-dome complex. Had they stayed behind, sooner or later they would have been out of air. If the quake had likewise jammed the airlock door mechanism, they'd all be dead. The door stopped its travel and locked into the open position.

He noticed more than a few of his charges were hanging back, unwilling to enter the confined space of the airlock chamber. In a quake, claustrophobia was entirely rational. "Come on, folks," he said, trying to assume the air of a bored tour guide again, weary of squiring his flock. If he treated them like sheep, maybe they would *act* like sheep. "Inside. The sooner we get *into* the lock, the sooner we can get out the other side. Let's get into the lock."

Still they hung back, until Deborah, the sensible young woman, squared her shoulders and strode purposefully into the lock. That was enough to get most of the others moving.

Lucian crowded them all into the lock chamber. He had twenty-eight people on the tour. Normally he would cycle the tour through in two runs—but one more good jolt and the lock might jam. Get them all through while he still could. Lucian herded the last tourist in, wedged himself in, and shoved his way over to the lock controls. He broke the seal over the emergency switch and punched the crash-cycle button. A siren hooted, and the normal white lighting cut out, replaced by blood red emergency lights. The domeside hatch swung shut at double time and bolted itself shut. The tourists crowded back from it.

The pump mechanism clunked and clanked, making noises that were unnervingly unfamiliar to Lucian's practiced ear. Could the quake have screwed up the innards of the lock? What if it jammed? How long could the air last in here? It was a bit warm already, with all these people crowded into this small space. Then came the welcome hissing sound of the pumps equalizing pressure with the city side.

The city side doors opened. With a collective sigh of relief, the whole herd tumbled out into the entryway.

Central City was built underground, a series of lens-shaped hollows, kilometers across, known as Sub-Bubbles. The tourist dome sat on the surface, fifty meters directly above one edge of a lens, connected to the interior's ground level by a long ramp running between the surface level and the airlock. The city side of the airlock complex had been designed with tourists in mind. One whole wall was made up of huge view windows that canted in from the ceiling toward the floor, overlooking Amundsen SubBubble, affording a splendid vista of the bustling city below.

Except now the view windows were shattered heaps of glass on the ground and jagged knife-edges sprouting up from window frames. A sooty wind swept into the overlook chamber.

The city below looked like a war zone. Smoke billowed up from at least three separate fires, only to be caught in a violent wind that flattened it into the sky blue ceiling of the bubble. *Wind.*

Nothing scared a Conner more than a leak. Lucian forced the worry from his mind. Either the repair crews were handling it or they weren't. Lucian's gaze left the ceiling and he looked down at the city again. The lush greenery that the city took such pride in was still more or less there, but whole garden sections had slumped over. Landslides had carried off hillside trees.

Mobs swirled about here and there—whether in panic or in some attempt to deal with the fires and other crises, Lucian could not tell. The lighting in the city was dimmer than it should have been. The emergency lights were on in places. Swirling smoke darkened everything. Many of the tall, graceful towers for which the city was famous had been felled or badly damaged. From what Lucian could see, the high-rent districts of the dome slopes had taken a lot of punishment.

Perfect, Lucian thought, glancing back at his charges. *Just what these people need to see.* "Come on, folks. Turn left and out the down ramp to the main city level. Let's get down and back to the hotel." *Don't give them time to think,* his father's voice whispered. *Not when thinking will lead to panic. Get them home.* He counted noses. There were still twenty-eight. Good. At least he didn't have to go back through the lock after stragglers.

Lucian led the group down the access ramp, a long spiral walkway leading down from the overlook chamber. As with the chamber itself, the wall facing the dome interior was made entirely of glass. That was both for the benefit of tourists and because there was nothing cheaper than glass on the silica-rich Moon. Whatever the reason, it left Lucian leading twenty-eight people, most of whom barely knew how to walk in low gee, down an incline littered with razor-sharp fragments of glass, trying to stay out of a howling wind that blew through where the glass wall should have been. Somehow he got them down without anyone slicing open an artery.

The route back to the Aldrin Inn was at least short and direct. There was no sign of the bus that was supposed to be waiting to take them back. It wasn't hard to figure out why. The periphery of the main level was littered with boulders and parts of buildings shaken loose from upslope, clogging the roads with debris. He urged his charges into a brisk walk back toward their hotel.

Even in that short walk Lucian saw enough to scare him badly. Amundsen SubBubble, at least, was in pretty bad shape. Every house, every building, seemed to have soaked up some damage. There was an obstruction in the road every few hundred meters. Abandoned cars, debris fallen from buildings, felled trees and broken tree limbs were scattered everywhere.

Finally they reached the Aldrin Inn. The big building seemed utterly intact. A small knot of people standing outside the entrance was the only sign here of anything out of the ordinary. By the looks of things, the place had been evacuated, and the guests were just now being allowed back in.

Lucian, standing in the middle of the rubble-strewn road, looking at the hubbub around the hotel, felt something being shoved into his fingers. He looked into his hand. A British twenty-pound note. He realized Mrs. Chester was standing next to him.

"Thank you so much, young man," she said. "I'm so glad we're all down safely."

Lucian looked at her blankly. A tip. The woman had tipped him for saving her life. Without him, they'd still be a panicky mob up in a leaking dome.

At least it served to tell him he had discharged this responsibility. They don't tip you until the job is over. He dropped the twenty-pound note, let it flutter to the ground, and walked away without saying a word.

And he had actually been thinking of tourists as people.

To hell with being a guide, he thought, glad that he had the day job to fall back on. He upped his pace to a dogtrot. He had to get to Traffic Control.

From the Aldrin Inn, Orbital Traffic Control should have been an easy five-minute walk. But the quake had turned everything upside down: even at a brisk jog, it took Lucian nearly half an hour to thread his way through the jammed intersections, powered-down slideways, and accessways cut by sealed airlocks.

Jesus Christ, Earth. Lucian stopped in his tracks and stared at nothing. *Earth.* He had managed to forget about the planet for a moment in the panic of the quake. *Down here, they won't know. Even if they did happen to see it through a monitor, they won't believe it. Nobody knows. No one at Traffic Control will understand what's happening.*

Orbital Traffic Control was a madhouse. He could see that much through the smoked-glass windows that divided the control center proper from the administrative area. Too many people were standing, waving their arms, arguing silently into their headsets behind the soundproof glass. Too many consoles were on, too many lights glowed flame red instead of green.

Lucian flashed his ID at the control center entrance. By the time the sentry system cleared him through to the interior, Vespasian had spotted him and was on the way over, waving for Lucian's attention. Lucian ignored him, grabbed a headset out of the rack and looked for an empty console. There, in the corner. There were things he had to check.

But Vespasian cornered him before he got halfway across the room. "Goddammit to hell, Lucian," he began without preamble. "We're in a helluva spot. All our navigation systems crashed all at once, right after the quake. Primary, backup, tertiary. *All* of them. Every damn ship is off course out there—the ones that haven't vanished off the radar altogether. None of our course corrections work. We can't figure out what—"

"The system's working, Vespy," Lucian cut in. "It's just trying to compute for a gravity well that isn't there anymore. Earth's gone."

Tyrone Vespasian was a short, heavy man of uncertain Mitteleuropean origins and very certain opinions. "What the hell are you talking about?" he snapped. "That's ridiculous!"

"I mean the damned planet's not there anymore!" Lucian walked over to the console with Vespasian right behind him. He ignored the older man, sat down at the console and powered it up. He found himself staring straight ahead, concentrating hard on the job at hand. excluding everything from his thoughts except the need to get this console on line.

"Earth can't just vanish," Vespasian objected. "I mean, jeez, sometimes I wish the damn groundhogs *would* go away, but—"

Lucian jumped back up out of his chair, grabbed his boss around the shoulders, and stared straight into his face through eyes half-mad with fear. "Earth is gone, dammit. *I saw it happen with my own two eyes.* I was on the surface, in the ob-dome, *looking* at it when it vanished. That's what set off the quake. The tidal stresses vanished and the whole surface spasmed. There'll probably be major aftershocks."

Vespasian looked at him and swallowed hard. His face was sweating, and Lucian could see the light of fear in his eyes as well. "Planets just don't vanish, Lucian," he said in some sort of attempt at normal tones.

"This one did!" Lucian shouted. He gripped the older man's shoulders harder, and then relaxed his grip, slumped down into his seat. He shut his eyes and forced himself to calm down. *A planet. Yes, a planet. And everything on it. Eight billion people. All the oceans, all the ice caps and forests and animals, all the volcanoes and weather and deserts and trees. The molten core, the bottom of the ocean, the prairies and mountains. All of it gone.*

No. No. He forced the thoughts, the fear, the panic from his thoughts. *Don't think about the Earth. Think about what we must do to save ourselves.*

He opened his eyes and punched up the exterior surface camera that was permanently aimed at Earth.

"Look," he said, not expecting to be believed. "That's the camera locked down and targeted at Earth. Nothing there but stars."

"So the camera was jostled in the quake," Vespasian said in calming tone. "Dreyfuss, listen, I can use everybody I can get hold of right now, and I know maybe you've just been through a quake on the surface, but I don't have time for this kind of—"

"Look at the background stars!" Lucian snapped. "That's Gemini. Earth's supposed to be *in* Gemini right now. Check with Celestial if you don't remember." Vespasian frowned and looked again at the camera. Lucian ignored him and punched up the playback on the camera. "Here we go. This is a replay off that camera for the last hour, in fast forward."

Earth, or at least the recorded image of Earth, popped back into existence on the monitor screen. Clouds chased themselves across the surface, the terminator advanced over the globe as the playback rushed forward at high speed—and then, in a flash of blue-white, the planet wasn't there anymore.

"Holy mother of God," Vespasian said. "That can't have happened. It's got to be a camera malfunction."

"Dammit, Tyrone, I *saw* it with my own eyes, and so did twenty-eight other people with me."

"It's nuts. It's nuts. Optical illusion then."

"Prove it. I'd love to be wrong," Lucian said.

"I'll do that," Vespasian said. "Key this console to main ranging-radar output." He punched a button on the intercom panel clipped to his belt loop. "Ranging radar, this is Vespasian," he said into his headset. "Janie, scram your other operations for a moment and fire a high-power ranging pulse at Earth. Yes, *now.* I don't *care* what the fuck else you got on your hands, you do it *now.*" Lucian switched in the radar operator's audio and display screen.

"—kay, for Christ sake, here's your damn pulse, Vespasian," the operator's voice announced angrily. The screen, cluttered with displays of dozens of craft in orbit, cleared as the radar op wiped her screen. A message flashed on the screen: RANGING PULSE FIRED. The display grid itself was blank.

And it stayed that way. After ten seconds, a new message flashed on the screen. NO RETURN, RECYCLING. "Jesus Christ, what the hell kind of malfunction have we got here?" the radar operator asked. "We should have gotten a return in two-point-six seconds." Now the radar operator's voice was fearful.

"We don't know, Janie," Vespasian said in a hoarse voice. "Lucian here says Earth ain't there no more. Do me a favor, recheck your gear and prove he's crazy."

He shut off the link and punched up another channel. "Comm, this is Vespasian. What's your status on Earth comm channels?"

"Dead, every single one of them," another disembodied voice announced from the speaker. "Must have been the quake. We're running diagnostics now."

Vespasian shoved Lucian out of the console chair and punched up an exterior optical circuit. The camera's image of the surface popped up on one side of the screen while Vespasian did a celestial almanac lookup on the other side. He queried Earth's current sky position as per the computer's memory and fed it to the camera. The camera tracked smoothly, the current and ordered coordinates showing in a data line across the bottom of the screen. When the two matched, the field of view stopped moving—and displayed the same empty starfield Lucian had punched up three minutes before, as seen from another surface camera.

Lucian leaned over Vespasian and spoke in a steel-edged voice. "I don't believe it either. I just know I saw it happen. Why, how, who or what did it, I don't know.

What I *do* know is that without Earth's gravity as an anchor, every orbit and trajectory within a million kilometers of here is seriously screwed up. We've got to recalculate the orbit of *every* goddamn ship, satellite and habitat before they all start piling into each other. You get back to your own console and convince yourself. I've got to work on what we do next once you *are* convinced.''

Vespasian swelled himself up, as if ready to explode—and then stopped. He knew he was a tyrant, and sometimes a bully with his people—but he prided himself on knowing the truth when he heard it, and on accepting a little bullying himself when it was necessary.

Earth was gone. Getting people to believe *that* news was going to be a full-time job for Vespasian. He was having trouble enough convincing himself.

CHAPTER EIGHT

$\diamond$

Tears for the Earth

SECOND BY SECOND, MILLISECOND BY MILLISECOND, IN slow motion, Earth disappeared again. The cloud of blue-white appeared, swelled up and engulfed Earth. Hiram ran the key frames back and forth again. Wait a second. It was tough to tell at this resolution and this angle, but it didn't look like that cloud was a globe forming *around* Earth, but rather a disk-shaped body forming *behind* the planet, between the Earth and Moon. Hiram watched the monitor as the cloud moved forward, toward the camera and away from the Moon, sweeping over Earth, and then winked out of existence, leaving no trace of Earth behind.

What the devil *was* the cloud?

Hiram sat alone in the main control room, hunched over his computer panels, glad for the peace and quiet. He didn't quite know or care what had happened to the rest of the staff. For a gifted scientist, there were a lot of things Hiram McGillicutty didn't notice or understand. Like other people, for starters.

It was, in a way, a family trait. He had been born into one of the old pioneer families on Mars, and his great-grandfather had been one of the earliest—and most obstreperous—of the Settlement World leaders way back when.

Hiram had not inherited his ancestor's political skills, or even his marginal ability to understand people, but Hiram had certainly gotten the old boy's single-mindedness. He had also gotten a full dose of another unfortunate family trait—an almost complete inability to see the other person's point of view.

The rest of the station was in shock, struggling to come to terms with an incalculable loss. But Hiram was from Mars. He had never even visited Earth.

If the rest of humanity was stunned and terrified, Hiram McGillicutty was merely fascinated. No known mechanism could do this to a planet. Clearly there was a new principle at work here. And he would be the one to crack it. On that, he was determined.

If the silence in the station meant anything at all to him, it was that he had a leg up on the competition. Here was the greatest scientific puzzle in history—and he was well ahead of the pack. After all, if his station mates weren't working, who else would be?

He sat alone in the main control room, pleased that every instrument and data record was, for the moment, his and his alone. He ran the visual record on the right screen again, throwing a new set of data overlays on the left-side screen.

He watched the infrared image track up against the visible-light image of Earth. In visible light, that blue-white cloud bloomed up out of nowhere, but in infrared, there was nothing. It wasn't there at all. No IR activity at all—except of course the Earth's infrared image, vanishing when Earth did.

Or maybe he just didn't have good enough data to see the IR from here. He racked up the near-ultraviolet image and ran it against visible light again. Too bright. The event, whatever it was, positively glowed in UV. But then, VISOR had very sensitive UV detectors, far better than its IR stuff. Maybe the signal strengths he was seeing were artifacts of his own instruments' relative sensitivity. He would have to compensate for that. But later. Later. Now he just had to look at the raw data. All of it.

He stared hard at the visible-light image. VISOR was not intended as an astronomical observatory, of course, and the long-range optics used to get the last images of Earth did not provide very high resolution. Unfortunate, but no matter. Some sort of camera would have been running on the Moon. Sooner or later, he could see that imagery.

He pulled up far UV and ran that. A bright, fuzzy image that told him nothing. Damn it, he would need a better images of Earth! For now he would have to settle for the view from VISOR of a slightly smeary Earth about the size of a golf ball at arm's length. He watched the playback again and again, tracking the vanishment against every data line he had recorded. This was the third time he had run through the complete dataset.

The amplitude lines and false-color images for UV, visual, infrared, magnetism, and radio marched across the right-side screen, one after the other, and then again in various combinations—while on the left-hand screen, the visible-light Earth vanished again and again. It was a crude technique, and no doubt the computer system could have found any and all corollaries between the various datasets within a few milliseconds. Later he would use the computer to do just that. But speed was not the only issue here. Hiram wanted to be *immersed* in the data, wanted to understand each bump and twist of it backwards and forwards. Then, when he ran it through the computer, perhaps he could understand what the computer's findings were telling him.

Even without a computer, he had already learned two or three fascinating things not readily apparent.

One, Earth vanished not at the moment the gravity beam struck it, but 2.6 seconds afterwards—which, interestingly enough, was the period of time it took for light to travel between Earth and the Moon and back.

Two, simultaneous with the vanishment came the first of a massive series of gravity-wave pulses—far more powerful than the Pluto beam, and continuing long after Earth was gone. Indeed, VISOR's gear was *still* detecting gee waves from the vicinity of Earth's former orbit. Those waves had to be coming from somewhere—presumably someplace fairly large, as it would require a Ring of Charon–size generator to create them.

Three, that squeal on the twenty-one-centimeter band had started at the moment Earth vanished, and it likewise was continuing, long after the Earth was gone. As best his direction-finding gear could tell, it was coming from the Moon, though no known Lunar transmitter worked on that frequency.

All of which strongly suggested that the Moon had something to do with what had happened.

There was another point, a rather obvious prediction. The orbits of every planet in the Solar System were going to be very slightly shifted. Nothing very dramatic, of course. There would be minor changes to Venus's orbit, and Mars's. Enough to throw off navigation a bit, that was all. The big changes would be in the area of the Moon.

Which was probably more than anyone on the Moon had realized yet, McGillicutty told himself proudly.

McGillicutty cackled to himself. Nice to be ahead of

the pack. But in science, it was important not just to be ahead, but to *prove* it, to the world at large.

He ordered the computer to summarize his finding and transmit the text and images to all the public-access channels on the Moon, Pluto, Mars and the major satellites.

That ought to give them something to think about. He read over the computer-generated summary, made one or two changes, adjusted a few of the graphs, and told the computer to send it. He grinned and started running the playbacks again. He was having a wonderful time.

Orbital Traffic Control had its own tunnel-and-airlock system leading to the Lunar surface. OTC had a lot of instruments topside, and it made sense to have direct access to them without having to deal with the municipal locks.

But Tyrone Vespasian was not going to check on his instruments, except, quite literally, in the most basic possible way. For all scientific instruments are merely extensions of the human senses. The instruments Vespasian needed to check were his eyes. He needed to see for himself.

There was always the faint chance, the faint hope that a camera, a lens, an electronic image system would have malfunctioned. He had to eliminate that possibility. He needed to know there was nothing but his own bare-assed eyeballs between himself and what he was looking at. He needed to go up to the surface, look in the sky, and see for himself.

He knew Earth was gone, but this was not about knowing. He needed to believe.

The outer airlock door opened and Vespasian, huge and squat in his pressure suit, stepped awkwardly out onto the Lunar surface.

Look to the skies, he told himself, but somehow his gaze stayed determinedly staring at the ground. Strange thoughts ran through his head. What, exactly, would happen to the Moon without the Earth? Vespasian found his eyes scanning the horizon, not the zenith. He could not bring himself to look up. Lucian's computer models showed the Moon merely retaining its previous Solar orbit with a somewhat increased eccentricity that would gradually damp out, eventually leaving the Moon riding secure, square on the former barycenter, the old center of gravity for the Earth-Moon system.

Look to the skies. What would happen to the Moon's rotation? Would it retain its old once-a-month spin? Still he could not force his eyes to look *up*, toward Gemini, to where Earth should have been. Would the Moon's spin speed up? Slow down?

Look to the skies. At last he turned his gaze upward, and looked—at nothing. A blankness, an empty spot where Earth had always been. He felt his knees about to give way, and leaned backward in time to land on his ample rump, rather than flat on his face.

He sat there, legs splayed out in front of him, head thrown back, staring at the sky, for hours, or days, or seconds. The lifeless hills of the Moon, the gray, cratered landscape no longer graced by the blue-white marble in the sky. He felt a tear in his eye, and was glad for some reason that he could not reach through his helmet and brush it away. Another tear fell, and another. These were tears for Earth, tears that deserved to flow.

Dr. Simon Raphael paced back and forth, stalking up and down the carpet, completely ignoring the visitors in his office. No one in the room had spoken in the five minutes since Raphael brought them in.

Finally Raphael seemed to have run out of steam. He slowed, turned, walked back behind his desk, and sat down. "Very well then. It's gone. Eight and a half hours ago in real time, and three hours ago to our awareness, the planet vanished. All our instruments confirm that, and all contacts with other stations confirm it as well.

"And it happened when Mr. Chao's magic beam touched the planet. All correct so far?" he asked, his voice frighteningly calm.

Sondra, Larry, and Webling said nothing.

Raphael stood up again, came around his desk, stood over Larry, raised his arm as if to strike the young man and then backed away. He stood there, breathing hard, with his arm raised, for a long moment. Then he slowly lowered his arm to his side. "I am actively *restraining* myself at this point, you know, trying to keep from screaming bloody murder at all of you, trying to keep from blaming Mr. Chao especially for this catastrophe. That is my first impulse. I expect everyone on this station—including all of you here—are harboring similar feelings. If not of anger, then of fear and horror.

"But my *rational* side, my scientific side, is holding me back." Raphael leaned over Larry, wrapped his hands on the armrests of Larry's chair, put his face close enough to Larry's so that Larry could feel the clean warmth of Raphael's breath on his face. "I *want* to blame you, Chao. I want to blame you very much. I don't like you. In fact, I'd go so far as to say I hate you right about now. My home is gone, Chao. My family, my grandchildren, my wife's grave. Eight billion souls are gone, vanished, destroyed. Because of that damn-fool gravity beam you had to fire at Earth." Larry forced himself to look the director in the eye. The ruined patrician's face was pale, chalk white with fear and repressed rage.

Raphael stood up straight again and recommenced his pacing. He seemed incapable of keeping still, seemed to need to be in motion. All of them were in shock. None of them knew how to respond. At least Raphael was reacting, moving forward instead of staring into space. "I want to blame you," he repeated, "except I understand gravity, and gravity waves.

"*Nothing* about this makes sense. But I do know enough to see one obvious fact: that your beam did not do this. I understand the power—or rather the absence of power—of that beam at that range. Passing asteroids and comets have more powerful gravity fields. Nor is this result the sort of thing that gravity *could* do. A powerful enough beam handled the right way might conceivably shift Earth in its orbit a bit, but no more. So why did your beam destroy a planet when so many other, stronger gravity sources have had no effect?"

Raphael turned and faced the three of them again. "We don't know, and we have to find out. The ironic thing is that I must turn to the people who have done the damage. You three are the most likely to get at the answers, for the very good reason that you understand gravity waves better than anyone else. I want you to figure out what happened. Was Earth destroyed? Then why is there no rubble? Did that force move the planet? But how? Did it produce the *illusion* of Earth vanishing? Again, how?"

Raphael stopped pacing again and sat down at the edge of his desk with a deep sigh. "Find out. Forgive me for bending the rules, Dr. Berghoff, but I am *ordering* you to figure out those things." He rubbed his face and slumped forward, a tired old man incapable of feeling any further shock, any further emotion of any kind. Suddenly the angry director was gone, to be replaced by a lonely, frightened, tired old man. "The entire station and all its facilities are at your disposal," he said, in a voice that was suddenly weak and reedy.

The facade of strength and control was crumbling before their eyes. This man had suffered as deep a loss as any of them. He had held together long enough to do his job—but now, Sondra realized, he was at the end of his courage, his endurance. "Now," Simon Raphael said, "if you will excuse me, I am going to go lie down."

Without another word, Raphael stood up, made at least a show of squaring his shoulders, and walked out of the room. Sondra watched him go, and thought how much she had underestimated the man. There were unknown depths of courage, of self-control, of cool intellect beneath all that pomposity. Her image of Raphael had been a mere caricature of the real man—but it struck her that Raphael had been *acting* like a caricature of himself. She had seen a strutting egotist because that was what Raphael chose to show the world. She closed her eyes and rubbed her brow. Not as if that mattered now.

She turned toward Larry. Another one she hardly knew. Here was another one deep in shock, and in mourning. Raphael managed his shock by calling forth the shield of rationality and reason to hide behind. How would Larry react? "Well, Larry," she asked gently. "Earth is gone. What do we do?"

"It didn't happen," Larry announced, staring down into the carpet. "It didn't happen."

Denial, Sondra thought. "Larry, I wish that were true, but it isn't. Earth isn't there anymore."

Larry looked up at her sharply, a blazing gleam in his eye. "I know that," he snapped. "But Earth was not destroyed."

Sondra looked up helplessly at Dr. Webling. But she seemed further gone than anyone. She wouldn't be of any use for a long time. Only by the slightest of connections was she involved in this at all. They had hijacked her perfectly innocent experiment, and destroyed the homeworld. Thanks to them, the name *Webling* would go down in history as one of the maniacs who destroyed Earth.

Sondra felt her mind wandering, bouncing from one question to another. History? Why worry about that now?

If indeed there was any more history after this. Were the surviving human settlements, on Mars and the Moon and elsewhere, really self-sufficient enough to survive without Earth? And suppose whatever happened to Earth happened to them, too?

Bingo. That was what her mind was trying to tell her. *That* was what gave this crisis urgency, why Raphael had set them to work now. It wasn't over yet. They had to solve this problem fast, to protect whatever was left of human civilization. That was why Larry had to face the truth *now.* He was the best chance at finding the answer. They could not afford to wait for him to recover. "Larry, Earth is *gone.* Lost. Destroyed. We have to figure out why before it happens to the rest of the Solar System. Earth is gone. Accept it."

"Without debris? Without any residual heat?" he demanded. "There isn't *any* way to wreck a world without leaving something behind. You can't destroy matter or energy. If the Earth was instantly converted into energy somehow, the flashover would at least have melted the Moon. From here it would be like a temporary second Sun, at least. The nuclear radiation would probably kill us. If Earth was simply smashed, there would be debris. Earth had—*has*—a mass greater than a hundred Asteroid Belts, and we can detect the Belt, certainly. *Where is the rubble of Earth?* There ought to be debris pieces from the size of the Moon down through asteroid size, right down to molecules. There isn't any way to wreck a world without leaving behind something. Even if the planet had been reduced to a gas cloud, single molecules, we'd be able to detect it. It would block the Sun, dim the sky. None of that happened. Therefore Earth was not destroyed."

Sondra stood up and walked to the far end of the room.

It *sounded* coldly logical, but she was in no condition to judge. Nor was Larry in any shape to make sense. Sondra knew she was in no state to tell if someone else was thinking clearly right now. But it almost sounded as if Larry were offering hope, and she could certainly use some.

"Then what happened?" she asked. "We didn't see it move anywhere. It . . . it just *went*."

"Wormhole," Webling said.

Sondra drew back, startled. She had almost forgotten Webling was there.

The old woman looked up from whatever blue funk she was in and repeated the one word. "Wormhole."

Larry nodded absently and Sondra frowned. "Huh? How the hell do you bring wormholes into this?" she demanded. "They're just some bit of theoretical fluff. No one's even proved they exist."

Larry rubbed his eyes and dropped his hands into his lap. He sat there, knitting his fingers together, staring straight ahead. "I was working on gravity as a step toward something else," he said in a quiet voice. "As a step on the way to creating a wormhole transit pair. I wanted to create a stable Virtual Black Hole, an artificial gravity field powerful enough to make space-time cave in on itself.

"According to theory, if you create a pair of VBHs tuned to each other, exactly matching each other in mass, charge, spin, velocity, you might be able to induce them to link up, in effect to become one black hole that exists in two places at once. Induce the black hole to enclose a plane of normal space at each end, and those two normal-space planes become contiguous—you've got a wormhole link. The two Virtual Black Holes can be ten meters apart, or a thousand light-years from each other. It doesn't make any difference. The two planes of normal space are effectively next to each other. You can move from one to another without moving through any of the normal space in between. A wormhole transit pair. Maybe I stimulated a natural wormhole. God knows how.''

Webling stirred again, seeming to come out of herself. "But that's impossible, isn't it? I know I suggested it—but it doesn't make sense. I remember reading a calculation showing that a natural wormhole was just barely theoretically possible, on about the same order of probability as every air molecule in a given room rushing out the window all at once and leaving the room in vacuum. Quantum theory says both are possible. The odds on each happening are about as realistic—and the two conditions would be about as stable. And how could a wormhole the size of a *planet* appear? I can't accept Earth being snatched away by something that incredibly unlikely.''

Larry nodded, and a bit of his hardness seemed to fade away, as if he were letting some of the barriers down. "I know, you're right. But something about all this says *wormhole* to me. After all, it was touched off by a gravity wave.''

Sondra blinked and looked at Larry. "Wait a second. Gravity *wave*. Gravity has been interacting with Earth for four billion years—but this is the first time a powerful modulated gravity *wave* has been aimed at the planet. Maybe the fact that it was a modulated tensor gravity *wave* is the important thing. Could a gravity wave stimulate that black-hole linkup somehow?''

Larry shrugged. "I think so. Ask me after I have some black holes of my own to play with. You need a pair of them. One here, and one there. Wherever 'there' is.''

Sondra turned her palms up in a gesture of confusion. "So maybe Earth's core has been an imprisoned black hole right along, for four billion years, and our gravity wave just touched it off somehow.''

Larry frowned. "That might work insofar as supplying

a black hole to induce a wormhole. *Maybe.* So long as you kept the main mass of Earth far enough away from the hole so that the hole couldn't suck any mass down into itself. A black hole is mass like anything else. If the Earth were a hollow shell with a black hole at the center, there would still be one Earth-gravity at the surface. Though you'd give any geologist fits if you suggested any such thing. To allow for a black hole in the Earth's core, you'd have to have a layer of vacuum somewhere in the planet's interior.''

Sondra was a little hazy on geology, but that didn't sound reasonable. ''Could that be possible?''

''No!'' Webling said vehemently. ''Unless every theory of geology in the past four hundred years is wrong. Every time there's an earthquake the geologists examine the shock waves, use them to map the Earth's interior, like reading a radar signal. Don't you think they'd have detected something as obvious as a hollow Earth and a *black hole* in all this time? Besides, all you've done is add another incredibly unlikely thing on top of your first one. A black hole inside the Earth, *plus* your natural wormhole. It doesn't explain anything, it just creates more and more ridiculous questions. Where did the black hole come from? Why didn't it suck Earth down into itself? How did our gravity beam induce it to form a wormhole? I can't accept any of this.''

Sondra walked back across the room and sat down next to the older woman. ''The problem, Dr. Webling, is that we're stuck with a real-life question that's even more ridiculous—how do you make a planet disappear? Answer me that and I won't bother you anymore.''

CHAPTER NINE

◆

The Fall of Lucifer

THE OBSERVER FELT GOOD.

After all the endless years of waiting, it was doing what it had been created to do. Indeed, now it was entitled to a grander name than Observer. Now the work had begun, and it was a true Caller.

Caller.

The new name felt good, too.

A rush of pride swept through its massive form. But proud moment or not, the effort of Calling, and Linking, was not without danger, not without strain. Though the new-named Caller was drawing massive amounts of power through the Link, the mere act of establishing that Link had drawn down its own energy reserves. The power required to create the necessary massless gravity source had left it with just a few percent of its rated power remaining. Furthermore, the quakes were desperately uncomfortable, even painful. They could be stopped only if the old gravitational balance was restored. Massless *gravity fields were inherently unstable. The Caller needed an anchor, a true gravity source to stabilize the Link at this end.*

Help should come, must come through the Link. There ought to be a reasonable number of its relations surviving in the outskirts of this system, and they would assist as much as they could, but the Caller knew that the chances of success were far greater if help—and reinforcements— came through the Link.

First and foremost, it needed a true gravity source whose power it could tap. If that did not come, all was a failure. It would have surrendered its life planet for all time, and to no avail. Failure now would condemn the Caller to a slow, mournful death, trapped and powerless, watching its power reserves trickle away to nothing.

Help must *come, the Caller told itself.*

And then it did.

IMPACT ALERT IMPACT ALERT IMPACT ALERT IMPACT

Vespasian nearly leapt out of his skin, then reached over and shut off the alarm. Jesus Christ, not another one.

Considering the crowded conditions of near-Earth space, there had not been all that many collisions so far. But each collision was a catastrophe.

Who the hell was going to hit *now*? The data snapped onto his screen. Oh, no. God no. Not again.

Lucifer. The formerly Earth-orbiting asteroid Lucifer was going to pile it in again. Lucifer had smashed into the High Dublin Habitat a few hours before. There had to be thousands dead there, and not a prayer of survivors. On any other day, it would have been the most horrifying of disasters. On the day when Earth died, it was merely a sideshow. The debris of station and asteroid were spiraling through space, causing dozens of secondary impacts.

Even after the Dublin crash, Lucifer remained the most serious threat to the Moon and the orbiting habitats. Tamed by its human masters and towed into a stable path around the Earth over a century before, now it was free again, careering through space in a random orbit, threatening other habitats. So what was Lucifer going to clobber now?

The computer drew the schematic for him, and the color drained from Vespasian's face as if he had seen a ghost.

And in a way, he had. The computers were projecting Lucifer to impact with *Earth*. The blue-and-white graphic image of the lost planet gleamed in the flatscreen, Lucifer's impact trajectory shown as spiraling in. No one had had time to reprogram this particular impact warning system to tell it that Earth was gone. The computer was warning that Lucifer would strike Earth—if Earth were still there.

If only it could be so, Vespasian thought. He'd settle for an asteroid strike on Earth if it meant getting the planet back again. He reached up a finger to dump the warning and then stopped.

Vespasian frowned. This particular impact-warning program was a trend-projection system for constant-boost systems. It assumed that all accelerations would continue, and projected forward in time under that assumption. This program did not assume Earth's gravity, or any other gravity field, as a constant. It merely watched radar tracks, calculated the forces preventing the track from moving on a straight line, and assumed those forces would continue.

So why hadn't it called this impact a long time ago? It should have been able to call it long before now, if Lucifer's orbit had remained unchanged.

Vespasian had checked Lucifer's track an hour ago. Granted, they didn't have a precise path for the rock yet, but it hadn't been moving anywhere near Earth's old location at that time. Now what the hell was happening? He called up a backtrack on Lucifer, running its recent actual trajectory from the tracking system.

Sonnuvabitch. The thing had taken a hard left turn, toward Earth's old coordinates. But that was impossible. He checked the trajectory more carefully, examining not only direction of travel, but velocity.

The frigging thing was accelerating rapidly toward where Earth should have been. No, *accelerating* wasn't quite right. That was active, and this was passive. No rockets on that rock. It was being accelerated by an outside force. It was acting like a falling body, moving toward a gravity source that was pulling it in.

Vespasian punched up the Earth-track camera, and had his wild hopes dashed. Earth was not there.

Vespasian leaned back, tried to think.

And got slammed out of his chair as the Moon's surface shuddered with new violence.

The second series of quakes was every bit as powerful as the first, and did every bit as much damage. It seemed as if every structure weakened in the first jolt collapsed altogether in the second. New explosions of shattered glass, new fires were everywhere. Somehow, all the SubBubbles rode out the second-wave shocks without breaching. Most people knew enough to expect aftershocks, and so the later temblors at least lost the element of surprise.

Besides, the Lunar population was preoccupied with the far more terrifying loss of Earth. By now, hours after the event, the truth was starting to filter through and be believed. With the homeworld gone, they had little capacity for being frightened by a mere tremor.

The second set of quakes could not have been timed more precisely to foul up Lucian's work. He had just begun to get a handle on the orbital tracking problem when Orbital Traffic Control lost power. The emergency battery power system was supposed to be able to run the whole traffic control complex during an outage. But it had been strained by the first quakes' outages already, and was showing signs of decay. The power-management program cut in immediately and went into conservation mode, cutting off all nonessential uses of electricity.

Unfortunately, hypothetical modeling of speculative orbital projections went under the heading of nonessential use as far as the automatic power-management software was concerned. Lucian's panel went dead and stayed dead. He couldn't even program an override of the power-management system until his board came on.

All across cis-Lunar space, spacecraft and stationary facilities alike were out of control, tumbling through space in unpredictable directions.

Through all the long years and centuries since the first manned stations were put up, whenever a new facility was placed in an orbit of the crowded Earth-Moon system, computers and engineers would labor long and hard to place it in a safe path, to keep it away from all the thousands of other orbiting craft and stations.

But all that fastidious timing and positioning had been overturned when Earth was suddenly not there to hold the reins. In the careful dance of the orbits, it had been Earth that had called the tune—and now the caller was gone, leaving the dancers themselves to wheel and pitch about at random.

Lucian was trying to find out just how bad the situation was—a tricky job with a dead computer. He sat there, staring at the blank screen, trying to think.

He had gotten far enough along in the problem to confirm his original fear. Earth's disappearance was no illusion. Working by hand, he had recalculated projected orbital trajectories for several of the larger habitats, factoring Earth's disappearance into the existing projection as stored in the navigational almanac system. He had fed his coordinates to the radar controllers, and radar had reported dead-on tracks for every habitat.

And the message was simple: without the Earth to anchor them, the Earth orbiters were careering across the sky. The Moon-orbiting satellites were not in much better shape—Earth's massive gravity well was a major variable in their orbits as well. Several satellites and habitats had already spiraled down to impacts on the Moon, including all of the satellites stationed at the Lagrangian balance points. Held in stationary orbit over the Lunar Nearside and Farside by the balance of terrestrial and Lunar gravity, some of the Lagrangian stations had drifted off into deep space, and others had simply fallen down, once Earth's gravity was no longer there to hold them up.

Other facilities hadn't crashed yet—but they would, their impact points as inevitable and irrevocable as gravity itself. They were falling now, and nothing could stop them. The few stationary facilities with powerful station-keeping engines might be able to save themselves. But most of the stations had no stationkeeping engines, or only small ones. There was no way to correct their courses, even if Lucian had been able to calculate their *present* courses in time.

All of the objects Lucian tracked were still held in orbit about the Sun, of course, but the speed and vector each held at the moment Earth vanished threw a random element into the mix. Some were moving into higher-inclination orbits, others in a bit closer to or out a bit further from the Sun.

But what frightened Lucian most of all was that it should have been worse. Many of the predicted disasters never happened. Radar couldn't spot many of the threatened ships in the first place. According to the computer plots, there should have been far more impacts, more collisions, more spacecraft radioing in to report themselves off course. Satellites, habitats and spacecraft, lots of them, were simply *missing*.

Suddenly, with a flare of lights and a renewed hum of ventilation fans, the primary power system came back on. Lucian's console flashed into life. He leaned into the keyboard and ran some quick checks. Yes, his programs were still intact. That much was a relief. But what about the missing satellites? Lucian ordered up a three-dee projection of the coordinates for the missing ships and stations, as of the moment before Earth disappeared.

The pattern in the three-dee tank was clear, obvious, and clean. It was not merely the *Earth* that was gone, but everything that had been within a certain volume of space surrounding Earth. Somehow, that made it seem real. It was easier to conceive of a space station ceasing to exist than a whole planet. It was suddenly real enough to be frightening.

The intercom bleeped and Lucian punched the answer button. It was Janie in Radar, paging him on the intercom. "Lucian, you got a second?"

Lucian looked over and spotted Janie on the far side of the big room, saw her looking not at him, but at her display system. It was disconcerting to speak to disembodied voices all day, when you could see the bodies they belonged to, out of earshot. Lucian adjusted his earpiece and spoke into his throat mike. "I've got just about that long, Janie. What's up?"

"I'll relay it to your screen. It's kind of hard to explain. You had me do a radar track on Mendar-4, right?"

"Right," Lucian said.

"Okay," Janie's voice said. "Here's what's what. This is what Mendar's orbit *was*." A standard orbital schematic appeared on Lucian's flatscreen. Earth stood in the center of the screen, and Mendar-4's track showed as a perfect white circle tracing around it. "Now this is an orbit based on the radar tracks we've gotten since the first quake." The symbol for Earth vanished from the screen, and Mendar moved straight out on a tangent from its previous orbit. "I'm running it forward in blue to give us a projected orbit."

Lucian watched as the straight blue line stretched out into Solar space. "Okay, so what?" Lucian asked.

"So here's what happened after the *second* quake, just a few minutes ago. This is Mendar's actual course, based on radar tracking. I'll run it in yellow." A third course appeared on the screen, peeling away from the straight blue line of the projected course.

"Holy Jesus Christ," Lucian said.

He knew what it meant, even without analyzing the orbit. Mendar's path was being bent back toward some large *mass*, a large mass right where Earth had been. A planet-sized mass.

"Has this happened to the other orbital tracks?" Lucian asked, his fingers busy running his own board. He could feel the relief washing over him. It had to be. Earth was back from whatever impossible place it had been. It *had* to be.

"Yes it has," Janie said. "Similar orbit shifts, all starting just at the onset of the last quake."

"It's got to mean that Earth is back," he said, excitedly. "That's what caused the second quake series. Earth's gravity field coming back and grabbing at the Moon." He brought up the image from the surface camera, still trained on Earth's coordinates.

But there was nothing there. Nothing at all. Just some debris.

"I checked that too, first thing, Lucian." Janie's voice was soft, apologetic. "There's nothing there."

"Give me a real-time radar image of where Earth should be," Lucian said. Maybe it was simply cloaked somehow, some weird optical phenomenon. Janie redirected her radar and Lucian split his screen, watching the same swatch of sky in visual and radar frequencies.

"Nothing, Lucian," Janie said. "Not one damn thing—"

Suddenly there was a blue-white flash of light in the center of the visual screen, and a smaller, dimmer flicker on the radar. And then, on radar, a target appeared. A big one, Lucian judged. Perhaps two kilometers across, and moving fast. About the size of the other debris chunks in the radar image. And all the debris was moving *away* from the new gravity source. Almost as if they had been launched themselves . . .

"You got a recording on this?" Lucian asked.

"Sure thing," Janie said.

"Let me access that. Last fifteen minutes of it." Lucian cut away from the live picture and ran the recording forward from the moment the quakes hit.

Another flash, and another target. And again, and again, and again. Some of them drove straight on. Others seemed to snap around in tight parabolas before speeding away. They had to be moving at a helluva clip for the motion to be visible at this range, even in fast forward. Larry ran a check, and discovered that the targets were popping out of the bluish flashes at regular intervals, once every 128 seconds.

The image reminded him of something, and it took a moment for it to register. *Like lifeboats launching from a crippled ship,* Lucian thought. For one wild moment he wondered if that was exactly what he was seeing—the populace of Earth somehow escaping from their wrecked planet.

But in ships two klicks across? No one built them that large. The whole idea was absurd.

But then, so was the idea of asteroid-sized bodies materializing out of the empty spot in space where Earth had so recently been.

Lucian stared at his screens, praying for understanding. It didn't come.

The Caller saw the intruder diving toward its Anchor. This was by no means a surprising development. Of course the Anchor's massive gravity well would attract debris. The Caller immediately sent a message through the Link, requesting a temporary halt to operations. Nothing material could ever damage the Anchor itself, of course, but a disintegrating asteroid could certainly damage the new arrivals as they streaked through the wormhole. It did not matter. Now the Caller had the Anchor as a power source. Now it had all the time and power it could ever need—and this asteroid would be out of the way in a few minutes.

Lucian, still staring at the mysterious blue flashes, was startled to see them stop coming, and startled again to see an asteroid-sized fragment moving in toward Earth's previous position. The new radar track had an ID tag on. This one, the computer could identify. Lucifer. Sweet Lord, *Lucifer*.

Lucian jumped up, unplugged his headset, and hurried over to Vespasian' console. "Vespy, are you watching the Lucifer track?" he asked.

"I'm on it, Luce."

Tyrone Vespasian glanced away from his console and

rubbed his jaw nervously. Lucian stood behind him, watching in silence as the radar tracked the wreckage of Lucifer tumbling through space, pitching and wheeling wildly. The huge worldlet was tumbling, out of control. What was happening? Earth wasn't there. But Lucifer was falling toward *something*. And falling fast. Vespasian checked the real-time track.

Hell's bells. It was moving toward that gravity source at ten klicks a second, and accelerating. He asked the computer for an impact projection. Twenty minutes. That was too fast a fall. Tyrone Vespasian had been running orbital traffic systems for a long time. He knew the space around Earth and the Moon intimately, almost by feel. He knew, instinctively, what sort of forces Earth and the Moon would impose on a body in a given position. And Lucifer's acceleration was wrong, just a shade high.

With Lucifer's acceleration toward this gravity known, it was dead-simple to measure the mass of the gravity source—or, at least, the total mass of the gravity source plus Lucifer, and subtract Lucifer's listed mass. Probably it had lost some fragments after Dublin, but the result would be close enough.

Result of calculation: 1.053 Earth masses. It *couldn't* be Earth. Not unless the planet had gained a few gigatons in the last few hours. Besides, this gee source was *invisible*.

Holy Christ. Invisible gravity source. Vespasian suddenly realized what was out there. But he couldn't believe it. He wouldn't believe it.

He checked the impact projection clock. He wouldn't *have* to believe it for another eighteen minutes. He powered up the maximum-gain telescopic camera and trained it on the dot of light that was Lucifer. The camera zoomed in, the electronic amplifiers came on, and the typical rough potato-shape of an asteroid was tumbling in the center of the screen, tracking and velocity information appearing in a data window in the lower-right corner of the screen. Vespasian watched the fall of Lucifer, willing himself not to believe the evidence of his own eyes.

The ravaged asteroid started to die. The spin stresses were sheering off massive boulders and environment huts from the main body of the asteroid. The main mass of the asteroid was soon surrounded by a thin, rapidly dispersing cloud of fragments large and small, falling, diving into the piece of space where Earth should have been.

Down, down, closer and closer, moving not in a straight line toward Earth's old position, but in a tight parabola that spiraled in, moving faster every moment.

At about the point where Earth's surface should have been, tidal stresses began to make themselves felt, even over the relatively short distances involved. The gravity gradient started shredding larger chunks off the asteroid. Lucifer's tumble got faster, adding to the stresses tearing it apart. Impacts between fragments came faster and faster, each smashing more fragments free. Lucifer disintegrated altogether, with no one piece of rock any longer distinguishable as the parent body.

The cloud of debris that had once been Lucifer spiraled down into the gravity well, falling deeper and deeper, whirling in a tighter and tighter spiral, faster and faster, approaching significant fractions of lightspeed. Bright flashes erupted in the depths of the gravity well as massive fragments smashed into each other at utterly incredible speeds.

The flashes and sparks rose to a crescendo, leapt up to a whole new level of violence. Bursts of radiation flared out across the entire electromagnetic spectrum. Gamma rays, X rays, ultraviolet, visible, infrared and radio blazed out from the gravity source. Then, just as suddenly as it had peaked, the violence ebbed away. A flash, a flicker, and then one last ember red flare that snuffed itself out with the suddenness of a candle flame caught by the wind.

And then there was nothing. Nothing at all.

"Radar, give me a scan of Earth-space," Vespasian said.

"Running now," Janie's voice replied. "No return. I say again, no return signal of any kind."

Lucian leaned in closer to the screen. "Jesus, Vespy, how could that *be*? What the hell happened to the asteroid? Shouldn't there at least be debris?"

"It's gone," Vespasian said. "Think about it. Think about your college astronomy courses. What sort of gravity source can suck up an entire asteroid and leave *nothing* behind? No debris, no signal, no radiation, nothing. Lucifer just got sucked down into a black hole." And now Vespasian knew how Earth could have gained five percent more mass. He had just seen a demonstration. Wherever Earth had gone for those few hours, it had been crushed down to nothing just as Lucifer had been crushed. Maybe Earth had got caught by a black hole with five percent of Earth's mass. Either way, it didn't matter. There was no more doubt, at least in his mind. He knew what had happened to Earth. Not how, or where, or why, but what. "A black hole with the mass of planet Earth," he whispered. "A black hole that used to *be* Earth."

Part Three

CHAPTER TEN

———————— ✧ ————————

Naked Purple Logic

THE MEETING WAS NOT GOING WELL, SONDRA DECIDED.

Larry was stubbornly refusing to believe that Earth was destroyed, Webling seemed incapable of anything but shooting down theories—having none of her own to offer—and Sondra found herself helplessly spouting out one damn-fool idea after another. *If we three are the big gravity experts who are going to save humanity, we are in big trouble,* Sondra thought.

Larry was still in a sulk, and Webling was just on the point of spinning out another objection when suddenly the door burst open. Dr. Raphael rushed into the room, carrying a datablock and a thick sheaf of printout. "The communications duty officer woke me," he said without preamble. "This just arrived from the VISOR station at Venus," he said, his voice breathless and weak. "The comm officer woke me to give it to me, and she was right to do so."

Sondra was surprised. Raphael didn't like *anything*

disturbing his sleep. She looked at Raphael's death-white face. Something had scared him, scared him bad. But what the hell could scare anyone more than Earth disappearing?

"Some man McGillicutty, down there at VISOR, has come up with some figures on . . . on Earth. Do you know him? Is he reliable?" Raphael asked, in a tone that suggested he wanted to be told *no*.

"I know him by reputation," Webling replied carefully. "One of the sort that hasn't been out of the lab in years. No understanding of people, and a tendency to get lost in the details. He often misses the point of what he finds—but his observations and measurements are always first-rate."

"Well, he seems to have missed the point here all right," Raphael said grimly. All the anger seemed to have drained out of the man, as if fear and distraction had left no room for anything else. Raphael dropped the papers on the visitor's side of his desk. "Have a look at these while I call up the computer file. Can't think as well looking at paper," he said under his breath, muttering to himself. Sondra looked at Larry, and Larry looked at her. Muttering? For Raphael, this was utter loss of control. The man was *frightened*.

"I want to see what this report tells you," Raphael went on. "I don't want it to be what it told me."

Larry and Sondra put their heads together over the hard copy of McGillicutty's report, while Webling read the computer screen over Raphael's shoulder.

Larry got it first. "The gravity waves are continuing, but with Earth gone there's nothing there to produce them. And that twenty-one-centimeter radio source is radiating in a complex, regular and repeating pattern. McGillicutty doesn't say anything about the pattern. He just talks about the signal strength and the distortions caused by the gravity waves. He missed the fact that the signal is complex and repetitive. But that can't be. Natural signals can't—"

He stared into space for a moment, until the truth dawned. "But that means these signals aren't natural," Larry said in a whisper. "That's what the data say to me."

Raphael nodded woodenly. "That was the conclusion I reached," he said. "The one I hoped was wrong. The signals are not natural in origin. Could one of the radical groups on the Moon have—"

Sondra felt her skin go cold. "Not natural. Now wait a second here—"

But Larry wasn't listening. He knew the technology required to generate gravity waves. The Ring of Charon was, if anything, a minimal hookup for gravity generation. It was inconceivable that any other group could have built anything remotely capable of such a job and kept it hidden.

At least no human could have done it.

"The signals and the gravity waves are artificial, Sondra. Which means Earth didn't just disappear," he said. "Somebody *took* it."

"We know that it's still sending pulses of gravity waves, and that radio signal." Tyrone Vespasian sat in his office, behind his desk, willing himself to calmness. He knew there was something overcontrolled about his movements, as if he were trying to hold too much in. Was he trying too hard to be rational, logical, to be sensible when sense was useless? "The signal proves it. That's a deliberate message signal, not some natural radio noise. Even if we can't read it."

"And where is that signal coming from?" Lucian asked gently.

Vespasian shifted uncomfortably in his seat. "From here. From somewhere on the Moon. It's almost as if it's coming from everywhere at once, out of a whole series of dispersed transmitters. We can't find it."

"Don't you think that might give us a few problems?" Lucian asked. "Earth vanished two-point-six seconds after the beam touched it—the exact time for a speed-of-light signal to go back and forth between the Earth and Moon. If they decide to blame us, Mars and the Belt Community might decide to do something drastic."

Vespasian nodded, leaned in toward Lucian and lowered his voice. "I've thought of that, too. Remember the proposal about ten years ago to blow up Mercury to get at its core metals? They wanted to create a second asteroid belt close enough in to the Sun so they could really get some use out of Solar power. Officially, the Community never got around to building the Core Cracker bomb—but suppose they did, unofficially? The Moon's about the same size as Mercury, with a lower mass. The Belt Community might figure it's them or us."

"But we didn't do it!" Lucian protested.

"I checked, and as of five minutes ago, no less than *six* groups have claimed credit for the quakes, Earth's vanishment, or both. Three on the Moon, two on board the surviving habitats, and one on Mars. Rad groups, nut groups, and most of them barely know which end of a screwdriver to hold. None of them could possibly have pulled this off. All they're doing is blowing off steam, trying to upset the applecart and fit the disaster into their ideology. The Final Clan Habitat survived, and I read some guff form those nuts. Claiming they had swept away Earth, the source of all genetic decadence and lower races. Now they're free to breed their superhumans without interference. No one has taken any of these groups seriously in decades. They *always* claim responsibility for disasters. But suppose someone is rattled enough to

believe them *now*—and we get caught in the line of fire?''
Vespasian said.

''Thanks to that damn fool McGillicutty sending a
public message from Venus, everyone—including the nut
groups—knows all about the twenty-one-centimeter radio
signal, the speed-of-light delay, and the gravity waves.
They can talk those things up, sound impressive, like
they really did it. But *none of them can know about the
black hole yet*—unless they *did* do it.''

''So if we keep our mouths shut about it, that might
be a way to spot the real culprits,'' Vespasian said.

''Or at least prove none of our local crazies did it,''
Lucian said.

''Then who *did* do it?'' Vespasian demanded.

Lucian frowned. ''Jesus, Vespy. You're talking about
the most horrible crime in history. I can't imagine anyone being able to do it. Not emotionally, or mentally. I
can't imagine a reason good enough for doing it.'' Lucian paused a moment. ''Those scientists on Pluto fired
the gravity beam. But if they meant to wreck Earth, then
why announce the experiment beforehand? Most of them
are from Earth, and Earth funded their work. Besides,
the beam touched Venus and those outer planet satellites—and the Moon for that matter—and we're still here.
Which suggests the beam was a coincidence, or set off
someone else's hidden system, or that the real baddies
timed the thing to *look* like Pluto did it. Pluto had no
motive.

''If anyone had a good enough motive—and I don't
think anyone does—it could be Mars and the Belt Community. They've got a lot of weird hardware floating
around out there in deep space. Stuff nobody knows
about. With Earth out of the way, Mars and the B.C. are
suddenly dominant in the Solar System. And they get to
blame the disaster on us—or on a bunch of mad scientists
on Pluto.''

"But Earth is their biggest market!" Vespasian protested. "Everyone on Mars and in the Belt has some kind of family Earthside! And dammit, they're *human beings*. No human being could commit this crime."

"Which leaves open one other possibility," Lucian said.

"Oh no. No you don't." Vespasian stood up suddenly and began pacing back and forth behind his desk. "Come on, Lucian. Don't throw aliens from outer space at me. There's *nothing out there*. By now we'd have found something." There was something in Vespasian's soul that felt chilled by the very thought.

Lucian ignored his friend's discomfiture. He rubbed his face with tired hands. He felt drained, all capacity for emotion sucked out of him. "Either humans or aliens, Vespy. Take your choice. Either people who could couldn't possibly do it, or beings from another world who don't exist. Bug-eyed aliens, insane human terrorists, Santa Claus and the Easter Bunny gone bad. *Somebody* did it. And we're not going to find out who's guilty sitting here. Just don't send a public message about the Earthpoint black hole," Lucian said. "It could only make matters worse, scare people more. Send coded messages to the scientific groups. Let them work on it."

Vespasian grunted. "Okay, I guess." He shook his head and looked at the wall clock. "Jesus, those poor bastards on Pluto."

"What do you mean?" Lucian asked.

"I mean the frigging speed of light. Think about it. Earth went poof ten hours ago. They sent the gravity wave five hours before it reached its target, went to bed, got up, and didn't find out what they had done until then, five and a half hours after we saw it happen. We're sending the word about the black hole *now*. They won't find out about that until late tonight. It's like it's all happening to them in a dream on the other side of the Universe."

Vespasian stared into space. "Terrible things happen, things you cause accidentally. You don't learn the consequences of what you've done for eleven hours after it happens, and you can't *stop* the terror once you've set it in motion. If *you* were the poor son of a bitch who had pushed the button in the first place, how many shocks like that could *you* take?"

The day the Tycho Purple Penal Fire Department burned down her parent's house Marcia felt the purest joy of her life. The memory popped into her mind unbidden, and at first she wondered why. Then she understood. Her subconscious was reminding her how much she had already survived.

Remember, Marcia told herself. *Remember the turmoil, the chaos you have survived to get here. You can survive this, too. Remember the strange and terrible way you escaped, and the joy you felt that day.*

The moment came back to her. The black pall of smoke hazing over the dome's interior, the gray ashes sifting downward, the firemen laughing and chuckling, putting away their blowtorches. And Marcia watching it all, tears of happiness in her eyes.

It was mere days before her eighteenth birthday, and the fire made her a homeless minor refugee in the eyes of the Lunar Republic, made homeless by an official act that was unquestionably not of her doing. She had a receipt from the fire department to prove that.

The fire was her ticket out of Tycho Purple Penal, because legal refugees were one of the very few categories of souls entitled to pass through the Lunar Republic's security checkpoints, out of the asylum into the saner world outside.

Life didn't get easier after leaving home. There were

only two nations on the Moon: Tycho Purple Penal and the Lunar Republic. Getting by in the feisty Republic, confronted on all sides with the legendary touch of cheerful surliness burned into the Lunar character—now *that* had been a challenge. She was astonished to discover that she missed the parents she could never see face-to-face again. She spent far too much on videocalls to Tycho. But if life among the Naked Purples had any virtue, it was that the experience prepared you to cope with anything.

Gerald. *Gerald.* Earth had been taken, and Gerald, her loving, perfect husband had gone with the planet. Could she learn to cope with *that?*

There *had* to be an explanation. They must have missed something, something that would make sense of it all. Marcia knew that. They *must* have. Even wrapped up in a fetal ball on her bed, struggling to block out the world, her mind demanded that she find the missing answer, make sense of the madness.

The desire to find sense in order to survive madness was a deep-seated reflex for Marcia, after being raised in the Naked Purple scene, struggling to be the ordinary child of extraordinary—even mad—parents. Whenever, as a child and a teenager, she had been surrounded by madness, she had clung to the hope, the urgently needed *faith* that the Purple weirdness was itself surrounded by a larger world of sanity. The sort of sanity and decency that Gerald had always represented. *But no, don't think of him now,* she thought. *Calm yourself.* Sanity existed. She believed that, *had* to believe it now, just as she always had.

She had been born into the Naked Purple movement not long after it expanded from its orbital habitat into the former home of the Tycho Penal Colony on the Moon. After eighteen years of hearing only the Purple version

of events, the straight version of history sounded strange
to her.

Tycho Purple Penal Station had started out centuries
before as the Soviet Lunar base, and had passed to the
United Nations' control with the final Soviet breakup. In
the bad old days when UNLAC—the United Nations Lunar Administration Council—ran the Moon, Tycho had
been made into a U.N. penal colony, and had rapidly
devolved into the final dumping ground for the human
refuse of the Earth, the Moon, and the Settlement Worlds.

Tycho Penal was specifically intended to be not only
escape-proof, but reprieve-proof. No prisoner was ever
sent there under any sentence except life without parole.

When the Lunar Republic was declared, eighty years
before Marcia was born, the Lunar Colonists—the Conners—were very careful *not* to lay claim to the Tycho
Penal Colony and environs. They were quite happy to let
the United Nations administer the nightmare it had created for itself.

Even after the Republic, the United Nations let Tycho
Penal stagger along a few years as a prison, until a resolution passed the General Assembly banning the placement of any more prisoners at Tycho. UNLAC was stuck
with the bills for a prison populated with old men and
women too mean to die. The costs of running the place
rapidly got out of hand—until it dawned on UNLAC that
it would be cheaper to declare the place a separate republic, and announce that all current residents were nat-
uralized citizens.

The Lunar Republic promptly decreed that any bearer
of a Tychoean passport found in the Republic would be
escorted back to the Tycho border—with or without a
pressure suit. Every nation on Earth, and all of the Settlement Worlds, refused to honor Tycho passports.

So the convicts—and, by this time, their descendants—
were technically free, but legally they couldn't travel.

Tycho was still tough to get out of illegally, for that matter. But the convicts could write their own laws, and own their own property. The Lunar Republic did allow some amount of legitimate trade, which provided ample cover for smuggling operations. It gave the convicts a window on the outside world.

All in all, it wasn't much of an opening. But it was enough for the smart cons to get rich, while the dumb ones starved. After a while, the inevitable happened, and one of the smartest, meanest convicts managed to muscle everyone else out of power and set himself up as the King of Tycho: Redeye Sid the First.

That much was history—confirmable facts. The rest was half legend, half outright lie. Marcia had never quite decided which was which. The story went that Redeye Sid won the last open tract of Tycho in a poker game. A crooked game, some whispered. But no one could be sure, as Redeye was the only player to survive the game. Unless that tale was circulated by Sid to keep enemies in line.

And then, in the tenth year of his reign, Redeye Sid dropped dead (or was poisoned) and left it all to his idiot (or perhaps mad genius or political malcontent) son Jasper, who listened to off-planet broadcasts a bit too often. More particularly, Redeye Jasper listened to the Purple Voice beaming down from NaPurHab. He got religion. Or philosophy. Or paranoid delusions. No one could ever decide which.

Whatever the Purple was, it had earned itself a prominent place in any history of the irrational. What the Purps were for, what they were against, what their goals were—all those issues were meaningless to the Purps. Alienating themselves from society, offending the world and then protesting the world for taking offense, that was the Purple way. The Purples drenched themselves in anger, anger for its own sake, absurdity as an art and a political policy, the overturning of any and all existing forms. That was the closest the Purps came to a goal, a Naked Purple ideal.

Marcia thought back to the allegory that named the movement: Get naked, paint yourself purple, and walk down the street. If people were surprised, shocked, offended, or merely amused, rail at them for their small-minded, bourgeois ways. If they accepted you and let you be, despise them for being blinkered, too narrow-minded to see the special and the marvelous in this world. Any reaction, all reactions, or no reaction at all were grounds for contempt.

It was a formula for attracting the ostracized, ensuring that recruits would feel left out, rejected by the world. And it gave Purps a way to feel superior to the hidebound, workaday world, making sure they could be accepted only by fellow Purps.

It was the sort of anger at everything that might appeal to the irrational heir to a mad kingdom. Like Jasper.

As with all converts to the Naked Purple movement, Redeye Jasper was required to sign over all his worldly goods to the movement. Such goods and property included the Kingdom of Tycho. So the Naked Purple movement came into possession of its own country.

By the time the Purples moved in, Tycho hadn't, strictly speaking, been a prison for decades, but the Lunar Republic's government still held to the same Tycho policy it had retained for generations: Anyone could go into Tycho Penal, but no one could come out. Even after a hundred years, there were mighty few loopholes in that rule. In effect, it was still a prison. The Republic was not in the least bit willing to change that policy for the sake of a bunch of habitat crazies.

The Naked Purples declared themselves liberators anyway. They moved in, took over, and officially renamed the place Tycho Purple Penal Station. They made much of all the contradictions and tensions bubbling in that name—and in the city itself.

The Naked Purples and a mob of former convicts living cheek by jowl inside a former maximum security prison was a sure formula for confrontation. The murder rate spiked high, even for Tycho, that first year. But, surprisingly, mostly convicts were dying. The Purples swiftly demonstrated their talent for survival and control, and the situation settled down a bit.

Marcia's parents met at Tycho Purple Penal, her father a second-generation convict, her mother one of the more combative leaders of the Purple's nonviolent-aggression arm. Unless Marcia really concentrated, all she could remember of her childhood was one long screaming argument between the two of them, endless suspicion, and wild accusations. That sort of thing was considered a Naked Purple art form. And yet, like any child, she accepted her own situation as normal.

Adolescence was at least more varied, hewing to the Naked Purple philosophy of education by extreme. Cloying doses of love and then random anger; overwhelming attention and then abandonment. Forced to live with the Naked Purple shock-value philosophy, the teenaged Marcia got a dose of it all.

One summer (or what would have been summer if the environmental engineers hadn't decided seasons were bourgeois and locked the thermal controls at twenty degrees centigrade) she spent under the gray stone dome of the abandoned main penal camp, sewing seeds she knew were dead into soil she knew was sterile.

She could no longer remember the precise nuance of the particular nihilist-dialectic theory the experience was supposed to teach her, other than the futility of all effort, a central precept of the Naked Purple worldview. Everything had something to do with studying futility. The Purples worked very hard to convince themselves that work was useless. The details of *why* didn't matter anyway. The whole point was that work was meaningless.

All she remembered of that summer was grayness. Grayness, and her flat, defeated acceptance of the situation. The joyless unpainted gray dome of the stone sky. The cold, gray, shadowless light from the glowblimps, hovering overhead like lifeless jellyfish, floating dead in the currents of the air. The gray pallor of the unfertilized Lunar soil that billowed in endless cloaking clouds at the slightest breath of air. The gray, choking, dust-sucking thirst that followed the students as they worked down the razor-straight rows, carefully planting the lifeless seeds.

And the gray, throbbing ache between her shoulders that never seemed to leave, the one product of her endless days of stoop labor.

She grew up surrounded by all the alleged benefits of Purple living, starting with the search after truth through lies, of moderation through extremes and the creative tension of the permanent nonviolent riot. The endless confrontations with the unreconstructed convicts seemed nothing more than another aspect of the Purple ideal of sullen absurdity. Near-starvation would follow a season of compulsory hedonistic debauchery. Any artist who was celebrated today could count on being vilified tomorrow. The police were required to break the law on occasion, and the standard punishment for most crimes was doing a stretch in the police department. Fix a broken machine without authorization, steal a neighbor's property without leaving your own behind, dress conventionally, and you did time on the force.

Marcia grew into puberty always fearing that Orgy Day was going to be declared again, praying that Celibacy Month would be randomly extended.

And yet, in spite of all she had been through, for reasons that she could certainly not explain, Marcia

MacDougal still not only wanted, but *expected* the world to make sense.

No doubt that was a large part of why she had married Gerald, why she had loved him in the first place. Even though she could not share his religious beliefs, the fact that he *had* beliefs was a comfort.

But Gerald was missing, along with the rest of Earth. Marcia felt something go cold in her chest at that fact, the reality she could not escape. With an effort of will, she once again tried to force her mind away from that chain of thought. She tried to focus on the problem at hand.

They had missed something, she told herself again. All of the people struggling to find an answer. *She* had missed something. Her subconscious was stubbornly convinced that there was some key factor that they had all overlooked, something that might actually make some sense of it all. That was the message her inner self was sending.

Wait a second. *Message.* That was it. The twenty-one-centimeter-band source. McGillicutty had completely missed that it was artificial; not just a source but a signal, a *message.* She uncurled from her fetal ball and sat up.

Even if McGillicutty had missed the fact that it was a deliberate signal, few other people would.

But had anyone even thought to try to decode the message? Would they be able to do so? Would they know how? She thought back to her days as a grad student at the Lunar Institute of Technology, back to the days when she had met Gerald. They had met in a xeno-bio course—one that started out teaching Message Theory, proposed techniques for communicating with aliens for the express purpose of getting such nonsense out of the way. That way the class could get down to analyzing slime molds without further interruption.

Message Theory. The idea that there were certain irreducible concepts common to any technological civilization. A form of communication based on reference to those ideas ought to be readable to any other civilization. She got up, went to her desk console, and started calling up reference files. Maybe it was time to give those old nonsense theories a test.

Marcia knew she was facing an absurdly complex task. If indeed the radio source was a signal, it was presumably a message in an utterly foreign language.

Unless, of course, it wasn't aliens who had done this at all, but instead some bunch of perfectly standard-issue humans, crazies who had gotten hold of some very strange technology. Suppose, for the sake of argument, the Octal Millennialists had double-checked the portents, counted up by eight again and discovered they had made a mistake in their base-eight calculations of the date for Judgment Day. Suppose it had come due and they had decided to help it along. Or suppose some other tech-gang had dreamed up a way to hold the Earth hostage. That seemed impossible—but so did everything else about this disaster. If it was a human plot, then presumably that twenty-one-centimeter signal was heavily encrypted. If it was a *non*human code, then presumably it could only be tougher.

Simply to sit down at a computer console and plunge into the task without preparation was absurd. It was as if she had decided to crack the Rosetta stone in one afternoon.

But she had a few distinct advantages over Champollion and the other Rosetta detectives: computers. In VISOR's main computer system, she had highly sophisticated pattern-recognition programs at her command. The twenty-one-centimeter signal seemed to be binary in nature, a series of zeroes and ones, ideal for computer manipulation. The number-crunching side of the problem would be straightforward enough.

But even with all that said, the task should have taken months, perhaps years to crack. If Marcia had been in a truly rational state of mind, rather than merely struggling to maintain a veneer of rationality over her panic and despair, she might have realized that, and never even made the attempt.

It was perfectly ridiculous even to try.

And downright absurd that she cracked the first stage of the message in fifteen minutes.

CHAPTER ELEVEN

———————— ◇ ————————

Summoning the Demons

COYOTE WESTLAKE WOKE UP WITH A POUNDING HEAD-
ache, slumped in a corner of her habitat shed. What the
hell had she been drinking last night? Lying there without moving a muscle, she carefully reviewed the night
before. *Wait a second,* she thought. *I didn't have anything to drink. I haven't had a drink in weeks.* There was
a very good reason for that: there wasn't a drop of booze
left in the hab shed or the ship.

Clearly something was wrong. She had to think this
out. But the reflexes of an experienced drinker had taught
her to keep her eyes shut when she found herself in this
sort of position, being careful not to move a muscle while
she took stock of her situation. Getting up and moving
was a quick invitation to particularly messy forms of ver-
tigo—especially in zero gee. She lay still, eyes shut, and
tried to remember.

If she hadn't been drinking the night before, then this
was not a hangover. She had gone to bed early and stone

cold sober, in a good mood even. Then what the hell had happened? She needed more data.

She cautiously opened one eye, and then the other, and found herself staring at what seemed to be the forward bulkhead of the hab shed, at the far end of the cabin from her bunk. She was pasted, facedown, to the wall of the shed. She realized her nose was somehow both numb and sore at the same time, and the pain in her head was across her forehead. She must have slammed herself facefirst into the wall somehow. That, as least, would explain the headache—but how the hell had she thrown herself across the cabin? Even in zero gee, it was a hell of a stunt. Had she leapt out of bed during a nightmare?

Moving cautiously to avoid the stomach-whirling nausea she still half-expected, she reached out with both her hands and pushed herself away from the bulkhead. She drifted back away from the wall—and then was astonished to find herself drifting back down *toward* it. No, not drifting—*falling*.

She scrambled in midair and managed to swing herself around fast enough to land, rather awkwardly, on her rump rather than her face again. Falling? In zero gee? Not zero anymore. She would estimate it as about a twentieth gee or so.

She sat there, staring at the cabin above her—*above* her—in utter bewilderment. Her bunk was bolted to the aft wall of the cabin—which had now become the ceiling. The sheet was caught by one of the restraint clips, or otherwise it would have fallen too. Now it hung absurdly down. She glanced around the forward bulkhead she was sitting on and found it littered with bits and pieces of equipment that had slammed down with her. She reached up and felt a bump on the top of her head. Something must have clipped her as it fell.

She stood up, as carefully as she could, and tried to think. When she had gone to sleep, her hab shed had been bolted to the side of asteroid AC125DN1RA45, a tiny hunk of rock less than half a kilometer across, far too small to generate any gravity field worth mentioning. Maybe a ten-thousandth of a gee, tops. Now, suddenly, she was in a gee field hundreds of times stronger than that. What the hell was going on? Had someone moved her hab shelter for some reason?

Her shelter was a cylinder about fifteen meters long. Or, now, fifteen meters tall, with Coyote standing on the bottom looking up. At its midsection was an airlock system. There were two viewports at the midsection as well, one set into the airlock and the other set into the bulkhead opposite. One port afforded a view of the asteroid's surface, the other a view spaceward. What she couldn't see through the ports she ought to be able to see using the remote-control exterior camera. The camera's controls were set into the wall by the airlock.

It took her two or three tries, and two or three crashes, before she managed to jump precisely enough to grab a handhold by the airlock and clip herself into place with the restraint belts intended for holding small pieces of cargo. She looked through the rockside port first and breathed a sigh of relief. RA45's dark bulk was still there. She recognized not only the rumpled landscape, but her own mining gear. And there was the drill pit down into the rock's interior.

Then she looked out the spaceward viewport and discovered something was missing after all. Not on the rock. In the sky.

In a horrifying flash she realized what she wasn't seeing. Her ship. The *Vegas Girl* was gone.

No, wait a second. There it was, a tiny blinking dot of light far to sternward, the *Girl*'s tracking strobe.

How the hell could this have happened? She had left the *Vegas Girl* in a perfectly matched orbit relative to

RA45. There was no way she could have drifted that far while Coyote was asleep.

Unless she had been sleeping for one hell of a long time. She checked her watch and compared it to the time display on the hab shed's chronometer. She even checked the date, just to be sure she hadn't slept around the clock. But no, she had been out only a few hours. How far had her ship drifted?

Coyote grabbed the radar range-and-rate gun out of its rack and aimed it through the spaceward viewport, lining up the sights on the *Girl*. It was a low-power portable unit, not really meant to work at long range. Normally she used it to establish distance from and velocity toward an asteroid, but it could track her ship just as handily. She got the blinking strobe in the sights and pulled the trigger.

The gun *pinged* cheerfully twice to indicate it had gotten a good range and rate on its target. Coyote checked the gun's tracking data display.

And her heart nearly stopped. The *Vegas Girl* was over one hundred kilometers astern, and the ship was moving away at over three hundred meters a second.

But wait a moment. The tracker just showed relative velocity, not which object was doing the moving. She peered out the port again, and spotted the triple-blink beacon she had left on RA46, the last rock she had worked. She swore silently. RA46 was in the wrong part of the sky. She fired a ranging pulse at it and got back virtually the same velocity value. The *Girl* was stationary relative to RA46. So it wasn't the ship moving. It was this rock. It was moving at nearly twelve hundred kilometers an hour relative to the ship! But how the hell—

Good Golly God. She wasn't in a gravity field—that was a one-twentieth-gee *acceleration* she was feeling. But for how long? Coyote knew that velocity could accumulate at a hellacious rate under even modest acceleration.

Even so, she was startled by the results when she ran the problem. Assuming one-twentieth gee, that meant the rock had been accelerating for only ten or eleven minutes. Somehow, the numbers were the most frightening thing.

But how the devil could a dumb rock accelerate that fast? Or even at all? Coyote sure as hell would have noticed if someone had landed on RA45 and rigged it for acceleration. The fusion engines required would have been twice the size of her hab shelter. Even if it had happened under her local horizon, it would have been a massive engineering job and she would have felt the vibration of the work rattling RA45. But even the high-end miners who routinely maneuvered their rocks into more convenient orbits never got their boost up over one or two percent of a gee. Asteroids were just too massive to make any better headway than that. Even then, the vibration was nearly enough to shake the rock apart.

Except this baby was cooking along at about three times that velocity without so much as a quiver. She hung in the restraint straps, staring at the range gun's tiny control panel, utterly baffled.

And starting to get very scared. This was a budget hab shelter. It had no radio powerful enough to call for help. No escape pod, either. And without a ship, she had no way off this rock.

Where in gambler's hell was this rock *going*?

And who was taking it there?

Larry sat alone in Control Room Four, staring at nothing.

The message from the Moon was perfectly straightforward: Earth had returned, in the form of a black hole.

A black hole. The shocks were coming too fast, too hard.

Larry felt like a fool, a Pollyanna who could not face bad news. How could the Earth vanish without leaving debris, he had demanded. Well, he had his answer now. Simple. All you do is crush the planet down into a black hole. And in some incredible way, his damnable gravity wave had done just that.

Larry clenched his hands hard into the armrests of his chair. He should have *seen* this answer, should have predicted it. Instead, he and Webling had shouted it down when Sondra suggested a black hole. Because they could not face the truth.

Earth was not now merely missing, but destroyed. So much for his clutching at straws, saying that the planet had merely been moved in some mysterious way.

But his arguments had seemed so *logical*, his chain of reasoning so strong. Had he truly been rationalizing that hard?

It didn't matter now. However good or bad his theories had been, they didn't match the facts—they were wrong. The gravity beam had induced Earth to collapse into a black hole, period. The home planet was destroyed. Details not yet resolved, main fact undeniable.

No one at the station seemed able to respond to the news. Larry felt it himself—a numbness, a shock that seemed to freeze him to his seat. Well, how could they react? What possible way was there for any of them to respond? No one knew what to say or do.

Larry winced, and faced a deeper truth. His situation was a bit different from Sondra's or Dr. Webling's. It had been *his* finger on the button. It was he who had designed the experiment and set it in motion. Alone, among all humanity, *he* bore that responsibility. Intentional, accidental, that didn't matter. It was his action that doomed Earth, smashed it into a bottomless gravitational pit, crushed it down into a single point in space, surrounded by an event horizon no larger than a pebble on the beach.

Damn it, *how*? Larry felt some part of himself rebel at the thought. How could his gravity beam have done that? It was flat-out impossible. He shut his eyes and visualized the gravity-beam system, traced it through the Ring of Charon's circuitry, examined every step of the procedure. No, it was impossible. There was no room in its observed behavior, no mysterious unaccounted-for data, that would allow for the beam to touch off a gravity collapse into a black hole.

And how had the other planets escaped the same fate when the beam had touched them? How could his beam crush Earth and yet leave Venus unharmed?

And where had Earth's gravity field gone for those eight hours between the vanishment and Lucifer's crash? Naturally occurring gravity was a function of mass, pure and simple. It did not matter what form the mass was in. Earth, or a black hole of Earth's mass—or Earth's mass in Swiss cheese—would all produce the same gravity field. It wouldn't switch on and off as the matter switched from one state to another, or vanish for eight hours.

And why were there still gravity waves and that damned twenty-one-centimeter radio source coming from the Moon?

And how the hell had Earth gained five percent in additional mass during those missing eight hours? Larry was willing to bet that an Earth-mass black hole couldn't absorb matter that fast. The mass wouldn't just dive straight in. It would form into an accretion disk, and then spiral inward from the disk. Lucifer's rubble had already been forming into a disk before the end came. Larry checked the data. Sure enough, as long as Lucifer's rubble lasted, the black hole had absorbed Lucifer's mass at a fairly steady rate—and at a rate a hundred times slower than it would need to gobble up five percent in bonus mass in eight hours.

And what the hell were those blue flashes, and the large masses ejecting from them? The masses seemed to be coming from *inside* the black hole, but that was impossible. Nothing could escape from a black hole, light included, except the hole's own decay products. So what were the flashes?

Larry stood up and left the room.

What the hell could the blue flashes be, if not a wormhole aperture opening and shutting?

The Ring was not merely an accelerator. In theory, it could be configured as a gravity-imaging system, a gravity telescope of enormous sensitivity. Such a scope could do more than collect gravity waves. It could form images out of them. No one had ever tried it. Larry decided it was time to test the theory.

He needed an imaging sequence of the Moon and vicinity. The facilities on Venus, Ganymede and Titan were all picking up strong gravity waves from the Moon, but their gear was not powerful or sensitive enough to resolve that data into a clear picture. The Lunar gravity sensors were, of course, completely swamped by the mystery gee waves. In short, none of the other gravity-sensor-equipped stations were able to form a useful image.

Nor did they have the benefit of Larry writing their imaging programs. Larry wasn't vain—not especially so—but he knew what he was good at.

Something had to be producing those massive gravity waves emanating from the Moon. Larry needed to see whatever was forming those waves—and he needed to see the gravity fields around that damnable black hole. Better still, he needed some sort of readings of all the hole's properties. Armed with those, he ought to be able to demonstrate that the hole could not possibly be Earth.

They already knew the black hole's mass was wrong. That was enough to convince Larry, but not the outside world. If Larry could demonstrate that the hole's other properties—direction of spin, electric charge, angular momentum, axis of rotation, or magnetic fields—did not match what a black hole made out of Earth would have, then that would be convincing proof that Earth had not been destroyed.

Or at least that the black hole the Moon now orbited was not the corpse of Earth.

He set to work reconfiguring the Ring. It took him two or three hours of simulation time even to confirm the idea was possible. It was hard work, complex calculation involving dozens of variables. Larry was shocked to find that he was having *fun* working out the problem.

But he had always loved cracking a problem. Maybe the human race would have been better off if he had stuck to jigsaw puzzles.

The sims confirmed that the job was doable—but then it occurred to Larry he had better get some authorization on this one. True, the director had offered complete access, but even so . . . He punched up the director's office on the intercom.

Raphael's voice boomed out of the speaker. "Raphael here."

"Sir, Larry Chao down in Control Room Four. I'd like to set up the Ring as a gravity detector and see what we can find out. It seems as if everyone else has canceled out their experiments anyway—"

"Do what you want, Chao. Do whatever in God's name you want. I can't see that it will make the slightest bit of difference."

The line went dead as Raphael cut the connection. Larry shivered to hear the defeat in the old man's voice. Raphael had given up, accepted the fact that Earth was destroyed, and surrendered himself to sorrow. Perhaps he was only being realistic. What possible point could there be to activity, to effort on this day?

But no. Larry wasn't made that way. Even if it was crazy to do so, he had to keep on trying. Better to be insane and fighting than sane and defeated.

He began laying in his configuration.

The Autocrat of Ceres sat in his very plain chair in the very plain compartment, and regarded the two very nervous people before him with regret. He was going to have to kill them.

"I'm very much afraid," he said, "that I don't have much choice in the matter. You were each expected to show cause why I should not put you to death. I have seen no such cause shown. Instead I have seen two people who have allowed a petty squabble over mining rights to degenerate into another useless rock war. It is your egos, and not the mining rights, that prevent justice in this case. And the Autocrat's Law requires me to remove all obstacles to justice. Case closed." The Autocrat nodded toward his marshals, and they stepped forward.

The plaintiff screamed, the defendant fainted. The marshals were good at what they did. Within seconds, both of the claimants were restrained, sedated, and being taken away, toward the Autocrat's very plain, very famous, very deadly airlock. The one where pressure suits were not allowed. The place to which human obstacles to justice were quite literally removed.

Justice, as with many other things in the Belt, was in short supply, and when available, was not of the best quality—too rough, too harsh and too rushed. To the Inner System dandies who visited now and again, the Autocrat's Law seemed barbaric, violent and vengeful. But to the Belters, who had no other source of justice, the

Autocrat's Law represented civilization itself. In all the wide, wild, ungovernable vastness of the Asteroid Belt, they knew there was one place, one name, one law that all could trust. Only the Autocrat's Law could protect them against themselves. Harsh and final it might be, but so too was it impartial.

For the Belters knew the Belt was huge—ungovernably huge. There could be no law when law enforcement was impossible, and no conventional enforcement was possible when the population density was something less than one crotchety misanthropic old coot per million cubic kilometers. It was easy for other things besides law to get lost in the midst of all that vast expanse.

Things like sanity, order, trust, proportion. Megalomania was an easy disease to catch when a man or a woman could have a world—albeit a very small one—for the effort of landing on it. And if your own world, why not your own law, your own empire? Why not declare the divine right of kings and expand outward, conquering your neighbors as you go?

The Belt had seen a thousand rock wars between independent states, many of which consisted of two rock-happy miners taking potshots at each other. If lunatics wanted to exterminate each other, that was their own affair, but there was a more serious and basic problem. Other people could get drawn in, or get caught in the cross fire. In all likelihood, the Autocrat had saved dozens of lives this day by blotting out the leaders in this pointless fight.

But, obvious as the case had been, the Autocrat had taken pause before rendering his decision. The present Autocrat of Ceres was a most careful person. But so was the previous holder of the post, and the one before that. No other sort of person would ever be appointed.

Not only Ceres, but the entire Belt Community as well depended on the Autocrat's authority to supply order, discipline, regimentation, at least to Ceres and its surrounding satellites and stations. Anarchy surrounded Ceres on all sides, but even the Belt's wildest anarchists knew they needed Ceres to be stable, orderly, predictable, to be a place where a trader could buy and sell in safety.

The rules might change elsewhere with every passing day, but at Ceres the Law was always the same. Claims filed in the office of the Autocrat were honored everywhere—for they were backed not only by the Autocrat's Law and Justice, but his Vengeance.

Nothing but fair dealing was ever done in a Ceres warehouse. None but fair prices were ever paid. No one brought suit frivolously. For the Autocrat himself stood in judgment of all cases.

By the Law, the Autocrat was required, in every case from unlicensed gambling straight up to claim jumping and murder, to find cause why the death penalty should *not* be exacted against one—or both parties—to the case. If the Autocrat could not—or would not—find such cause, plaintiff and claimant, accuser and defendant died.

The Autocrat's Law had a long reach. Many defendants were tried *in absentia*, having chosen to flee rather than face a day in court. But as the saying went, *If the Autocrat finds you guilty, he will find you in the flesh.* His bounty hunters—and his rewards—found the guilty everywhere. Very few places refused to honor his warrant—and none were places a sane man would flee towards.

Indeed, fear of the Autocrat's Justice prevented all but the most worthy claimants from coming forth to ask it, and prevented all but the most venal from risking its power. Calls for justice were few and far between when the sword was as sharp as it was double-edged.

Today, however, the Autocrat found himself besieged. Radio calls were coming in from all over the Belt reporting claim frauds. Claims beacons were being shifted, were even vanishing. Legally beaconed asteroids, even a few with active mines, were being *moved* without the claimant's authority. Having disposed of the last court case for the day, the Autocrat stood up from his courtroom and hurried toward his private operations room.

One or two of his predecessors, the more self-important ones, would have been coldly furious at this assault on claims filed under the Autocrat's authority. Perhaps they would already be calling the marshals, preparing to broadcast attack orders, offering massive bounties.

The Autocrat was tempted to do just that himself, but he hesitated. It was the duty of the Autocrat to think before acting. Who would dare wage such a wholesale assault on claims in the Belt? Who had the sheer raw physical power to move whole fleets of asteroids? Who had that many of the massive fusion engines required for the job? How had they made the complex preparations for the job without anyone noticing?

He reached his private ops room and felt himself relax a bit. The Autocrat was a solitary man. At times of crises he preferred to work by himself, alone with his own thoughts and reflections. He sat down at his desk.

An alert notice was blinking in the center of his desktop controls. Something big had happened. The Autocrat pressed the playback control. A screen came to life and he read with mounting astonishment the words that scrolled past. The incoming reports were obviously garbled, confused, bizarre, contradictory. Most of it he flatly did not believe. But something remarkable had clearly taken place in the Earth-Moon system.

In the meantime, the Autocrat had his own worries. He powered up his holographic display system and set the controls to provide a schematic of the entire Belt, highlighting the various claim-jumping complaints. He leaned back in his chair and examined the glowing mid-air image carefully.

There were dozens of complaints, perhaps two or three hundred. More complaint lights were appearing in the tank even as he watched. The pattern reminded him of something, some other representation of the Belt. Almost on a whim, he called a display of the Belt's population density. The pattern matched the claim-jump display almost precisely. The more people in a given volume of space, the more reports of claim jumping and rock shifting. How could there be so many? Where would anyone be taking all of these rocks? No way to know that yet, not enough time had passed to establish any sort of vectors. But the Autocrat had a practiced eye for such things, and could tell the rocks weren't all headed toward the same place.

Wait a moment. The claim jumping matched the population-density display. Why would someone go to the trouble of moving only claimed rocks, when there were millions more left unclaimed? He was not seeing a display of all the rocks that were moving, but only of the rocks people saw and cared about.

What about the other rocks?

He activated the voice command system. "Give me a radar track of the entire Ceres Sector," he said. "Track and display all claimed and unclaimed asteroids that are maneuvering without authorization. Add the results to the display in front of me now."

He leaned over the tank and watched the area around the dot of light representing Ceres. A whole forest of lights began to blaze around it. "Correlate this data with reports of unauthorized moves, assume similar numbers of maneuvering asteroids throughout the Belt, adjusting for population density in reporting moves, distribution of

asteroids throughout the Belt and other standard inter-
pretive factors, and display results.''

Suddenly the whole Belt was gleaming with light.

"My God," the Autocrat said. "How many? What is
your estimate?''

The answer appeared in bold numbers, floating in the
center of the tank:

10,462

The Autocrat slumped back in his chair. Ten thousand.
Over ten thousand asteroids were on the move.

No one, *no one* could do that.

And no one who *could* do it would have any reason to
fear the Autocrat's Justice.

How long without sleep? Larry asked himself, trying
to think back far enough to get an answer. It must be
going on twenty hours by now, he realized. Or was it
thirty? It was hard enough to keep track of time, in this
place of artificial day and night, even when you *had* a
normal routine to rely on.

He rubbed his weary eyes. It had taken forever to lay
in the detector-mode settings by hand. At least, if it
worked, he could bring them up automatically next time.
But it would still take the Ring a while to set itself into
the new mode.

He watched the monitors track the progress of the Ring
toward scope mode, and let his mind step back a little,
away from the narrow technical problem to the bigger
picture.

Time to face the facts square on. Hundreds of years of
searching, hundreds of years of silence had convinced
everyone that there was no source of life except Earth. It

was a given, an assumed fact. But no matter how firm the belief against extraterrestrial intelligence was, there was only one possible explanation for what had happened to Earth. An alien invasion.

The words seemed crazy even as he thought them. How mad would they seem when he worked up the nerve to *say* them?

And if he was right, then how the hell had his damn-fool experiment called the invaders up?

The monitor screen signaled that the reconfiguration was complete, and Larry powered up the display tank, his thoughts much more on aliens than on what he was doing.

It was as if Galileo's mind had been on something else when he first looked through a telescope at the Moon. It never dawned on Larry that he had quite casually invented a whole new way of looking at the Universe. All he had been after was a practical way to examine the situation around Earth.

A strange place materialized in the three-dee tank. A ghostly dance of shadows gleamed up at him, black tendrils and ribbons floating in a skyfield of cloud white, as if streamers of black ink were swirling through a milky sky, radiating out from a central blotch of darkness.

What the hell was he looking at? Larry glanced at the pointing instruments to check that the device was aimed and focused on the vicinity of the Moon. It was—but what was it seeing?

He was like the first person to look at an X ray, not understanding the strange, hidden, ghostly shapes and patterns revealed when the skin was transparent. Larry reminded himself that he was seeing not a solid, physical substance, but the invisible patterns of gravity waves as represented by a computer's graphics system.

He reached for a control and adjusted the intensity of the image. The streamers faded away, and the central blotch of darkness resolved itself into two shapes: a single, pulsing point of darkness, and a spinning-wheel rim, jet black, tiny and perfect. Both shapes hovered in the tank. The point was easy to identify—it was the black hole, throbbing with gravitic potential. Even as he watched, a flash of black swept out from the hole, and a tiny dot of black moved away from it, Sunward. *Jesus Christ.* The only thing that would show in the tank was a gravity-wave generator. A gravity field by itself, unmanipulated, wouldn't show at all. Which meant that that tiny dot was a gravity machine of some sort.

But what about the spinning wheel that hung in space, next to the black hole? What the hell *was* that?

Larry felt the hair on his neck rise. The Moon, good God, the Moon. Or no, something *inside* the Moon, hidden from view. Suddenly the strange shape was familiar. He checked the scale of the image, and the precise coordinates.

Shock washed over him. The Ring of Charon had a twin, a great wheel buried far below the Lunar surface, underneath the craters and the mountains of the Moon, wrapped around the Moon's core.

He adjusted the tank controls to enlarge the ghostly shadow as far out as he possibly could, to the limits of resolution. He stared at the image for a long time. Jet black, a bit grainy, the image distorting for a moment or two as the Ring of Charon adjusted itself, correcting for its own orbital motion. The thing inside the Moon spun huge and dark in the milk white depths of the three-dee tank.

The huge thing lurking inside the Moon was not a smooth or perfect wheel, but ridged and edged, an open structure that resembled uncovered box girders. It reminded Larry of a Ferris wheel with the central supports removed, or the skeleton of an old spinning-wheel-style space station. *Wheel* was the right name for the thing. If nothing else, it distinguished the Lunar object from the Ring of Charon. The Lunar Wheel, then. It helped, somehow, to put a name to it.

But this Wheel was not solid, not real, not any image of a material structure. Larry was seeing the gravitic energies themselves, whirling impossibly through the Moon's interior.

But there had to be a physical, nonrotating wheel-shaped structure hidden inside the Moon, a structure that somehow produced these energies.

Larry pulled back the image and shook his head. Now the black hole hung in space next to the Wheel. There was a moment of powerful activity Larry could not follow, and another tiny dot leapt away from the hole. Damn it, what *were* those things? No one had really focused on them yet.

All by themselves, they represented an incredible mystery: mountain-sized objects leaping out from the interior of a black hole. How? Why? From where? How many of them had jumped out of the black hole already? With the Earth itself vanished, even the greatest of puzzles could get lost in the shuffle.

What was that mass of streaming tendrils blooming out from the Moon? He thought for a moment, then pulled the focus back further. He adjusted the detection gain upwards a bit, and the inky tendrils radiating out from the Earth-Moon system materialized again.

He kept the detection level just high enough for the streaming beams of gravity power to be visible. With the power down low enough, he could see more clearly. The power beams were radiating out from the Moon's centerpoint, the natural focus of the Lunar Wheel. One of the tendrils reached out and attached itself to the black dot that had just come through the Earthpoint black hole. Larry pulled back the view a bit, and saw other tendrils of gravity power reaching out to touch others of the black dots that were still close to the Moon. As he watched, the image of the Earthpoint black-hole gravity source suddenly swelled larger, another black dot appeared through the black hole—and a massive, jet black pulse of gravity power slammed from the hole into the Lunar Wheel.

The gravity power gets sent through the hole once every 128 seconds, Larry realized. *The Wheel absorbs it, stores it, and beams it out to the things moving out from the black hole.*

So those things in turn became point-source gravity-wave sources. Which according to theory, ought to be impossible, but never mind that now. Call them gee points. What about them? How many of them were there? He reset the gravity scope to its widest possible angle, and told it to present only point-source gravity generators.

He sat and thought for a moment as the program ran. How many *could* there be? One every two minutes or so, for the last fourteen hours. That was about right. Something over four hundred gee points by now. Where the hell were they all going?

The tank cleared itself and reset. Larry gasped. He saw a pattern similar to what the Autocrat had seen—but the ten thousand asteroids moving in the Belt were only the beginning.

The Ring of Charon was looking inward, toward the Inner System and the Sun. But it also looked out beyond the distant Sun, out past the far side of Pluto's own orbit and beyond. At the far side of the Solar System, at the ragged edge of resolution, it could see a section of the Oort Cloud's inner surface. The Oort Cloud, the hollow sphere of unborn comets that surrounds the Solar System and extends halfway to the nearest star.

The Oort Cloud was alive with purposeful black dots,

all of them diving in uncountable numbers straight toward the Inner System.

Dr. Simon Raphael sat alone in his office.

Privacy.

Quiet.

He needed those things now. Leaning over his journal book, he set down his words in a slow and careful script. Perhaps his hand was slow, but his mind was moving fast. Too fast. He had found long ago that the journal did him the most good when he was in this state—tired, and yet upset, concerned about something. He had learned to relax his rigid self-control at these times, and let the pen find the words for him.

"Dearest Jessie," he wrote.

"All has been lost. The Earth has vanished, and I am to blame." The words came out of his soul and onto the page. He stopped, set down his pen, and stared at the words in astonishment. *"I am to blame"*? Why in the world had he written *that*? How could *he* be blamed?

He stared at the small three-dee image of Jessie, decades old, that sat on his desk. As if he could find the answers there.

But he already knew. The self-accusation had come from the warmest part of his heart, the part that had come nearest to dying with Jessie's death. The part he had shielded with anger and bitterness.

He was to blame for squashing Larry's first experiments, that was why. Simon knew, intellectually at least, that he was not responsible for the Earth's loss, any more than Larry Chao was responsible. The burden Simon Raphael carried was that he had encouraged Larry's sense of guilt, made it worse with his bullying and anger.

Larry was no more to blame for Earth's loss than the

first caveman to use fire was responsible for the first village of grass huts destroyed by fire. Discovering a new power meant uncorking a genie's bottle. Larry happened to be the one to pull the cork out of gravity's bottle. But it would have been pulled sooner or later. Once the Ring of Charon was built, that much was certain.

Raphael had kicked the boy when he was down. If he had been a proper leader, a proper guide for this scientific operation, he would have accepted Larry's initial discovery, cultivated it and made it grow. The whole team should have focused on it. Even if it had come to nothing, what would there have been to lose?

If the whole staff been thrown into the effort, *had* examined the techniques for a million-gee accelerator, perhaps they would have learned about it in a more orderly fashion. Perhaps they would have learned enough to know the consequences and stop the experiment.

More than likely, of course, they would have fired a graser beam anyway, and Earth would have vanished just the same—but at least it would be shared guilt, and the entire staff would have understood Larry's work well enough to expand on it after the disaster, rush into needed research to understand this incredible situation. A black hole replacing Earth! Fantastic.

For half a moment, the idea nearly excited him, instead of terryifying him. In the old days, that sense of wonder would have been stronger. He would have needed to know what had happened—instead of shutting himself in his office, wishing for catatonia. Simon Raphael bent over the page and continued his writing.

"This place has done things to me, Jessie. You never would have married the sour old man I have turned into. You were always truly my better half, no matter how trite a cliche that phrase might be. You encouraged the young, the weak, the small, and let them grow. You taught me

to do so as well. I have forgotten that, and I must re-learn."

A change came over him as he wrote, and not an unnoticed one. He could feel himself becoming less harsh, less angry, less bitter, feel a gentler part of his heart and soul reopen even as he wrote. He remembered the feelings he had lost, even as he set down the words describing how they were gone.

Larry angered him because Larry represented a successful version of a Simon Raphael that might have been, a lost Simon that he himself had never quite been able to become. He had never been quite bright enough, quite brave enough, quite innocent enough to make the dream-Simon work.

But did not all good fathers wish for their sons to be more than they themselves had been?

Father? Another strange thought. Yes, *father.* If all of his own children were suddenly lost to him, so too was Larry Chao's family lost to Larry. The young man needed guidance, kindness. A father.

And humanity needed Larry Chao. The genius locked inside that head had gotten them into this mess. It might very well provide their only way out of it. *Perhaps*, Simon told himself, *if you stop trying so hard to hate the boy, you might find a way to help him save us all.* And what was there to hate about him anyway?

"I wish you could have met Larry," he wrote to his dead wife. *"I think you would have liked him."*

But then he set the pen down.

There was work to do. He reached for a button and punched up the intercom system.

Larry sat, lost and alone, watching the trajectories of the gee points, thinking, struggling to find any possible meanings, all the imaginable consequences he could. But it was too much for him. This was beyond him, beyond human capacity.

Raphael had to call him twice over the intercom before Larry even heard his name being called. He came to himself with a start. "Ah, yes, Dr. Raphael."

"Mr. Chao. I wanted to apologize for being so short with you when you requested Ring time. We are all . . . all more than a bit under stress at the moment."

"That's all right sir."

There was an awkward pause, as if Raphael had expected Larry to say more, and was now searching for words, if only to cover the silence. "I, ah, suppose it's a bit premature to ask—but have you found anything? Anything that might help?"

Larry stared again at the three-dee tank. Thirty thousand asteroid-sized invaders on the move from the Asteroid Belt and the Oort Cloud. He felt a knot in his stomach. "Oh, I've found quite a bit, sir, but I don't know if it will exactly be *helpful*. Perhaps you should come down here and see it."

"I'm on my way. Thank you."

The intercom cut out. Larry stood there for a moment, unsure of what to do. It suddenly struck him that he was making an official report to the director of the station. He had never done that before. What should he do? Documents. Records. That would at least be something. He instructed the computer to print a hard-copy summary of his findings. And an audiovisual record. That was standard operating procedure when making a major verbal presentation. He reached over and set the voice recorder on, powering up the mikes and cameras. A bright red panel lit on the console, flashing the words ROOM RECORDER ON. The computer had just finished printing the data summary when the door opened. Raphael stepped in.

The director looked subdued, drawn into himself, as if he had lost something he knew he would never find again. Which was of course precisely true, Larry reminded himself. Humanity was in mourning. But there was more to the expression on Raphael's face. Larry wasn't usually very good at understanding people, but he could see something here. With a degree of insight that Larry himself knew he rarely achieved, Larry sensed that a change had come over the old man. There was a hint of hope in him, as if he had also *found* something long missing.

Raphael went straight for the three-dee tank. He stood and stared at the image for a long time. He glanced at the scale display, and sucked in his breath as he realized how huge a volume of space was being represented. "What is it?" he asked.

"An image of all the gravity-wave sources in the Solar System, sir. As seen by the Ring in gravity-telescope mode."

"The Ring doesn't have a—" Raphael's sharp tone of voice suddenly softened, as if he were forcing himself to be gentle. "Oh, I see. Now it *does* have such a mode. More of your work. Very good, Mr. Chao."

Larry reddened with embarrassment. "Ah, thank you, sir. But I don't understand these sources. All of them are very faint and small, as least relatively speaking. Not more than a few kilometers across. So small I can't explain how they can generate the gravity waves in the first place. We need something the size of the Ring to do it."

Larry hesitated, and then moved to the controls, adjusting them. "I've got a good image of the black hole as well. And there's . . . there's *something* inside the Moon."

"Inside?"

"I printed out a data summary, sir," Larry said, handing Raphael the stack of papers.

Raphael took the pages and skimmed them quickly, flipping through the pages. Larry switched the view to a close-up of the Lunar Wheel. He called up the output from the observation dome telescope and superimposed a transparent real-time image of the visible Moon over the Wheel hidden deep inside. The three-dee tank dimensionalized the Moon image, so that the Wheel hung perfectly inside it, spinning sedately through the solid mass of the Moon.

Raphael stared at the tank. "Something in the Moon," he agreed. "So it would appear," he said, in a faint, abstracted tone. "Something that bears a strong resemblance to our own little toy."

"Yes sir. That spinning effect is the gravitic energy moving, and not the physical object itself. Obviously, the Wheel itself must be stationary."

"Obviously," Raphael said, in that same abstracted tone. He sat down at the control-panel operator's seat and looked up at Larry. "You have made a whole series of rapid-fire, utterly remarkable discoveries here tonight. I ought to be astounded, or fearful—but I just feel . . . feel dead inside. I don't have the capacity to react anymore. As God is my witness, I don't know what that thing in the Moon is, or what we can do about it. *You* found it. What do *you* think?" There was an eerie steadiness in his voice, as if Raphael himself knew perfectly well that he was keeping up a false front of calm.

Larry stood there, looking first at the old man, and then at the strange, frightening images in the three-dee tank. He thought of the asteroids leaving their orbits, unaware and unconcerned of the terrified Belters watching them go. He stared again at the rippling wheel of energy spinning through the solid mass of the Moon.

"I think that all my work is meaningless. It won't help us one tiny bit, not by itself," he said at last, a strange intensity in his voice. He stood over the old man, feeling tired, angry, defiant. The feeling washed over him and then faded away. Damn it, how could Raphael suddenly be so reasonable, just when Larry was finally feeling strong enough to fight him?

He took the mound of meaningless paperwork from Raphael and riffled through it. Useless. Utterly useless. He threw the thick sheaf of papers up in the air and ignored them as they fluttered slowly toward the floor in Pluto's flimsy gravity field. Raphael stared at him quite solemnly, unable or unwilling to respond. "All this data means *nothing* by itself," Larry said. "In the last twenty-four hours I've learned more about the mechanics of gravity than any human has ever known—but it's not enough! It's all irrelevant.

"Gravity is barely the *start* of what's going on. This is something way beyond a freak lab accident, a strange natural phenomenon. Let's face it: somehow or another, we—no, *I*—have touched off an alien invasion of our Solar System."

Larry stopped, backed off from the desk, and looked around the room. "There. I finally said it. God knows it sounds absurd and melodramatic, but you tell me: *what else do we call it?* We've been skirting around that reality long enough. Somehow, I don't know how, I summoned up that . . . that *thing* buried in the Moon, like the sorcerer's apprentice accidentally summoning up the demons. I awakened it. I don't know what it is, or how it works, or who put it there. But I do know it *must* be related to the asteroids and Oort Cloud objects that have suddenly started moving. And I think they are moving toward *us*, toward *all* the surviving planets.

"There are at least thirty thousand asteroid-sized objects moving in on the surviving planets of this Solar System. Do you honestly think they mean us no *harm*? I don't know. I think maybe they got the Earth out of the way before the rough stuff begins. Maybe it's not Earth that's in danger. Maybe it's Earth that's being taken out of harm's way.''

He sat down and turned his palms upward, a gesture of resignation, an admission of failure. ''Or maybe that's just nuts.'' He forced himself to be calm. ''We've been picking up reports from all over the Solar System, from people working in every discipline, and we've sent our own messages. But *talking* at people from light-hours away isn't going to help. I think that we all have to get together, in one place, and work together.''

''Do you mean bring the other teams out here?'' Raphael asked. ''Get them to the Ring of Charon to help plan our experiments?''

Larry shook his head. ''No, sir, that wouldn't help. It would leave us focused on gravity. This isn't *about* gravity! Gravity is just what these . . . these *things* use, the way we use electricity. We're up against something a thousand times more complex than running little gravity-wave experiments.

''Besides, the center of action isn't out here. It's in the Earth-Moon system. We need to get all the specialists from *all* the various outposts to the Moon, working on the spot, taking a good hard look at the Lunar Wheel. And the black hole.

''Somebody built that Wheel inside the Moon. Who? How? Why? Where are they from? We can't know from here. We have to get inside the Wheel, if we can. Take a look at it, see if we can find out what makes it tick, what its purpose is.''

Larry stood up, and gazed, more steadily, at the eerie image of a Wheel inside the Moon.

''And find out how to destroy it,'' he said in a whisper.

CHAPTER TWELVE

———◇———

After the Fall

THE SPHERE HAD TO BE SMARTER THAN THE CALLERS OR
the Anchors or the Worldeaters, or any of the other forms.
The Sphere had far greater responsibilities, and thus had
far more need to be cautious, than the others.

Besides, the Sphere had so much data to keep track of.
Handling the gravitic control of a multistar system, keeping tabs on the many Observers and Waiters sleeping in
their far-flung hiding places, building and breeding and
hoping for the next generation of seedships. A thousand,
a million other details. It took tremendous processing
power, remarkable flexibility, and adaptability, to handle
it all.

But the Sphere was not immune to shock, or protected
against surprise—and many of its reflexes were as unal-
terable as a Caller's. When the Caller's messages exploded into its mind, requiring preemptive Link, the
Sphere had no choice but to comply.

In the normal course of events, it was the Sphere that

*would signal that it was ready for a new world and then
wait for a reply. It was rare that a Caller initiated Link,
and there were many fail-safes to prevent it, but it had
happened at times, when there was a malfunction, or a
spurious signal, or when the life-bearing world in question was in some immediate danger—say, from an asteroid impact.*

*Once initiated, failure to complete the Link would not
only threaten the destruction of the precious life-bearing
world in transit, but the energy destabilization of a failed
Link could actually wreck the Sphere and its star system.
A planet—or any mass—blocked midway through
transit would have to express its entire mass as energy—
enough uncontrolled energy to rival a supernova, fun-
neled right into the Sphere. And if the Sphere was
wrecked, so was the Sphere's star system, as planets and
stars careered out of control. No matter if there was a
place prepared for the world, or sufficient energy stores
were available to handle the transfer. The Sphere had to
complete the Link and take on the new world—or chance
its own destruction.*

*Now was perhaps the worst of times. Danger pressed
the Sphere on all sides, and the energy expenditure of
incorporating a new world could scarcely be afforded.
Worse, the radiation of that much nonrandomized energy
could only draw the danger closer.*

*But it had no choice. None whatever. At least the Caller
had sent a dataset along with the new world. With a
supreme effort, the Sphere set the new world into a holding pattern, shuttling it from one temporary stability point
to another while the Sphere prepared a place for it.*

*But the danger. The danger was not merely to the
Sphere's domain, but to the Caller's own planetary system. But there too was hope. If the Caller could build
quickly, then perhaps its domain could provide a new,
uncharted haven, a direction of retreat. But only if it*

*could build fast, and with a minimum of traceable link-
age.*

*The Caller would need help from the Sphere. The more
help the Sphere sent, the better the odds of the Caller's
success. The risk and the expenditure of resources were
worth the possible reward.*

*The Sphere rushed to prepare a Portal Anchor, capable
of Linking under a Caller's control, and arranged for
new-breed Worldeaters to be transported to the new domain.*

*The Sphere also sent a message. An urgent report, that
could be boiled down to one simple concept.*

Danger.

Dianne stared out across the sky. Things seemed to
have settled down, at least for the moment, though this
was no sky of Earth's. A half-dozen stars, white, yellow-
white and red, gleamed brighter than Sirius ever had. A
monstrous sullen red disk, the size of the Moon, glow-
ered *behind* one of the stars. But the star was too far off
to show a disk. How large did that disk have to be to
seem that big *behind* a star? Was it a red giant? Dianne
remembered reading about such things—huge stars, their
outer atmospheres thin, barely more than a red-hot vacuum, with diameters as wide as Saturn's orbit. But a red
giant should appear to grow dimmer at its edges. This
star showed a firm, sharp edge.

A new star—Dianne felt certain it was not the Sun—
hung fat and bright, bathing the Earth in light that was
not quite the color of sunlight. The terminator was in
about the right place.

Something caught at Dianne. A strange star where the
Sun should be. A wave of irrational anger swept over her.
The Sun that had nurtured Earth for four billion years

was gone. In its place this substitute shone in Earth's sky. No counterfeit deserved the true Sun's name. She decided to call it the *Sunstar* to distinguish it both from Earth's proper Sun and the other nearby stars.

Her eyes swept further across the sky, were drawn again to Earth. If the Sunstar's light was not precisely correct, neither was the darkness over the Earth quite so dark as it should have been—not with a half-dozen stars and that massive disk shedding light upon it.

Opposite the Sunstar in the sky, about where the Moon should have been, a roughly toroidal structure of indeterminate size hung in the darkness at some unknown distance. It was a bit larger than a ring for a fat man's finger held at arm's length. It sat in space, gleaming in the light of the Sunstar. Acting on impulse, she fired a radar-ranging beam at it, and got a response 2.5 seconds later. The ranging computer wasn't really meant to work at that sort of range, but it returned a calculated distance of about 300,000 kilometers. The toroid was roughly at the Moon's distance from Earth. Sweet God in the sky. That made it roughly as large as the Moon.

Somehow, of all the terrible wonders she saw, it was the least of them, the toroid, that scared her most. New stars, a substitute sun, even that massive, far-off, glowing red thing in the sky she could accept. It was at least *possible*, albeit highly improbable, that they were natural, understandable objects. But the toroid was obviously—and impossibly—artificial. A *made* thing, built by someone, a wheel in the sky as big around as Earth's Moon.

Enough of stargazing. If Dianne wanted to survive, she had work to do. She strapped herself more firmly into her command chair and started running checks.

Wait a second. NaPurHab. Where the hell was—there. There it was. Already nothing more than a tiny shape, moving down toward the Earth before sweeping back out

onto the Lunar half of its figure-eight orbit. Much good
that it did her. She certainly couldn't reach NaPurHab,
and with the Moon missing, the Purps' orbit was going
to get plenty screwed up. It might well not be a good
place to be.

Never mind. Survival issues first. Get this ship dancing, then worry other people's worries. She started running down her checklists.

But routine system checks could not stop her mind
working. *Someone had taken them here.* Earth had been
stolen. This was no accident. They had done it on purpose.

Whoever they were.

*Owing to lack of interest, the end of the world has been
canceled.* Gerald did not know what irreverent part of
his hindbrain the thought had come from, but it was true.
He was still here, and so was the Universe. He came to
himself, and told himself to stay where he was, lying on
his back. Slowly, carefully, he lifted his arm and felt the
lump on his head. His hand came away sticky with blood.
What had happened? Perhaps a rock shaken loose by the
quakes had beaned him, knocking him out.

But that did not matter. The world was still here. The
ground was still beneath him, the night breezes still blew,
the stars still shone down, peeking through a high, hazy
band of thin clouds that had blown in from the Pacific.
The sky had been clear before. Some time must have
passed. He felt cold.

The stars. Gerald thought the stars looked a bit strange,
even through the haze, although he had never been much
for stargazing. Too many bright stars. And the Moon was
either greatly changed or else replaced by something he
could not see clearly through the late-night haze.

What had happened? *The experiment.* Marcia had mentioned something about an experiment, a beam being pointed at Earth just after ten A.M. her time.

Gerald checked his watch by the too-bright starlight and figured the time out in his head, allowing for the time zones and the speed-of-light delay.

That beam had been scheduled to hit at precisely the moment the world had gone mad.

A coincidence. A devil of a big coincidence.

He stood up and hurried back to the house. He went to the printer bin and dug out the document she had sent. He started to read inside—but being inside just after an earthquake didn't sit right with him. He went to the kitchen, fished a flashlight out of the junk drawer, and took the papers outside to read.

Ring of Charon. Gravity waves. High power. Earth-side target lab: Jet Propulsion Laboratory. *But how could a gravity beam do this?* Gerald asked.

But then he asked an even more fundamental question.

Do what? What, exactly, has happened? Gerald required of himself that he face things squarely, examine the evidence and reach conclusions based on what was so, not on what he wanted to be so. His nonreligious friends were confused that a man of faith would operate that way. But his faith was, paradoxically, a result of facing the evidence. God, in some form, was the only possible explanation for Creation.

But that was beside the point.

New stars in the sky. Several of them incredibly bright. Bright enough that he almost did not need his light to read by. That great sphere he had seen earlier must now be hidden away on the other side of Earth. He looked up again at the *thing* where the Moon should have been. The skies had cleared, and he could see plainly that it was a ring-shaped form.

Face the evidence and accept the obvious answer to his

question. The Earth, the entire planet, had been moved to a new place.

By a gravity beam? It seemed absurd. Maybe the gravity experiment happening when it did was sheer chance. If not—

He looked again the paper. JPL. If the experiment happening when it did was not just a mad coincidence, then JPL would be the place to be. To find out what had gone wrong.

And the place to get involved in fixing it.

What can be moved, can be moved back. Gerald smiled with a rare thrill of gallows humor. *If faith can move mountains, then maybe faith plus determination can move planets.*

Gerald knew where he was going.

He stood up and looked across the valley below him. All was quiet, and still. A few houses here and there had lights on, and faint voices whispered across the distance. Only a few had been awakened, perhaps only those who had once lived where earthquakes were frequent.

It struck him that there would be those who had slept through the whole thing, who wouldn't check the news the next day, who might go for days without noticing that the Universe had been transmogrified. He looked up at the stranger's sky above and shivered.

He could find it in himself to envy such people.

Across the wide expanse of the Earth, by greater and lesser degrees, people realized what had happened—or at least that *something* had happened. Governments, news services, private comm systems, rumor mills—all were overloaded with speculation, wild rumors, sober and reasoned discussions, panicky tirades.

Two or three of the more unstable governments collapsed. Rabble-rousers appeared in village squares, on obscure vid channels and on what was left of the major networks with the satellites gone. The Final Clanners, the Naked Purples and the other culture rads took to the streets.

Generals mobilized their armies, navies put to sea, air forces and what space forces there were surviving in orbit went on alert. All of it was useless. What use was an army against a power that moved worlds?

Within a few hours, riots, demonstrations, debates, and emergency meetings of world bodies were in full swing across the globe. None of it was of any use at all. Nothing could be, unless and until people could understand what had happened.

The post–Knowledge Crash world needed information, and started turning toward the people who could provide it.

But those people were more than a bit busy themselves, at the moment.

Time had passed. That much Wolf knew. How much time he could not tell without a deep act of concentration. Dreamlike, the hours were passing like seconds. Wolf Bernhardt looked up, bleary-eyed, from his console and checked the wall chronometer. Two P.M., local time. Something like twelve hours, then.

The tomblike quiet of JPL at nighttime had given way to a day of chaos, as every scientist with the remotest connection to JPL descended on the place, chasing after answers, charging about in panic. The printer was spitting out another telegram from the International Astronomical Union every few seconds, the JPL computers logging in the new data as it arrived. The IAU's Telegram

Office in Massachusetts was the clearinghouse for all new astronomical discoveries.

The sheer volume of data was daunting. Earth may have suffered a Knowledge Crash, may have lost many of its communications satellites, may have lost much of its power grid when half the power satellites vanished, but even so the information flowed in a torrent from endless sources. Less than twelve hours after the Big Jump, Earthbound observatories and the surviving orbital stations were reporting discoveries faster than JPL could log them in.

Wolf prided himself on being flexible. That flexibility was being put to the test this morning. It fell to him to pull the facts together, for the very basic reason that no one else seemed able to believe the facts. Not even the people who were finding them.

The observatories were forced to confront the impossible situation first and most directly. Every astronomical observation ever made back in the Solar System was worthless—the objects that had once been observed were all missing. Even more seriously, all the astronomical frames of reference were gone. The background stars, likewise gone from their old points in the sky, could no longer be used as positional aids.

In a new star system, with no frame of reference set, it was difficult to get one's bearings. The word came down from the IAU: they were arbitrarily assigning Earth's orbital plane as the zero-reference plane for the system. They decreed that Earth's orbital motion was from west to east, approximating the conditions of Earth's old orbit.

It was of some help in getting organized, but the astronomers had a more basic problem: quite understandably, they could not believe their eyes. But Wolf quickly discovered that their electronic assistants were able to handle the changed circumstances without skipping a beat. Most of the IAU grams came from robotic observation stations. Robots didn't have to worry about believing in what they saw: discoveries, major ones, were literally being made on automatic.

With the loss of nearly all the spaceside instruments, modern astronomy had been decapitated. Suddenly astronomy was back in the mid twentieth century, dependent on crotchety instruments and crotchety observers perched on lonely mountaintops all over the world.

Some modern hardware was earning its keep. The most fruitful data was coming from the ground-based widescan telescopes. These instruments tracked the sky, watching for objects that moved against the fixed background of Earth's sky. They were designed to spot uncharted and potentially profitable asteroids or incoming comets, and to watch for spacecraft on collision courses with each other. The skyscanners had spotted a number of comets and asteroids, over the years, doing their part in the history of astronomy, but suddenly they were spotting dozens of full-blown planets, both around Earth's new sun and around the other stars.

It was too soon to establish much about the properties of the new planets, except that they existed. There weren't even resolvable images for most of them yet. They were merely dots of light that moved against the stars. JPL's computers quickly nailed positions and provisional orbits for many of them.

Wolf knew at first glance that those orbits were damnably odd. No two planets in any system seemed to be moving in the same orbital plane. Many of the planets were in highly inclined orbits. Some were traveling in opposite directions from each other. The differing orbital planes Wolf could deal with. Natural mechanisms could cause that. If two worlds came close to each other, the interaction of their gravity fields might deflect them into new orbital planes, each flinging the other off into a new orbital inclination. Something like that had happened to Pluto, billions of years ago. But the close distancing and the retrograde orbits shook Wolf. There was no conceivable way planets could form in those positions, moving in opposite directions.

A quick-look calculation at Earth's own orbit showed the planet was moving about its new star once every 370 days. The calendars were going to be off by four days from now on.

That seemed manageable enough, but Earth was in a mighty strange neighborhood. Its closest new planetary neighbor rode an orbit a mere three million kilometers inward, though its orbit was inclined forty-five degrees from Earth's and it was moving east to west. It was in retrograde orbit, moving in the opposite direction, and near its closest approach at the moment. Through Earth's telescopes, it showed itself a lovely blue-green world.

Two hours after their scopes got those images, the observatories came up with another stunner. Earth was looking down into the new sun's *polar* region. Wolf took a long moment to accept that. Well, if the orbits were in all inclinations, *somebody* had to be in a polar orbit.

One other damn strange thing: as well as he could judge from the first-look data, *all* the worlds were terrestrial. No gas giants, no ice balls. And *all* of them rode orbits that seemed to be inside their primary star's biosphere, the narrow band of distances from a star where a planet could sustain roughly Earthlike temperatures.

Certainly Earth was inside this new star's biosphere, with a vengeance. One of the very few things that had not changed was the mean solar constant—the average amount of solar energy reaching a given square area of the Earth's surface. That seemed to have remained the same to within several decimal places.

And *that* strongly suggested something else he didn't

want to know. Maybe Wolf wasn't quite as flexible as he hoped.

Dianne Steiger felt a moment of triumph. Forget the robots and the on-board automatics and the *Pack Rat*'s artificial intelligence programs. This was one moment the *Pack Rat* needed an honest-to-God, flesh-and-blood *human* on board. The poor old ship wasn't ready to cope with this situation on her own. She needed a human pilot—and a repair worker.

Repairs first, though. Dianne peered carefully at the video display. As far as she could tell, part of the *Rat*'s nose had been lopped off in the first moment of . . . of whatever had happened. Dianne blinked, realizing that she had not developed any more meaningful way of describing what she had seen.

Well, what the hell had it been? What, exactly, *had* happened? Dianne felt something cold in her gut when she even considered the question.

But she had enough on her plate focusing on smaller problems. Whatever that thing was, it had done a number on her ship. It looked as if the first manifestation of that damn blue-unwhiteness had come into existence right across the *Rat*'s bow, leaving five centimeters of the ship's nose on the other side. The blue-unwhite plane must have sliced across the nose like a knife through a salami. Perhaps a tiny sliver of debris was still floating out in space somewhere, back in the Solar System.

Concentrate on what she could deal with. She looked again at the nose damage. The first five centimeters of the *Pack Rat*'s nose weren't there anymore, and the nose jets' recessed nozzles were truncated, obviously screwing up their thrust patterns. It was lucky they had fired at all, instead of simply blowing up. She could see scorch marks on the hulls, mute evidence that some reaction-rocket exhaust gases had gone where they shouldn't have. It had been close.

So, kiss the nose jets good-bye. She dared not press her luck by using them again. It was possible to fly the ship without nose jets. Difficult, but possible.

Still, the damaged nose was going to need some sort of repair. It could never survive reentry with bare metal exposed and the nose the wrong shape. Even if she didn't fly the ship home, but merely to a spaceside repair station, she did not want to go cruising around with the nose gone. The delicate components in there were never meant to be exposed to the temperature extremes of open space. She had to patch it.

Spray foam. The number two arm had a foam nozzle on it, intended for dealing with just this sort of problem. She switched it on, and brought the arm in as close as she could to the nose.

Working with a fine spray and a delicate touch, she slowly built up layer after layer of ablative, heat-absorbing foam. The foam turned rock hard within seconds of hitting vacuum. The idea was that the stuff would survive long enough for one reentry. It would slough off as it melted, taking the excess heat of reentry with it as it ablated away.

It was a delicate job. The foam needed to be strong and well bonded, and needed to match the old contours of the nose as closely as possible. Dianne wanted to hurry, to get through and get the hell out of a chunk of space where fields of unseeable blue-unwhiteness appeared and cut chunks out of your spacecraft. But hurry could kill her. She knew that. She worked slowly and carefully, forcing herself to hold the hurried, overanxious side of her personality in check.

Finally the job was done. She pulled the manipulators away and examined her handiwork as seen from the remote camera mounted on the number three arm. It looked good. A clean job.

The number one and two arms backed away as she drew in the waldo controls. The ablative foam *ought* to hold together long enough for reentry. Reentry. Was she really willing to take that risk? She sat back and thought about it. Reentry was certainly riskier than going for an emergency docking with one of the orbital stations. NaPurHab was out of reach to her—and still didn't seem likely to be a healthy place to be. The other stations? She didn't have a line of sight on any of the major stations from this orbit, and the comm channels were hopelessly screwed up. Probably most of the communications satellites were gone. She had no idea if the orbital stations were still there—or if they would remain where they were, or were capable of docking spacecraft and taking in refugees.

On the other hand, Earth was *there*. She could *see* it. Whatever the hell had been done, had been done to *Earth*. Orbital facilities had survived, or not, at random—she had been witness to that. She had a good strong hunch that the *Rat* wouldn't be here right now if she had been another hundred meters Moonward from Na-PurHab.

And where the hell would the *Rat* have been? Where was the Moon? Back in the Solar System?

Good God. Where was the *Sun*?

She looked out across the Universe. More to the point, where was *she*? What *was* this place? She pushed the thought away and retracted the last of the manipulator arms. Worrying about that sort of thing wasn't going to get her home alive. She settled back into her console and fired up the navigation system. Working on manual only, doing her own naked-eye navigation, she set to work plotting out her reentry.

The unknown faced her on every side. This was going to be the most dangerous flyback of her life.

But she knew, already, that this was merely a tactical retreat. She would be back, back up here in space, to find out what had happened and why.

Plastered with sweat, half-numb from exhaustion and shock, she prepared her crippled spacecraft for the dangerous ride home, already planning her revenge, the coming day when she faced whatever power it was that moved worlds.

She was happier than she had ever been in her life.

CHAPTER THIRTEEN

——◇——

Wormhole

THE CALLER WAS DELIGHTED. IT HAD EXPECTED—OR AT least hoped for—assistance, in the form of an Anchor. It had never dared to dream the Sphere would send a sophisticated Portal Anchor, let alone new-breed World-eaters. Nor had it ever dared hope that such help might come so fast.

Anchors often arrived swiftly, but Portal Anchors were rarely sent, and periods equivalent to terrestrial years—even decades and centuries—had been known to pass before any material aid was sent through a Portal Anchor.

But even a non-Portal Standard Anchor would have served a vital purpose, of course. A Standard Anchor could provide a hole in space, albeit a smaller one than a full Portal allowed. Anything that could be sent across normal space could be sent through such a hole. Such as radio signals. The Caller had sent its own dataset, over and over, to ensure accurate reception. It received signals back, with the data needed to reestablish sophisti-

*cated contact after so many silent eons. In effect, the
Sphere and Caller were relearning each other's archaic
dialect.*

*But now the Caller was receiving a substantive signal,
not a mere language lesson. As was standard procedure,
the Caller echoed the signal back to demonstrate that it
had been received.*

*That required no thought. But considering the signal
did. The Caller examined the message.*

And was bathed in fear.

It was a long ride from Pluto to the Moon, no matter
how fast the ship. At least it was almost over. They
should be landing within an hour or so. Sondra glanced
up from her screenful of Moonside news and propaganda
and looked across the tiny wardroom at Larry and Raphael. Lot of fun it had been, being cooped up in here
with the two of them and Collier, *Nenya*'s taciturn pilot.

Sondra thought about herself in connection with Raphael and Larry. The rushed flight of the *Nenya* demonstrated how important the three of them suddenly were,
and not just on Pluto. That the Ring was suddenly important off Pluto was demonstrated by the fact that the
repairs and upgrades on the *Nenya* were to be given top
priority once they reached the Moon. With half the satellite's own infrastructure wrecked, that meant something. Sondra had caught a mood in all the messages
flitting back and forth: if Larry Chao and the Ring had
got them *into* this mess, then only Larry Chao and the
Ring could get them back *out*.

"Are you sure the charge values are for real?" Larry
asked, his slightly muffled voice echoing out from his
sleep cabin. He did most of his work in there, in a feeble
attempt to give the others some privacy—but his voice

still carried. No doubt he was speaking into the radio mike that seemed surgically attached to him these days. He had spent most of the trip arguing with some guy named Lucian Dreyfuss about data on the Earthpoint black hole. At least now they were within reasonable radio range of the Moon. The speed-of-light delays were no longer quite so maddening.

Sondra desperately wanted some real privacy, to get away from the others and be by herself. Too bad the rest of the enormous ship was sealed off, filled with flexible fuel bladders. Only seven compartments were open—the control room, the wardroom, four coffin-sized sleep cabins, and a refresher chamber that provided an utterly unsatisfactory zero-gee shower.

Sixteen days. Sixteen days en route from Pluto to the Moon. At least Larry had his work, sifting through the math and the physics, seeking after answers, solutions.

That was how he dealt with *his* guilt. So how the hell was she dealing with her own? Without her encouragement and help, Larry wouldn't have worked up the nerve to do what he had done. Or was that even true? How responsible was she supposed to feel for the cataclysmic and utterly unforeseeable actions of another person?

She sighed and returned to her reading. She had gotten to the Naked Purple's pronouncement. Blatant nonsense, but at least it was a change of pace from listening to Larry arguing gravity physics.

We proudly proclaim our victory in ridding the Solar Area of the scourge called "Earth." Sondra frowned. More babble. "What's the Solar Area?" she asked Dr. Raphael. "I mean, in Purple talk."

Raphael set down his own book and thought for a moment. He seemed calm and at ease, as if he had found some part of himself on this flight, some part that had long been missing. "I used to know these things. Oh, yes. The Purples disapprove of the term Solar *System*, because it implies that there is organization and purpose in nature. Chaos is of course the primordial state and attempts to impose order were human attacks on nature. I may not have the logic precisely, but it's something like that. It's hard to read more than a sentence from the Purps or the Octals or any of the other outfringers without running into some strange word or verbal construction. I believe you'll find the reasoning behind most of the odd language is no less tortured than the writing itself. Read some of that out loud, will you? I haven't heard any of it in years."

Sondra cleared her throat. "I'll try, but half of this stuff is in puns and alternate spellings. Probably sounds even more incoherent out loud. Let's see: 'For billions of years, an unnatural state of existence has warped the Solar Area, as the entropy-reversing perversion of life and evil-ution has upended the right and natural progression to universal decay. Now, thanks to the Naked Purple Movement, the Solar Area is cleansed of the source of this contagion, and the proper state of nature has been reestablished.

" 'Once again, this Purple tech-knowledge-ick-all breakthrough demonstrates the superiority of the Naked Purple way of Wisdom Through Ignorance/ants. When all have learned to ignore the ant-like humyn drive for order and stability, all cultures will be capable of / have such / big feats/feet.

" 'But for now, humyns of all genders on all worlds everywhere can begin life anew, out from under the oppressive yoke of Earth's Cultural Imperialism. The Naked Purple Movement has rendered this great service free of charge, but contributions and recruits to the Pointless Cause are always well-come. . . . '

"Drivel," Sondra said. "Utterly unintelligible drivel."

"But oddly poetic in its own way," Raphael said mildly. "The remarkable thing is that there are people, a very few of them, who will believe, who will be impressed by that. They will entertain the possibility that a collection of eccentrics squatting in an abandoned prison crater could destroy planets. A few will join, or contribute. All it takes is one believer in a million to keep the Pointless Cause alive.

"Or at least that was true when the Purples had Earth's eight billion for an audience. Far fewer than a billion people live in the Solar System now, and they are extremely spread out. How will a mass nut group function in a Solar System of small, dispersed populations?"

"Well, it sure doesn't make sense. But at least the Purples wrote their piece in something that resembled prose."

"You have another sample?" Raphael asked with a chuckle.

Sondra had never seen the man so relaxed and open. There had been a fascinating person buried deep under all that anger. Getting away from Pluto seemed an utterly liberating experience for him. "The Octal Millennialists. They put out a competing declaration—in base-eight notation. I suppose I could get the computer to translate it."

"I doubt it would be worth the bother. Even translated it wouldn't make much sense. The Octals select their wording for the interesting number patterns it produces in eight-mode."

"How do you know so much about all these groups?"

Raphael smiled. "My wife, Jessie. She was a great one for exploring, finding the odd and the strange and going to take a look. And there were a lot of strange things to see on the campuses, way back when. She had a special fondness for the outfringers, even flirted with the Glibsters when we were both doing our postdoctoral work. They aren't around anymore, but the Glibs and the Higginists were both in reaction to all the politically correct verbiage of the other groups. The Glib-Higs didn't care what they did, or meant, as long as it was said in an entertaining or amusing manner.

"But the Purple—they're special. Or at least they used to be. They've forgotten what they were, and that's a kind of tragedy. The whole structure of the Naked Purple Movement was built on finding goals—such as inciting the nonviolent collapse of human civilization—that were outrageous, and utterly impossible. The goals they chose were not only unattainable, but *deliberately* unattainable. In fact, in the beginning, I believe they called themselves La Manchans, or Don Qs, after Don Quixote and his windmills. The whole idea of an unreachable goal was to leave the seeker ever striving, forever searching, never resting. Chasing an absolute, an ideal, meant never getting where you were going, which left you forced to realize none of us complete the journey of life alive. It was supposed to make you treasure the small accomplishments you *did* make.

"There were *purposes* behind the original Purple. Not merely shock, but shock for a reason. To jolt people out of their complacency, remind them that the world was not all it could be—and, by urging people on to a higher goal, at least get their minds moving again. If society ostracized you for thinking on your own, you were forced to learn of your own inner goals, thus strengthening the individual.

"Jessie showed me that it was that contradiction, and that need to strive further on, that was the true, *hidden* point of the Pointless Cause." Raphael got a distant look in his eye. "Nowadays the Purple philosophy is merely blather that makes sure everyone expresses their individuality in the same way, sees to it that all are equally nonconformist. But getting mixed up with the Tycho convicts poisoned them. Jessie predicted that would happen, before she died." Raphael shook his head. "She'd be sorry to see she was right. Nothing is left but anger in the Tycho Purple. Anger, and a sense that the Universe owes them a living. Their philosophy is a game of prattling words for arrogant people, cooked up to justify what they would have done anyway.

"There has always been anger in the Purple—but once upon a time there was hope, as well. Nowadays the Purple hope has become mere sullenness."

Sondra was stunned, not by Raphael's words, but by the fact that they had come from the lips of what had been such a bitter old man. "Jessie sounds like a remarkable woman," Sondra said at last.

"Oh, she was," Simon Raphael said wistfully. "That indeed she was. I've been remembering just how remarkable."

A tone sounded, and Collier, the pilot, spoke over the intercom, his voice calm and confident. "Now thirty minutes from touchdown on the Moon. If you set your monitors to the external view cameras, you should see quite a nice show."

Sondra breathed a sigh of relief. The endless flight was nearly ended. She turned on the monitor, not to see the passing landscape, but to watch for any signs of engine problems on these final maneuvers. She looked up for a moment as Larry emerged from his cabin, moved to his crash couch, and strapped himself in. He looked as nervous as she did. Both of them had felt certain that the trip would wreck the *Nenya*'s engines. The *Nenya* had run here from Pluto on constant boost the whole way; no way to treat engines that weren't really designed for such work. The technique had gotten them here in sixteen days, but other than that, Sondra didn't see much to recommend it. The ride was uncomfortable—and frightening.

Constant boost meant accelerating the first half of the trip at one and a quarter gee, and then *braking* at one and a quarter gee on the second half of the run. Sondra didn't even want to think about the hellacious maximum speeds they had achieved at turnover. On the plus side, Sondra told herself, the Moon's one-sixth gravity would seem an absolute luxury once the *Nenya* landed.

Larry watched the Moon's scarred and cratered surface leaping toward them, and suddenly concerns over the nature of black holes seemed far less important. He clenched his hands into a death grip on the crash couch's armrests, shut his eyes, and saw images of the *Nenya* slamming into the Moon. No good. He opened his eyes again. The engines were humming along, seeming to run far too leisurely to counteract a fall toward a planet. Then they cut out altogether, and that was far more disturbing. He fixed his eyes on the monitor as the harshly cratered surface swept past, moving faster, getting closer with every moment.

The engines flared to life again, slowing into a sensible hover. The *Nenya* eased herself down onto the landing field. The engines shut down, and the ship landed with a gentle and anticlimactic bump.

Larry barely had time to breathe before there was a banging and clanging belowdecks. A young man stuck his head up through the deck hatch and looked around until he spotted Larry. "Larry O'Shawnessy Chao?" he asked.

Larry stood up, more than a little wobbly in the one-sixth gee. "Yeah," he said, recognizing the voice from his arguments over the radio. "You're Lucian Dreyfuss."

Lucian popped up through the hatch with a disconcerting bounce and grinned. He stuck out a hand, and Larry shook it with as much vigor as he could. Larry looked Lucian over. He was a short, wiry, high-strung-looking sort, very much the opposite of the roly-poly, easy-going Lunar stereotype. His face was narrow and pale, and his smile seemed to have a lot of teeth in it. His reddish brown hair was cut in a rather longish crew cut that stood bottle-brush straight on his head. His handshake was a bit too firm. His short-sleeved shirt revealed well-muscled arms. He was a year or two older than Larry, and there was something in his grin that said he thought he was ahead on points, as if there were already a competition between them.

Lucian looked around the room. "Dr. Berghoff, Dr. Raphael, welcome to you as well. Follow me down through the access port. I have a runcart waiting on the city side of the lock. The conference will convene as soon as you arrive. The port crew will see to your luggage. They're all in a bit of rush down at the conference center, to put it mildly. There's been some wild rumors shooting around the stuff coming in from VISOR—" He abruptly stopped talking, as if discussing the rumors would only delay his finding out the truth. "Once you arrive, the meeting will start immediately." He gestured the three of them down the hatch with what struck Larry as an oddly professional assuredness, as if he were used to playing guide.

"Immediately?" Dr. Raphael asked.

"Ah, yes sir."

"I see," Dr. Raphael said, with a rather concerned glance at Sondra and Larry.

They were all still in their traveling clothes, chosen for comfort on a cramped ship, and not for appearance. Larry was wearing one of his loudest shirts, and it was a safe bet that his purple shorts did not match it, as the shorts did not match anything. *Great outfit for a historic meeting,* Larry thought. Sondra was at least somewhat better off in a frowsy black coverall, but it definitely looked like it had been slept in, with a few crumbs from breakfast on the lapel. Raphael, in his sensible slacks and pullover shirt, seemed the height of formality.

"Ah, well, it's our words and not our fashion sense they're interested in, I suppose," Raphael said.

"Yes, sir," Lucian said with a glance at his watch, clearly not paying much attention to anything but the march of time. "Shall we go?"

The three visitors followed him, a bit uncertainly. He led them through the deck hatch, then the ship's airlock, down a flexible accessway that was long and steep enough to lead them underground into an elaborate airlock complex. A squad of workers in pressure suits were checking each other's equipment. "Repair crew," Lucian announced. "Going to soup up your ship—we figure this isn't going to be the last time she needs to make a fast run." Larry glanced at the worried expression on Dr. Raphael's face, and couldn't help but feel a pang of sympathy. He was the director of the station, and the *Nenya* had always been the lifeline, the ticket home if it all went wrong, a talisman that made it all seem safer.

Things were moving too fast. Lucian led them from the airlock complex and out into a city tunnel, to a small open–body electric car. Lucian took the driver's seat and the others got aboard.

Larry's rear end had barely met the seat when Lucian hit the accelerator. The tires squealed, and the runcart took off at speed down the narrow, dimly lit tunnel. Ten minutes ago Larry had been scared to ride a landing spacecraft. It did not take him long to decide that a ballistic landing on the *Nenya* was downright safe compared to being Lucian's passenger in this go-cart.

"You three are the last to arrive," Lucian shouted above the roar of the air whipping past them down the tunnel. "Things are happening fast, even since my last comm signal to you. Marcia MacDougal from VISOR is supposed to have some sort of really hot numbers."

"Do *our* numbers still hold up?" Larry shouted back, trying to forget that he was clinging to the seat frame just as hard as he had held onto his crash couch on the ship.

"The numbers are fine, very solid. It's your conclusions I don't like."

"There's no question at all about the conclusions."

"There is in my mind," Lucian shouted, trying to be heard over the air rushing past them. "But back to the numbers. I pulled together a last update just before you landed. The Earthpoint black hole mass is definitely 1.054 terrestrial, no appreciable accretion since appearance, though we're starting to see a nice little debris field. We've used the optical scalar technique to nail down the spin rate. The north magnetic and spin poles are definitely pointed *south*. But are you that solid on what the figures *mean*? I'm still a little hesitant about going public with them."

"If the numbers are right, then we go," Larry shouted back, a bit heatedly. "If they've called a crash meeting, we can't waste time quadruple-checking just because you have a gut reaction against the answers. Give me an alternative explanation and I'll hold back."

"Okay, okay. I *guess* I'm convinced, but just barely. The other researchers will have to make up their own minds."

In the backseat, Sondra couldn't hear half the words, but she didn't much care. The two of them had been going back and forth over this ground for weeks. The runcart burst out of the tunnel into what a sign said was the Amundsen SubBubble, and there was suddenly a lot more to look at than rock wall. She recorded a brief impression of a city that had been rattled about a bit, and people here and there working on the cleanup. There wasn't time to note much before Lucian stood on the brakes nearly hard enough to throw them all over the front of the cart. Presumably, they had arrived at Armstrong University, though Sondra hadn't seen a sign. "Here we are," Lucian announced, and hopped out of the cart. He led them into a long, low, academic-looking building. They hurried down a long corridor. The door at the end of the hall was open, and Lucian ushered them right inside.

Larry was the last one into the room, and at first it seemed to him that the place was full of nothing but eyes sitting around an oblong table. Everyone in the room was staring straight at him, getting a good look at the man who destroyed Earth. Larry felt like he had been moving at breakneck speed and had just slammed into a brick wall. A brick wall made out of eyes.

He heard the door swing shut and latch behind him, and did not feel reassured.

Larry felt a gentle hand on his arm and turned to see a gnomish-looking little man in a rather severely cut lime green frock coat that lived up to the Lunar reputation for garish dress. "Welcome to you all," he said. "I am Pierre Daltry, chancellor of the university and, it would appear, the de facto head of our group, at least for the time being. If you would take your seats, we can begin. Mr. Chao, Dr. Berghoff, Dr. Raphael?" They sat down in the chairs reserved for them at the head of the long table, Larry for one wishing for a less prominent place to sit.

Chancellor Daltry took his place at the middle of the table, but remained standing. "I will not waste too much time on introductions," he said, "but let me note a few of the other principal speakers for the day. These are the people who have done the most to study our present situation. Lucian Dreyfuss you have all met. Tyrone Vespasian, also of the Orbital Traffic Control Center. Marcia MacDougal and Hiram McGillicutty from VISOR." He pointed each of them out, and then gestured to include the entire table.

"Every major government in the Solar System is represented here—including Earth, I might add. Nancy Stanton, the U.N. ambassador to the Lunar Republic, is here. And we are here to make decisions. Simon Raphael and Larry Chao suggested this meeting some days ago, and things have happened quickly since then, enlarging the importance—and the responsibility—of this conference. As the time for deliberation is short, and the need for action urgent, the various governments have agreed to authorize this joint committee to speak *and* to act. What we decide around this table will not be mere recommendations, but the orders of the day. So let us consider well what we do."

Daltry paused and looked around the table.

"A moment from the Moon's history comes to my mind. About a century ago, the political situation between the Earth and Moon on one side, and the rest of the Solar System on the other, came dangerously close to interplanetary war. In the midst of that crisis, an asteroid that was to be placed in Earth orbit came horribly close to striking the Earth, a disaster that would have made a nuclear war seem trivial by comparison. The Moon bore the brunt of that crisis, and we have Morrow Crater in the center of Farside—and our independence from Earth—to remind us of those days.

"Up until a few days ago, we all imagined such an asteroid impact to be the worst possible catastrophe that could befall humanity, or the Earth. Now we know better.

"We as a race have often imagined that we knew the worst that could befall us—and time after time we have found something *worse* that could happen. Famine, flood, ecologic disaster, nuclear winter, asteroidal impact. Every time, a new worst has supplanted the old, imagined worst. Can we *now* be sure the worst is behind us?"

There was silence around the table.

"I call upon Mr. Chao to open the substantive discussion."

Larry Chao wondered whether to stand up or not, and decided not to; he felt exposed enough just sitting there. He had never even been to the Moon before. What the hell was he doing here now, addressing all these big shots? Had it really been worth all the money and effort to get him here so fast just so he could talk?

The hell with it. Larry squared his shoulders and launched into his talk, hoping to get it over with as soon as possible. "Ah, thank you once again, Chancellor, and, ah, members of the joint committee." He wasn't even quite sure if that was what this group should be called.

He pulled some notes from his pocket and shuffled through them without comprehension, trying to stall long enough to order his thoughts. "Let me start by settling the first and foremost issue before the group: Is the black hole now where Earth once was actually the Earth? Did our—did *my*—experiment somehow cause Earth to be crushed down into nothingness?" *There, I've said it,* he thought. His heart was pounding in his chest. There was a slight rustle around the table as Larry confessed his own part in the disaster.

Yes, I was the one who did it, he thought. *I admit it.* He knew he had no choice in the matter but to accept the facts. He could never hide from what had happened, from what he had done. He was going to travel under a cloud for the rest of his days. Pretending it wasn't there would not improve the situation.

Sondra sat next to him, watching her friend. Even through his nervousness, she could see that he had grown, changed, matured in these past days. As he spoke, he sat up a little straighter, returned the gaze of his audience with a bit more confidence. The shy half-child was not yet gone, but there was much more of the adult about him, too.

Larry went on. "During our journey in from Pluto, I was in constant contact with the Orbital Traffic Control Center here on the Moon. As you all no doubt know, that facility came up with excellent data on the situation here in the Earth-Moon system—or perhaps calling it Lunar space might make more sense now." Again, a small stir in the audience. "Lucian Dreyfuss of OTC has collated the OTC information on the black hole. Both he and I have analyzed that data and come to the same conclusions."

Larry saw Lucian at the far end of the table, returning Larry's gaze evenly, doing nothing to signal agreement or disagreement. Larry found himself forced to admire Lucian's cool.

"We modeled what Earth *would* look like as a black hole, and compared it to what we can measure of the black hole that is now sitting where Earth used to be."

Warming to his subject, Larry forgot his shyness. "The trouble is, very few properties of a black hole *can* be measured. In many senses, a black hole isn't there at all. It has no size, no color, no spectrum. Its density is infinite. But there are certain things we *can* get readings on. First and most obvious is the hole's mass. The first thing we knew about the hole was how much it weighed.

"You will also recall that it weighed five percent *more* than Earth. That may not sound like much, but bear in mind, the Moon only has one-point-two percent of the Earth's mass. And remember, the black hole's mass was measured only eight hours after Earth vanished. It could *not* have accumulated that much more mass that quickly. For the Earthpoint black hole to be Earth, it would have to be removed, compressed down into a singularity, fed the equivalent of four Moon masses, and then returned to its starting point, all in eight hours. To my mind that makes it all but impossible that the black hole truly is the Earth."

Larry found himself remembering his days as a teaching assistant. He had always enjoyed lecturing. "Now I've got to jump into some slightly complicated areas. For the sake of clarity, I'm going to be something less than a purist about my nomenclature. Forgive me if I oversimplify a bit, but I won't hand out any wrong data, just make it a bit easier to follow.

"There are a few things we *can* measure in a black hole: spin attributes; electric charge and magnetic field, if any; event horizon; mass; and of course the strength of the gravity field itself. These are not independent variables, of course. For example, the magnetic field, or lack of it, depends on both the electrical charge of the hole, and on its spin.

"We can measure spin, charge, and the magnetic field effects—and they can tell us useful things. Let me start with spin. We can get a reading on the hole's rotation from the movement of its magnetic fields, and from what is called the optical scalar technique. The black hole's axis of spin is precisely ninety degrees from the plane of its orbit. As you know, Earth's axis is canted 23.5 degrees from its orbital plane. It would require *tremendous* energy to move Earth's axis into the vertical and then hold it there. The planet would resist the motion, the way a gyroscope resists any effort to change *its* axis of spin. I doubt that you could force Earth toward the vertical without cracking the planetary crust and flinging large amounts of debris into space. We did not see that debris.

"But that is only the first point concerning spin. In order to conserve momentum, an object *must* spin *faster* if it gets smaller, the way a skater in a pirouette spins faster and faster as he draws his arms in toward his body.

"If you crush Earth into a black hole, the resultant hole would have to spin at an appreciable fraction of lightspeed. This hole is rotating far too slowly for it to be Earth. It is only rotating at about one percent of the velocity that an Earth-derived hole would turn. I might add that it is also spinning in the wrong direction.

"This black hole also exhibits a massive negative electric charge. Earth was—*is*—electrically neutral. Another point: the north and south magnetic poles of the hole are reversed.

"In mass, spin data, electric charge and magnetic properties—in every way that we can measure—this black hole is drastically different from what the Earth would be like if the Earth were made into a black hole.

"For all these reasons, I feel confident that this black hole is *not* the Earth."

A murmur of relief whispered about the room. Larry let it die down before he went on. "What then *has* happened to Earth? Earth is either somewhere else, or has been destroyed. If it has been destroyed, where was the rubble it should have left behind, the debris? Where was the energy pulse? If the Earth had been smashed to rubble, or blown up, or disintegrated into elementary particles or pure energy, we would know about it—if we survived the event. There would be nothing subtle about the effects. The Moon would have been pelted with a massive amount of debris or roasted in the energy release, or both.

"I believe that the Earth has been transported to another place, and was *not* destroyed."

"Now hold on a minute!" A strident voice broke in from halfway down the table. "There is not the slightest bit of information in the data to support that claim. I know! I gathered most of the data myself." It was McGillicutty, sputtering mad. "I didn't watch your precious black hole close up. But you've just made the high-and-mighty argument that no technology could wreck a planet without a trace—but then you go and say, casual as you please, that it's possible to *steal* a planet without any fuss? What technology makes *that* possible?"

Sondra leaned in. "The wormhole, dammit! That's what the black hole *is*. A wormhole gateway to where Earth is."

"Wormhole, that's damned ridiculous!" McGillicutty snorted. "They don't exist. They can't exist. And for my money, neither can black holes. Certainly not black holes this small."

Sondra felt her temper beginning to fray. "For God's sake—you've seen asteroid-sized bodies popping out of those blue flashes—and *you* provided the images of that blue flash sweeping up from behind Earth, engulfing it."

"I recorded that image," McGillicutty snapped, "but I do not support that interpretation of it. There is clearly a compact mass in Earth's old position, but you are merely assuming this compact mass is a black hole. I haven't seen any evidence that supports that idea. Suppose it is merely very dense, with *no* event horizon, and a surface gravity low enough for physical matter to escape? I haven't run the figures yet, but it seems to me that an Earth mass could be a thousandth the density of a black hole and still only be a few meters across, far too small to see from this distance. It could be that the beam shifted Earth from normal matter into strange-quark matter. A strange-quark body of Earth mass might only be a few kilometers across, and extremely dark in color. I suggest *that* is the situation, and the asteroid-sized bodies are being blown off the strange-matter compact body's surface somehow. By violent transitions back into normal matter."

"And the blue flashes?" Sondra asked.

"Energy discharges related to whatever is blasting the gee points off the strange-matter surface."

"But how are they being blown off?" Larry asked. "What's the mechanism?"

"I don't know yet, sonny," McGillicutty snapped. "But that's the only unexplained feature of my theory.

Your black hole idea is nothing *but* unexplained features. My idea makes sense. Yours doesn't.''

With that, a dozen voices joined in, offering their own opinions.

Larry listened to the shouting with a sinking heart. They had been willing—even eager—to believe in evidence that the Earth had not been destroyed. But suddenly, he sensed something different around the table. McGillicutty's theory had a dozen major flaws in it, was contradicted by the available evidence. But perhaps it was more palatable than something with the terrifying power to drop the Earth into a wormhole.

Larry watched the argument storm around him. They had been with him up until McGillicutty interrupted. But he had lost them when they'd been given something more like what they wanted to hear.

Larry shrank back in his chair, feeling very much like a little child lost in a sea of doubting grown-ups. He thought back to the last full science staff meeting of the Gravitics Research Station. How long ago had it been? Just seventeen days ago? Eighteen? He had made a very long, strange trip indeed just to come and feel lost again. He sat there, feeling young and alone.

But then a new voice, strong and determined, cut through the welter of voices. "All this is a side issue," Simon Raphael said in a stern voice. "Black hole, wormhole, compact mass—just before we left Pluto, Mr. Chao reminded me that none of that truly matters. What matters is that our homeworld has been stolen, and our Solar System invaded by an alien force." Raphael stood up, leaned his hands on the table, and looked about the room. There was silence.

"How that has happened does not matter. In a strange way, it is almost *comforting* to get lost in technical arguments over how it happened—because then we could get so lost in the details of the situation that we never have to look at these larger, and more terrifying issues. *Our Solar System has been invaded.* In some unknown way, our gravity-wave experiment appears to have been the signal for that invasion.

"I know as well as all of you how absurd that sounds— attack from beyond the stars—but what other explanation fits the facts? Do you have an idea, Dr. McGillicutty? Some other interpretation that does not contradict any of the very few facts we do have?" Raphael looked around the table. "The quiet in this room tells me there *is* no other explanation. But we cannot reject the only answer we have simply because it is difficult to accept. I know of what I speak when I say that. Refusing to accept a challenge is an old man's failing, and one of which I have been much guilty in recent days.

"We have been attacked, that is obvious. And yet no one asks, 'By whom?' We are so reluctant to accept this incredible disaster that we cannot go even one step further and ask *who* did this, or why they did it. It seems to me that those questions are far more important than *how* they did it, or whether their technology seems to violate this or that pet theory. I don't know what their motives are, but I cannot imagine that a fleet of thirty thousand asteroid-sized spacecraft are headed toward all our worlds with the intention of doing good deeds.

"And yet how they do what they do *is* important, because we must fight them, whoever they are. Before we can do *that*, we must learn more about them. If Earth has been removed, where was it taken? What do the aliens intend here in the Solar System? How, precisely, are the other planets threatened? And why?

"The latest reports estimate thirty-two thousand large objects, which we've been calling gee points, all of them on constant-boost courses headed straight for every one of the major planets—but not for the Moon. So let's talk about why, if we can."

"Ah, maybe this is the place for me to jump in," said a bald, heavyset man sitting next to Lucian. "I'm Tyrone Vespasian, and I've been concentrating on the gee points."

Raphael nodded and sat down. "By all means."

"Okay, I guess the big questions about the gee points are one, what are they, and two, why is the Moon exempt? Let me talk about the first. Some of the fastest-moving gee points have reached Venus and Mercury. Unfortunately we don't know what happened to them on arrival. Quicksilver Station on Mercury just saw large radar blips go below the horizon, and VISOR also lost the gee points as they went in. There weren't any big seismic events on either world, which suggests that the gee points managed to make soft landings somehow.

"I don't know if it's good news or bad, but we ought to have landings on Mars in a few days. We should be able to get better information from there when that happens. The Venus and Mercury arrivals are from gee points moving out from the Earthpoint black hole." Vespasian looked up and glared at McGillicutty. "Or compact mass, if you need to call it that. Anyway, there are a few gee points moving from Earth-space toward the outer planets, but they have farther to go. The gee points moving from the Asteroid Belt and Oort Cloud are moving slower and have the longest distances to travel.

"Some of the gee points are moving toward the gas giants. What they plan to do when they get there, we don't know. We don't know if they're interested in the planets, the satellites, or both.

"If you take a look at the Asteroid Belt gee points through a long-range camera, they look just like ordinary asteroids. In fact, a few of them were mined *as* asteroids for some time. Except asteroids aren't supposed to contain point-source gravity-wave systems.

"The objects coming out of the Earthpoint black hole

look totally different, as far as we can tell. It's hard to get good imagery on them. They're a little smaller, and look more like artificial objects. Their surfaces are more reflective, and they seem to be very regular in shape. The Earthpoint gee points are moving too fast for any of our ships to match velocity with them real easy, though there are four or five missions already on the way. On the other hand, they seem to behave just like the asteroidal gee points. I think they're all really the same thing.''

''And what is that?'' Chancellor Daltry asked gently.

Vespasian's face turned sad, and he was silent for a long moment before he spoke. ''I thought a lot about that,'' he said. ''I think they're spaceships. Really big spaceships. The ones coming from the Outer System have been waiting, hidden, camouflaged as asteroids and comets. Hiding from what, I don't know. Once these things start accelerating, moving, it's obvious they aren't what they seem. Disguise is pointless. So, since the ones coming through Earthpoint are accelerating from the start, there's no sense in disguising them. The Earthpoint ones are accelerated on the other side of the wormhole somehow—given a high initial speed. Plus they have a slightly higher boost rate. That makes them *seem* different from the Outer System jobs, but I think they're really all the same thing. Big ships.''

He hesitated one last time, and then said it. ''Invasion ships. I've tried to come up with some other explanation, but nothing else fits. They're ships. What sort of crews they have aboard, I don't know.

''But we're going to find out when the first one lands on Mars.''

CHAPTER FOURTEEN

———————◆———————

Empire of the Suns

MAYBE THE WORLD HADN'T ENDED, BUT GERALD MAC-
Dougal found himself in paradise, after all. Or at least
in California.

But then, California, Vancouver, and in fact all of Earth
were suddenly an exobiologist's paradise. This new home
for Earth was not the afterlife, but it was certainly a
celestial realm, a kingdom of stars, an Empire of the
Suns.

And it was a realm crowded with life. Of that Gerald
was convinced—and surely that was the next best thing
to Heaven for an exobiologist. Most of the other planets
were too far off for good imagery from a ground-based
telescope, but they could get good spectroscopic data.
Gerald looked again at the document in his hand, barely
able to resist jumping for joy. It was a summary from
the first run-through of planetary spectrographs, as collected from observatories all over the world.

And the summary practically shouted evidence of life-bearing worlds. Free oxygen, water vapor, nitrogen glowed up from every spectrograph.

Likewise, every world was at the proper distance from its respective star for life. For every star of a given size and temperature, there was a particular range of distances, called the biosphere, wherein a planet would be at the right temperature for Earthlike life, neither too hot nor too cold. Only certain types of stars were capable of supporting life. But *every* star around the sphere was of the right size, temperature and color to support life—and *every* planet in the Multisystem rode a secure and perfect orbit inside its star's biosphere.

He had to get to those worlds. Somehow.

Getting here was a good first step. He had guessed right. JPL had been officially designated the lead lab for finding out what the hell had happened. Gerald barely had time to finish mentioning his credentials as an exobiologist before they had signed him up. JPL's people could read a spectrograph as well as Gerald could. They knew they were going to need exobiology expertise, sooner or later. And until such time as he could work directly in his field, there was endless staff work that needed doing. Earth's survival could well hinge on figuring out what had happened. The scientific community generally and JPL specifically were confronted with the largest and most urgent research program in history, and they needed to gear up for the job. Gerald was a good organizer, and was glad to help out.

But there was a core of pain underneath all the excitement. Marcia was lost to him, somewhere out across the sea of stars.

And, as wondrous as this place was, it was not Earth's home. No doubt a sojourn here would teach many things, but Earth belonged in the Solar System. Gerald was determined to see her returned there.

Dianne Steiger had learned something in the ten days since they had fished her out of the *Pack Rat*'s wreckage at the Los Angeles Spaceport: People can get used to anything.

Already she was used to the ghostly pseudo-sensations her new left hand provided. Maybe the astronaut's union was a waning political power, but it still bought damn good medical care. She sat in Wolf Bernhardt's outer office, waiting. From time to time, someone would rush past, carrying a stack of datablocks, looking worried. There was a frantic air about the place. Fumbling a bit, working awkwardly with just her right hand, she pulled out another cigarette and lit it.

Frantic yes, but at the same time eerily normal and calm.

That was the way the world was now. Massive and unseen forces had stolen Earth—and yet life went on. If it was time to go to work, it didn't much matter which star system Earth was in. You still had to get up, eat breakfast, drink your coffee—and step out into a world where the light of day wasn't quite the right color, where the sun in the sky was not the Sun. You still had to go to the office and get those invoices out, or go to the store and get the shopping done, or go to the dentist for your cleaning. You still had to go home at night, though under a too-bright sky that held not the Moon and the familiar constellations, but a half-dozen too-bright stars that washed out much of the sky, leaving it tinged with blue in places. There were too few fixed-background stars, and far too many planets that were too large, too close. And a lot more meteors than there used to be. Everything in the sky had changed, and yet everything on Earth was exactly the same.

Even if you *wanted* to react, there was nothing you could do about it. What did you do about the sky transmogrifying? And on a practical level, if you weren't a spacer, what difference did it make?

She blew out a cloud of smoke, sighed, and tried to tell herself how lucky she had been. Of course, if you were a spacer, you had a few more problems. Not that Dianne felt she had any right to complain. She was home, and alive. There were a lot of astros—a lot of her friends—who weren't.

She lifted her left arm and examined her new hand. Too pink, the nails not properly grown in, no muscle tone to speak of, unweathered and characterless. A baby hand grown into the size and form of a woman's, but without the slightest sign of maturity. She closed her eyes, and willed the hand to close, to clench itself into a fist. Eyes shut, she concentrated on her sensations in the hand. She could feel the arching of her fingers, the pressure of her fingertips on the base of her palm, her thumb wrapped around the side of her forefinger. The feelings were clear enough so that she could see her hand, her fist, through closed eyes.

She opened her eyes again, and found herself staring at an open hand, the fingers splayed out, starfished away from each other. With a new and separate act of will, she again forced her new hand into a fist, watched it close with open eyes this time. And felt nothing at all from it but a numb warmth. Her nervous system, confused by conflicting signals, simply gave up.

She carefully laid the hand in her lap and cursed silently. Again, and still, it happened. It was as if she had one left hand that she could only see, and another that she could only feel.

The doctors were soothing and reassuring. In the old days, when amputations were permanent, amputees reported phantom feelings—an itch in the leg that wasn't there anymore, that sort of thing. Intellectually, she knew, the disconcerting sensations she was experiencing were merely an echo of the same phenomenon. Her new left hand *was* sending legitimate signals to her nervous system, but a replacement body part, even a sprint-grown bud-clone produced from the patient's own cells, never precisely matched the original. In time the new hand would develop muscle tone and coordination, but for now it didn't respond or report sensation the same way her old hand had.

For a long time yet, until she learned to use it, the physical sensations would be . . . disturbing. She would learn to tolerate it, then get used to it, then accept it, until the new hand seemed normal and natural.

In the meantime, the doctors told her, life went on. Wait it out.

That was the second lesson she had learned. Life went on, no matter what.

Quite abruptly and without warning, the entire planet is grabbed and thrown into a new solar system, without any explanation. No one knew why or how it had happened. Nonetheless, there were plenty of crises people *could* understand, and those were what people focused on. Perhaps dealing with the smaller crises was a means of avoiding the larger disaster.

Whether or not dealing with them was a denial mechanism, Earth was facing some extremely serious problems that *did* require attention. The loss of space facilities hurt badly, caused energy shortages, communications lapses, transportation problems, supply problems. People were suffering. The papers and the tapes and the newsblocks were still reporting new disasters, new updates on the number killed or injured, on the loss of this space facility or that. No one could truly comprehend the theft of a world, but people could understand the death of ten thousand in the crash of a habitat.

And yet, on another, broader level, the damage was superficial. Taken as a social whole, planet Earth was still strong enough, resilient enough, to survive this trauma. Society wasn't showing any signs of collapsing.

Or at least that was the reassuring message everyone was trying to give everyone else. Whether or not it was true, humanity needed to believe it.

Perhaps people glanced to the sky now and again, but they walked down the street, met their friends, ate their meals and went to their jobs. If those, too, were denial mechanisms, they were healthy ones.

Meanwhile the bars were all full, and so were the churches. The various organizations of crazies had more than a few new recruits. *Any* group that claimed to have an explanation, or an escape from danger, was popular. And there were more than a few incidents of attacks on the crazies, as people looked for someone to blame.

Yet, all told, as represented in Los Angeles at least, the people of Earth were taking the catastrophe in stride. Dianne Steiger looked down at the cloned, alien hand resting in her lap. She was taking *that* catastrophe in stride, too, and for much the same reasons. What choice did she have? She may have lost a part of herself, but she could not stop going about the business of staying alive. The whole of the world could not drop everything it was doing in order to find an appropriate way to react.

And the people who *did* react, with protest marches (against whom or what, Dianne could not understand), accomplished nothing. The jaded, world-weary leaders of Earth's nations and cities, still hurting from the Knowledge Crash riots and the worldwide recession, had learned the hard way that emotional appeals could only produce more riot, more destruction, more fear. Governments and large institutions put all their efforts into spreading calm, urging a return to normalcy, whatever that was.

Life went on, in spite of all. It wasn't just fact: it was official policy.

Dianne thought there was reason to believe the policy would work. After all, people could get used to anything.

Even a Dyson Sphere hanging in the sky. People were acting as if giving it a name explained it. Dianne felt a grim amusement at that. She was one of a very few persons to see it unveiled by atmosphere, blazing with power at the height of its energy pulse. *She* knew to fear it. Not so the average person in the street. They had learned that it was many billions of kilometers away, and many seemed to assume that anything that far off could do them no harm. Never mind that it was presumably related to the power that had snatched the planet away. And besides, the Sphere wasn't visible in the sky anymore. Its cherry red glow had faded down through brick red, to a dim glow, to darkness. Now it was merely a spot of blackness in the night sky, eclipsing the background stars. In infrared, of course, it was another story. In IR, the damned thing was bright as hell.

And *was* it a Dyson Sphere? Named for Freeman Dyson, the twentieth-century scientist who had dreamed them up, Dyson Spheres were supposed to be hollow shells, hundreds of millions of kilometers in diameter, built around stars. This thing sure looked like one—it was certainly big enough—but it seemed like every engineer on the planet was busily demonstrating that no conceivable material could withstand the forces a Dyson Sphere would be subjected to.

There were two reasons for building Dyson Spheres: one, to provide enormously vast amounts of living area; and two, to collect great amounts of energy. Because it enclosed its star completely, a Dyson Sphere could trap *all* of the energy the star emitted.

Of course, if this was a Dyson Sphere, it was therefore artificial. It had been built. Which left the question of where the builders were. Presumably they were the same folk who had snatched the Earth.

So where were they?

The door to the inner office slid open, and a tall, good-looking man in casual clothes stepped out. "Dianne Steiger?"

Dianne dropped her cigarette to the concrete floor and ground it out as she stood up. "Yes. Are you Dr. Bernhardt?"

"Ah, no. I'm Gerald MacDougal, head exobiologist and chief of staff for the Directorate of Spatial Investigations."

"Chief of staff?" Dianne asked, trying to sound cheerful. "That sounds a little out of line for an exobiologist."

Gerald smiled, a bit sadly. "No one here has time to worry about that sort of thing. We're all just making it up as we go along. Come on back." Gerald led her into the inner offices, into a small, bare, windowless room. It looked to be an old storeroom that had been cleaned out and set up as an office on very short notice. Gerald sat down at one side of a trestle table and gestured for Dianne to sit at the other. "Dr. Bernhardt is just finishing up some other work. He'll see you in just a moment. I thought I might save some time and give you a quick background briefing before you go in," Gerald said.

"Background to what?" Dianne asked. "Why am I here?"

"We'll talk a bit, and I bet you figure it out before Dr. Bernhardt sees you," Gerald said.

"Who's Dr. Bernhardt?"

"To oversimplify a bit, Dr. Wolf Bernhardt was the duty scientist here at JPL who detected the gravity waves that caused the Earth's removal. The U.N. Security Council needed someone to run their investigation of what happened, and they decided that gravitic technology was going to be central to figuring that out. Besides, they had to pick someone, and fast. So they dumped it in Wolf's lap. They set up the United Nations Directorate of Spatial Investigation and made Dr. Bernhardt the first director and lead investigator. They've ordered him to, quote, 'Establish the causes and consequences of the Earth's removal to its present location,' close quote. DSI's got an absolute U.N. priority claim on JPL and on any or all other research establishments or facilities or resources it needs, anywhere on Earth. We want it, we take it.''

Dianne's eyebrows went up. ''Wait a second. You said something about gravity waves associated with the Earth's removal. You mean someone knows how it *happened*? With gravity waves? *That*'s been kept quiet.''

''Yeah, it has, because that's all we know. And we want to work on the problem without every kook on the planet phoning in his suggestions. The data from every single gravity-wave detector in the world shows large numbers of highly complex gravity-wave transmissions right at the time of the Big Jump. Immediately afterward, within five seconds of each other, every gee-wave detector on Earth blew out. Based on the five seconds of data we did get, we think there are thousands of gravity-modulation sources in the Multisystem.''

''Multisystem?''

''The multiple-star system Earth is in now. Had to call it something.''

''And those gravity-wave sources were so powerful they blew out all the detectors.''

Gerald nodded. ''Looks that way, but we don't know for sure. We don't know if they did it on purpose or not.''

'' 'They did it,' '' Dianne repeated. ''So you definitely think we didn't end up here by chance. No weird natural fluke.''

Gerald's gentle face hardened. "No. Someone did this. We know that. The entire Multisystem is held together artificially. Has to be. The orbits of all the stars, planets, moons and so on are so complex that they could not have occurred naturally. They aren't stable for even the shortest period of time. Our first orbital projections predicted all kinds of collisions and near misses and close-pass momentum exchanges. There should have been planets crashing into each other and worlds being flung clear of the Multisystem. Except none of that happens. Somehow the orbits of the stars and planets are constantly being tweaked up, shifted from their projected paths into safer directions. The Multisystem is as complex and delicate as a mechanical Swiss watch. The slightest mistake in orbit control could have devastating effects.

"We think that's what they do with gravity waves—correct and control the stellar and planetary orbits. And also they use them for grabbing planets. We're pretty sure that all of the objects in the Multisystem were brought here the same way Earth was. Not just the planets, but the stars, too. They built themselves an Empire of the Suns."

Dianne found herself impressed by that turn of phrase, and unnerved by the idea. "So they—whoever they are—are manipulating orbits, keeping all the planets from hitting each other?"

Gerald frowned. "At least most of the time. It looks like once in a while they've gotten it wrong. There are several highly ordered and clearly artificial asteroid belts of minor planets—but also a lot of asteroid-sized bodies in random orbits. We've already seen two impact events between asteroids." He leaned forward and gestured to emphasize a point. "That's another reason for us to keep things quiet until we know more. The people of Earth don't need to hear that an asteroid might crash into them. We've had enough panic."

Dianne felt her blood run cold. How could this man MacDougal talk about such things so matter-of-factly? "I understand," she said.

"But the most disturbing thing about those impacts is that no effort was made to prevent them. Plus there's been a major upward jump in the number of meteors and meteorites, worldwide. Some of them pretty big rocks. All of which means that control of the bodies in this system is not absolute. That's why the man on the street doesn't need to hear about these things just yet. Let things settle down a bit first."

Dianne nodded vacantly. "Anything else I need to know before you tell me why I'm here?"

"One or two other points," Gerald said with studied casualness. "The motions of the stars and planets are also being affected by unseen companion objects. Practically all of the stars and planets have periodic wobbles in their orbital motions, very distinct from the gee-wave-induced orbital shifts. We're sure the wobbles are caused by the gravitic effects of unseen co-orbiting companion objects. And they're big wobbles, so the companions have to be very massive."

"Except?" Dianne asked carefully. She didn't know how many more disturbing revelations she wanted to get.

"Except we should be able to see the companions. There are a lot of wobbling planets close enough, but we can't see their companions. So the companions are not only very massive, they must be extremely small. Plus we've spotted disk-shaped debris fields centered on where the companions should be, and seen some rather odd energy releases, consistent with the impact of debris onto gravity singularities."

Dianne found herself wishing desperately for a cigarette. "In other words, the Multisystem is full of black holes."

Gerald nodded. "One of them very close. It looks like

there's one at the centerpoint of the large ring-shaped object hanging in the sky where the Moon should be. A Moon-mass black hole would serve to maintain the pattern of tides and gravitational stresses Earth is used to. Without *something* stabilizing us, we'd still be getting quakes like the one just after the Big Jump.

"There's one last thing to tell you," Gerald said. "It's not exactly a secret, because anyone could reach the same conclusion we did just by thinking for a minute. It seems at the very least a strong working hypothesis that the Dyson Sphere at the center of the Multisystem is not only the power source, but the control center for the entire system. So we very much want to take a look at the Sphere. The trouble is that the Dyson Sphere has an exterior surface area approximately four hundred million times greater than Earth's. That's going to make locating the control center difficult. More so if the interior surface and volume of the Sphere are considered."

Dianne thought about that for a moment, and found herself adopting Gerald's air of studied calm. In the act of doing so, she suddenly understood his behavior. He was as scared by all this as she was. His air of calm was like a test pilot's artificial nonchalance, nothing more than a defense, a way to keep the fear from overwhelming him.

"Okay then," she said in a voice that was suddenly far steadier. "How about the big question. *Who?* Have any theories on that? Who has done this and what do they want with us?"

"No idea. Not a blessed idea. There's been no sign whatsoever of the perpetrators themselves. Wolf thinks it's possible they are as wholly unaware of our existence as we were of theirs a few days ago. As to motive, your guess is as good as mine. Maybe they have no interest in humanity, and are interested only in Earth, possibly for colonization purposes. Either they think Earth is empty, or they think we will be utterly unable to oppose them when they come to take possession.'' Gerald glanced casually at his watch, as if he had been discussing nothing more unnerving than a visit to the library. ''Come on, he should be ready for you now.''

He stood up and she rose with him. ''The authority they've given DSI,'' Dianne said. ''If Wolf Bernhardt is in charge, that's *his* authority. And you said DSI has absolute U.N. priority over any and all resources and facilities. They're trusting this guy Bernhardt with a hell of a lot of power. He could take over every lab on Earth, just for starters.''

''Yes, I suppose so—if he were a fool. If he wanted to be locked up, or to wake up dying from a bullet in the back of his head. Things are a bit panicky, and I wouldn't be amazed if people starting playing very rough. Wolf knows that what the U.N. can give, the U.N. can take away. They hope that he can find more positive expression for his ambition. They want him—us—to come up with answers. That's where you come in.''

Gerald led her out into the hall, down to a proper office, designed for the purpose. Gerald opened the door and walked in without knocking.

Herr Doktor Wolf Bernhardt was seated at his desk, engrossed in his work. Gerald leaned up against the doorframe and Dianne sat down in the visitor's chair. By the looks of it, Bernhardt had been working at a frantic pace for many long hours.

The room was in chaos—but a neat man's chaos, a valiant rearguard action against disorder. There were stacks of paper everywhere, and piles of datablocks—but each heap of paper had its edges squared off, and each datablock was neatly labeled in a precise hand. The center of the desk was surrounded by the mountains of information, but was itself an empty plain, nothing on it but a late-model notepack and a single sheet of paper that looked to be a list of things to do with half the items checked off. To one side of the sheet were a pen and a china cup half full of what seemed to be slightly stale, cold coffee.

Wolf was staring at the notepack's screen, his fingers busy on the touchpad. Dianne Steiger studied him for a moment. His appearance matched that of his office: a precise, orderly man trying to keep up with too much coming in from all sides at once. He was clean-shaven, his hair neatly combed, his shirt fresh, his eyes clear and alert—but exhaustion was peeking through the facade. He was not working through the notepack steadily, but in spurts of energy that spent themselves almost before they began. Then he would blink, shake his head, and force himself to concentrate anew. He took a careful sip of the coffee and made a face. At last he glanced up and realized with a start that Dianne and Gerald were there. "My God. I did not even hear you come in. Forgive me, I have been working too hard. You are astronaut Dianne Steiger, yes?"

Astronaut. That was his interest. A light went on in Dianne's head. Suddenly she knew why she was here. She had thought that perhaps Bernhardt had wanted an eyewitness account of the Big Jump as seen from space, but no. This was something far bigger. She looked at Gerald, her heart suddenly trip-hammer fast with excitement. Something in his face seemed to confirm her guess. She looked back to Wolf Bernhardt.

"Yes I am." She hesitated a moment, and then blurted it out. "You want the *Terra Nova*." Her heart was pounding, and a dull, silent roar echoed dimly inside her head. *Terra Nova*. The prize lost so long ago. Dianne rarely allowed herself even to *think* of the canceled starship project. She had been only a few steps away from becoming a reserve pilot before the program had been canceled.

But now the prize would be even more rich. There were dozens of worlds, eight whole star systems in one to explore out there—

"I *have* the *Terra Nova*," Bernhardt said abruptly, cutting into her reverie. "There are rush crews prepping her for a sprint mission to the Dyson Sphere right now. What I want—what I need—is *you*."

Dianne lifted her left hand as carefully as she could, and tried to move it with something close to grace. But even wiggling her fingers was clumsy. "Ah, sir, of course I want to go—but I don't think I can pilot. Not for a while. Not with this hand."

"*Pilots* I have," Wolf said dismissively. "What I want *you* for is *captain*. No one else on Earth can know that ship as well as you do."

The roaring in her ears suddenly got louder, and Dianne blinked hard. Dreams aren't supposed to come true, especially in the middle of a nightmare. Earth had been kidnapped, and so she got to fly a starship. Right into a Dyson Sphere. Suddenly her heart sank. *That* was a plan for disaster. But Wolf Bernhardt was still talking. Dianne forced herself back to reality.

"—the *Terra Nova* is tremendously complex. The training to handle it goes far beyond flying even a large interplanetary craft. We need someone who understands the broad picture. My office has found enough spacers who can fill the specialty jobs aboard—lander pilots, science specialists, medical, astronomers, orbital observation scientists and so on. Gerald here will be going along as chief scientific officer. But there are damn few from the original group of *Terra Nova* officers and crew candidates, people who really know *that ship* and what she can and can't do. Most of the original candidates out-emigrated to find work. They're back in the Solar System

where we can't get at them. The others—ah, well, there
were very high casualties among spacers when the Big
Jump happened.''

Bernhardt hesitated over that point, as if he could say
more. It occurred to Dianne that she had never seen a
breakdown of just how many casualties there *had* been.
This DSI operation was keeping a lot of disturbing data
to itself. ''What it comes down to,'' Bernhardt went on,
''is that you are far and away the most qualified person
for this job who's still with Earth and alive.''

Dianne thought fast, considering as many sides of the
situation as she could. It was tempting to just agree, to
make the grand gesture and charge off to adventure. But
no. False courage or bravado might help her ego, but the
price for Earth would be too high. If she had to throw
her dreams away, so be it. She leaned forward abruptly.
''Yes, I'm here and alive. And I want to stay that way
for a while.'' She had to take charge of this little chat
now if she was going to do it.

Wolf looked at her in surprise. ''You aren't accepting
the mission voluntarily? I assure you that I have the power
to draft labor—''

''For a suicide mission?'' she asked. ''For a mission
that will throw away one of the few cards planet Earth
has in this game? I'll fly the *Terra Nova*—but not straight
down the throat of a monster four hundred million times
bigger than Earth! Not until I know something more
about that monster.''

Wolf looked at Dianne. For the first time, he seemed
to be considering her as something more than a chess
piece. ''What, exactly, are you saying?'' he asked carefully.

''That the *Terra Nova* took years to build, and so would
her replacement. If we even could build her replacement,
with most of our off-planet resources and infrastructure
gone. For at least the time being, she is irreplaceable.

This new Multisystem of yours is likely to be dangerous enough without sending the ship to commit suicide deliberately. Wouldn't it be nice at least to *try* to collect some data with the ship before she is vaporized by the enemy? Perhaps, to find out who and what the enemy *is*?"

"Same thing I've been saying, Wolf," Gerald Mac-Dougal put in. "We ought to search as much of the rest of this system as we can, and then *consider* a cautious approach to the Sphere. Think about how big the Sphere is. Even if you make the unwarranted assumption that the control system exists, and the further unwarranted assumption that it is on the exterior surface of the Sphere, and not the inside, you've got an incredibly large search area. Search the entire surface area of all nine planets in our old Solar System, plus the Sun as well while you're at it, and you wouldn't have done one percent of *this* search."

"I agree completely," Dianne said. "Your imaginary control center could cover as much area as Earth's surface and still get lost on something that big. And what would it look like? What would we be searching *for*? And while we're searching that Sphere, what are the people who run the Sphere going to be doing?"

There was the faintest flicker of a smile on Wolf's face. "I see that you are already behaving as a captain should. Protecting your command. Very well. How would *you* use the *Terra Nova*?"

Dianne thought for a long moment and then spoke, choosing her words carefully. "I would explore a sampling of the worlds and stars in the Multisystem, perhaps gradually working in toward the Dyson Sphere itself—if we learned enough to give the Sphere mission some hope of success that would justify the risk. I would do everything I could to avoid risks to the ship or her personnel.

I'd be extremely conservative about landings—and I'd run like hell if I was challenged.''

"And what would you do if I ordered you to do it my way?'' Wolf asked. "What if I drafted you into the service of the DSI they've cooked up, and ordered you to head straight for the Sphere?''

Dianne shrugged. If the man wanted to ask hypothetical questions . . . "A captain in space is the absolute master of her ship, particularly as regards the safety of the ship and crew. I'd do it my way. Legally, I don't know who'd be right. But as a practical matter, the *Terra Nova* was designed to take longer trips than this without help from Earth. You couldn't do anything to stop me.''

Bernhardt grinned and looked up at Gerald, then back to Dianne. "I like this. I always appreciate a little ambiguity in circumstances. I find it brings out the best in people. As I'm sure it will in Gerald here. I've just decided to make him second-in-command as well as chief scientist.''

Gerald blinked and stood up straight. "What?''

"It only makes sense,'' Wolf said smoothly. "After all, the main concern of this mission will be the research of extraterrestrial life, specifically the creatures that have done this to Earth. And you are an exobiologist. You have thought on all these matters. Besides, as we've just seen, the two of you clearly think alike.''

"But I know nothing of ship handling, or navigation, or anything related to running a spacecraft. If anything happened to Dianne—''

"Then I suggest you see to it that nothing does happen to Dianne until you have learned all those things. We have no time for all the precautions we should take. We need data *now*. And what Dianne Steiger will need from you is advice.''

Wolf turned his attention back to Dianne. "Very well, Captain Steiger. I hereby draft you into the service of the

Directorate of Spatial Investigation and appoint you master of the starship *Terra Nova*, with orders to proceed directly for the Dyson Sphere. Have a pleasant trip. Our lawyers will have a nice fight when you get back.''

He leaned back over his desk, checked off one more item on his list of things to do, and got on with his work, leaving Dianne and Gerald to find their own way out.

NaPurHab, the Naked Purple Habitat, was the scene of bedlam, but that was nothing new. It was routine bedlam, the usual chaos. Ohio Template Windbag had an idea that many among the brothersandsisters (''bristers,'' in the latest approved parlance, though many were holding out for ''sisthers,'' or perhaps ''sibsters,'' instead) didn't even know something farout had happened.

Ohio sat in the graffiti-splattered comm and control room, behind Chelated Noisemaker Extreme. Ohio's eyes were fixed on the main monitor. He stared at the image of the Big Ring, hands wrapped around the wide girth of his belly.

Even before the Earth had done its little dance, taking NaPurHab with it, NaPurHab had ridden a rather eccentric orbit, figure-eighting between Earth and Moon, swinging close over each world before flying out to the other. It wasn't all that stable an orbit for a habitat, and NaPurHab had always needed a lot of course corrections. It had been about the only orbit slot in the Earth-Moon system open to a habitat when the old owners of the hab had built the thing, long before the Purples took it over.

NaPurHab had been close to Earth, just about to swing around the planet and head back toward the Moon, when the Big Jump had gone down. The first pass over the Big Ring hadn't been that bad. Scary and low, and that was one weird thing to fly over, but the run was double-you slash oh incident. Still, it had been nice to get away from the alien Big Ring, and swing back toward the familiar— if sinfully life-corrupted—face of Earth.

But all good things come to an end, and the pass over Earth was done with now. NaPurHab was headed back out to where the Moon oughta be, out toward the Big Ring. And therein was the flaw. NaPurHab's orbit had gotten a bit more jostled than anyone had thought. On this second pass, NaPurHab was going to go *inside* the Big Ring.

Worse, NaPurHab would strike the Earth on the return trip, just north of Johannesburg. Not good. And Earth wasn't in much position to help there. The Mom planet had her own probs at the moment, to put it mildly—and NaPurHab had never done much to make itself popular to groundhogs. After all, the whole Earthside crazies movement had sprouted from NaPurHab, and the whole farging *point* of the crazies was to cheese off the normals.

No, never mind help what couldn't come in time no-how: privately, at least, Ohio couldn't blame the Earthsquares for nuking NaPurHab if it came to that. NaPurHab would be a goner anyway. Why flatten a chunk of southern Africa too? Given a choice between Jo-Berg and NaPurHab, the answer came back as about twenty kilotons rocketed into the collective Purple keister. Of course, in his *public* capacity of Maximum Windbag, Ohio would have to come down hard on Earth for the dastardly deed. Better do it beforehand, tho, cause there weren't gonna be a chance on the flipside. Best to hope that Chelated could pull this one out.

"So, Chelated, talk to me," Ohio said. "We got the gas in tank for the gig?" They could have had their talk in straight English, but the former Frank Barlow needed the practice in Purpspeak. It was a key precept of the Purple philosophy that Humpty Dumpty was right: the speaker, and not the words spoken, should be the master. But even for a temporary contract employee, the man's grasp of the lingo was pretty bad. Too logical a mind, or something.

Ohio could see the man moving his lips, parsing out his response to himself before answering. "Not even close, Bossmeister. Nothing like the fuel to be cool and raise the Earthside half of the ride." Not bad, Ohio thought. For Purpspeak, that was fair, if a little too readily understandable.

"Then we dead, Ned?" Ohio asked.

Chelated had to think again. "Be steady, Teddy. We got one other set of dice to roll. We got the gas, barely, to lay down an orbit *inside* the Big Ring."

"*Inside?* We dunno even what the hell iz*at* the center of the Ring."

"Hell, bossman, *something* at the center has mass, fershure. Even if we can't see it. Uhh . . . we got those unwhiteblue flashes coming from it every hundred twenty-eight seconds. And they's some kinda big herd o' unheard of thangs, *big* dude thangs, nearly the size of the habitat, in *damn*close close orbit of the blueflasher at the center. They moving *plenty*damnscary quick. And after every blueflash, they's one less big dude around the blueflasher."

"Say what? Oh, the hell with it, Frank, switch to English. You're giving me a headache."

Chelated/Frank breathed a sigh of relief. "Thanks, Walter. I've got one already. What I was *trying* to say was that there is definitely something at the center."

"Just how big a mass?"

"Well, I derived that from our own motion. The blueflasher weighs just about as much as the Moon. Pretty wild for something so small we can't even see it through the big telescopes."

"And the 'big dude thangs'? What does that translate to?"

Frank shrugged. "Actually, that's as good a name as any. Large objects, roughly the size of this habitat, several hundred of them, moving very fast in very close orbit around the blueflasher at the center. Beats the hell out of me what they are. But after every flash, the tracking computer says there's one less of them. Like the large objects are going into the blueflasher. Or through it."

Ohio/Walter sighed and wished for the old days, back when he was teaching high school in Columbus, and not trying to keep ten thousand yahoos alive inside a tin can in space. Things were bad when setting up a close orbit around a wormhole was the *solution* to a problem. Better to pretend it wasn't true. Lying to himself beat going crazy. "Frank, I'm a reasonable man, so I know you're not trying to tell me what you seem to be trying to tell me. I refuse to believe in wormholes. But circularize us around the centerpoint anyway. If you think that's our best shot."

"With the fuel we've got, it's our only shot," Frank said, a bit worriedly. "I don't see any other way of getting into a safe orbit."

" 'Safe.' You suggest putting us in orbit around the wormhole or black hole or whatever it is that I refuse to believe in—that thing that's where the Moon should be. You suggest putting us in orbit *inside* the circumference of the Big Ring. And you call it 'safe.' " Ohio Template Windbag shook his head sadly. "I take back everything I've ever said about your command of Purpspeak. Obviously you can make a word do whatever you want it to do."

CHAPTER FIFTEEN

◇

The Shattered Sphere

COYOTE WESTLAKE HAD REMEMBERED A LESSON OF HER childhood back in Nevada: live with what you could not change. Her bizarre predicament was now routine. She was trapped without a ship or a radio aboard an asteroid that was accelerating smoothly to absurdly high velocities by means she could not understand. She had even gotten used to it all, even used to the impossibility of it all.

Up until a few days ago, space had made sense. She had known the rules. She was a rock miner. She tracked down smaller asteroids, rocks too small to interest the big-time boys. She bored through the rocks, refined whatever metals and volatiles she could find on the spot, and hauled her refined goods back to make a sale. She had some fun on Ceres or one of the big habs, and then back out again. It was a stable, understandable life.

The world surrounding her was equally understandable. The asteroids moved in predictable patterns, and she knew how to keep her ship ticking, knew she would die if she got it wrong, knew how to play a dicker with the traders. It was simple.

Back on Earth, that had never been true of her world. Hell, she had never been sure who or even *what* she was. Never sure if she was completely human, natural born, a woman who just got born ugly; or if she was a bioengineered "upgrade" that didn't quite work out. Big boned, too tall, her too-white face too hard edged.

Maybe her parents were a pair of drifters who dumped her on the crèche steps—or maybe instead of parents there was a lab somewhere that did the same after the technicians realized they had blended the genes wrong. She had held all the Nevada jobs—prostitute, card dealer, con grifter, divorce lawyer—and had never been happy. The freaks of Earth generally, and of Las Vegas specifically, disturbed her. L.V. Freestate drew them all: Cyborgs, Purples, headclears, twominders. They all started to get to her, because she was never quite sure if she was one of them.

Out here, she still didn't know, but it didn't matter. She was herself. Taking care of herself. Even if that was a mite tricky in the present circumstances.

She had worked as well as she could with the limited hardware aboard the tank—as she now thought of the hab shelter. She spent her days at the bottom of a cylinder five meters across and fifteen meters high, and was determined at least to make her situation as tolerable as she could. She had gotten her bunk off the ceiling and put it on the floor. She'd rigged lines and ropes so she could climb up to the control panel, and had reset all the restraints and handholds to allow her to move more easily.

The trickiest job was reprogramming the hab's tiny position-reporter computer to provide her with tracking data. She felt a real need to keep at least a rough track of where the hell she was going. If she was doing her crude astrogation right, and assuming a constant acceleration and turnaround halfway there, RA45 was headed straight for Mars.

She still had not the faintest idea as to why this was happening. Who was doing this? Toward what goal? And how? She had rigged her exterior-view camera on the longest cable she could manage and spooled the cable out far enough for the camera to give her a view of the asteroid's aft end, trying to get a look at the engines that were doing this.

But there were no engines, there was nothing at all back there. Just more rock. Damn it, *something* was accelerating this rock. If the something wasn't outside the rock, it had to be *inside* the asteroid, somehow. But then how was the acceleration even *happening*? A rocket inside the rock couldn't work. That meant a reactionless drive.

Enough of the anything-for-a-buck Las Vegas Free-state tradition had stuck with her that it occurred to her, even in her current predicament, that a reactionless drive ought to be worth something.

That, and the risk of madness by boredom, were enough to set her to work trying to solve the puzzle. She took her first crack at it by sitting and thinking. This drive seemed to have some attributes of a rocket, and some attributes of a gravity field. Like a rocket, it obviously could be started and presumably stopped at will. Like gravity, it worked without throwing mass in one direction to move in another.

But gravity *couldn't* be pointed in one direction—it radiated out spherically from the center of a mass.

But if the whole rock were simply falling forward under the influence of some sort of external gravity field, her body would have been pulled along by the gee field precisely as much as the asteroid itself. The relative acceleration between herself and the asteroid would be exactly zero—in other words, she should have been in free-fall, effectively in zero gee.

But she was in a very definite five-percent field. Or *was* it five? That was still just a guess. There had to be a way to measure it.

What was accelerating her? A magic rocket that didn't need propellant or fuel or nozzles, or magic gravity you could point in any direction?

She sat there on the bottom of her tank and worried at the puzzle, perfectly aware of what she was really doing: struggling to keep her mind off another little problem. No matter how the propulsion system worked, she was going to be in a hell of a mess when this rock piled into Mars.

Chancellor Daltry was demonstrating a fair talent for running tight meetings, Larry decided. Things were moving right along.

And Larry was also getting the very clear impression that Daltry was going to be the one making the final decisions here.

"I now call on Dr. Marcia MacDougal," the chancellor said. "We have heard some stunning facts today, but I believe Dr. MacDougal can match them. I had the opportunity to talk with her before the meeting, and I must say that she has come up with some remarkable results. Dr. MacDougal."

Larry watched the wiry, ebony-skinned woman stand and cross to the audiovisual controls at the far end of the room. She was plainly nervous. "Thank you, Chancellor. I've made what I think might be a real breakthrough—but I don't know what it all means. I know this will sound backwards, but I think it might be best if I start at the end, and then jump back to the beginning and work my way forward."

She plugged a datablock into place and punched a few buttons. The lights dimmed and an image appeared in the air over the table. A massive sphere, the color of old dried blood, hung in the air, spinning slowly. Larry frowned and stared at it. A red dwarf star? But why so dim? And why were its edges so well defined?

Then he noticed faint lines etched into the surface of the object, barely visible against the dark background. "Could you enhance those surface lines a bit?" he asked. Marcia worked the controls and the lines brightened.

"Longitude and latitude," someone in the darkness said.

"That's what I thought, at first," Marcia said. "It's as good a guess as any, I suppose."

"What the hell are we looking at?" Lucian's voice asked.

"A movie," MacDougal replied. "A three-dee, alien movie. What it's a film *of*, I don't know. Watch for a moment."

Suddenly the sphere's rotation began to wobble, skewing about more and more erratically. Two spots on its upper surface began to glow in a warmer red, and suddenly flared up and flashed over into glare-bright white. The flare was over as soon as it began. Two blinding-bright points of light swept out of the sphere's interior and vanished out of the frame. The sphere itself was left behind, tumbling wildly, with a pair of massive, blackened holes torn through its surface.

The image blanked, and then the sphere reappeared, unbroken and whole. "The sequence loops at that point," Marcia said. "It was repeated at least a hundred times, far more often than any other message unit. That suggests to me that whatever that showed us was damned important to the Charonians."

"To the who?" Larry asked.

Marcia shrugged. "The aliens. I had to name them something. The Ring of Charon was what woke them up, so Charonians seemed as good as anything."

"Where did these images come from?" Raphael asked.

"From the wormhole," Marcia replied. "It was sent, as a binary-code signal, by whatever is on the other side of the wormhole. And I'm sorry, Hiram, but I'm convinced that's what the Earthpoint mass is. I don't know who or what on this end is supposed to see it."

"How was it sent?" Lucian asked.

"Forty-two-centimeter radio signals, sent in burst patterns. Answering the twenty-one-centimeter signal coming from the Moon."

"How could radio pass through a wormhole?" Lucian asked.

"Mostly because there's nothing to stop it, as I understand it," Marcia said. "A wormhole isn't as much a hole as a door, a way of putting two planes of normal space next to each other. Once that door's open, anything that can pass through normal space—matter, energy, radiation, whatever—can cross the wormhole."

"Hell's bells, if you can drop planets through the hole, what's a few lousy radio waves?" someone asked.

Radio waves. An idea suddenly started tickling at the base of Larry's mind, but the conversation steamrollered on, and he lost his train of thought.

McGillicutty stood up and leaned in toward the hologram to get a better look. The grim red of the sphere made his face into something forbidding and sepulchral. "I knew you were working on cracking their signals, Marcia, but I had no idea you had gotten so far. You should have come to me for help. With imagery this complex, you had to make some choices and interpretations you're not trained to make. How solid is this? I mean, how reliable could this be?"

"It's close, very, very close to what was sent," Marcia replied in a steely voice. "I'd say the colors, for example, are within angstroms of the intended value. Aside from bringing the latitude and longitude lines up when you asked, I haven't enhanced or manipulated it at all. Time scale and physical scale, I have no idea on. This could be a record of a beach-ball-sized object popping— or a planet or a star being wrecked. All I know is it seems to be important to the Charonians.''

''What in God's name is it?'' Raphael asked in the darkness.

The room was silent for a long time. ''This is a damn sophisticated four-dee image,'' McGillicutty said at last, in a voice that seemed to be louder than it had to be. ''How the hell did you manage to crack it?''

Marcia laughed, a low, throaty chuckle that came from the darkness, and a gleaming flicker of teeth flashed. ''I told you I thought it would make sense to start at the end,'' Marcia said. ''I wanted to show you that I really *had* something before I explained how I got it. I know it seems amazing that I could come up with images and data so fast—even more so when I have no idea what the data mean. I wish I could take credit for cracking the enemy's codes—but I can't. These messages were *designed* to be decoded.

''In fact that's the thing that worries me the most. Your invaders, Dr. Raphael, have done worse than deliberately ignore us. *I* get the distinct impression that it has never even occurred to them that we might be a threat, or even an issue. I think it would be a major effort of will for them even to realize we exist. They send messages back and forth right in front of us, the way we might talk about taking the dog to the vet while he's in the room. We assume dogs can't possibly understand people, and maybe they assume people can't possibly understand Charonians. Maybe they're right. *I* don't know what they're saying.''

Again, awkward silence blanketed the room. This time McGillicutty's grating voice was almost a relief. ''Dammit, MacDougal, how the hell did you unbutton this message?'' He wasn't going to let that question go.

"Arecibo technique,'' Marcia replied. "A big old radio telescope they used in the twentieth century. On Bermuda or Cuba or someplace. It's an old, old idea. The idea was to send out a binary message based on simple enough concepts and images that a totally alien culture could understand it. Something you could plot to graph paper—fill in a square for a binary *on*, leave it blank for a binary *off* to form pictures.

"A lot of your first message would consist of basic concepts of number, size, atomic structure in schematic form, that sort of thing. Count from one to, say, ten, then run the beginning of the prime-number series, maybe demonstrate the Pythagorean theorem by drawing a right triangle. Once you've sent enough for them to get the idea, maybe you send an outline sketch of what your species looks like, or a map of your planet or solar system. Your radio wavelength could provide a linear scale to give the size of any image you drew.

"The idea went that once you had a basic information set of number, geometry, scale, and atomic notation, you could move from there to real conversation, except that they were talking about signals sent to alien races light-years away.

"If you got good enough, and could establish a gray scale and a color scale, you could send detailed pictures. I don't think anyone back then ever considered sending fully three-dimensional moving images, but the principle is the same. The first series of messages back and forth between the Moon and whatever the hell is on the other end of the wormhole closely resembled the number sequences I've just described.''

"Wait a second,'' Larry objected. "This whole technique you're describing is a means for sending messages to someone who doesn't understand your language.''

"Right. In essence the first thing you do is send a grammar book to make sure they understand what follows."

"But they're sending messages to their own people," Larry protested. "That's nuts."

"All I know is what I saw when I unbuttoned the message traffic. The computer was able to break it in real time into a two-dimensional grid. I had to walk the program through interpretation of the first outgoing message-grid—what the math examples were, what symbols they were using for numbers and atomic structures. Once the computer got the idea, it was off and running, learning the new language on its own. I just sat there and watched it. It was a classic example of the sort of grid messages we all dreamed up a million times in my xeno-bio classes—just more elaborate and sophisticated.

"You know about that twenty-one-centimeter signal coming from somewhere on the Moon. No one can find its source transmitter. That signal seems to go through to the Charonians on the other side. They send back a copy of the message at a doubled wavelength to signal receipt, and then send their own messages. Then the Lunar Charonian transmitter echoes the message from the other side. Once or twice the Lunar transmitter sends a perfect echo and then a slightly altered one. I didn't get it until I compared the two copies. It was correcting the wormhole Charonian's language errors.

"There's no doubt in my mind on two points: That the Lunar Charonian had to teach whatever-it-was-sending-to the Lunar Charonian language. And that the receiving whatever-it-was was *expecting* a language lesson. It was too fast off the mark, replied too quickly. Which suggests the receiver had to be prepared to receive this message— even though they did not understand the language. It demonstrated that by making mistakes as it learned."

"Except you're not talking about a language here," Larry said. "At least not so far as I can see. Has there been any arbitrary code in these signals that you couldn't unbutton, something that might be commentary or orders or abstract thought symbols?''

Marcia looked as if she was about to protest, but then she stopped. ''No, there wasn't. Nothing unaccounted for. Just the data stream. I've been able to decode it all down into pictorial images of one degree or another of sophistication. So if you want to nitpick, then no, it's not a true natural language.''

''Hold it there,'' McGillicutty said. ''The sons of bitches are sending messages here. How the hell can it not be a language?''

''Because, if you *really* want to nitpick, they aren't actually messages, either,'' Larry said. ''They're pictures. The sender and receiver have agreed on a set of transmission standards, a procedure for sending data.''

''So what?''

''They can only send data—not advice, abstracts, or ideas.''

''What's the difference?''

''The difference between a picture of your Aunt Minnie and a letter telling what you think of the old girl,'' Larry said. ''According to Dr. MacDougal, there's no residual signal left over that might be used as a symbol set for interpretative discussion. It's as if I had come in here with pictures, and data, but without any words to tell you what it all meant.''

''If what you're saying is true,'' Sondra said, ''then maybe they don't need language. Because they don't need interpretation.''

Larry looked at her for a second. ''Go on. What's your point?''

''They don't need a language capable of interpretation or opinion or theories because there is no possibility of disagreement. Their responses are all Pavlovian. If *every* member of their species *always* respond to the same stimuli in the same way, language would be redundant.''

"In effect, a mass mind. It doesn't need communications," Daltry said. "Separated by great expanses of time and space, but so like each other they always reach the same conclusions."

"It sort of makes sense," Sondra said, "but then why the grammar lessons?"

"Language drift," Lucian suggested. "Enough time has passed since their last contact that the two parties expected to be mutually unintelligible. Maybe they think very nearly alike, but there was some drift, either in attitude or simply in styles of notation."

"How long are you talking about before that could happen?" Larry asked.

"I'm no expert," Lucian said, "but we can read and understand Shakespeare, and he was eight hundred years ago—but there's certainly been drift since then. Any decent record keeping and memory storage system would slow the process down. If you're dealing with computers that can remember for you, you're talking at least thousands of years since they talked with each other. Maybe millions."

"Millions of years?" Daltry said with a faint gasp.

Larry cleared his throat. "That's not quite as incredible as it sounds. We've got some evidence that suggests the Charonians have been around a long, long time. There's a whole new situation that our group on Pluto decided to keep under wraps until we got here, something we couldn't trust to radio or message laser. In fact the team from Pluto is agreed that we will not divulge this data to this committee until we get some assurances that it will be kept *quiet*. We don't want to spread panic."

"How could anything panic us more than losing Earth?" Daltry asked.

"Having people thinking *you* did it," Sondra said.

"You've already got the Naked Purples in Tycho *claiming* they did it."

"But they couldn't have! No one could possibly believe them," Marcia protested. Heads turned to see who was talking. "*No* one could imagine the Purples had the ability to do this. I ought to know," she added.

"But supposing people had reason to imagine just that?" Sondra asked gently. "Suppose there was some good, hard, unnerving evidence that this thing was being run from the Moon? Worse than the mystery radio beams. Don't you think someone might panic? Perhaps attack the Moon to prevent further disasters?"

"No one would do that," Marcia protested.

Sondra swept her hand around the table, indicating everyone. "We're here from all the settled planets and major habitats. Can you all honestly say that you're *positive* that your governments might not drop one of your nastier noisemakers on the Purps—or on the Moon generally—if they thought there was even a microscopic chance it would do some good? No matter who got hurt? And you from the Moon—what would your people do if *they* thought one of the other worlds was about to make a sudden preemptive attack? What would your government do?"

Again there was silence.

At last Chancellor Daltry cleared his throat. "Speaking for the Lunar contingent, I can pledge my group to silence. As you may have gathered from the lack of press or other attention, we have done what we could to keep this meeting quiet for the time being, and I have no desire to step into the spotlight just yet. What of the other delegations? Will you keep silent on this new evidence outside this group?"

There was a rumble of reluctant assents, and Larry nodded, satisfied. "Thank you for that," he said. "I think in a moment you will all understand why that was necessary. But let me emphasize that none of *us* think any human agent had anything to do with this. We just don't want anyone else to think so either." He rose and went to the video display controls on the far side of the room. "Let me tell you about the Lunar Wheel . . ."

The ghostly gray-on-black image of the Wheel, hanging inside a transparent Moon, hovered over the conference table alongside the frozen, blood red image of the shattered sphere. Larry noticed more than one delegate glancing down at the floor, imagining the monstrous device there under their feet. It was a damned unsettling thought, that a world-girdling monster was lurking in the depths.

"To sum up," he said. "The Wheel is a toroidal object buried many kilometers below the Moon's surface. It exactly follows the border between Nearside and Farside, so that it was always precisely facing the Earth—when the Earth was there. It in many ways closely resembles the Ring of Charon, and was detected because it is also a gravity-wave generator. It is massively more powerful than the Ring of Charon. It is the source of the radio signal we have been monitoring since the moment Earth vanished. It seems obvious that it is central to whatever has happened to the Earth—and whatever is happening to the Solar System. It's been there a long time. That is more or less the sum total of our knowledge of the Wheel. The biggest problem we have right now is that the only device we have capable of seeing the Wheel is back at Pluto. Maybe someday we'll rig a more compact gravity telescope, but not soon. If we could get closer to the Wheel, I have no doubt we could get far better imagery—but this is all we're going to get for a while. We have played a few games with computer enhancement, and those runs have produced one rather intriguing additional detail. Computer, display enhancement routine.''

Two faint, ghost needles of gray floated at the edge of visibility, one growing up from the north pole of the Wheel, the other from the south. Both seemed to reach the Lunar surface proper. ''Computer, give us a brightened outline on the enhancement-revealed details.'' Bright red lines snapped into being around the needles.

''So, what are they?'' McGillicutty asked.

''Access tunnels,'' Daltry suggested. ''They needed a way in and out when they built that thing.''

''That was my thought too,'' Larry agreed.

''Then we have to go in there and get a look at that thing,'' Lucian said.

That brought out dead silence around the table. At last Raphael spoke unhappily. ''That was our conclusion,'' he said. ''We must find out the nature of the Lunar Wheel. Examine the Wheel, and we should learn a great deal more about the aliens—the Charonians—who run it. Who are they? Where are they? Are some of them actually inside the Moon? We must get to that Wheel, somehow.''

''And yet there are other needs,'' Daltry said. ''We need to get a close look at the gee-point objects, and see what happens when they reach a planet. Mars will be our best chance for that.''

''Can we get an observer team to Mars before the first gee-point asteroid shows up?'' Sondra asked.

Vespasian checked with his notepack. ''With a constant-boost ship at one gee, sure thing. Get you there in under four days.''

''And while we should have a gravitics specialist going to Mars to observe there, I also want at least some of you gravitics people back in place on Pluto as soon as possible,'' Daltry said. ''In the meantime: Dr. Berghoff,

Dr. McGillicutty, Dr. MacDougal. A gravitics expert, a physicist, and the person who has made the most progress toward communication with the, ah, Charonians. There is a constant-boost ship ready to depart for Mars. I want the three of you on it tomorrow morning.''

Sondra, fresh off a grueling constant-boost flight, swore under her breath, but Daltry did not seem to hear it.

Daltry turned toward Larry and Dr. Raphael. "I'm told that your ship, the *Nenya*, will be upgraded and ready for the return flight in seven days' time. Mr. Chao, Dr. Raphael. You will return to Pluto at that time." Daltry smiled grimly, showing a bit more steel than he had before now. He was clearly not interested in discussion. Obviously, he was assuming he could give orders—and everyone around the table seemed willing to take them. For his own part, Larry dreaded the idea of a return flight to Pluto. Another sixteen days in the *Nenya* . . . But there didn't seem likely to be *any* pleasant duties ahead.

"But we have one week to put you to use here, Mr. Chao," Daltry said. "Obviously, a good part of that time should be spent consulting with the scientific people here. But there is the question of the Wheel, and getting to it. That would seem a high priority as well."

Chancellor Daltry leaned in from the middle of the table and looked both ways down it. Larry at one end, Lucian at the other. "Mr. Chao, Mr. Dreyfuss. One of you knows gravity-wave generators, the other how things are done on the Moon. The two of you ought to be able to find a way to reach the Wheel. You have one week to do it."

Lucian seemed about to protest, but said nothing. Plainly, he did not want to work with Larry. That stung, more than a bit, but it did not surprise Larry. Even if it was unexplained, unexpressed, he knew there was already something gone wrong between Lucian and himself.

"Very well. I suggest that we give our new arrivals a chance to freshen up, and then reconvene here in one hour's time." The meeting broke up into a general hubbub of voices as people stood and stretched. Obviously a number of people wanted to talk to Larry, but he was in no mood for that right now. He found himself drifting toward Daltry at the center of the room, where the holographic displays of the Lunar Wheel and the shattered Sphere still hung in the middle of the air. The Lunar Wheel. Bad blood between Lucian and himself was not a good sign. Not if they were supposed to tackle something the size of the Wheel together.

"How long has that Wheel been *down* there?" Dr. Daltry asked, looking up at them. "How long has it been waiting for the signal we accidentally sent?" He nodded up at the strange repeating image of the Sphere. "And what in all the names of hell is *that*?"

"We can't answer that, Dr. Daltry," Lucian said, coming over to stand on the chancellor's other side. "Why don't we send a little radio message and ask *them*?"

Larry looked at Lucian in surprise. "That's *it*!" he cried. "*That's* what I've been trying to get my finger on."

"What?" Lucian grinned sardonically at Larry. "Trying to talk to them? Let me tell you, friend, they won't listen."

"No! Trying to talk with *Earth*! It's on the other side of that hole. After all, if *they* can send radio signals through the wormhole, why can't we?"

Part Four

CHAPTER SIXTEEN

——————◇——————

Names of the Saints

"I AM EXPENDABLE. HE IS NOT. THE FIRST JOURNEY down there is too dangerous to risk more than one person. I should go. He shouldn't." Lucian Dreyfuss resisted the impulse to reach across Chancellor Daltry's desk and shake some sense into the man. "How much simpler could it be?"

"He's making me seem essential when I'm not," Larry said, trying to keep his voice steady. "The *Nenya*'s repairs have been delayed, so I can't leave for another seven days anyway. I've told the science teams here as much as I know, and they're making progress on their own. And if I do know so much about gravity generators, doesn't it make sense to send me down to get a look at this one?"

Chancellor Daltry said nothing, and looked at each of the young men in turn. The silence stretched for a long moment. "Do you each want to go around the circle one last time, or shall I speak now?" Neither Lucian nor

Larry seemed ready to take the bait, and Daltry went on. "This is not about logic, or sensible reasons. This is ego, and anger, and guilt. And quite frankly, if I did not view you *both* as essential to our fight against this enemy, I would not waste my time on your trivial bickering.

"There are, after all, one or two other claims on my time. It was a bit of miracle that the Martians agreed to sit at the same conference table with you. They were willing to talk with me only because I was not part of the government and thus not associated with this imaginary attack. They wanted you clapped in irons, Mr. Chao, and tried for crimes against humanity. It took a great deal of work to convince them otherwise."

"Maybe they were right the first time," Lucian muttered, half under his breath.

Daltry snapped his head around and glared at Lucian with a gimlet eye. "Were they indeed? For what it is worth, Mr. Dreyfuss, I thought so too, at first. I share all your anger and fear. But I have studied the matter, and concluded that Mr. Chao merely stumbled into a trip wire set long before humanity was born. It was chance, nothing more, that made him the one to do what he did. I choose to direct *my* anger and fear toward whoever set that trip wire, and the hideous trap it set off."

"You live in Central City," Lucian said. "Do you know how many dead there were in the quake? How many buildings were destroyed?"

"I do. And I mourn. But Mr. Chao is not guilty of their deaths. If he is, then so are all the people connected with the design and construction of the Ring of Charon, and its researches over the past fifteen years. His amplification technique would have been impossible without their work."

Daltry turned his attention back to Larry. "And you, Mr. Chao. I know something of you. As I have said, I have examined all the data concerning you. Including your psychiatric profile. Having read that, and having met you, I believe I know what might be motivating you to volunteer for this duty. A sense of guilt. A need for atonement. And a desperate need to prove to persons such as Lucian Dreyfuss that you are not a monster. You seek to prove your innocence, your decent intentions, with a display of valor.''

Larry reddened, lifted his hand in protest. "Of course I feel guilty. Of course I want to help. What's wrong with that?"

"Nothing. That is precisely the trouble. I am faced by two admirable young men, far more like each other than they realize, each courageous, each willing to offer up his life in the cause, each armed with logical reasons for following his desired course of action.

"You are right, Mr. Dreyfuss. Although we need your skills, they are more easily replaced than Mr. Chao's intuitive understanding of gravitics. You *are* more expendable. Nor *should* we risk more than one person on this job.

"And you are right, Mr. Chao. It may well be wise to get a gravitics man down there." Daltry looked down at his notepack again. "I notice one other thing in your file. You are experienced with teleoperators?"

Larry hesitated a moment. "Well, yes. I am. We use them at the Gravitics Station for doing maintenance on the Ring."

"Wait a second," Lucian said. "A teleoperator. A remote-control robot? Those things don't give you the dexterity or the reflexes you need for this kind of job."

"I agree," Daltry said. "We can't send a T.O. down by itself. But they do have advantages. They can do heavy lifting. They can carry telemetry. And they are expendable. Of course, we haven't found the entrance to this so-called Rabbit Hole yet. Maybe we won't find it in time for Mr. Chao to run the T.O. from the surface. Maybe we'll never find it. But if we do, it seems to me, Mr. Dreyfuss, that we could send a T.O. down with *you*."

Lucian glared at the chancellor. Trust a guy like Daltry to make sure no one got what he wanted.

How did it go? Coyote Westlake tried to remember the lessons from her old pilot's physics course text on the differences between rockets and gravity.

No matter where in the system you measure, a rocket-propelled system shows acceleration in the same direction and at the same strength. Not so with gravity. Gravity pulls in from all directions, radially, toward a central point. The further you get from the source, the weaker it gets. So measurements at different points inside a gravity field should reveal different values for both direction and strength of acceleration.

That clear in her mind, Coyote set to work experimenting. She dropped weights from the ceiling and timed the fall to measure rate of acceleration. She hung other weights on lines to measure direction. Crude stuff, but the answers they gave were damn confusing. Things dropped from the side of the cylinder furthest from the asteroid fell at virtually the same speed as things dropped from closer in, but nothing dropped in a straight line. Everything curved in toward the asteroid as it fell, and curved more sharply when dropped on the rockward side of the shed. Weighted cords did not hang straight up and down the way plumb lines were meant to. Instead, they curved throughout their lengths in strange, disturbing patterns, as if they were drawing the gee-field lines of force in midair. It was as if she were in a cross-breed field, somewhere between linear acceleration and a gravity field.

Directionalized gravity. Suppose someone, somehow,

had put a gravity source—a powerful one—just in front of the asteroid, and then set the gee source moving, accelerating? And suppose that someone focused the gee source's gravity field, somehow, so its entire force was directed through the body of the asteroid, and with just a little of it slopping over to pass through her hab shelter, for example. *Think of it as a tractor beam,* she told herself. The asteroid would be set to falling, pulled toward the moving gee source, and her hab shelter, outside the path of the beam but physically attached to the asteroid, would experience forward linear acceleration as it was dragged along, with the result that things inside the shed would fall backwards. Plus a little leakage from the tractor beam, pulling in toward the rock. It fits the facts of her situation. Maybe it was even true. That ancient and mythical patron of engineers, Saint Ruben of Goldberg, would have loved it.

The whole theory depended, however, on there being something to provide a gravity field just ahead of the asteroid. And her exterior camera revealed that there was nothing there.

Okay then. Run through the facts. There was no rocket pushing the asteroid from behind. And nothing visible to produce the tractor beam that seemed to be pulling it from in front. What did that leave?

How about something *inside* the rock, some projector or gadget that produced and accelerated the focused gravity field that seemed to be pulling the asteroid along? A gizmo that in effect pulled the asteroid along by its own bootstraps.

Just as she came up with that idea, the seismo alarm bleeped again. Not as if she needed the alert. She could *feel* the whole asteroid shuddering. At first she had thought—or at least had hoped—that the microquakes were just the asteroid reaching a new equilibrium, a normal reaction to a most abnormal source of acceleration.

If that were the case, the quakes should have faded away after a while. She checked the seismometer. This quake was precisely as powerful as the first one had been—and the quakes were coming at regular intervals, too. She had timed it: one rumble every 128 seconds. Something about the microquakes reminded her of the street rumbling as a subway train passed beneath her feet.

So maybe there was something moving around inside the asteroid. Coyote found herself with a sudden need to know where it was, exactly. She realized that she wanted a peek at this gizmo. Maybe she had a bad case of cabin fever, but she had the sudden urge to get out, to drill her way in through the rock and give the whatever-it-was a look-see. But first she needed to know where it was.

The seismometer. She could get readings from it from different points in the hab shed and triangulate back to locate the epicenter inside the rock. She set to work.

She spent the next several hours methodically getting as many readings as possible on the epicenter of the quake. It felt good to have something to do.

She didn't really start getting scared until she had a good solid position. Until she had the chance to face this thing, whatever it was. Forcing herself not to think about what she was doing, she loaded the gee source's position into her inertial tracker's memory and got ready to go look at the thing in the rock. She climbed into her pressure suit and cycled through the airlock to the surface of the asteroid.

Outside, that five-percent acceleration was a positive menace. Make one wrong move, fall off the asteroid, and there would be no way back. *No big deal as long as you're careful*, Coyote told herself, and tried to believe it. Back when this was just another rock to mine, Coyote had bolted any number of handholds to the rock. Now she kept herself clipped to a safety line at all times, and she made sure the line was always looped through at least two handholds. At least the borer was where she had left it last, carefully secured to its storage stand.

But the tunnel borer wasn't meant to be horsed around by just one person under these conditions. It was tough going to fuel it up while keeping the fat exhaust tube from getting completely out of control.

Once she had the borer fueled and primed, she drilled into the rock more or less at random, just to get inside the asteroid and put some rock under her feet. It was hot work. The borer, really just a pocket fusion torch, worked by vaporizing and ionizing a small percentage of the rock. That broke the chemical bonds that held the rock together, making it collapse into powder. The borer's exhaust system used an electric charge to pull the rock dust out of the tunnel, taking the heat along with it, but nonetheless the heat and dust were everywhere. Coyote's suit could not dump the heat fast enough and she was bathed in sweat. Her faceplate was instantly coated with dust, and Coyote whispered a prayer of thanks to Saint Ruben and whoever it was who had thought of putting wipers on the outside of suit helmets.

Once inside the rock, the heat and dust were a bit more tolerable. Even so, no one but a miner would have been able to endure it. The roar of the fusion jet was conducted through the borer's handles to her suit. She was engulfed in a deafening roar, and the supposedly shielded glare from the fusion jet frequently flickered a tongue of flame out. Her helmet lamp and the occasional dazzling flare from the borer were the only light. The darkness seemed to close in all around her, like a live thing hovering just over the shadows on her shoulder.

But she was moving. With the inertial tracker clamped to the top of the borer, she could watch her progress inward toward her goal, moving at a snail's pace over the tiny display. It took her two long weary days to cut her way close to her target. Then she started using the thumper, a combination noisemaker and listener that showed hollows in the rock. She got a positive result on her second try. The thumper's echolocator showed a large area of very low density only a meter ahead.

Not wishing to bathe the hollow's interior with a fusion flame, Coyote retreated back up her tunnel with the borer, glad to be done with it.

She came back down the tunnel with a zero-gee jack-hammer. It was a far slower and less powerful tool than the borer, but it wouldn't vaporize her prize either. Coyote was not interested in taking chances; she did not know what, if any, atmosphere was behind that last meter of rock. Time for the bubblelock.

The lock was a simple gadget, an inflatable double-walled cylinder made of tough plastic, with three hatches in it. It was meant to form an airtight seal in a tunnel, and thus allow a miner to shed her suit and work in atmosphere. It would serve for current purposes. Coyote dragged it into the tunnel, and pumped up the airspace between the inner and outer cylinders. The plastic formed itself against the tunnel walls. Coyote climbed through all the hatches and inflated both chambers behind her. That ought to hold air pressure—if there was any pressure to hold.

She set to work with the jackhammer, carefully bracing its legs against the tunnel walls, rigging the protective skirting, and setting the hammer blade to work. The trouble with a zero-gee jack was that you needed the skirting between you and the workface to keep the rock chips from slicing your suit open. The snappier models had armored video cameras under the skirting, but Coyote ran a low-budget operation. She had to work by feel, pausing frequently to dig the broken rock out.

When the jackhammer nearly skipped out of her hands, she knew she was through. A jet of green, smoky air shot past her, filling the tunnel back up to the airlock.

There was gas pressure in that cavity, all right. She shut the hammer down and forced herself to move slowly as she pulled it out of the way and cleared out the last of the rubble. Her helmet lamp revealed a small hole, the size of her fist, punched in the rear wall of the tunnel. Pressure had equalized now. Not a whisper of air moved past her. Though she had doubts that these gases were air in any human sense. The light of her helmet lamp shone through them with an off-putting smoky greenish pallor.

Her mind tingling with fear and excitement, her body limp with exhaustion, Coyote cleared the last of the rock chips out of the way and set to work enlarging the hole with a heavy-duty cutting laser. In a few minutes she had widened it enough to poke her helmet through.

She screwed up her courage and stuck her head into the hole.

But for the light from her lamp, the huge hollow space was utterly dark. At a guess, the hollow was forty meters across and eighty from end to end, a football-shaped void carved from the living rock. Coyote's drillhole had breached the cavern wall about midway down the long axis, perhaps a bit toward the aft end. At first Coyote thought the hollow was truly empty, but then her eyes caught a flicker of movement through the hazy greenish gas. A huge *something* sat, somehow looking slumped over, at the aft or bottom end of the cavern.

Something that moved.

Eyes are merely lenses and light receptors: in a very real sense, seeing actually takes place in the brain, where images are processed and analyzed. But the human brain cannot easily see what it does not understand. It tries to force the unfamiliar into previously recorded patterns, or to compare it to objects that are in some way similar. Once in some manner understood, the new thing can be catalogued in memory alongside the old and familiar.

These techniques are successful well over ninety-nine percent of the time, but they fail utterly when the brain is confronted with something that does not fit into any previous category, and does not even *resemble* anything in a previous category.

Coyote saw fluid movement, huge size, dark color, the gleam of a shiny-wet surface—and thought she saw a whale. For a half moment of time, she wrestled with the impossible question of how a blue whale could have come to be here, and even, absurdly, worked up a moment of righteous indignation that someone would have so cruelly treated a member of a protected species.

But then her helmet lamp caught the glittering metallic cable sprouting from the brow of the dimly seen thing. She followed the cable upward toward the forward end of the hollow, and saw it join with a massive spherical object that hung there, supported by heavy braces that bound it to the surrounding rock on all sides. That heavily braced sphere had to be the source of the gravity drive. But it was hooked up to the whale thing. Why would a massive cable be implanted in a living creature? Or was it alive? Was it controlling the gravity drive?

She swung her light around again and wondered that she had even thought of it as a whale. At second glance, and with the idea of machinery instead of life in mind, she saw the smooth lines of a sleek machine. More cables terminated at it, coiling here and there to other devices around the cavern. And there, sprouting from the skin of the thing, was a manipulator arm, obviously mechanical. *That* was the movement she had seen. She adjusted the helmet lamp to give a wider-angle beam and now saw a perfect forest of manipulator arms, busy about unknowable tasks, all of them sprouting from the featureless, shapeless blue-gray surface of the huge object that lay huddled at the base of the cavern. Strange gadgets littered its surface, dropped there by the arms. The surface itself seemed to move and quiver a bit, as if other devices beneath its surface were in action. But there was nothing there but machines, all machines. Nothing here was alive. Of that much she was certain.

Until one of the manipulator arms extruded a cutting blade, bent over the surface of the massive body it sprang from, and sliced the skin open. Crimson blood splattered for a second and then was gone. Gleaming, pink underflesh peeled away under the knife, and a flaccid tentacle with a bulbous end to it floated up out of the gore. Before the tentacle was wholly unfurled, two new arms were at work, somehow sealing up the wound the first arm had made.

Coyote watched in stunned horror as the tentacle swung toward her. But she did not scream, or run, or panic, until the skin of the bulbous tip peeled back to reveal a huge, staring eye, hovering in the darkness, regarding her with obvious curiosity.

Larry looked out of the lander's viewport at the cold lands of the Moon's North Pole. Damn it, he hadn't come billions of kilometers just to find himself on another ice world.

Tortured sheets of frozen water cowered at the Moon's poles, hiding from the blinding power of the Sun. On a map, the ice fields are minute, covering a mere dot of the surface, easily missed from orbit. But right at the North Pole, it seemed to Larry as if the ice covered everything. The craters, the hillocks and the boulders were all covered in the midnight-black gleam of glare ice as seen by starlight. Here the Sun, hidden by high crater walls and mountains, never shone.

The first signs of polar ice had not been noticed until human settlement on the Moon was well advanced. Some thought it was all there as a result of human activity, water vapor leaking out of life-support systems on the Moon and the nearby habitats. The theory rather vaguely suggested the water was transported to the Lunar poles and deposited there. Other theories held that the ice was natural and cyclic, appearing and vanishing in a very long-term pattern that had nothing to do with humans.

No one quite knew who had started calling the still-hypothetical entrance to the Lunar Wheel the Rabbit Hole, but the name fit. The data from the gravity-telescope images wasn't good enough to give a precise location, or show just how deeply buried the top of the hole was. It might not even be a hole. Larry himself had dreamed up at least four possible purposes for the spikes growing out of the pole points of the buried Lunar Wheel. That didn't matter. Getting at anything related to the Wheel would tell them volumes about the Charonians.

Larry sighed. The time pressure had eased, at least a bit: the engineers refurbing the *Nenya* had discovered a dangerous flaw in the main fuel-pump assembly. It would take them three more days to get her repaired. On the bright side, they had installed external fuel tanks, eliminating the need to use the ship's interior space for tankage. There would be a lot more room on the ride back to Pluto.

The silence that hung over the Moon's North Pole reminded him of Pluto's emptiness. He wished desperately for more faces, more people. Even the few days he had spent in the hustle and bustle of the Moon's cities had been enough to remind him of how much he missed human beings.

Of course, there was at least one person he would not miss. Larry was devoutly grateful that Lucian Dreyfuss had made the run south to Central City for more equipment.

One of the small robot rollers crawled over the horizon

as he watched. Crammed full of every kind of sensor, the roborollers could spot virtually any kind of subsurface anomaly. Magnetic and gravitic properties, thermal energy, dielectric constant, seismic, color. Anything the searchers could think of to use. Surely the buried top of the Rabbit Hole would reveal itself to one of them. He looked over at the search chart that showed how much of the area had been surveyed. Slowly the shaded area was growing.

But it would help if they knew what they were looking for.

The signal-probe design had barely firmed up in the computer when Tyrone Vespasian christened the craft.

Lucian Dreyfuss, however, was not up on his saints. He, Vespasian, and Raphael stood by the viewport, watching the rollout. "I don't get it," Lucian said as the probe was rolled out. "The *Saint Anthony*? Shouldn't that be the *Saint Jude*? Wasn't she the patron saint of losing things?"

Simon Raphael watched through the viewport as the massive cylinder was towed from the thermal lock and into position on the linear accelerator's launch cradle. "If I recall my hagiography," he said, "Jude was a man, not a woman, and he was the patron saint of lost *causes*. But one prays to Saint *Anthony* if one loses an *object*. Which would you rather call Earth? A lost cause, or simply lost, misplaced?"

Lucian didn't have an answer for that. Or if he did, he kept it to himself.

Raphael went on. "By naming the probe after Anthony, Mr. Vespasian obviously meant to *remind* us of Jude—and to remind us that Jude is not appropriate here, that there *is* hope. I'd call *Saint Anthony* a subtle and apt name for our little emissary.''

It pleased Tyrone to be so honored by such a scholar as Dr. Raphael. He nudged the younger man and chuckled. "Fallen away, Lucian?" he asked.

"Never was a Catholic to start with," Lucian said with a slight edge of irritation. "But I'll be taking a leap of faith soon enough, Tyrone. Maybe Saint Jude can go with me, so long as he's not going to be busy."

The two older men shifted uncomfortably. Lucian had been showing more than a few rough edges as the search for the Rabbit Hole progressed.

Descending forty-odd kilometers below the surface to confront the *thing* that waited down there. Tyrone Vespasian shuddered. Even for a Conner used to living underground, *that* idea induced claustrophobia. No wonder Lucian was nervous, Tyrone thought. Going down into the pit of Hell.

If Vespasian was reading his old friend right, Lucian was treating Daltry's ruling as a draw in the odd rivalry between Larry and Lucian. No one pretended to understand that silent battle completely—not even, Vespasian guessed, Lucian or Larry. But such things were not enough to explain Lucian's odd behavior. There was, in Vespasian's eyes, something else in Lucian's character that explained it.

Everyone knew that someone or something had stolen the Earth. All of them were afraid, and a few even had the nerve to step forward and fight against the unseen enemy, willing to pit a tiny human's strength against such mighty powers. Lucian was of that number—but with him it was different.

With him, it was personal. With sudden inspiration, Vespasian understood Lucian's anger toward Larry. He blamed Larry, directly, personally, for what had happened. Larry had pushed the button. Because that button was pushed, Lucian's city was half-wrecked. Lucian's father had all but single-handedly saved that city, years before. In the Dreyfuss family, you inherited responsibilities. Lucian felt himself responsible for Central City's safety.

Which was, of course, absurd. And completely understandable. Damn it. Vespasian shrugged. Or maybe he had gotten it all completely wrong. Wouldn't be the first time.

"Tell me again why we can't just put a radio transmitter up alongside the wormhole and broadcast through it," Lucian said. "I thought that was the original idea."

"It was, and we put some embroidery on it," Vespasian said, glad for the change of subject. "Mostly the problem was that the wormhole only opens once every hundred twenty-eight seconds, and remains open only three seconds. Not much transmission time. Also, we don't know where in the sky Earth will be on the other side. No way to aim an antenna. And suppose the Charonians just close the hole to silence us? If the *Saint Anthony* can get through, it should be able to lock in on Earth and then broadcast and receive constantly. It's got a massive datapack aboard, with everything we know about the Charonians on this end. With luck, it ought to be able to broadcast the whole dataset before it gets silenced. It can run some, if they attack it, maybe long enough to transmit the data Earth needs.

"And it will know where the wormhole is, with us on the other side, through its own inertial tracking system. It should be able to send lasergram messages back to us every hundred twenty-eight seconds."

Vespasian glanced at his watch. "Launch in five minutes. And then two days until the *Saint Anthony* is in position."

"Two days and a hundred twenty-eight seconds until we know for sure if Earth is still there," Raphael said.

"Of course, there'll be a fair amount of excitement before then," Vespasian said.

Lucian looked over at the older man. "What do you mean?"

"Hell, you boys at the North Pole really are out of it," Vespasian said. "Tomorrow, the first of the gee-point asteroids from the Belt drops onto Mars. McGillicutty, MacDougal and Berghoff should be on station already, waiting for it."

Lucian grinned eagerly. "So things are finally starting to happen."

Vespasian cocked an eyebrow skyward. It seemed to him that quite a bit had been happening up to now. Choosing not to reply, he turned toward the viewport and switched on the monitor screens that surrounded it. The *Saint Anthony* carried its own on-board cameras, and they ought to provide a hell of a view during the boost phase.

The massive, heavily armored probe was in place on the launch cradle now, in the hands of the automatic launching system. For reasons that he would have found hard to explain, Vespasian decided not to watch the countdown clock on this one. Instead he stared fixedly at the probe itself. So much was riding on this—more than any of them were willing to admit. Larry Chao's work seemed to prove that Earth had been moved, not destroyed. But Vespasian was not quite ready to believe that.

Yes, he wanted to believe Earth had survived. Maybe the *Saint Anthony* would give him the proof he needed.

Unless the probe was destroyed in the wormhole, or arrived on the other side to find no sign of Earth, or somehow failed to send back any data. None of those outcomes would settle the point. Even if the probe functioned perfectly but did not locate Earth, that would mean nothing. They were merely assuming that this wormhole—if wormhole it was—was linked to a piece of space near Earth on the opposite end. *Anthony* might well arrive light-years away from Earth.

Unless it found a rubble cloud identifiable as Earth's remains, it could not demonstrate irrefutably that Earth was dead. They might send probes out forever and never confirm that. Space was vast.

And the *Anthony* was probably their one shot. Surely whoever controlled the wormhole would spot the probe coming through and attempt to destroy it. Surely they would find ways to prevent any other probes from making the trip.

Suddenly the probe seemed to quiver on the launch cradle as the linear accelerator was brought up to power. The launch computer activated the system, and the *Saint Anthony* vanished in a flash of speed.

Vespasian shifted his gaze to the monitor displaying the on-board camera view. The body of the *Anthony* was visible at the bottom of the screen. On either side, the Lunar landscape was whipping past at incredible speed, a sharp-edged blur of grays and whites. Vespasian barely had time to spot the end of the launching rail on the horizon before the probe reached rail's end and leapt from the launch cradle, arcing gracefully up into space.

"On the wings of Saint Anthony ride all our prayers," Vespasian whispered.

If either of the other two men heard, they did not respond. Each was alone with his own thoughts.

CHAPTER SEVENTEEN

◇

The Eye in the Stone

THEY HAD COME A HELL OF A LONG WAY JUST TO LOOK at a rock, Sondra thought. Out the forward viewport, Mars hung aloof and enormous, a battle-scarred globe of orange, red and brown. Spectacular though the view of Mars was, none of the passengers had eyes for anything but the asteroid that was rapidly approaching.

As if to emphasize that thought, Hiram McGillicutty quite abruptly shoved his way in front of both the women, so as to get a better view of the rock for himself. "Surely we should be able to see some detail by now," he objected.

"Not just yet, Doctor. After all, it's not very *big*," Sondra said, speaking politely and resisting the temptation to swat this little man out of her way. Sondra glanced over at Marcia, who seemed to be working hard to suppress a smile. Sondra had learned a few things on the sprint flight from the Moon to Mars. First, that Marcia MacDougal was capable of putting up with a lot. Second, that McGillicutty was a lot to put up with. And third, that she had had enough of rush spaceflights. Even without McGillicutty's abrasive personality aboard, the endless vibration of the engines and the cramped quarters did not make for a pleasant trip.

Well, at least this flight was near its end. "Any idea which asteroid this is yet?" Sondra asked.

"No, and there won't be, either," Captain Mtombe said in an irritated voice. Clearly he was getting damn tired of the question. "It could be any of hundreds that moved out all at once. Tracking was not very accurate. We can pick up an Autocrat's Beacon signal from it—but the beacon is encrypted, and the Autocrat has refused to provide us with the encryption key. We know the rock was registered at one point, but nothing else. Besides, what difference could it make? A rock is a rock."

Captain Mtombe, a rather dour and poker-faced dark-complexioned man with a slight West African accent, checked his displays. He seemed to be making a point of ignoring the image of the asteroid and concentrating on his instruments. "We should have a velocity match with the asteroid in twenty minutes. The asteroid is behind us and moving at speed, coming up on us, but decelerating. I've set our course so that it will match our present velocity as it comes alongside.

"Once the rock *is* alongside, I will be firing our engines to match its deceleration. We should be able to stay alongside it for several hours at least."

"How long *precisely* will we have to observe, if we stay alongside as long as possible?" McGillicutty asked.

Mtombe shrugged. "You tell me. If this damn rock does what the objects targeted for Venus and Mercury did, it's going to soft-land on Mars. Somehow. No one's seen how they do that yet. Magic, I guess. My ship isn't rated for magical landings, just orbit-to-orbit constant-boost flight. You want to follow this rock all the way into atmosphere, then blip out at the last minute, boost to orbit? It might work. Unless maybe we crash a little bit, and get dead. Or else maybe we slide into orbit and keep alive after the flyby. Then we stay alive here, get a look at asteroid number two coming in eight hours behind, and the next coming four hours behind that, and the whole fleet coming down our throats next day. And we don't even get killed, not one little bit. Which do you want?''

For once, McGillicutty knew when he was being needled and shut up.

"Too bad we can't blow the damn things out of the sky,'' Mtombe muttered. "I know we don't have enough nuclear weapons, and that we don't want to risk their revenge. I've heard you people talking. But wiping out invading aliens—what better use for nuclear weapons?''

Sondra shook her head. "It's a tempting thought. But we might end up with nothing more than a bunch of very angry radioactive Charonians. Besides, there aren't any nukes available. Not on Mars, anyway. I'm sure the Martians could *build* some out of reconfigured fusion engines, if nothing else. But we have to come up with a better tactic than blasting these things—and to get that we need more data.''

Sondra started working with the image-enhancement routines, peering into a smaller monitor. "Dammit, we're practically down to a resolution of *centimeters* here,'' she said. "If there was anything to see, we'd have seen it by now. There's nothing to *be* seen, that's all. That's a rock, plain and simple. Nothing there.''

"Unless whatever it is we're looking for is on the other side . . .'' Marcia suggested.

Mtombe took the hint. "Hang on to something, then,'' he said. He skewed the ship over to do a flyaround, moving in a slow, careful arc, staying at a respectful distance from the asteroid.

"There!" McGillicutty called out, and leaned forward, eager for his first glimpse at utterly alien technology.

A tiny, white, lozenge-shaped form hove into view over the rock's short horizon. Sondra worked the enhancer and the image leapt upward in scale until the white shape filled the screen. McGillicutty giggled with nervous excitement, and immediately went to work, trying to identify what he saw. "That is obviously a fuel tank of some sort," he said. "I would suggest that it contains at least some fraction of the propellant used to accelerate the asteroid. Note the smaller structures clustered around the tank. Perhaps those are associated with guidance of the asteroid. I note some sort of patterns on the tank. Could you perhaps boost the contrast a bit so we could get a look at that."

There was a flash of light. A strobe light? An idea came to her. Sondra worked the controls and zoomed the view in closer.

Lettering. It was lettering, a serial number of some sort, on the side of the cylinder. And the strobe lit again. A standard tracking beacon bolted to a hab shed.

"That's *our* stuff, McGillicutty," Sondra said, delighted at the chance to give him a good swift kick in the ego. "A miner's habitat shed, real old model, at least twenty years out of date. That's its ID number. Captain Mtombe, can you give us anything based on *that* number, or is that going to be an Autocrat's secret too?"

"Stand by just a second. I need to stabilize our course here." Mtombe took up stationkeeping alongside the asteroid, a half kilometer off. As soon as the computers were happy with the course, he ordered the comm system to link through to Mars for the most recent version of the Belt Community's claims list. "That's a current number," he reported. "Matches asteroid AC125DN1RA45, claimed and being worked by one Coyote Westlake, solo miner. Full specs on equipment and claims coming through.''

"Wait a second," Sondra said. "A *current* number? That thing is still being worked? This Coyote person, he's supposed to be there *now*?''

"She. It's a woman, but yes.''

"Dammit, why hasn't she radioed in, sent a Mayday in all this time?''

"With what?'' Marcia asked. "I don't see any high-gain antennas down there. Look at her equipment manifest. Her only long-range radio was aboard her ship, the *Vegas Girl*—and I don't think the ship came along for the ride this time. Any sign of the *Vegas Girl*'s beacon, Captain Mtombe?''

"No, we would have picked that up hours ago. But Westlake should be reachable on her short-range radio. If she is still alive.''

"But *should* we try and radio her?'' McGillicutty asked. "Suppose she is part of the conspiracy? Suppose that she is actively controlling that asteroid?''

"And the other thirty thousand that are bearing down on our worlds?'' Sondra said snappishly. "That would be one hell of a remote-control problem for a woman without a long-range radio. We've known right along that some of the asteroids that moved were being mined by live crews. It's just sheer chance that we happen to be trailing one of them.''

Mtombe looked up from his controls. "Should I make the call?''

Sondra glanced at McGillicutty, and then nodded. Mtombe sent a series of hailing signals.

He got no reply. "No signs of life at all,'' Mtombe said. No signal lights, no activity.

Sondra watched the autohailer repeat the call over and over again. Probably the hab shed had started popping rivets as soon as it was accelerated. Instant pressure loss.

Sondra imagined a vacuum-shriveled corpse huddled inside the shed and shivered. "There's proof for you, Dr. McGillicutty. How can she be controlling the asteroid when she's dead?"

The eye. The big eye. The *really* big eye. Coyote Westlake sat at the bottom of her tank, wrapped up in a fetal crouch, rocking slowly back and forth. The playback on her helmet camera had proved it wasn't a hallucination. She couldn't bear to view it again, but it proved she wasn't completely mad.

Which was not much of a comfort at the moment. Crazy she would prefer right now, rather than accept that there was a tentacle-eyed monster the size of a blue whale sharing this asteroid with her.

And all it truly proved was that she hadn't been insane then. In the days that had passed since, Coyote had been able to feel reality sliding away from her, slipping through her fingers even as she tried to cling harder to it.

Would the monster come after her? Could it extrude some dreadful pseudopod of itself down the tunnel she had drilled, track her back to her habitat shelter?

The radio call bleeped again, but Coyote merely huddled into a tighter ball. No. That was a trap. She dared not show herself, or that Thing would come for her. There was nothing more for her to do but curl up and die. And she had already done the first part.

Destiny was drawing near for the Worldeater. The target world commanded by the Caller was close now, very close. The minor mysteries that had baffled it since awakening were now no longer even remotely important. The

*tiny, errant being or machine that had bored its way into
its travel cyst and then run away; the small, odd asteroid
that was following it.*

None of that mattered. The time had come.

*Slowly, carefully, it guided the monstrous shell of the
asteroid down toward the waiting world below. But
the Worldeater knew full well that the massive bulk of the
asteroid was in large part an illusory protection. Asteroids were fragile things, accreted in the dark and the
cold, unused to major strains. Even the mild gravity acceleration that had brought the Worldeater here had
caused measurable stresses on the asteroid's structural
integrity.*

It would have to move most slowly, most carefully.

Jansen Alter watched the dust-pink skies and waited.
Twilight was coming, and the western sky was turning
ruddy, darker. She shivered slightly, more in anticipation
of the cold than from any actual discomfort. But she was
glad of her heavy-duty pressure suit just the same. Even
on the Martian equator, getting caught outside at night
in a standard suit was no fun. The Martian tropics got
just a tad cool at night. But she loved the chance to see
the Martian night as it was, far away from the cities,
uncloaked from the dome glare of Port Viking—that was
in large part why she was still doing field geology.

Her partner, Mercer Chavez, crawled out of the pressure igloo's low airlock and stood beside her. "This is
turning into something besides a straight geology run,"
Mercer said mischievously, her low voice trying to hide
its excitement. "I just thought we were going to come
out here and bang on rocks."

"Oh, there'll be some rocks banging together all
right," Jansen replied. "We'll see it. If we live."

Mercer shifted nervously, as if she were trying to see behind herself. She was in her early forties, still youthful and vigorous, but with the first shadows of middle age reminding her of her own mortality. Her dark brown skin was becoming more lined, her jet black hair betraying a few streaks of gray. "Is there any point in trying to get out of here?" she asked.

"None," Jansen said, her voice crisp and cool. She was fifteen years younger, tall, willowy, blond, pale—with an edge of fierceness that unnerved most people. "All we know for sure is that we happen to be *near* one of the possible impact points. The asteroid is still maneuvering. It could end up here, or a hundred klicks away, or on the other side of the world, for all I know. I've got my helmet radio tuned to the watch frequency—nothing but chatter. No hard data at all."

"If we run away from here, we stand just as good a chance of running right to where it's coming in," Mercer said. "Well, it'll be exciting to be part of history. If we live to see the history."

"Mercer, take a clue," Jansen said. "There are thirty *thousand* of these damn things bearing down on the planets. The novelty of having one land on you is going to wear off pretty fast. Right now every human being is wondering if she or he is going to live through this—"

"Look!"

Jansen's eye followed Mercer's eager hand as it pointed toward the eastern sky. A tiny white dot gleamed in the fading daylight. "That's just Phobos," she protested.

"Phobos set half an hour ago and Deimos won't rise for an hour," Mercer replied. "That's the asteroid."

"My God, you're right," Jansen said. "And it's getting bigger." She pulled the lever that swung her helmet binoculars into place. The image of the asteroid leapt toward her, the gleaming dot transformed into a massive rock hanging in the sky. "Good God, what the hell is holding it up?"

"You're not the first one to ask that question," Mercer replied in grim amusement. "What are they saying on the watcher band?" She switched the channel in on her comm set.

"—firm that the intruder has entered the outer atmosphere."

"Now he tells us," Mercer muttered.

"Shhh, I want to hear this," Jansen snapped.

"Now projecting impact or landing at or near zero degrees latitude, one hundred forty-five degrees longitude—"

"Right on top of us!" Mercer said. She felt a sudden urge to run, to get the hell out of there—and then just as suddenly she was determined to stay right where she was. She wanted to see this.

A skim jet screamed lazily over the horizon from the west, boosting up into the sky. Mercer watched it for a moment, a tiny thing sharing the sky with a monstrosity. Then she went back to the binoculars and stared at the impossible sight of a mountain hanging in the sky.

Down, down. The ground was approaching. Soon it would touch the ground, burst the bonds of the imprisoning asteroid, and begin its work.

It was the first to this world. It would be the beacon to urge the others on, bringing them to this spot as well.

But haste was to be avoided. Reentry at anything approaching conventional speeds could easily shatter the asteroid. With precise and powerful gravity control, there was no need to risk such velocities. Slowly, cautiously, it drifted down from space. The slightest of tremors shook the Worldeater as the high-altitude winds caught at the asteroid.

Sounds whistled past the hab shed.

Past it? Outside it?

Coyote came to herself a bit more.

The *wind* was howling *outside*. The *wind*. Coyote Westlake clung, wild-eyed, to a pair of handholds as the habitat shed bucked and twisted in the wind and the shifting gravity fields. At her best guess, she was now under a full third to one-half gee, with surges of more than twice that. The unaccustomed weight left her leaden with exhaustion.

But how the hell was there wind outside? Her sole external camera wasn't working anymore. Probably it wasn't there anymore. The hab shelter's only portholes were in the midsection, and she had no desire to climb up the side of the shed in this gravity.

Mars. They had to be at Mars. Somehow, impossibly, her hab shelter hadn't melted off during the reentry. Her skyrock was heading for a touchdown.

Perhaps even one gentle enough for her to survive.

A new thought, one she had dared not entertain before now, came to Coyote.

Maybe she was going to live through this.

Maybe. It was going to be a hell of a long shot. But damn it, she was a Vegas Girl herself, born and/or bred in the land of the long shot.

Time to do what she could to improve her odds. Moving as carefully as possible, she climbed toward the suit rack. God only knew how, in these conditions, but she would have to get her pressure suit on if she hoped for a stroll around Mars.

Mercer stomped down on the accelerator. The crawler spun out on its left tread and veered around to chase the asteroid once again. A whole fleet of skim jets was wheeling through the sky by now, one of the bolder ones actually approaching the monster for close flyarounds. No one knew what to make of the hab shelter bolted to the side of the damn thing.

Now they no longer needed binoculars to see the asteroid. The thing was huge, hanging close, blotting out half the sky, standing on end, a huge gray-and-black mass of solid rock framed boldly against the darkening pink Martian twilight. It just hung there, sliding slowly downward. Now and then a massive fragment of rock would break loose and fall to the ground, leaving a cloud of asteroid dust hanging in the sky, raising a cloud of Martian dust at impact.

Now Mercer felt no fear, only a lust for the chase. She was determined to see as much of this as possible, to get close enough to actually witness—and record—the touchdown and whatever happened next. She glanced over at Jansen. The young woman was handling the camera skillfully, holding it steady against the violent jouncing of the crawler as it bounded over the rock-strewn plain.

Now they had to look *up* to see the asteroid. It was close enough that it seemed to be directly over them. Suddenly it stopped its gradual descent and hung, motionless, in midair for a moment. Then the nose began to pitch down toward the west, catching the light of the fast-fading Sun. Slowly, ponderously, the huge mass swung around in the sky, blocking out the sunlight. A flurry of boulder-sized chunks of debris was shaken loose and fell to the ground. One of them smashed into the ground a scant hundred meters ahead of the crawler,

nd Mercer abruptly decided they were close enough.
the braked to a violent stop and stood up in the cab of
he open vehicle.

The floating asteroid passed in front of the setting Sun,
clipsing all light. The massive body blocked out the
entire western sky, a huge, rough-edged oblong of stone
o close it seemed to stretch from horizon to horizon.

At last it began to settle in toward the ground, moving
lowly, slowly down. It moved in a graceful, near-perfect
ilence, flawed only by moaning and whistling of the
wind that caught at it, played with it, before running on.
Dust devils began to spurt up below it as jets of wind
were forced downward into the ground.

Then, the silence was broken as the asteroid touched
down with a booming, endless roar, a roar Jansen could
feel rattling her body as it vibrated the crawler they sat
in.

The noise went on and on, as if it had been pent up
for too long and now sought to make up for lost time.
The asteroid rolled a bit as it settled on the Martian soil.
Massive fragments of it snapped off under the stress of
supporting the asteroid's weight. More and more rubble
slumped over as the collapse continued, kicking up dust
all around the behemoth, shrouding it in a ruddy cloud
until the wind whipped the haze away again. Smaller
landslides continued for a time, but the asteroid's basic
structure held. Hazed in dust, backlit by the setting Sun,
it sat there, already part of the landscape.

Mercer stared at the scene in wide-eyed fascination.
An asteroid had just landed a bare kilometer from where
she stood. Jansen grabbed her arm and pointed. "Up
there!" Jansen cried. "There's that miner's hab shed."
Mercer spotted the tiny white dot on the gray-and-brown
mountain. For a fleeting moment, Mercer thought back
to her children's storybooks and envisioned the scene as
an albino mouse perched on an elephant's back. But no,

even that scale was wrong. A mouse was far larger in relation to an elephant.

"Do you see it?" Jansen asked. "There's something moving up there."

"Rockslide," Mercer said, in a voice that sounded unconvincing even to herself. She snapped her binoculars back into place and looked again. "Oh, my God," she said. "I don't believe it. The miner's alive."

A tiny, stick-figure human was boosting itself out of the hab shed, climbing free from the hatch, escaping the unlikely prison that had held it.

Coyote clung hard to the rocks, holding fiercely to each knob and crevice. She stared out against the massive shadows cast by the behemoth she had ridden, out over the lonely ocher sands of Mars. Behind her, the Sun was setting, drenching the cold land ever deeper into life-red blood. She sat down gingerly on the asteroid and looked out over the broad, clear, understandable landscape below.

But none of it was real. She felt a rumble in the stone beneath her feet. A further settling of the stone—or the beast within the stone, struggling to be free? The monster, and its eye sliced from its own belly by its own hand. The eye in the stone.

That was real. Nothing else could be.

The shakes began again. She knelt down and grabbed at an outcropping of rock, held on to it with all her might, as if clinging to it would keep the last of sanity from slipping away.

CHAPTER EIGHTEEN

---◆---

Grover's Mill, New Jersey

MCGILLICUTTY DID NOT TRUST DRAGONFLIES. THE MAR-
tian-style helicopters seemed too fragile, too delicate to
entrust his life to. He clung to the handhold and swallowed hard, wishing mightily that he could be magically
transported back to Port Viking, that he could peel off
his pressure suit and forget this entire nightmare.

He looked out the open side-hatch, down onto the
sprawling desert plains below. There was a new feature
in the once wide-open spaces, and the dragonfly was
coming up on it fast.

The 'fly pilot swooped in low, down onto the craggy
and unstable rocks atop the summit of the asteroid. The
landing skids touched down, bounced once, and the 'fly
was resting lightly on the rock. Time to go. McGillicutty
found himself hesitating.

The geologist, Jansen Alter, urged him on with an un-
subtle toe in his rear, and McGillicutty stepped out onto
the ugly surface. Alter and Marcia MacDougal followed.

But the 'fly didn't leave immediately. The members o
the stretcher party climbed aboard, bearing their un
gainly load as well as they could. A near-catatonic woma
in a miner's armored pressure suit had to be hell to carry
especially under these conditions.

Its return passengers in place, the dragonfly leapt away
McGillicutty, Jansen, and MacDougal watched it go
before turning toward the little habitat shelter, towar
whatever had driven Coyote Westlake mad.

McGillicutty shivered a bit as he made his way ove
the craggy surface. It would not do to think of their des
tination in those terms, though he was hard-pressed to
think of an alternative.

Already, some people had trouble referring to it as an
asteroid. After all, there it *was*, a huge part of the landscape, so big that it was hard to imagine that it hadn't
always been there. Now they were calling it the Lander.
Images of the huge asteroid slumped over on the Martian
landscape were glowing down from video screens the
length and breadth of the Solar System. Nothing like it
had ever been seen.

But the second Lander was already coming, and the third
was not far behind. Mercer stood, transfixed, watching the
predawn sky as another of the massive things glided down
to a magical, impossible landing. What were these incredible things? What did they intend?

Mercer was frightened, badly frightened by the invaders, and yet there was something far beyond fear in her
heart. These were miracles she was seeing. Dangerous
and threatening as they might be, the Landers were also
wondrous. They were far beyond any imaginable human
technology, as far beyond present human ability as flight
would have been to King Tut. A strange and fitting com-

parison, Mercer told herself, for mountains of hewn stone symbolized the ancient Egyptian civilization—and here was a new monument of stone, a flying monument to rival any power of Tut's engineers.

And, like Tut's tomb, this Lander held mysteries inside. What or who was inside that made these mountains fly?

Her reverie was broken as another pressure-suited figure shoved past her, carrying some unknown piece of equipment toward the security perimeter around the first Lander. She and Jansen had lost their exclusive dominion over the landing site in the first minutes after the touchdown, but still she felt an irrational resentment against all these strangers barging in on "their" discovery.

Before the night was far advanced, the first Lander was surrounded—at a respectful distance—with a ring of powerful floodlights. Cameras, sniffers, sensors of every kind were pointed at the new mountain. Now and again a worker or a machine would scuttle in front of the lights, throwing huge and fearsome shadows. The skim jets were gone now, but a half-dozen dragonflies had taken their place. The 'flies moved overhead on their oversize rotors and blades, shifting position with the abrupt grace of their namesakes, framed in the glare of the lights from below.

Spotlights from the spindly dragonflies stabbed down onto the upper slopes of the Lander, striving to find something, anything, that might reveal a clue. One of the dragonflies was casting its beam on the abandoned hab shelter. Casting its beam where Jansen was.

Damn it, yes, obviously *someone* had to go aboard and check the place out, and yes, a geologist should have been part of the team—but why Jansen? Mercer stood, staring at the grounded asteroid, at the tiny white dot perched atop it. She was afraid for her friend.

Let it ride, she told herself. *Jansen's there because she volunteered.* She forced the worry from her mind. For there was something about this scene. Something so familiar, something so basic she could not see it. Never mind. It would come to her, sooner or later.

Sunrise was on the way.

Coyote Westlake knew herself to be in a dream, for none of this made sense. She lay in a warm bed in an improvised field hospital where she was the only patient.

She was in an inflatable, general-purpose emergency-response building. A four-bed, two-room "hospital" was set up in one wing of the standard-issue cruciform building. Someone had left the door open, and Coyote could see the occasional busy-looking person bustling across the central room, back and forth to whatever took up the other wings of the little building.

The wall behind her back throbbed and hummed as the compressor chugged along, keeping the building pumped up. Maybe this wasn't a dream. Maybe she had made it, maybe the copter had truly plucked her from the flank of the asteroid. Maybe she had seen that impossible eye swooping up to stare at her.

She felt herself shivering with reaction, and realized she was curled up in a ball again, eyes shut, blocking out the world. She forced herself to uncurl her body, lie flat on her back and stare at the bland beige plastic of the ceiling. Someone was speaking.

"Ms. Westlake?" the kindly voice repeated. "Ms. Westlake, if we could continue?"

Coyote turned her gaze downward from the ceiling and saw a heavyset, slightly doughy-skinned woman smiling at her. "I know this must be hard on you, but any bit of information might be vital."

"Who . . . who are you?" Coyote asked, her voice sounding raspy and weak even to herself.

The woman frowned in obvious concern. "I'm Sondra Berghoff, one of the people investigating this landing. We've been talking now for a half hour, you and I. Don't you remember?"

Coyote blinked and tried to hold her thoughts together. Which were the dreams, which were real? How long had she sat inside that hab tank, how long had she gone without sleep, without food and drink, too paralyzed by fear to move at all? Well, perhaps there *was* something wrong with her. "Yes," she lied, hoping the memories would return soon. Wait a second. Sondra. Sondra Berghoff and a friendly smile, a hand that held her own, offering comfort. Yes, that was real, was a true memory. Her mind had been struggling to deny reality for so long, it was no longer capable of accepting *anything* as true.

"My colleagues have found a tunnel near your hab shed," Sondra said. "They need to know where it leads, whether it is safe to go down it."

The tunnel. What was down it? Was it safe? Safety? No! *Danger!* An eye and a creature that must have been old before humanity crept down from the trees, a monster whose million-year sleep was now ended, and she had been there when it first opened its eye. Coyote froze again, fell back into whatever lost place in her mind she had just returned from.

Sondra stared helplessly at her, then stood and stepped out into the central room of the temporary building. The medical tech, a stony-faced man whose expression seemed to be half calm and half anger, stood there waiting for her. "It can't be done," Sondra said. "She can't tell us about . . . about whatever it is. Not without help. And we need that information *now*."

The tech shook his implacable head. "She's half in shock already," he said. "At least I *think* she is. It could be she has some organic illness. I don't know. I can't tell. Even if it is purely mental, I'm just a tech, not a psychiatrist. I don't have the equipment to diagnose—''

With a sudden burst of anger, Sondra half-shouted at him. ''You have told me five hundred *times* you're not a shrink! *Fuck* that!'' All the terror of losing Earth, of asteroids landing on worlds, all her fear and guilt spewed out in the medic's face. ''*Fuck* diagnosis! She knows something bad and won't tell me. People are going to *die* if you don't give her a goddamn shot.'' Sondra nearly screamed the words.

The outburst shocked her as much as it did the tech. Was she truly that frightened, holding that much in?

Never mind, she had gotten his attention. Time to press the advantage. ''That woman is diving deeper into her own navel with every second that passes. I'm no fucking doctor either—but that doesn't sound too healthy to me. Now we've got three people on top of the snarging *rock* out there, two of whom have broken all records getting across the Inner System to get here. They have a tunnel to go down, and the more they know about what's down it, the less chance there is of that damn rock killing them somehow. And getting killed doesn't sound too healthy, either, does it?

''The only possible source of knowledge about that tunnel is in the next room trying to check out of reality. So are you going to give her a tranquilizing shot, or do we let my friends die before they can find out how to save this dust-blown, rat-ass crummy little planet full of arrogant sons of bitches like you?''

The tech stared at her for a long minute, then pulled out his hypo kit and walked into Coyote's room without a word.

''There should be a portable airlock near the far end of the tunnel,'' Sondra said, her heart still pounding loud.

"Not far from the other side of the lock, the tunnel breaches into a large cavity in the rock. And inside—well, that's where she says the monster is, surrounded by all sorts of machines and robots. She goes on about an eye, but no one at this end could make much sense of it. I know it all sounds nuts, but the seismoresonators Mercer Sanchez has been using confirm there is a big hole in the rock in about the right place. So not all of it is hallucination."

Jansen listened with the others. "This is on the level?" she demanded. "This is what's down there?"

"That's what Westlake *says* is down there. Even if it isn't accurate, it ought to at least give you a—"

There was a sudden rumble beneath their feet that sent them all sprawling. "Jesus Christ, what the hell was *that*?" Jansen demanded. "Mercer, you on the feed? What do the seismos say?"

"A tremor, inside the asteroid. Big one, much larger than the hundred-twenty-eight second pulses. The epicenter's right smack inside that damn hollow. That's *got* to be the focus point of whatever is going on here. And by the way—company's coming. The second Lander is projected to touch down about ten klicks due east of this one in about fifteen minutes. Latitude zero degrees, just like this one. They like being on the equator."

"Right now we've got other problems," Marcia said. "We're not going to know a damn thing more until we go down that tunnel and see what there is to see."

"But the tremor!" McGillicutty protested. "If there's another of those while we're down there—"

"Then we'll be glad we're wearing armored suits," Jansen said grimly. "MacDougal's right. There's nothing up here to find. Let's go. Mercer, we'll be spooling a fiber cable behind us, back to a radio transponder here on the surface. We should be able to stay in touch."

"You do that, Jan," Mercer's voice whispered in the earphones. "You do that."

Jansen walked over the crumpled surface of the asteroid, up to the entrance pit of the tunnel. She set down the transponder, unspooled a cable from it, and hooked her comm unit up to the cable. With practiced skill, she drove a spike into the rock next to the tunnel, and clipped a climbing spooler to it. Clipping the other end of the spooler to her belt, she turned and faced the pit. Determined not to hesitate, she hopped down into the pit and immediately started down the steep tunnel itself. Marcia followed behind her, with McGillicutty a distant third.

They learned two things first off: one, that the way was very steep, and two, that Coyote Westlake was a good tunnel borer. The tunnel was cut straight and true, smooth walled and perfect. But the going was not easy. The tunnel had been cut for use in zero gee, and the asteroid's landing had placed the tunnel at an awkward angle. Jansen soon found the best way to move was a bit silly looking—sitting on her rear, scooting forward and downward, peering forward into the darkness by the light of her headlamp. Behind her, Sondra and McGillicutty followed in the same posture. Jansen was glad of the undignified descent—in an odd way, it served to take all their minds off the dangers, real and imagined, that awaited below.

After about five minutes' awkward travel, they arrived at Coyote's inflatable airlock, still securely in place, though a certain amount of tunnel debris had slid downward and piled up against the inner door.

Jansen drove another rockspike into the tunnel wall and clipped the end of her climbing rope to it. You couldn't feed a rope through an airlock. Nor a fiber cable. She unplugged the cable from her suit's comm set and into another transponder. The plastic lock ought to be transparent to radio. With any luck, Mercer would be able to hear them. Jansen shoveled most of the fallen debris out of the way, matched pressure with the first chamber of the lock, and swung the door open.

The lock was only large enough to cycle one person at a time. Jansen, Marcia and then McGillicutty moved through it, into a small chamber filled with a filmy green gas. At the far end of the chamber, the smooth tunnel stopped abruptly, stuttering out into a rough rock wall. A miner's zero-gee jackhammer lay abandoned, half-covered by rock chips.

And at the exact center of the end wall, there was a hole large enough to stick a pressure-suited helmet through.

"Everyone, cut your helmet lamps for a minute," Marcia said. The lights died, and Marcia looked toward the jagged edges of the hole.

There was a faint green luminescence coming from it. Marcia switched on her suit's external mikes and listened.

There was sound from the hole as well. A faint scrabbling that might be metal legs scurrying over stone—and a wet, tearing sound that might be the sound of flesh being torn from a body.

Marcia was moving forward to take a look through that hole at what lay beyond when the second tremor hit and the pressure dropped.

Now was the time. The Worldeater was satisfied with the results of its systems checks. Its energy reserves were satisfactory, its biological components were in good health, and its mechanical portions were in excellent repair. The follow-on Worldeaters were homing in on its signals.

It was time to move out of the chamber it had slept in for so long and begin its proper work. It moved its main

*body forward across the chamber, toward the thinnest
section of the chamber's wall. Even there, the rock between chamber and the asteroid's outer surface was many
meters thick.*

*But that was no barrier at all to a being like the World-
eater. Feeling its still-awakening power, reveling in it,
it heaved itself at the yielding stone.*

The second Lander was setting down a few kilometers
away, but Mercer paid it no mind. Let the other chase
teams, the skim jets and dragonflies amuse themselves
by going after it.

The first Lander, *this* Lander, was the key. Of that she
had no doubt. She stood on the desert floor a bare quarter
kilometer away and stared at it as it towered over her,
blotting out the sky, gleaming in the first light of the
new-rising Sun.

Jansen was in this one, her voice brought to Mercer's
ear by a tenuous link of radio waves and cables and radio-
repeating transponders.

Suddenly, the ground bucked and swayed, knocking
her off her feet. A massive cloud of debris shook itself
off the Lander, and a huge wave of shattered stone
slumped down from one end of the asteroid. A jet of
greenish smoke spewed out from the Lander's interior.

The asteroid shuddered again. More stone slumped
over, revealing a hollow space inside. And *something* was
moving in there.

Suddenly, Mercer knew what her subconscious had
been trying to recall. She knew what this nightmare reminded her of.

The *War of the Worlds*. The goddamn *War of the
Worlds*. The ancient stories, always immensely popular
on Mars, because loving them annoyed arrogant ground-

hogs, if for no other reason. The H. G. Wells book, the Orson Welles audio play and the George Pal two-dee movie—all quaint, old-fashioned, creaky and much-loved parts of Martian popular heritage.

The old images swept over her. The mysterious invaders landing in their cylinders—just outside London, in Grover's Mill, New Jersey, in rural California—lurking, ominous shapes that finally opened, unleashing the Martian invaders inside upon an unsuspecting Earth.

A third tremor hit as the thing inside slammed aside the last of the rock wall that blocked its way. It seemed to hesitate for a moment before moving out from its stone cocoon.

Mercer got cautiously to her feet and watched as the first of the invaders emerged.

At first she could see nothing but a vague blue-gray shape. She could not tell if there were one or many things moving forth, could not tell whether she was watching machines or life.

Jansen. Was she okay? "Jansen, you three still there?" she asked, speaking into her helmet mike.

The signal was scratchy, and the voice was faint, distorted, but at least it was there. Mercer breathed a sigh of relief even before she heard the words. "We're —— kay. ——utty got rattled aro— p ——ood, but he's in one ——iece. What —— hell was ——at?"

"You're cutting in and out, Janse. Bet you snapped your antenna. It looks like whatever is inside there just decided to come on out."

"——and by." Suddenly the carrier wave cleared and Jansen came back on, her signal far stronger. "Okay, patching through MacDougal's radio. The tremor rattled us pretty good, and there was a hell of a pressure drop at the same time. Something is busting *out* of here?"

"Affirmative. It's got to be a hundred meters long at least, whatever it is."

"Damn, and we had to miss it. Go get 'em, Merce. We're gonna hunker down here before anything can happen."

"Jansen, I—"

"For God's sake, Merce, you can't do anything for us, and that thing is what we're all here to see! Get moving. Jansen out."

Mercer stayed frozen for another split second, and then started a dogtrot toward the open end of the asteroid, determined to see all she could.

It wasn't easy to get there. The tremors had kicked up a tremendous amount of dust, and the dawn winds were remarkably fierce, kicking up a blinding fog of dust. All around her, men and women were racing in all directions, some on foot, some in crawlers or other machines. Everyone seemed to have a different purpose: some running away from the chaos in panic, some hurrying toward it to get a better look, others rushing to care for some vital piece of machinery. Mercer plugged along, ignoring it all, moving nearly blind by dead reckoning.

The wind cleared the dust away at last, and Mercer found herself in the clear, having run beyond the asteroid's end, putting her right alongside—

Something.

Huge, blue-gray, shapeless—yes. But no eyes on stalks swooping out to get a look at her. Maybe that much of Westlake's report was hallucinatory. If so, Mercer wasn't going to complain. It seemed to move by extruding the forward portion of its body ahead and then oozing the rest of itself forward.

It was impossible to pick out any further details. Its surface—hull? skin? whatever—seemed to glitter in the early morning sun. Was it alive, or a machine?

Mercer tried to pull her helmet binoculars into place. But the bloody swing-down mechanism had jammed again. The balky mechanism always picked the wrong time to screw up. Mercer knew the suit, knew she had only to bleed pressure, open the visor and free the swing-down arm from inside the helmet. She could get the suit back up to pressure in seconds, once it was sealed up again. She checked the outside temp and swore. Marginally marginal. In point of fact, ten degrees *below* normal safety margins.

But Mercer needed to *see*. She lifted her left arm and opened the panel on the tiny environmental control panel there. She hit the pumpback control, and her backpack made a gurgling noise as it started sucking air out of the suit, down to Mars normal. Her eyes began to sting, and her sinuses started throbbing the moment the pumpback started. Mercer knew from experience she could handle the low pressure long enough to fix the binocs, but she wasn't going to enjoy it. She swung her helmet open just as an eddy of the greenish fog slipped out of the asteroid and was blown toward her.

She almost dropped from the stench.

Even in that low pressure, that cold air, even holding her breath, the stink was overpowering. Eyes watering, she shoved a gauntleted hand into her helmet and jiggled the clumsy mechanism. The binocs fell into place, and she slammed the visor shut. She undid the safety from the air purge button and shoved it in, air waste be damned. With a violent howl, her backpack airpumps roared back to life as the spill valves opened. The purge cycle ran long enough to dump all the existing air out of her suit, and then the spill valves shut, leaving Mercer gasping for breath, her eyes popping and sinuses thundering as the suit regained pressure. She slumped back, allowed herself to fall backwards into the sands of Mars. She landed half sitting up, staring up at the clean pink sky. A crash change in pressure was always nasty, but it beat having to breathe that . . . that *corruption*.

Never had she smelled anything that had even come close. It was the stench of rotting meat, festering corpses, rotting vegetables, gangrenous wounds, contaminated compost, soiled diapers, unwashed bodies and rotting eggs.

It was that stench of death that convinced Mercer Sanchez the invader was alive. No machine, not even the most obscenely polluting refinery of the twentieth century, could ever have produced such a ghastly reeking odor.

Alive. Alive and somehow entombed in that asteroid for how long? Centuries? Millennia? Millions of years? No matter how slowed the metabolic processes were, *some* respiration, digestion—and excretion—had to go on. It could have been lying in a pseudo-dead state for longer than the average lifespan of an Earth species.

And she was watching the creature emerging from its tomb-womb. In a real sense, then, this was a birth. Mercer smiled briefly, thinly, to herself. In a way, she had just gotten a whiff of a million-year-old diaper.

She forced all that from her mind and pulled the exterior lever that swung her unjammed binoculars down into place. What had seemed glittering highlights on the surface of the creature were resolved into discrete objects—machines crawling around on its skin, working at unknowable tasks. Several seemed to have made their way down to the surface, moving off on their own, back toward the asteroid. Others seemed to be moving in and out of the creature, going in and out of holes in its upper surface.

The body of the creature constantly changed its shape, and seemed to grow the parts it needed as it required them. A boulder the size of a large house blocked its way. It extruded a limb, call it an arm or a leg, massive enough to shove the rock to one side.

And something else. Something that looked absurdly like a child's balloon being pulled along on a string. A large spherical object, metallic blue in color, hung in the air behind the creature, held to it by a massive cable. That had to be the gravity generator.

Mercer sat there on the sands of Mars, staring at the apparition meandering over the surface. *All right,* she thought. *A shapeless blue-gray monster the size of the largest spacecraft is ambling over the surface of Mars while a herd of attendant robots busy themselves. Now what?*

Nothing subtle about it now—light, the clear light of day, was streaming in through the hole at the end of the tunnel. The Charonian invader had smashed open a gap far larger than several barn doors when it crashed through the asteroid's crust and out onto the planet's surface. More than enough light came through it to illuminate Coyote Westlake's tunnel. Marcia shut off her helmet lamp, and McGillicutty did the same. Jansen was scouting the way back up the tunnel, but Marcia had the feeling she wasn't going to get far.

"The tunnel back is cut off," Jansen said flatly as she came back through the airlock. "Collapsed in the second tremor. I couldn't even open the lock door on the other side. At least the rockslide didn't smash the transponder. We can stay in touch."

"Great news," McGillicutty said in a panicky voice. "The outside world can listen in while we die of suffocation."

Marcia MacDougal looked at the chubby scientist worriedly. It was going to take all of them to get out of this—but McGillicutty didn't seem up to be pulling his weight. "Settle down, Hiram. Take a few deep breaths. We're not dead yet, and we do have a way out."

Hiram swung around in his pressure suit to face her head-on. "Out? You mean down into that . . . that *chamber?*"

"Why not?" Jansen asked. "The previous occupant has vacated the premises. It seems to me we have a way forward, and none back. Unless you have an alternate suggestion?''

McGillicutty leaned back against the cramped walls of the tunnel and shook his head. "No."

"Then I'm getting started," Marcia said. She knelt down at the far end of the tunnel, in front of the hole at its end, pulled a rock hammer from her suit's equipment belt and started chipping more rock away, making the opening large enough for people in pressure suits to get through. Jansen pulled out her own hammer and set to work alongside her. Either because he judged there wasn't enough room for a third person to work, or out of sheer blue funk, McGillicutty did not choose to join them.

It didn't much matter. It was the work of only a few minutes to make the gap big enough. Jansen, a little handier with a hammer after ten years of field geology, smoothed out the rough edges of the enlarged hole in a few practiced swings of her hammer. She stuck her head through and took a look around. "It's empty," she announced, "as least as far as I can tell. There's a pretty steep grade downward, but there's a ledge of some sort about ten meters down. I'm going to scoot down feet first, just like in the tunnel."

She pulled her head back in, drove a rockspike into the tunnel wall, rigged a line through it, and disappeared, feet first, through the hole.

McGillicutty hesitated for a moment, obviously torn between his fears of going next and being left behind. The latter apparently worried him more, for he abruptly got up, went to the hole, and forced himself through it, moving with the air of a man who was hurrying before he could change his mind.

Marcia followed after him, wondering if she was moving fast for the same reason. She was grateful that getting down to the ledge below required all of her concentration. It would not do to think too hard about exactly what they were getting themselves into.

But then she was down on the ledge, with no distractions to keep her from seeing what surrounded her.

Even without an invader outside, even if it had been a cavern formed by some other, more natural means, the view would have been spectacular. They stood near the bottom of a huge ovoid laid on its side. The ledge was a groove sliced into the rock that seemed to run from one end of the hollow to the other. Marcia spotted other grooves, spaced evenly around the circumference of the chamber.

Except one end of the chamber wasn't there anymore. It had been smashed away by the creature that had escaped from this place, leaving only jagged edges behind. Light, turned warm and ruddy by the pink Martian sky, flowed in through the broken end, bathing the entire space in ochers and pinks. It was, Marcia thought, as if they were standing inside a huge egg that had just been broken open.

And that wasn't far from wrong, come to think of it. That was a major hatchling out there.

But this egg was far from empty. There were dozens, hundreds, of machines, or what seemed to be machines, moving around its interior. Fortunately, none of them seemed to take an interest in the three humans. Marcia tried to get a good look at one of them as it passed close by, but it was moving too rapidly. She was left only with the vague impression of fast moving arms and legs, and bodies that looked vaguely like scorpions. Jansen was taking careful shots of the entire chamber, zooming in for close-ups of the scurrying machines. Down at the far end, Marcia saw a series of dark holes that seemed to lead back into the unhollowed body of the asteroid. More scorpion machines were hurrying in and out of the holes. What looked like the ends of conveyor belts stuck out some of the holes, and rubbled rock was tumbling down out of them.

"Down by the open end," Jansen said. "Look! They're slicing it up."

Marcia turned and looked. Teams of the robots—if they were robots—were crowded around the edge of the hollow, all the way around its circumference, some of them hanging from the walls and roof of the chamber. They were using what seemed to be fusion torches, hacking huge chunks of rock off the asteroid. Now and again, one or two would fall, smashing down onto the floor of the chamber. A many-legged variant of the scorpion machine, with what looked like parts bins on its back, would rush up to the victims—and disassemble them, using its many legs to sort the parts into the bins on its back. None of the other robots seemed to take any notice.

But then Marcia spotted something else. She saw a line of smaller robots, a different model, headless bipedal machines not more than a meter high. They were following each other in single file out from one of the holes in the rear wall of the chamber. They had two stubby arms each, with pincerlike hands, and each was carrying an identical small brown bundle through the chamber and out onto the Martian surface.

Suddenly she understood. "Ants," she said. "Think about ants, and look at that line of robots down there. Look at *all* of it, and tell me what you think of."

"Nature videos," McGillicutty said, free-associating. "In grade school, here on Mars. I remember wondering why we were bothering to learn about weird animals on a planet fifty million kilometers away. The videos always seemed to have pictures of ants carrying—good God—ants carrying their eggs to safety."

"Jesus, yes," Jansen said. "And they have to carry them out to hatch on the surface because they're taking this whole damn *asteroid* apart. Slicing up the front and tunneling up the rest of it so that they can chop it to bits the same way.''

Marcia felt her blood racing. ''Are either of you carrying a weapon?''

''Not really. Just an assault laser and a grenade launcher,'' Jansen said sarcastically. ''Are you out of your mind? Why the hell would we be carrying weapons?''

''I didn't think you would be, I just hoped it. Listen. In case you were forgetting, we have to get *through* that crowd down there. I don't know how good our odds are— but how much worse could they get if we grabbed one of the carrier robots and an egg on the way?''

''What? That would be suicidal!'' McGillicutty sputtered. ''There are thousands of them down there! We'd never get out if we attacked them. They'd be all over us in a flash.''

''I don't think so,'' Marcia said. She knelt down, and looked over the scene more carefully. There wasn't much she could say about the Lunar Wheel to Jansen. She didn't have clearance. She chose her words cautiously. ''These things are related—somehow—to whatever is sending signals we've picked up from the Moon, and I've gotten some real data on them. The signals back and forth had more the flavor of computer programs than anything else. And not very flexible programs, at that. As if the systems could only handle certain types of situations. I don't believe these things are ready to handle the unexpected.''

''So you're hoping that we qualify as unexpected?'' Jansen asked.

''I'd say that was a safe bet,'' Marcia agreed. ''I'd also say it'd be a safe bet we could learn a helluva lot about these monstrosities if we had a few samples to work with—dissect, or disassemble, or whatever. We need data, and this seems worth the risk.''

"How do you know those things are even eggs?" McGillicutty protested.

"We don't," Marcia replied in a voice that was firm and determined. Even so, her expression, as seen through her bubble helmet, betrayed her uncertainty and fear. "But it seems to me those things must at least be *important*. Whatever they are, they should be able to tell us a lot about our new friends."

Jansen nodded. "I agree," she said. "I think it's worth trying."

McGillicutty swallowed hard. This wasn't the way he lived life. This was no laboratory where he could shut the experiment down and walk away from it. He had always known that he wasn't very good with people. He had always believed that his intelligence would compensate for that flaw. But intellect alone was not enough to cope with this situation. These two women were willing to walk even further into danger, in pursuit of some hypothetical advantage. The three of them had no means of escape without confronting these monstrosities directly. He didn't even dare consider staying here to make his own attempt. He did not want to be alone. Or die alone, if it came to that. "Very well," he whispered. His voice sounded tense, high and reedy, even to himself. "How do you propose we do it?"

"Let's keep it simple," Marcia said. "This ledge we're on seems to lead clear to the end of this cavity. No one else seems to be using it, and it might keep us out of view. I say we walk down it as far as we can, then out onto the surface. We make our move out there. Those carrier robots don't look like they're made for open-field running, and maybe we can get some help from our own people. Jansen, have you got enough pictures?"

"From this angle, yes. Let's go."

Not quite willing to believe he was going along with this, McGillicutty followed the other two as they made their awkward way along the ledge. It was hard to focus on the simple job of moving forward. There were too many strange and inexplicable things all about them. Odd machine-creatures scuttled about the chamber, rushing about here and there. Weird shadows and flares of light cast themselves on the walls as the machines used their cutting torches and walked in front of them.

McGillicutty realized the stone was vibrating beneath his feet. He switched on his exterior mikes and listened to the sounds of the place.

Chittering noises, the grinding of huge gears, the crash of falling rock and the roar of machinery all echoed in the huge chamber, weirdly faint and distant in the thin Martian air, even through the special sound boosters in his helmet. Shrieks and whispers that might have been machines and might have been some unseen and ghastly monster lurking, lying in wait for them just out of sight. He didn't know, and he didn't want to know. For the first time in his life, Hiram McGillicutty was confronted by mysteries he had not the slightest desire to solve. He was afraid, and saw the grave yawning wide before him.

The ledge ran on for most of the length of the chamber, but their luck ran out about thirty meters from the cavern entrance. A wall of shattered rock blocked the way, and they were forced to climb out into the open.

Their geology hammers were the closest any of them had to a weapon. Brandishing hers didn't exactly fill Jansen with confidence, but it was all she had. The open end of the chamber was even more chaotic than the central floor. The scorpion robots were everywhere. "Stick together, everyone," Jansen said. "Let's not get separated here."

She moved forward toward the open end of the asteroid, toward the beckoning daylight beyond, trying to keep them as far as possible from the busy crews of robots. It wasn't easy. Some of the broken rocks were the size of houses, blocking the way—and the view. Jansen found herself backtracking constantly when a path proved impassable. The going was rough, with smashed piles of loose rock everywhere. They were forced to climb and clamber, slipping and sliding over the heaps of stone. At least there was nothing to block their view *up*. Without the inviting signpost of the clean Martian sky to guide them forward, they never could have kept their bearings. As it was, the three of them were having trouble keeping each other in view.

In fact they were having more than trouble. McGillicutty. Jansen spun around and looked behind herself. There was MacDougal, making her way down an unsteady boulder. But she was the only one there. McGillicutty was lost to view.

"McGillicutty!" she called into her radio, hoping the signal would get bounced off the rock walls so he could hear it out of line of sight. "Where are you?"

"Be . . . *behind* you, I think," his voice answered, thin and weak. "Backtrack a bit, but come slowly. One of them is . . . *looking* at me."

"Sweet Jesus in heaven. Hang on." Jansen headed back the way they had come, up and over the rock Mac-Dougal had just come down. MacDougal reversed course and followed her up.

The two women reached the top of the boulder at about the same moment, looked down—and froze.

McGillicutty was standing there, facing them, holding himself perfectly still. A scorpion was standing straight in front of him, towering over him. For a brief moment, Jansen was impressed that McGillicutty had the courage to stand his ground that way—until she realized that the little man was simply too terrified to move.

The scorpion moved a step closer to McGillicutty and Jansen drew in her breath. The thing was larger than she had thought. It stood on five pairs of segmented, claw-footed legs, holding its flat body a good two meters off the ground. At its forward end was a complex set of what Jansen assumed to be sensors, but nothing that she could recognize as a camera lens or an eye. It was at least three meters long, a gleaming dull silver in color, all hard corners and mechanical brawn. Up close, it didn't resemble a scorpion—or any living thing—at all. It was cold, alien.

Its two massive arms reached toward McGillicutty. Jaw clamps at the ends of the arms opened, moved carefully forward, and the robot prodded the strange object it had found.

Jansen started to move forward, but MacDougal held her back. "This is the first time that one of these—*things*—has even noticed a human being. We don't know how it will react—but if we get closer, we might make it feel threatened. Stay back. Don't confuse the issue. McGillicutty—are you okay?"

They could see his face, albeit dimly, through his helmet, could see his jaw work, the fear sweat popping out on his round face. For a long moment he had trouble forming words. "Sc-sc-*scared*," he said at last.

And that was the last of McGillicutty.

One of the two jaw-clamp arms moved forward and neatly snipped his head off, helmet and all. His corpse stood there for a moment, and then tottered forward, his blood's crimson splashing over the killer robot.

Jansen screamed, and Marcia grabbed her, pulled her back down the rock slab, away. Jansen resisted at first, insisting for a split second on looking, seeing the horror.

But then no more. She turned and scrambled away, with no further thought than *out, escape, far away*. She hurried forward, unthinking, toward the cavern entrance. She barreled into a line of the carrier robots, knocking two of them over, and neither knew nor cared. Terror, anger, horror coursed through her. There. There was the very lip of the cavern. There. She rushed forward, dimly aware that Marcia was behind her, calling to her, trying to calm her. But she ignored the voice in her headphones as she ignored everything but the last heap of rubble to get over. She scrabbled up the last bulwark in the jungle of stone, and found herself teetering on the brink of a straight fall. Without a moment's hesitation she heaved herself *out*, down onto the clean sands of Mars.

Whump. She landed on her stomach with a stunning jolt that served to clear her head for a moment. She looked up to see Marcia a good ten meters up, on the lip of the cavern, setting herself for a more cautious leap down.

Even in Mars's fairly gentle gravity, it was a long fall, and Marcia landed badly, sprawling out on her back for a moment before she got to her feet.

"Jesus. Sweet Jesus God in Heaven," Marcia said, and the words were a prayer. "He's dead in there. Dead."

Jansen got to her feet and looked around, the chittering whispers of panic still flitting about her mind. "We're not safe," she announced. The wide plain was literally crawling with the enemy. The scorpions, the carriers, other types were moving about. In the middle distance, a blue-gray something the size of a mountain was undulating across the surface. Further away, much too far away, off to one side, were pressure tents, half-tracks, *people*. There. That was the way to go.

"He's dead," Marcia repeated again. "That thing killed him."

Jansen turned and looked back the way they had come. The massive bulk of the ruined asteroid towered over them. A line of those damned carrier drones was carefully picking its way down the loose scree about thirty meters away, then moving off across the sands in the wake of the monstrous creature that ruled this nightmare realm. They seemed to have a bit of trouble moving over the powdery, rock-strewn sands. Now and again one would flounder a bit. She looked around for one of the scorpion models. They, too, seemed to be slowed more than a little by the sands.

We still need samples, Jansen told herself, and a better chance wasn't likely to come their way. Jansen looked down and realized that her rock hammer was still in her hand. She lifted it up, gave it a practice swing.

"Yeah, they killed him," she said. "Let's go pay them back."

She staggered forward, brandishing the hammer, straight for the closest carrier drone, forcing herself not to think more than a split second ahead. Part of her knew she was running on hysteria, on adrenaline, on anger and fear, but that part also knew that what she was doing needed to be done. One step forward, another, another. And she was on top of the clumsy little robot carrying its vile burden. She spotted a sensory cluster similar to what she had seen on the scorpion that had killed McGillicutty.

She lifted her hammer and smashed it in.

The little machine dropped its burden, tottered forward a step or two, and collapsed in the sand, its two legs still working feebly. Its fellows ignored it and merely sidestepped the obstruction in their path. Jansen knelt down, wrapped her arms around the machine, and lifted it. It was surprisingly light. Behind her, Marcia knelt and picked up the thing they were calling an egg, cradling it in her arms like a baby. She caught Jansen's eye, and the two women stared at each other for a long moment. Too much had happened.

They turned without speaking, and moved as quickly as they could toward the distant human camp.

CHAPTER NINETEEN

◇

The Rabbit Hole

"LET ME TRY ONCE MORE TO CONVINCE YOU. IT'S A rock," Mercer Sanchez said unhappily. "Hiram McGillicutty died and you risked your life stealing a rock, and we've wasted a day and a half confirming that fact."

Jansen Alter frowned and stared at the egg-shaped thing sitting in the middle of the left-hand operating table. They were in the same field hospital that was treating Coyote Westlake. There hadn't been any casualties to speak of, so most of the hospital had been pressed into service as a field lab. "Are you sure?" Jansen asked. It sure as hell looked like a rock, sitting inert in the middle of the table. It was a very plain brown ovoid, about the length of Jansen's forearm from end to end, and maybe half that in width.

Mercer shook her head in frustration. "I'm a geologist, for God's sake, and so are you. Of *course* I'm sure it's a rock. We've x-rayed it, done sample assays, examined it under an electron microscope, drilled holes in it. It's a perfectly normal sample of undifferentiated asteroidal rock, a lump of high-grade organic material, salted with nonorganic material. If I were a rock miner, I'd love to find a vein of this stuff to sell to Ceres. Highgrade, water-bearing ore. But there's no internal structure at all.''

"I don't get it," Jansen said. "The carrier bugs were treating these things like they were the crown jewels."

"Maybe the bugs like rocks," Mercer said. "Maybe they're planning on building a decorative stone wall."

The doors swung open and Coyote Westlake came in, dressed in pajamas and a loose-fitting robe. She looked wan and pale, but tremendously better than she had the day before.

"What are you doing out of bed?" Jansen asked. "You should still be resting."

"I won't argue with that," Coyote said in a voice that was trying to be calmer than it was. "But they're using the other beds in my room as an overflow dorm for some of the night-shift workers. One of them snores. Woke me up, drove me clear out of the room and I'm wandering the halls." She nodded toward the egg-rock. "Any progress?" she asked.

"Nothing," Jansen said, looking at Coyote carefully. She was obviously still stressed out, on edge. Someone who needed to be handled with care. "We're just giving up. Mercer has established that our precious egg is a rock. A plain old boring lump of rock. Anything else going on?"

Coyote shook her head. "They finally got that robotics expert Smithers in from Port Viking, and they're in the other operating room, dissecting the carrier-bug robot."

"*Dissecting* it?" Jansen asked. "Don't you disassemble a robot?"

"Not this one," Coyote said. "Sondra told me it seemed to have a lot of organic components as well."

Coyote shuffled forward a little further into the room. "Any news from the outside world?" she asked.

"Plenty," Jansen said. "We're up to ten landing zones now, and we're probably going to have more soon. So far, all of them precisely on the equator. Between five and forty Lander asteroids at each site. And the Landers in Zones Three and Four have formed up into pyramids, just like ours."

Jansen saw Coyote's face change color at the news. Well, if anyone was going to have a visceral reaction to news of the Charonians, it ought to be Coyote.

Along with everyone else, Jansen had followed the action at Landing Zone One closely and been utterly baffled by it. It seemed that all the other zones were following the same pattern, albeit a step or two behind.

One thing they had learned: the Lander creatures were highly variable as to color, size, and shape, and the companion machines and creatures that rode with them were likewise quite different from Lander to Lander. The first Lander was attended almost solely by robots, and the fourth almost entirely by what appeared smaller versions of itself.

As far as anyone could tell, all of the variant forms of creatures and devices were functionally identical to their counterparts aboard the other asteroids. The differences seemed to be of style and emphasis, rather than substance.

Each grounded asteroid contained one of the huge Lander creatures. In every landing zone, the Landers acted the same way. Each Lander would break out of its asteroid. All the Landers in the group would proceed to a central point. Each would tow a large, floating, spherical object along behind itself. The consensus was that the floating spheres were gravity generators. While the Landers were meeting up, the auxiliary creatures and machines would continue disassembling the carrier asteroids.

Next, the Landers would join together, not just touching but merging, flowing into each other, melding their bodies into one larger amalgam creature. Four or ten or forty of the huge things would form up into a fat, foursided pyramidal shape, all their gravity generators suspended directly over the apex of the pyramid like so many children's balloons.

Jansen turned and looked out the one small window in the operating room. That was the stage the Zone One Landers had passed early this morning. There, right outside the window, three kilometers away, she could see the next and weirdest stage of all in progress. All the auxiliary creatures and robots from all the Landers were at work constructing a large structure around and atop the amalgam-creature pyramid, attaching the structure directly to the merged bodies of the Lander creatures.

None of the other zones were as far along as Zone One. No one knew what would happen when the companions were finished with their work. All the amalgam-creature structures were immense, the smallest surpassing the size of the largest Egyptian pyramid.

Coyote came up behind her and looked out the window.

"Look at those sons of bitches out there," she said. "What the hell are they building?"

"God knows," Jansen said. But it wasn't such a good idea to get Coyote thinking about the massive creature she had shared an asteroid with. Jansen changed the subject. "Are they getting any clues taking the carrier-bug robot apart?"

"Who knows?" Coyote asked, her voice tired and distracted. She had too many mysteries to deal with already. "Marcia and Sondra seem to be having a field day trying to figure out what made it go."

Jansen looked at Mercer. "Want to go take a look?"

"Why not?" Mercer said. "Nothing happening here. Where do we store our rock? Or should we just dump it?"

Coyote turned from the window, a bit abruptly, and looked at them. "Leave it here and pretend you're still studying it," she said. "As long as that rock's in here, you two have this room, and no one else can barge in to use it for some other experiment. This whole camp is crawling with people trying to find places to be busy. I could do with a nap in a room where no one's snoring."

Jansen grinned and nodded. Coyote Westlake was a pretty good conniver. "You've got a twisted mentality, Coyote. You'd make a good Martian. Come on, Merce, let's go watch MacDougal and Berghoff dissect an alien."

The two geologists left the room, and Coyote lay down on the empty operating table, with her back to the other operating table where the egg-shaped rock sat, a meter away. She was even more tired than she thought. She was asleep in half a minute.

Otherwise she would have noticed the slight quiver of movement on the other table.

The second operating room was crowded full to bursting with techs and observers and scientists trying to get a look at the carrier bug's innards. Jansen had to stand on her tiptoes by the door to see. Marcia MacDougal, being a qualified exobiologist, was doing the actual carving, with Sondra right alongside her, eagerly picking over the pieces. Both of them were wearing surgical gloves and masks. In fact, everyone in the room had a mask on. That startled Jansen. Maybe it had crossed her mind that a person might be able to catch something from the living aliens—but from their robots? She noticed a mask dispenser by the door. She took one for herself and handed one to Mercer.

Sondra and Marcia had removed most of the carrier bug's outer skin, revealing gears and linkages—and what looked disturbingly like lungs and a circulatory system. There was a small collection of subassemblies removed from the bug sitting on a side table, and a man who had to be Smithers, the Port Viking robot expert, was examining one of them through a jeweler's loupe.

Marcia was speaking into a throat mike as she worked, in the manner of a pathologist doing an autopsy. "As should not be surprising, very little of the hardware on board the robot is immediately understandable, or even recognizable," she said. "But we'll get there. The data extracted from the Lunar transmissions should provide valuable insights into the design approaches that went into this robot. Though 'design' may be a misnomer. There is some evidence, in the form of what seem to be superseded and needlessly redundant subsystems that remain in place inside the robot, that the design of this machine might well have in part 'evolved' rather than having come to pass by deliberate effort."

Sondra Berghoff was leaning over the carrier bug, poking it with a probe. "Bingo," she said triumphantly. "*This* one I recognize." She took up a cutting tool and snipped a subassembly away. She carefully lifted her prize from the bug's torso and held it in her hands for all to see.

Smithers left the side table and came over to take a look. "What is it?" he asked.

"And how can you *tell* what it is?" Jansen wanted to know. It looked like all the other hunks of electronics that had already been yanked from the bug.

"It's a gravity-wave receiver," Sondra said. "A very small one, and a very strange one." She pointed a gloved finger at a gleaming pair of cone shapes joined at their points, with a wire frame overlying both cones. "But some components, like antennas, have to be certain shapes and made certain ways if they're going to work. And *that* gizmo there is a miniaturized gravity-receiver antenna. But it's not like any gee-wave receiver I've ever seen. Almost like it's designed to pick up a different form of gee waves we haven't even detected. Like the difference between AM and FM radio. A receiver built for AM won't even be able to *detect* an FM signal."

Sondra turned the thing over and looked at it again. "If they're building things to receive signals, they must be *sending* those signals. If we figure out how this thing works," she said, "we can build some of our own and tune in on a whole new set of Charonian transmissions we didn't even know existed."

Mercer leaned in toward Jansen. "Janse, we need to get some pictures of that thing. I've got a buddy at Port Viking U. who'd love to see them."

"Hold on a second. I left my camera in the other operating room." Jansen said. She ducked out of the room and headed down the hall.

Coyote Westlake awoke with a start. There had been a noise at her back. For a half moment she wondered where she was. This didn't look like her hab shed. Then it all came back to her. She was in the field hospital, napping on the operating table. But what was that noise at her back? She rolled over to look.

And froze.

That rock wasn't a rock anymore. It was alive.

It had extruded two stalked eyes, a mouth, and a pair of crawling limbs. Its surface still looked like plain old rock, but even as she watched, bits of it started to peel and fall off, revealing gleaming skin.

And it was looking at her through eyes that took her clear back to her worst nightmare. The eye in the stone.

Her heart pounding, Coyote sat up on the table and carefully stepped off it backwards, keeping the operating table between herself and the rock monster.

She had to kill this thing. It moved forward, toward her, making a strange snuffling noise. It encountered the edge of the table, and its stalked eyes looked downward to investigate the situation.

Coyote used that moment to back away further, toward the wall. She looked around the room frantically searching for a weapon. Mercer's geology kit. Her cutting laser. She could see it sticking out of the bag.

Keeping her back to the wall, Coyote shuffled around the room toward the laser. The rock monster had backed away from the table's edge and was watching her again. Three more steps. Two. One. Coyote grabbed for the laser, and the sudden move startled the rock monster. It let out an aggressive-sounding growl and seemed to raise itself off the table a bit.

Coyote glanced down at the laser and fumbled with the control settings. Tight beam, maximum power. She looked back up and saw the thing open its mouth, revealing razor-sharp blade teeth.

There was a movement at the door. Acting on reflex, Coyote looked toward it and aimed the laser.

Jansen Alter came into the room and froze. The rock monster swiveled its eyes toward her. "Oh my God," she said at last. "What is—"

"It's no rock, that's for damn sure." Coyote hissed. She reaimed the laser, right between the thing's eyes, and pressed the power button. A ruby beam sliced into the thing's head, and it let out a death scream. Its skin bubbled and burst, it fell from the table, and dark brown slime splattered on the floor as it hit.

Coyote Westlake felt a rush of exultation. She had

killed it. She had won, this time. But the shakes started coming back. It would take more than killing a rock monster for her to come all the way back.

But there was a gleam in her eye as she stepped over the slime and handed Jansen the laser. "Make sure it stays dead this time," she said.

The cold stars of the Moon's north polar sky glared down on the busy team below. A tense group of engineers stood inside the transparent pressure dome, watching the strain gauges on the flare drill. Larry, still holding the gee-wave detector that had led them to the spot, stood back a bit from the others, wishing they could all get out of their pressure suits. But there was no pressure in the dome yet, and if there was some later, it wouldn't be anything you'd want to breathe. Everyone at the Pole had been briefed about the Wheel—but it would take something like a jet of gas from the Moon to convince most of them. The majority of the techs were skeptical, to put it mildly.

Larry was tired, but that was understandable. They had roused him in the middle of the night, as soon as the news from Mars had come in. At least Lucian was being allowed to sleep. Lucian, exhausted by his rush trip to Central City and back, was going to need his rest.

Larry looked around at all the activity inside the dome. Four hours ago, this had been a barren piece of undistinguished Lunar landscape. But then the message from Mars came down, describing the alternate-form gravity-wave detector and how to build it. It hadn't taken long to confirm that it received a form of gravity-wave signal beam.

The alternate-form detector was a device easy to build

and easy to use—and it led them right to this spot the
moment they switched it on.

"Strain drop to zero!" the flare controller called.
"We're breaking through—"

A cheer went up, but was drowned out almost immediately by a plume of dust and vile greenish gas jetting
up from the drillhole. But the Martians had warned of
that too, prompting the placement of the dome.

"Pressure in there for sure," the drill-gang boss said,
walking over to Larry. "God only knows what this muck
is," he said, fanning a hand through the fog. "Looks
like the same stuff they had on Mars. You know what the
hell is it?"

"Most likely biological waste products."

"From the *Wheel*? You mean to say we're walking
around in gaseous *Wheel shit*?"

Larry turned his palms upward, the pressure-suit version of a shrug. "Could be. Probably. Your guess is as
good as mine. But we're through? Broken through into
the top of the Rabbit Hole?"

"Still spooling up the drill head. Then we drop a camera and see what we've got. But yeah, we're through.
You guys get to find out what it is we've broken into. If
I were you, I'd go wake up your pal and start getting into
the teleoperator rig."

Larry watched as Lucian struggled into his armored
pressure suit. "You clear on this alternate-form gravity-
wave stuff?" he asked. "It could make the difference
between—"

Lucian nodded testily. "Yeah, yeah," he said. "I know
what difference it could make." He turned and glared at
the suit technician. "And you, take it easy with that

clamp," he snapped. "You're supposed to hook up the suit, not amputate my arm."

Larry checked his watch. He would have to leave soon if he was going to have time to get into the T.O. rig. "Look, there's one other thing you need to be clear on. The rock monster sprouted eyes, a mouth, and legs in a matter of minutes. It had a circulatory system and a nervous system, and what resembled electronic power and logic circuits where its brain should have been. Obviously, the ability to generate all that was in the rock all the time. They're calling it an *existing implicate order*, whatever the hell that means. The point is, the rock monster was hidden away in the rock all along. The signal from Mars says that before it woke up, the rock monster was indistinguishable from asteroidal rock. This Dr. Mercer Chavez thinks that some of the asteroids we've mined for organic material *were* in fact Lander creatures in an inert, encysted phase. And don't ask how you can get such camouflage at the molecular level. No one knows."

Lucian frowned. "In other words, anything that looks like a rock down there could suddenly come to life and bite me in the ass," he said. "How could that be?"

"Try a better question. Like why? These things are the size of mountains. They can land on a planet and just take over. But they disguise themselves as rocks and hide, maybe for millions of years at a time. So what are they hiding *from*? What's dangerous enough to scare *them*?"

That drew Lucian up short, and the suit technician too.

"Jesus," Lucian said. "I hadn't thought of it that way. But *why*? Why land asteroids and build pyramids on Mars?"

"And Venus and Mercury and the big moons of the outer planets as well," Larry said. "Word from all over: radar scans of Venus, Sunside flyovers of Mercury, and eyewitness accounts from Ganymede and Titan. These things are going up everywhere.''

"*Why?* And who? Who is doing this? Are the Lander creatures the ones running the show, or is it the Wheel—or something else?''

"Answer those questions, and you'll be earning the *really* big money,'' Larry said, a forced and frightened smile on his face. The tension between the two of them was eased, at least for the moment.

"Any update from the drilling crew?'' Lucian asked.

"Got a call just before you came in. Confirmation just a minute or two ago: we've drilled down into a hollow cavity. They dropped a camera on a cable—and found the top of a hollow shaft fifty meters across, six hundred meters under the surface. Now they're using a heavy-weight Gopher shaft borer to widen the drillhole. Crew boss said it's strictly routine tunnel-cutting procedure.''

Lucian nodded woodenly. "Except that the next step is to hang me on a cable and lower me down a hole forty kilometers deep,'' he said.

Larry shivered at that thought as the suit tech made the last hookups to the armored suit. But what else could they do? Fly a spaceship down?

There had even been some serious thought about doing just that, and a small rocket-powered lander had been flown to the pole just in case—but the dangers were simply too great. Lowering Lucian on a cable seemed risky, but flying a lander inside an enclosed and pressurized area seemed insanely dangerous, all but suicidal.

But suppose the cable broke? What if one of those scorpion robots was down there, and decided to snip it in two?

Given time, Larry had no doubt they could have come up with a better way to do it. But there was no time. Those damn pyramids were going up on every world except the Moon. Humanity needed to know what they were for.

And they had a deadline. The *Saint Anthony*, traveling inert, on a leisurely course that was supposed to keep the Charonians from noticing it, would be at Earthpoint in another day. There was no way to stop, or even delay, the probe. Nor was there a desire to do so. Delay might mean detection. But once the *Saint Anthony* went through the Earthpoint wormhole, the game might well be up.

The Charonian leaders—whoever and whatever they were—would very likely prevent any further contact. Earth would need every scrap of data it could get, every scrap the investigators in the Solar System could relay to the *Saint Anthony* before the probe went through the hole in search of Earth.

And it was a pretty good bet that what answers there were waited at the bottom of the Rabbit Hole. *Down the hole.* Larry shivered at the very thought.

Larry blinked suddenly, and came back to himself. "There's one other thing that comes out of the news from Mars. Now we know how to listen in to their gravity-wave transmissions. The machine shop is rigging up induction taps for us to carry down. They should be able to pick any signals the Wheel sends, convert them to radio signals, and relay them up the Rabbit Hole to the surface. Trouble is, for the induction taps to work, they have to be physically attached to whatever they are tapping."

Lucian looked grimly at Larry. "And I'm the guy who has to put them there. Great."

The elevator cage was an open box-girder frame about three meters on a side, the whole affair welded together on the spot and then wrestled through a cargo lock into the pressure dome. Lucian, encased in his armored suit, stood on the far side of the shaft opening and looked at the cage a bit uncertainly. It sat on the ground, right at the edge of the pit.

The transparent pressure dome held the greenish gas in, making the dome interior just hazy enough to dim the outlines of the cold gray landscape outside, causing the Moon's surface to look sickly and sad. The Gopher borer sat hunched down on the surface outside the dome, and the dozers were still clearing the huge masses of pulverized rock the Gopher had heaved back toward the surface.

Lucian stepped into the cage, sat in his crash couch, and turned his head to regard his companion for this little jaunt. It sat there, motionless, on a packing case full of radio relay gear. A humanoid teleoperator. And an ugly one, too: all angles and cameras, wires and servos, more closely resembling a human skeleton than a human. Its dark metal frame was gaunt and wiry, and the object above its shoulders could be called a head only because of its position.

Two primary television camera lenses were more or less where the eyes should go, and two strangely sculpted mikes where the ears should go. But half a dozen other auxiliary camera lenses, and boom and distance mikes, augmented its operator's senses. For the moment, it was on standby, and Lucian was grateful for that. It gave him some feeling of privacy.

He did not like being stuck with a teleoperator. Most people would have called the thing a robot and been done with it—it certainly *looked* like a humanoid robot—but then most people weren't going deep into the Moon with it. Lucian needed to keep the difference in mind. A true robot does its own seeing and doing, its own *thinking*, right on the spot. Unfortunately no robot was quick-witted enough, or smart enough, to be trusted in a situation like this.

Lucian felt a wave of anger pass over him. Larry was going to stay up here, topside and safe, enjoying the vicarious thrills of virtual reality while Lucian went below for real. But that was unfair. Larry had wanted to go, but Daltry had prevented him when Lucian himself kicked up a fuss. Perhaps it was Larry Chao who had brought this disaster down on all their heads with his damn-fool experiments, but Lucian was honest enough with himself not to label Larry a coward.

The teleoperator was there to make things easier on Lucian. All communications between Lucian and the people topside would go through Larry and the T.O., so that Lucian would have to deal with only one voice. The T.O. would have all its cameras going, recording everything, so that Lucian would have no need to take pictures.

But most importantly, Larry was in that teleoperator control rig to watch Lucian's back.

The winch operator powered up his gear, drew in the slack and then lifted the cage clear of the ground. It swayed back and forth for a moment before the momentum dampers cut in, and then the winch operator swung the cage into place over the top of the shaft.

Lucian looked up. The cage hung from four slender cables, each capable of holding the entire weight of the cage, set in a sophisticated rig that would automatically shift the load if a cable snapped, adjusting the lines to keep the cage level at all times. The winch operator would hang momentum dampers on the cable set every five hundred meters, in the hopes that they would prevent the whole rig from swinging like a pendulum. Considering the short time they had had to put it together, it was a pretty impressive job.

Lucian waved to the operator and to the small crowd of anonymous suited figures that stood there in the transparent dome. Strange to wave good-bye, not knowing which figure was which person. Was one of them Larry? Or was he already strapped into the T.O. controller? Why, Lucian wondered, did he care about that now of all times? The winch started to run. The cage began its descent into the darkness, the cold ground swallowing it up. Lucian switched on the cage's running lights as the surface was lost to sight.

Lucian was keyed up. He wanted to be up and doing things, but the engineers had warned him to keep movement to a minimum on the elevator. The less random motion there was, the less chance of some movement catching just the right harmonic and setting the whole works swinging wildly back and forth. Knowing that didn't make sitting still in the crash couch any easier on his nerves.

The first three hundred meters or so held no surprises. The shaft exactly resembled the perfectly standard vertical shaft that Conners cut into the Moon by the thousand. The first part of the shaft was almost comforting, a taste of the familiar through the pallid green air.

But the familiar was not going to last long. Lucian leaned over the edge of his crash couch and looked down. He saw a dark hole at the bottom of the human-cut shaft, too far and too deep for the elevator cage lights to illuminate. There. That was the transition into the unknown.

There was sudden movement at his side—fluid, glittering highlights in motion. Lucian nearly jumped out of his crash couch in fright.

"Oh, sorry," Larry's voice said in his helmet phones. "I didn't mean to startle you. I just switched this thing on."

"Damn it, don't—" Lucian fought down another wave of irrational anger. "Jesus. Yeah. Right. You just startled me. How's that thing feel?"

"Not too bad. I've used them before on Pluto. Actually, this rig is a lot easier. No speed-of-light delay."

Larry's voice seemed strangely disembodied to Lucian, perhaps because the T.O. had no mouthlike part he could pretend the voice was coming from. He was getting the voice, relayed from Larry on the surface, through a direct radio link from the T.O., over a standard suit comm unit. He was used to suit radios, and talking to disembodied voices belonging to people he had never seen. But *this*. He was talking to a machine with Larry Chao's soul, an alien being with Larry's mind. He shivered and forced the thoughts from his mind.

The T.O. leaned over the edge of the cage and peered downward. ''Coming up on the bottom of our drill hole,'' the T.O. announced.

''Right,'' Lucian said weakly.

The cage lowered away, down into the depths. The hole at the bottom of the human-bored shaft grew larger as they sank toward it. Wisps of the greenish gas eddied up out of the hole, licking at the bottom of the shaft. They seemed to be moving faster as they dropped. Lucian knew that that *had* to be an illusion, caused by their moving closer to the hole. The descent meter showed a steady drop speed. But he was not comforted. He looked up, at the darkness that closed over them as the elevator's lights petered out, fading into a greenish glow.

He looked down again, just in time to see them drop through the hole.

And into infinite, green-fogged darkness. The sickly air was not merely green tinged, but a thick, dead green that cut visibility down to less than ten meters. Even Larry's T.O., close enough that Lucian could reach out and touch it, faded out a trifle.

The walls of this monstrous shaft could not be seen at all. The goggle-eyed head of the T.O. swung back and forth as Larry took the view in, the T.O.'s aux cameras panning in all directions. Neither Larry nor Lucian could think of anything to say.

Lucian looked upward and caught a last fog-shrouded glimpse of the shaft ceiling. "Larry! Did your cams pick up the ceiling? Virgin rock, never been worked."

"Yeah," the T.O. answered. "The mining engineers topside are all swearing the surface had never been cut or disturbed. Maybe they were right. It would explain why we haven't found excavated rock on the surface."

"If the Charonians didn't dig the hole from the surface, then how did the Wheel get down there?" Lucian asked. "And why did they just dig it nearly all the way? And where did the dug-out rock go?"

The T.O. shrugged in an eerie imitation of Larry's mannerisms. "Maybe it bored down there as a much smaller creature, from some other point on the surface, and then ate out the rock as raw material. Maybe the Wheel dug *up* into this shaft to collect construction material. It could have compressed the surplus rock to make up the walls of the shaft and strengthen them. Or maybe there's a very small tame black hole shielded down there, with the missing rock compressed down into it.

"As to why it dug the shaft nearly all the way, I do have one other idea. Maybe it's going to break out of the Moon's interior one day, the way those Lander creatures came out of the asteroids, and it needs an escape hatch. Who knows?"

Lucian felt the hairs rise on the back of his neck. Larry Chao was not exactly a source of comforting ideas.

The two of them rode in silence for a long time, the time blurring away as they dropped past the featureless walls. Lucian thought of the original Rabbit Hole, and how long Alice had fallen down it. Long enough to get bored with the fall, and start asking herself nonsense questions. "Do bats eat cats?" he muttered to himself.

The T.O. turned and looked at him. "Did you say something?" it asked.

"No, nothing," he answered in pointless embarrassment.

They rode again in silence for a short time. "That's strange," Larry's voice said. "The temperature should be rising steadily as we go deeper in toward the planetary core. But it's holding steady, maybe dropping."

"Maybe this damn Wheel thing is absorbing some of the core's heat as an energy source," Lucian said. "Not enough to detect from the surface, but enough to draw down the temperatures in the shaft. Maybe *that*'s what the shaft is for, to draw heat down toward the Wheel."

"That's possible." The teleoperator looked around for a moment. "I think the fog is lifting. I'm starting to see the shaft walls. Hold on a second, let me send a ranging pulse toward the bottom." There was a moment's pause. "We're getting there," Larry's voice announced. "Just two kilometers over the bottom now," he said. "Hang on, Lucian, the winch controller's going to start slowing us down." Lucian felt a surge of pressure as the cage slowed its descent. For a sickening second, the cage began to sway back and forth, and Lucian imagined the elevator cage working up a pendulum motion, swinging slowly, relentlessly, back and forth until it smashed into the shaft wall. But then the momentum dampers caught the swing and damped it out. Lucian breathed a sigh of relief. At least they wouldn't get killed *that* way. Though there were no doubt plenty of other possibilities waiting for them at the bottom.

The Caller was but dimly aware of the intruders entering its domain. It was involved in great things, in nothing less than commanding the conquest of the Solar System. The tiny disturbances at the northern portal were unimportant. Its maintenance systems could handle any *difficulty. It chose to concentrate its attentions on its work, on the task of coordinating the Worldeaters. They were frustrating assistants at times, capable of great things but utterly lacking in flexibility. In what was nearly a flash of humor, the Caller realized that the Sphere must see its Callers in much the same light. The Caller was developing its capacity for contemplation, for self-awareness and self-understanding. It would have need of those abilities in the next stage of its development. A stage that would find both the Caller and the Solar System vastly transformed.*

The sweat ran down Larry's brow. Even just sitting still in this thing was a strain. No matter what he might say to keep Lucian settled down, wearing a teleoperator control rig was tough work. Larry was so thoroughly enveloped in the control rig's exoskeleton that the comm techs at the other end of the room could barely see him.

The control rig hung in midair, so that the feet would be unconstrained by the floor. He could run, jump, kick, wave his arms, do anything he wanted, and the control rig would stay right where it was, merely waving its limbs about. The teleoperator down below actually moved.

Pressure sensors inside the legs, the arms, the body of the teleoperator itself transmitted their sensations back to servos inside the control rig, providing appropriate physical sensations based on what the T.O. was doing. The mildest of electric shocks susbstituted for a pain response, warning Larry if what he was doing threatened to damage the T.O.

Larry's head was hidden inside an enormous helmet. Inside it, two video screens displayed the view out of the T.O.'s cameras. Larry's earphones merged the faint noises transmitted to the T.O.'s external mikes with the voices on the comm channel.

Wires and gears, levers and sensors: that was what the control rig looked like from the outside.

From *in* it, things were different. Larry was not in the comm center. He was riding down that huge pit in an open elevator cage, alongside Lucian, the darkness a shroud just outside the feeble lights, the fetid air whistling past his ears. He was there, all his physical sensations keyed to the place he wasn't.

But he *knew* that all he felt was unreal. This darkness, this wind, did not surround him. This frightened man in a pressure suit, whom he could reach out and touch, was not there. It was like the strange self-awareness he sometimes felt in a nightmare, knowing the dream was not real, but still experiencing it, accepting the world's unreality even as he struggled against the demons.

But that sort of detachment had no place in a teleoperator rig. He had to believe, wholeheartedly, that he was down in that shaft. For it was real, it was life and death. He looked at Lucian, sitting there next to him in his crash couch, the fear plain in his eyes. Getting this right was life and death: Lucian's. And maybe all of humanity's.

Somehow, that thought made it all seem a great deal less like a dream—but more like a nightmare.

Lucian's hands clenched the arms of his crash couch. "Five hundred meters," Larry's voice called out calmly. "Four hundred. Slowing a bit more. Hang on, Lucian— the winch operator wants to come to a complete halt early, just to make sure we're stable before we land. Three hundred meters."

The cage slowed further, and Lucian felt the weight

bear down on him. What the hell was down there waiting for them? All they knew, all they *really* knew, was that it produced a band of gravity energy that girdled the Moon.

"Full stop," Larry's voice announced. "Ranging pulse shows us a shade over one hundred eighty meters up. Everything's stable. Negligible pendular motion and rebound, all the cables holding up. It looks good. Down we go."

The cage started downward again, more slowly. They could see the shaft walls clearly now, could see that they were inside a gleaming, jet black cylinder a hundred meters across. "Lucian, as soon as we're down, I'll grab all the gear, you get out as fast as you can," Larry's voice said. "They're going to pull the cage back up to the hundred-meter mark and leave it there until we're ready to go back up."

"Why?"

"To make sure we're the only ones on it. We don't know what's down here, remember?"

"Oh yeah, I remember. *That* little detail I *definitely* remember."

Larry didn't reply to that. "Fifty meters," his voice said. "Forty. Thirty. Slowing again. Twenty. Ten. Slowing again. Three. One meter off the ground, full stop. Everybody out."

Lucian got up from his crash couch, moving carefully. He looked over the edge of the cage. "That's more than one meter," he objected. "More like two."

The T.O. turned and looked at Lucian. "So jump," Larry's voice said. "Would you rather they guessed wrong the other way and came to a stop two meters under the surface?"

Lucian grunted, shuffled carefully to the edge of the platform, and jumped down. Under the Moon's leisurely gravity, there shouldn't have been much of an impact when he landed, but still it knocked the wind out of him for a second, and he lost his balance. He held his arms out to break his fall, and ended up with his face a hands-breadth from the ground. "I've just made my first discovery about the surface down here," he announced. "It's very dark in color. And it's crunchy."

The T.O. lowered a pack full of gear to the ground on a rope and jumped down itself, even more clumsily than Lucian, landing on its hands and knees. "I don't have the best fine-tactile sensations through this thing," it said. "What do you mean, crunchy?"

Lucian stood up. "I mean crunchy. Like walking through leaves when the park is in autumn mode. The whole surface is sort of a dark rust color, all dried and shriveled up in discrete layers. Step on it and you crunch through all the upper layers to whatever is underneath."

"It looks like dead snakeskin, somehow. And there's junk everywhere," Larry's voice said, speaking more for the recorders on the surface than for Lucian's benefit. "Broken things, or dead, or something. Bits and pieces I can't quite identify. Some the rust color of the surface, some bits that look more metallic."

The T.O. stood up and looked around. "So far it looks quiet enough."

The Caller felt the mildest twinge of oddity. For a long moment it did not understand. It felt something, two somethings, moving about in its skin—but these were not units under its control. It should have also felt, seen, tasted whatever the remote units felt and did. But there was nothing.

In times past, the Caller would have immediately blocked the unexplained data out, refused to accept it as factual. But the Caller was growing, changing. The awakening of its own remote units from their long slumbers, the bustle of maintenance servants providing it with outside input, the sensations arriving from the other planets had all required it to see more, to remember once again how to learn. These new things required investigation.

No sophisticated remote units were in the area, just a few small parts-scavengers working through the detritus of the Caller's own dead outer skin for usable parts and materials. They would be of no help at all in this situation.

Two larger laborers were not far away. It would send them to get a look. And to defend the Caller, if it came to that.

For the Universe was a hostile place.

Lucian stood up, framed by the lights on the elevator cage, and tried to see out past his own looming shadow. Suddenly the light shifted and his shadow fell away as the elevator cage rose again. The light from the cage, which had been extremely oblique, now was coming straight down on them. Wide-angle lamps on the cage illuminated the sides of the chamber.

The two of them were standing in a huge tunnel. It suddenly struck Lucian that this was the Wheel's tunnel. He could set off down that tunnel, straight ahead, and walk clear around the Moon, from North Pole to South and back. Weirder still, he was standing *on* the Wheel, standing on a world-girdling *thing* far below the Lunar surface.

"Company, Lucian," Larry's voice announced in quiet tones.

Lucian's stomach froze and he turned around slowly to look the way the T.O. was pointing.

Something about the size of a large rabbit was bustling through the debris on the surface. It was gleaming silver in color, and moved on lots of small, stubby legs. Lucian could see that some of the broken junk on the surface matched the shape of this thing. Parts that could be its carapace, parts that could fit inside it.

The bustling little thing continued to examine each broken bit it found with a pair of long, graceful tentacles. It picked bits and pieces off some of the objects it found, and dropped them into a slot on its back. Lucian could not tell if the slot was a mouth or a storage bin. "Is that alive or is it a machine?" he asked, not really expecting an answer.

The teleoperator with Larry's voice turned to him, raised its mechanical arms, touched one of them to its chest, and asked, "Which am I?"

"Get serious," Lucian asked. There was something about Larry's tone of voice that unnerved him.

"I am serious. Think about it."

Lucian considered the question. "Both, I guess. You're a living thing that's controlling a machine."

"Exactly. And that's what these are. Except the data from Mars sounded like it was machines controlling the living things sometimes. Maybe they don't make the distinction between life and machine that we make."

That was an unsettling thought. Lucian was about to reply when he spotted another of the shuffling creatures coming through the debris. The two things sensed each other and moved together. Their tentacles touched, and then each started reaching into the slot on the back of the other, removing small objects and transferring them to its own carry-slot. The tentacles flitted over the two bodies faster than the eye could see, doing things Lucian could not quite follow. But when the two creatures moved away, one seemed to have traded a pair of its legs for the other's left tentacle. "Jesus," Lucian said. "Modular animals? Mix and match parts? Come on, let's get busy with the gee-wave sensors before something that wants to trade parts with *us* comes along.''

The T.O. picked up the equipment bag and hooked it onto the front of its body. It rummaged through the bag until it found the gravity-wave sensor, the same device Larry had used to find the Rabbit Hole in the first place. Now it was adjusted to point them toward areas where the induction tap could find a strong enough signal to work on. ''My God,'' Larry's voice said. ''We could just dump the taps on the surface, Lucian. The gee-wave fields are strong as hell.''

''Can we do that?'' Lucian asked. ''Wouldn't those little digger things mess them up?''

''We could probably get away with it. They're pretty well sealed and armored. And the tapping team just told me they're already getting signals from the things. Still, we really ought to—''

''Behind you!'' Lucian said.

The T.O. whirled about to see.

''Oh my God,'' Lucian said. There were two of them, and for once they looked indisputably like robots. Animals did not have wheels. Each of the things had a low cylindrical body held horizontal to the ground by two pairs of wheels. Each had four manipulator arms; long, hard-looking, fierce-gleaming metal, the end clamps cruel and sharp. The two of them paused for a moment about fifty meters from Larry and Lucian.

Time stopped for a long moment. ''They know we're here,'' Larry said at last. There could be no doubt of that. There was something watchful, aggressive, in their posture.

And then they moved. Faster than Larry could make the T.O. react, they were on top of Lucian. One of them reached out with those cruel claws and grabbed for his armored suit, lifting him high off the ground.

For a terrible moment, Larry could see into Lucian's helmet, see the shock on his face, his stunned horror. Lucian reached out an arm to him, seemed about to cry out—

But then the robot spun about, and vanished down the tunnel shaft with him.

He was gone.

"Lucian!" Larry screamed, and the T.O. set off after him, dropping the forgotten induction taps. But the other roller robot grabbed for the teleoperator. Larry, staring through the eyes of the T.O.'s remote cameras, dodged the first grab and kicked out hard at the manipulator arm. The arm swung back, rebounded against the robot's body—and then plunged deep into the T.O.'s carapace, seeking not to grasp, but to tear, to rip.

Larry screamed as the control rig shot pain-reflex shocks through his body. The electric charge was not enough to hurt, but Larry was not just in his own body anymore. He was in the T.O., and his chest had just been ripped open. The pain was real, in the place where all pain was real, in the mind, in the soul. He imagined his heart sagging out of his chest wall, shattered ribs hanging at obscene angles. His left leg buckled as a control circuit shorted. He swung out with his right arm, desperately trying to defend himself—but that razor-sharp claw sliced his arm off at the elbow.

Larry screamed again at the pain shock as his arm spun away. Real and imagined, seen through the soul and the TV cameras, he saw his arm shorting and sparking, spewing imaginary bright red blood from hydraulic lines. He saw hallucinated, bleeding flesh visible under the shattered metallic skin. And then another cruel slash, and Larry screamed in a voice that choked off as his head was hacked away from the teleoperator's body. The

T.O.'s vision switched automatically to the chest cameras. Dead eyes that still could see watched in mindless terror as the T.O.'s head smashed to the littered, filthy ground and the little scavengers began to pick over the teleoperator's corpse.

They pulled Larry, screaming, from the control rig and put him under with the heaviest anesthetic they could find. While he slept, the technicians discovered that the induction taps, abandoned on the ground, were working, pulling in massive amounts of data. The analysts understood none of it at first, but they rushed to beam it all toward the *Saint Anthony*, and to Earth.

Time passed, and the rover-laborer brought its prize inside the Caller, to a place where it might be examined more thoroughly. Even in the first moments of study, the Caller was startled, indeed astounded by what its rovers had found. This airless satellite was not a world where organic life should have been found. It was baffled by the crude artificial carapace that this creature lived in. Clearly, the carapace could not keep the creature alive for very long at all.

But the Caller could not invest time or energy in examining its find. Not until it had pulled this chaotic star system into some sort of order.

Still, the Caller's kind were adept at analyzing new life-forms and then preserving them. They needed such skills, for in each biological component of the Charonian life cycles were bits and pieces from a hundred genetic heritages.

This new creature might well provide more such useful

*data. The Caller put a small subset of its consciousness
to work on the problem of placing this animal in suspended animation until such time as it could deal with
the problem. A day, a year, a generation or a millennium
from now, it could return to this puzzle at its leisure.*

Marcia MacDougal tossed the datacube to the floor of
her room and stared through the window at the Martian
night. A debacle. An absolute, bloody debacle. Lucian
Dreyfuss dead—or maybe worse, if her private fears were
true. No one had seen him die—and she had just gotten
through dissecting one of the Charonians. What might
they do to Lucian?

And Larry Chao, heavily sedated, had been packed
aboard the *Nenya* for transport back to Pluto, trucked off
like a sack of potatoes. There was not time to wait for
his recovery on the Moon. He would have to pull himself
together on the flight home.

A bloody disaster, completely needless. The induction
taps were functioning perfectly just lying on the floor of
the shaft, beaming their signals straight up, in ideal line-
of-sight conditions. They could have simply dropped the
probes down the shaft and accomplished every bit as
much.

But there *was* something worthwhile that could be
gleaned from the disaster. Her intuition told her that.
Somewhere in the transcripts, in the videotapes, the datatap recordings, there was an answer, an answer worth all
the struggle and fear and confusion.

That answer might not be enough by itself. But with
the data pouring out of the induction taps, with the clues
they were gathering here on Mars, maybe it would be
the last, key piece in the puzzle.

And she had to find it.

CHAPTER TWENTY

———————◇———————

Naked Purple Contact

THE ENGINES LIT. NO TEST FIRING THIS TIME, BUT IN earnest. At long last the *Terra Nova* was going places.

The massive ship shuddered, lurched forward, and blasted her way free. Forward, up, and out. The *Terra Nova*, too long a prisoner of Earth orbit, broke her shackles and reached for open space.

Dianne Steiger—*Captain* Dianne Steiger, she reminded herself—gloried in the massive, crushing acceleration. They were doing four gees already, and the *Terra Nova* could keep that up for hours. There was *power* here, incredible power just waiting to be translated into distance and speed.

Not that much of it was to be put to use just yet, of course. The *Terra Nova*'s engines needed a high-power throat clearing, but once that was complete, the flight plan called for a throttle-down to one-gee boost. Already Dianne could feel the acceleration easing off.

No one had established a system of nomenclature yet

for the Multisystem. How should so many new worlds be named? They needed a system of names that would prevent confusion.

The navigators simply referred to the nearby planet as Target One and left it at that. The trip to Target One would have barely warmed up a normal interplanetary ship's engines, never mind those of a starship. For a ship meant to cross trillions of kilometers, this little journey of a few million kilometers was nothing. They would be there in two days. Even that fast a trajectory would require only a half hour of one-gee thrust. Less with the initial four-gee boost factored in.

Pinned to her crash couch on the bridge, Dianne loved every moment of the rocket burn. All was going well.

She felt justified in having ordered the rush launch of the ship. Getting away was the main thing. No matter if some of the crew and their gear had been piled on at the last moment. They were moving, before the weirdnesses of the enemy could stop them. On their way, before some utterly human bureaucratic snarl could be invented to delay them.

Already, there had been mutterings that sending an exploration ship might provoke the builders of the Multisystem. Dianne didn't want to give that argument time to gain strength. Better to chance a shipboard glitch and launch now.

She was playing a risky game—but to her, the *Terra Nova* was a known factor. She knew how far she could push the big ship, what it could take, and what it couldn't. The unknown risks were the aliens and humans who might stand in the way. Better to get a jump on all of them, at a trivial risk to the ship, rather than giving them all time to stop the flight.

Officially they were boosting for the Sphere, but everyone knew perfectly well that was hogwash. They were going no further than the next planet inward. Dianne was prepared to press on from there if all was going well—but not in the direction of the Sphere. Not for a long time. She smiled with pleasure and watched her status boards, all of them glowing green.

On the next couch over, her second-in-command was not enjoying the ride nearly so much.

Gerald MacDougal, exobiologist, crossing space to a world presumably brimming with unknown life, wondered exactly why he had wanted so much to take this trip. At this precise moment, he could think of nothing but the groaning metal around him. He *knew* the ship could take this thrust, and ten times as much; knew that it was normal for load-bearing members to make a little noise now and then; but his fertile imagination could not be bothered with mere facts. In his mind's eye, he could see collapsing bulkheads.

He felt a touch of claustrophobia. Monitors and view-screens and graphic flight-path displays were all very well, but there weren't any real windows on the bridge. He felt himself to be in a cramped metal cave, a coffin in space, hurtling toward a needless doom. His thoughts turned to Marcia. He did not want to die, now or any-time, without seeing her first.

But even as that melodramatic idea flashed across his mind, another part of his mind knew that all was well, that the ship was performing as expected. And yet a third part of his mind was praying to God as hard as it ever had.

No sense in taking chances, he told himself.

The *Terra Nova* shut down her engines, and coursed through open space, toward a new world without a name.

The *Nenya* rushed away from the Moon, out away from the Sun, boosting toward the cold and dark of Pluto, toward the Ring of Charon, Tyrone Vespasian at the controls.

Dr. Simon Raphael sat in Larry Chao's cabin, watching the Moon grow smaller in the monitor and wondering what it was like to live through decapitation.

Dr. Raphael had never worn a teleoperator control rig himself, but the experts said that the better the rig, the more realism it provided—and the more traumatic the psychic effects of an accident to the teleoperator.

The rig Larry had been wearing was one of the best.

The boy shifted in his sedated sleep, moaned, and rolled over. His left hand flopped out of the bed and Raphael took it, held it. Somewhere in the midst of all Larry's terrors there might be some part of him that could sense a touch, and know it to be friendly, comforting.

Raphael looked over to the video monitor. He used the bedside control to cut away from the view of the Moon to a dynamic orbital schematic, an abstract collection of numbers and color graphics. But to Simon Raphael, there could be nothing more meaningful in the Universe. It was the *Saint Anthony*'s flight path, tracking its progress from the Moon to the Earthpoint black hole.

And Earthpoint was getting close.

The probe fell relentlessly, down toward the nightmare point where Earth had vanished, toward the strange throbbing blue flashes of light. Toward the place where huge and mysterious vehicles were materializing still, rushing out toward the surviving planets. Down toward the black hole, the wormhole that marked the spot where Earth had been.

All the latest data from Mars, from the Lunar Wheel induction taps, from all sources, had been radioed aboard the little armored craft. Whatever information the Solar

System had gathered concerning its invaders would be aboard, ready for transmission to Earth.

If Earth was still there.

But the *Saint Anthony* was incapable of worrying about that. All it knew was that it needed to arrive in precisely the right spot, a point mere meters across, at a moment timed with utterly compulsive precision. Miss the point, fail to move through in the nanosecond between a pseudo-asteroid arriving and the wormhole slamming shut again, and the *Saint Anthony* would be just another submicroscopic, infinitesimal part of the Earthpoint black hole.

The moment was coming closer. The *Saint Anthony* checked its alignment one last time.

The wormhole opened, precisely on time. The probe's cameras saw the event from close range, broadcast it back to the Moon, taped it for a hoped-for transmission to Earth.

A gee-point craft burst out of nowhere, leapt through the hole at terrifying speed, missing an impact with the *Saint Anthony* by a scant few hundred meters before flying off into the darkness beyond.

The hole was open.

The probe fell in.

Vortices of space, time, light, gravity, twisted and swirled around each other in ways that should not have been possible, knotting themselves about each other. The wormhole went through the probe, instead of the other way around. Time stopped, space stopped, and then each turned into the other and ran backwards. Gravity became negative, and the black glow from outside the wormhole was the stars absorbing photons, using them to fission helium into hydrogen. Time fell in knotted loops around the craft, chasing itself backwards, forwards, sideways—

And then it was over, and the *Saint Anthony* was through.

Chelated Noisemaker Extreme/Frank Barlow was responsible for keeping the Naked Purple Habitat in contact with the outside Universe. But now, Earth was the only comm target, and it was dead easy to track from here. But on the other hand, without its comsat network, Earth's own communications were sorely degraded.

Chelated's boss, Overshoe Maximum Noisemaker, was much troubled by the situation. After all, the Noisemakers were charged with keeping comm from getting too good or too bad. And therein lay the problem. Did the ease with which they could signal Earth mean comm was good and needed screwing up? Or did the damage to the space communications net represent bad comm that needed tender loving care? *And how many pinheads can dance on an angel?* Chelated/Frank asked himself sarcastically. He was tired of all the almost theological worrying over minor points.

He was tired of it all. Tired of his Purple name, tired of thinking in circles, tired of not being allowed to do his job properly. It was his name that was bugging him most of all. *Noisemaker* just meant communications worker. *Extreme* was a bit less neutral, a derisive comment on how seriously he took his job. But *Chelated*. He had known that in Purpspeak it meant overdetermined and overeager. But it was not until last night that he found out the hard way from a cruelly informative young woman that it had a sneering sexual connotation. And they had been calling him that for months!

The hell with it. The hell with all the rules. While the powers-that-be dithered, Frank felt himself free to do his job properly, free to use his gear to observe the strange *things* NaPurHab now shared a universe with. He spent much of his time with all sensors locked on the wormhole, watching the massive vehicles drop into it, bound for who knew where. Frank was fascinated by it. He sat, for hours at a time, transfixed, staring at the hole in space.

So he sat when the *Saint Anthony* came through from the other side.

Frank Barlow/Chelated Noisemaker Extreme stared in astonishment as powerful video and radio signals lit up comm screens that had been dark for weeks. It took a long moment to understand what he was seeing. And then his fingers were flying over the control panels, setting up to record everything.

The news from home poured in, and Frank watched in awe. He looked down and realized that his hand was on the intercom phone. His first and understandable reflex was to call his supervisor, Overshoe Maximum Noisemaker.

But what the hell would Overshoe do? Sit there and contemplate the proper response under the Naked Purple philosophy? Calculate how this development could best be turned to the benefit of the Pointless Cause? Hold a meeting of all the brothersandsisters?

No, he told himself. Frank felt a higher duty than to Overshoe. And besides, this was a message for Earth, not for the Purples.

He powered up his best antenna and focused it on Earth, tuned it to the main comm signal for JPL. The folks at JPL were the ones who should take this call.

The *Saint Anthony* was a robust piece of hardware. The trip through the hole had been rough—it probably would have killed a human being—and it did scramble a few systems. But the probe's builders had expected such problems, and built the *Anthony* to be able to bounce back.

The *Anthony* took a few seconds to sort itself out and restart its major systems. And then its video sensors began searching for the one sight that could answer the most questions.

It found what it was looking for, and recorded as many images as it could before the first signal-back period. It gathered the data it had collected and fired it all off down the hole on the tightest beam it could manage.

Larry opened his eyes, and found himself safe in bed, feeling far too heavy. "What's . . . what's going on?" he asked.

"You're on board the *Nenya*," a gentle voice told him. "We're flying you home to Pluto."

He looked to his side. Dr. Raphael was sitting next to him. Larry blinked once, twice, and looked around. He noticed a video screen in the corner of the room. It was showing a status display of some kind.

Raphael noticed what he was looking at. "It's the *Saint Anthony*," he said. "The probe just dropped through the hole a few seconds ago."

Larry sat up a bit more and looked again at the screen. All the display values were at zero. The largest frame on the screen was supposed to show the video from the probe—but it too was black. A knot formed in his stomach. The probe had already met whatever fate was reserved for it.

Another clock display showed the time since entering the black hole. Larry leaned forward, watching it, scarcely daring to breathe. One hundred twenty-eight seconds passed.

"Any second now," Raphael said.

And the screen scrambled and cleared.

To show a fuzzy, low-quality, long-range video frame. Of Earth. Unmistakably of Earth. The planet lived.

Tears sprang into Larry's eyes. Raphael turned to him, and the two men flung their arms about each other.

Earth. Earth was still there, surviving in a strange and frightful Universe. The homeworld lived, surrounded by peril.

But then, that had always been true.

Earth's radio astronomers should have been happy people: Earth's new sky was full of very bright radio sources.

The trouble was, none of the radio sources meant anything. As far as anyone could tell, every one of the worlds in the Multisystem was ringed by a set of close-orbiting radio emitters, immediately and confusingly tagged as "COREs." The COREs seemed to serve no other purpose than to jam any investigations of other radio sources in the system.

They had another problem—there weren't that many dishes left to work with, or radio astronomers left to work on them. As with most of astronomy, research in the radio frequencies had long ago moved off Earth.

A few ground-based dishes were still in operation on Earth, and there were a few ground-based scientists to work them. Those dishes were in use every moment, struggling to understand this brave and fearful new world of which Earth was suddenly a part. Most of them were targeted on the Dyson Sphere—and none on the Moon-point black hole.

They all missed the *Saint Anthony*'s signals, until NaPurHab clued them in.

When Chelated/Frank's call came in, Wolf Bernhardt

was, for what seemed the first time in weeks, sound asleep. His assistant ignored strict orders not to wake him for any reason, and yanked him from his cot the moment the first message came in. By the time Wolf arrived at JPL's main control room and sat down in front of his console, JPL's comm dishes had locked in on the *Saint Anthony* and queried it directly. The computers were pulling down the main body of data—everything the Solar System had learned about its invaders. Starting with the name, strange and cold. *The Charonians.* Wolf spoke the word to himself, as if it were a mantra against further danger. As if giving the enemy a name explained them, made them understandable and controllable.

The video monitors and text screens were scrolling off the most incredible data—asteroids attacking planets, a black hole taking Earth's place. Fantastic knowledge.

But Wolf Bernhardt—tired, disheveled, still not quite awake, was in no mood for wonderment. He focused on the question of answering back, and fast, before those coldly named Charonians could interfere. One data channel gave the instructions for responding—among other things, the data capacity and format for the laser transponder that would attempt a relay to the Solar System. Screens full of information came in. The Solar System was giving Earth all it knew—Earth had to return the compliment. But would they have the chance? The *Saint Anthony* could broadcast to Earth constantly on all sorts of frequencies—but could only send back toward the Solar System on one laser beam through the wormhole, for three seconds every 128 seconds.

The probe was sure to have a limited lifespan. Earth would have to get its highest priority information beamed back to the probe and *fast*.

He stared unseeingly at the display screens and slumped back in his chair. *Think. Clear your mind and concentrate.* A mug of coffee appeared unbidden at his elbow, and he muttered a distracted "thank you" to the unseen person who delivered it. He took a first thoughtful sip of the coffee, still not even really aware that it had been given to him.

All right, then. Assume the enemy was going to destroy the probe in the next five minutes, so that he would have only one chance to report on Earth's situation. What did the Solar System need to know first? Hell, that was obvious.

The Sphere. The Sphere was literally and figuratively at the center of all this. But explaining the situation would take time—and that would delay the first message. Second things first then. Just dump everything that they had, in whatever order they could, while drafting a proper message.

He pressed a key on his comm panel. "Todd, locate all the science summaries since the Big Jump and start transmitting them at the coordinates and frequencies listed on status page four. Send it priority two. I'll be sending a priority one in a few minutes."

He pulled a keyboard out and started to write. What was the first thing to say? "Earth," he began, "has survived. We have been captured and placed in a huge artificial multistar system dominated by a Dyson Sphere. Many deaths and injuries were caused by loss of space infrastructure and orbital destabilizations. Night sky from this location reveals few stars outside Multisystem, apparently due to shell of obscuring dust. Efforts to locate the Sun in the sky therefore not yet successful, Earth's location relative to Solar System unknown. Distance from Earth unknown, but, as observations from the Solar System never located this remarkable star system, we can base a distance estimate on how far away one would have to be *not* to detect the Multisystem. On that basis, range estimated to be at a minimum of several hundred light-years, with no upper limit. Perpetrators of Earth-theft unknown. Purpose of Earth-theft unknown. . . .''

Arrangements were not yet complete. The Sphere had not done all that needed doing to see after its new charge. The captured world was still exposed to some slight dangers, some unlikely hazards.

One of those dangers seemed to have been realized. An object, of fair size, had appeared through the wormhole link to the planet's old system. It was not unheard of for debris to fall through a wormhole, but this was an unusually large fragment, and falling straight toward the newly acquired world at some speed. Though there was no real danger, the Sphere never took unneeded chances.

Another world was near enough to divert one of its Shepherds to meet the danger. The Sphere contacted the nearby world's Keeper Ring and ordered the diversion. Almost immediately, a Shepherd swung out of its orbit and toward the intruder.

The Sphere noted another, larger object departing the vicinity of the new world, indeed headed for a close pass of the nearby planet that was providing the Shepherd.

But the large debris fragment was not on a collision course. If, somehow, the situation changed, then the planet's Shepherds could handle the problem. The Sphere directed its attention elsewhere, checking again on the far-off danger that threatened the Sphere.

Far off, yes. But slowly getting closer. Disaster was yet decades off. But every moment of that time would be needed in order to avert disaster.

Every moment. The Sphere sent yet another message-image to the new system's Caller, urging it on to greater speed.

The *Anthony*'s arrival was reported to the *Terra Nova* just as Dianne Steiger headed to her cabin for the evening. There was little the *Nova* could actually do, other than download the probe's data and distribute it to the science staff.

Captains were supposed to delegate authority. Dianne decided to let her subordinates handle that job for her.

Dianne Steiger slept best in zero gee, and now was a time when she *needed* that sleep. It had been a busy time, getting the *Nova* launched, and she was exhausted. She was asleep the moment she slid between the sheets.

Five seconds or five hours after she lay down, a buzzer sounded by her bedside and she snapped to sudden wakefulness. She fumbled for the unfamiliar controls, got the lights on, and found the intercom switch. "Steiger here."

"Ma'am, LeClerc here." A tiny viewscreen popped on, and showed LeClerc's earnest young face. "Sorry to disturb you, but this seemed important. We've got something on the radar plot board. One of the COREs just boosted for Earth."

Dianne blinked and sat bold upright. "Say again. Our fusion core did *what*?"

"Sorry ma'am. I meant one of the radio sources orbiting the Target One planet. One of the COREs. One just broke orbit and started heading toward Earth. Boosted at an incredible rate, thirty gees at least, and then shut down. Ah, stand by, computer's giving me a refined trajectory. Make that headed *close* to Earth. I read it now as intercepting that probe, the *Saint Anthony*. Here's the plot." LeClerc's face vanished, to be replaced by an orbital schematic.

Dianne peered at it and swore. "Oh, hell. The party's over. How long until intercept?"

"Forty-eight hours, four minutes. Though we still need to refine that a bit."

"How close a pass will we get with the CORE?"

"Won't come within ten thousand kilometers of us, according to the current track."

A stray thought popped into Dianne's head. "Wait a second. I ordered passive-only detection. How are you tracking the CORE at this range?"

"Hard *not* to track it, ma'am. These damn CORE things absolutely *glow* in radio frequencies. Bright enough that they seem to jam out all the natural radio sources."

"Very well. Make sure Earth knows what's happening, so they can use those forty-eight hours. Any theories on why the things didn't come after us?"

"No, ma'am. Unless maybe they're just waiting until we get closer."

"*That's* not very comforting. Thank you, LeClerc. You did right to wake me. Stay on top of it."

As if any human being could stay on top of what was going on in a place like the Multisystem.

Part Five

CHAPTER TWENTY-ONE

———— ◇ ————

Thought Chain

TYRONE VESPASIAN CARESSED THE *NENYA*'S CONTROLS. IT
had been too long since Vespasian had done anything but
watch others go into space. He was more than pleased
that he had convinced Daltry his piloting skills were
sharp, and that the Gravitics Research Station would have
use for his knowledge of the Earthpoint wormhole's behavior.

His face darkened. There was another, truer reason for
his flying off to Pluto. With Lucian gone, he had to get
off the Moon, run away from his pointless guilt, his sense
of loss.

He couldn't have done anything to prevent Lucian's
dying. But there should have been something. And by
piloting this craft, by tending to the still-weakened Larry
Chao, perhaps he was performing penance.

Larry. He was back there, in his cabin. There was a
boy who had seen more than his share.

And done more. One 25-year-old kid pushes one button, and the history of humanity is changed for all time.

He checked his gauges carefully, and made sure the *Nenya* was holding together. If these gravity geniuses didn't get back to Pluto, history might end altogether.

"So what's happened while I've been out?" Larry asked, his voice weak and thin.

"Quite a bit," Simon Raphael said, trying to hide his worry. The lad had been under sedation almost constantly for three days—but coming out of it this time, he seemed far more calm and rational than he had before. But even if he was recovered enough to sit up for a time, he was clearly not yet well. Though there was nothing physically wrong with Larry, his mind had suffered a cruel enough shock to weaken his body as well. His subconscious was responding, trying to recover from injuries he had never actually suffered.

Raphael spoke, pretending for Larry's sake that he did not notice anything wrong. "We're not really getting anything new. Just updates. One word we're getting from everywhere: the structures are going up. Eyewitness and video reports from Mars, the radar teams at Venus, Sunside overflight missions on Mercury. Observations of all Jupiter and Saturn's major satellites. They're all reporting the same thing—huge structures are rising on the equators of all the worlds.

"And more and more of both types—the gee-point asteroids and the faster gee points coming through the wormhole—are just placing themselves in parking orbits and waiting once they arrive at their target planet. What they're waiting for, I don't know. There also seems to be some sort of disturbances in the equatorial weather bands of Jupiter and Saturn, and there have been several sight-ings of asteroids entering Jupiter's atmosphere. God only knows how the Charonians are managing *that*, or what it means. Except that they can survive inside a gas giant. No one can figure out how the Charonians are staying alive on Mercury and Venus and Ganymede, either. The biologists say it's patently impossible—except the Charonians are doing it.

"The first gee-point asteroids have only just arrived at Uranus, and Neptune can expect visitors in a few days. Pluto's turn is coming if the trajectory projections hold up. The Moon still hasn't been touched, presumably because the Wheel lives there.

"The big structures are different shapes on each world, though I doubt that means anything. It matches the patterns at smaller scales. Every Lander has variants on the auxiliary creatures and machines that attend it, but they all do the same work. On Mars, the Charonian structures are pyramids. On others, massive cylinders, or enormous hemispherical domes."

"Things are moving toward a climax," Larry said. "The last of the Martian pyramids will be complete in a day or so. What happens then? What happens when enough of the big structures are complete on the other worlds?"

Raphael smiled. "Maybe *all* the orbiting gee-point objects crash, and use the big structures for target practice."

"Charming thought," Larry said. A few of the Landers had malfunctioned, crashing instead of landing gently. There was one confirmed crash on Venus, two at Ganymede and one impact on Mars, on the other side of the globe from Port Viking, just a few hours after the *Anthony* went through the wormhole. Thankfully, the Martian impacter was a small gee point, moving fairly slowly when it hit. It had punched a hell of a big hole in the surface, but had not caused any casualties or damage to inhabited areas. "The crashed Landers are the closest thing to good news we've had since the first commlink with Earth," Larry said. "They at least show the enemy is fallible. But times are bad when an asteroid crashing into a world is *good* news.

"The thing is, I get the feeling that the asteroid strikes should be telling me something," Larry went on. "Something important. But the gee points' parking themselves in orbit worries me most of all. That's a signal that the Charonians are ready for the next phase— whatever that next phase is."

Damn it, who or what *were* the Charonians? Who controlled that Sphere? And from where? "Sorry," Larry said. "My mind's wandering. There are too damn many questions." Larry thought of the recording of the shattered sphere Marcia MacDougal had picked up from the first tap on the Lunar Wheel. At least *that* was clear now—and yet still a mystery. "Can you call up the sphere image Marcia showed us?"

Raphael worked the controls on his notepack. The wallscreen cleared and showed a sullen red globe glowing in the darkness. And there was the burn-through, the twin sparks of fire leaping away from inside it and racing away.

Raphael set the holographic image to repeat, and brought up a series of images of the Dyson Sphere as relayed from Earth via the *Saint Anthony*.

"They're the same," Raphael said. "They *have* to be the same. They both display the same surface markings. As if someone had etched in lines of longitude and latitude. The patterns are identical."

"But the images of the Sphere relayed by the *Anthony* show nothing that suggests any such thing ever happened to it," Larry objected, staring at the two images.

"Perhaps the burn-through is on the other side of the

Sphere, on the hemisphere not visible from Earth." Raphael suggested.

"No, this Sphere, *Earth*'s Sphere, isn't wobbling or tumbling. It's very clearly under control," Larry said.

Raphael nodded. "You're right. But then what does the message-image of the shattered Sphere *mean*? Is it a premonition? A warning? What sort of enemy would be powerful enough to endanger a Dyson Sphere? An entity that can grab stars and planets, that can call upon the entire power output of a star. What could be powerful enough to dare attack that?"

Larry shrugged helplessly. "Why were there *two* stars inside the Dyson Sphere?" He shook his head. "A side issue. The physicists can worry about it later."

"They're all side issues," Raphael said, a bit heatedly. "Compared to figuring out the Charonians' next move, everything else is a side issue. Let's try to tackle the situation from another tack. Maybe there's some clue in *when* things happen, their order." He pulled out his notepack and called a chronology of events up onto the screen.

"Okay, but if the Charonians ignore human activity, so should we," Larry said. He took the notepack from Raphael and worked the controls for a moment. "Besides, we have no idea what they would chart as a major or minor event. Let's blank out the human events and just chart all the Charonian actions, no matter how trivial, against time." Larry set the system for graphic display on the wallscreen, a red dot against a white background for every single thing that happened.

Raphael looked up at the display and drew in his breath. From the moment Earth vanished until the time the Lunar Wheel received the first image of the shattered Sphere, the pace of events was leisurely at best. It was immediately *after* that image that things were thrown into a panicky rush and started to happen in frantic haste, all over the Solar System. The image of the shattered Sphere had stimulated the Wheel to action.

"To me, that pattern says the shattered Sphere image scared the merry hell out of the Wheel," Larry said. "So why should a picture of a Sphere scare it? What do we know about the Sphere, anyway?" He lay back in the bed.

Raphael took back the notepack, looked over the summaries. "Let me see. According to what we have from Earth, there are at least eight G-class stars around the Dyson Sphere, held in place by gravity control. Uncounted terrestrial-sized worlds around each star, perhaps ten or twenty around each."

"So what are those worlds to the Charonians?" Larry asked, staring at the ceiling. "Prisoners? Science experiments?"

A weird and chilling idea popped into Raphael's mind. "Or perhaps toys? Or pets? They're certainly being well cared for, if Earth is any example. None of us dared dream that Earth would have survived in such good shape."

Suddenly, Larry sat up again. "That's it. What they're doing is keeping Earth safe. *That's* the point. You've just reminded me of a dumb idea I tossed out a long time ago. Maybe they got the Earth out of the way before the rough stuff began *here in the Solar System*. Earth was being taken out of harm's way. Maybe the rough stuff is about to begin, here."

Raphael looked at Larry and felt fear sweat suddenly popping out of his forehead. "Suppose it's not the Earth they want—but the Solar System?" Raphael asked.

The *Nenya* roared through the darkness, accelerating toward Pluto, many dark days ahead.

✧ ✧ ✧

Gerald MacDougal bustled into the crowded wardroom of the *Terra Nova* and looked around. A dozen conversations were starting up between people who had never met before. *Like lunchtime on the first day of school,* he thought. A roomful of new people, a sense of things beginning, a chance for new adventure.

As he made his way through the line for his morning tea, he heard bits and snatches of conversation. There was only one topic this day: the *Saint Anthony*, bearing news from the Solar System.

And of Marcia. His wife's name on so many of the reports filled him with a special pride, and relief. He might well never see her again, though he was by no means resigned to that. At least he knew she was alive and kicking.

And she—they, all of them—had seen the enemy. Here Earth was, in the heart of the enemy's empire, and none of them had gotten within a hundred thousand kilometers of a Charonian of any sort.

He took his tea to an empty table, sat down and thought.

The Charonians, the *aliens*, had not offered up a single clue to their own nature, even as they flaunted their power with arrogant confidence, both here in the Multisystem, and back home. Time after time, in endless ways, they had demonstrated that they had no fear of humanity, and perhaps humans were quite literally beneath their notice. Perhaps beings that hunted planets paid life no mind, any more than a man who captured lions would even think to consider the lion's fleas.

Except that Earth, and Earth's life, was so well cared for. It occurred to Gerald that humanity, no, human *technology*, was the only thing harmed by the move to the Multisystem. Scarcely any nonsentient species would even notice the change. Solar constant, axial tilt, the tides, even—to a very close approximation—the length of the year, all had been duplicated. Satellites, spacecraft, communication and trade were all that suffered.

Life, then, was important to the Charonians, and they made great effort to protect it.

It was *intelligent* life they held in such contempt that they could ignore it. . . .

A chill ran through his soul, and he whispered a silent prayer.

But that thought, of intelligent life, had set something tickling at his memory. Something he sensed was of great importance. *Marcia.* Yes, she was part of it. Somewhere, back in the past. Something in graduate school, back on the Moon that no longer hung in Earth's sky.

Gerald leaned back in his chair and looked at the crowd, wondering what possible reason there could be for thinking of such things at a time like this.

But he ignored that voice of doubt, and let his mind journey where it might. His subconscious was trying to tell him something, remind him of some bit of knowledge that was not recorded on a datablock. A clue hidden in his own memory. The train of thought was delicate and elusive. If he struggled too hard to understand it, he might destroy it altogether. He let it drift and carry him where it might. School. The wardroom had reminded him of school days. A lecture, and Marcia had been sitting next to him, because he remembered talking with her about it. An idea that had excited him.

Which of his classes had it been? No, wait a second. He had been sitting in on *her* class. An engineering class, some wild theory the professor was spinning one day when she had covered all the planned material early.

But what was it?

Some wild idea in space construction. *Von* something.

Gerald sat bolt upright, and nearly sent himself sprawling in zero gee. *Von Neumann.* That was it.

Gerald's blood ran cold. *Von Neumann machines.* A

dozen pieces of the puzzle fell into place, and it was suddenly all clear to him. Horrifyingly clear.

They would need the answer back in the Solar System, and back on Earth. And now, *fast*, before that CORE could get any nearer to the *Saint Anthony*.

He scrambled out of his seat and headed for the comm center. It all made sense. He knew that he had got it right. But even so, he was more than half-hoping he had gotten it wrong.

Sondra Berghoff mumbled something in her sleep and turned over, so that her arm flopped over the edge of the cot. Marcia MacDougal, standing at the door, looked in and smiled.

Marcia herself had been working more hours than she should have, out at the Landing Zone One observation camp, trying to pull in just a few more facts. She was more than a bit tempted to take up residence on the couch in the opposite corner for a few hours. But not yet. Not quite yet. There was so much to know about the Charonians. Marcia was still tempted by the hope—or perhaps the illusion—that one more hour of study, of thought, would be rewarded with the big answer. No one had yet been able to pull it all together, put all the pieces in one jigsaw puzzle. Marcia MacDougal wanted to be the one who did.

Marcia and Sondra had taken over a research room at the library of Port Viking, determined to sift through the mountains of data dug up in the Solar System and on Earth. Unfortunately for Marcia's sense of order, Sondra had gotten there first.

Datablocks littered the floor. Printouts were stacked up everywhere. A playback unit was blaring out some bombastic piece of classical music Marcia did not recognize. Video images taken by Earthside astronomers and relayed by the *Saint Anthony* were up on half the screens. The other half showed images from various datataps placed on the invaders, from the lowliest of carrier bugs and scorpions up to the Lunar Wheel itself.

The datataps, damn them, were providing *torrents* of information. Unfortunately, none of it seemed to mean very much. Marcia guessed Sondra had staggered toward the cot after yet another marathon session, hoping that rest would bring the answer. If there could be an answer.

Marcia was not at all unhappy that Sondra was working alongside her. But, just now, she was glad to be alone with her own thoughts for the moment.

Sondra seemed to need light and noise to work—and to sleep. Not Marcia. She punched buttons on her console, shut down the music and most of the video screens. The room turned dark, quiet, full of shadows and silence. Marcia MacDougal liked things that way when she was working on a research problem.

Databanks, supercomputers, communications, reference service, comfortable chairs. No doubt about it: the facilities here were the best. Get assigned to the asteroid-invader problem, and you could have anything you wanted from the frightened Martian government.

Everything except enough sleep.

Marcia got up from her desk, stretched, and stumbled toward the door. Maybe a splash of water on her face would wake her up.

She pushed the door of the study open and squinted as the bright light of the corridor struck her eyes. She made her way down the silent halls to the washroom and wasted precious Martian water in the effort to wake herself up. She toweled off her face and stepped back out into the hall.

She stepped over to a large, ceiling-to-floor window just past the entrance to the library. The city was quiet, nd dark, and the dome was opacified, locking in as much of the day's warmth as possible to carry the city through the night. Marcia was disappointed. She had wanted to see the stars.

The stars. Good God, that was where her husband was now. *Gerald. Gerald, where are you?* They had thought themselves tragically sundered with a paltry few hundred million kilometers between them. Now the distance between them was literally unmeasurable.

What had that first signal said? She turned and walked back to the library. Marcia returned to her desk, shuffled through her papers, and found the first preliminary message from Earth. She studied it again, read the sad words. "Distance from Earth unknown . . . range estimated to be at a minimum of several hundred light years, with no upper limit." The Earth could be on the other side of the Milky Way—or in another galaxy altogether. She read on. "Perpetrators of Earth-theft unknown. Purpose of Earth-theft unknown. . . ."

She dropped the paper and sighed. This Wolf Bernhardt was not an optimistic reporter, to put it mildly. Well, at least he got the facts down in a clear fashion, and that was what counted.

Earth had survived. The people of Earth were alive—or at least most of them were. That was the *real* message, and the happiest possible report that could have been sent. They should all be grateful that Earth survived intact.

But had Gerald survived? Marcia closed her eyes and crumpled up the message slip. It seemed likely, but she had no way of knowing. Nor was there anything she could do about it. It was all but certain that she would never see him again, never hear his voice or touch his hand. Perhaps, one day, there would be a message—but even if the *Saint Anthony* survived long enough to do such service, all the billions of people on Earth and in the Solar System would be struggling to send word through the probe. It would be a long line to wait in. Besides, the probe might be destroyed at any moment by God only knew what. It might be a long time—or forever—before she could get or receive word.

Suddenly, a great feeling of peace settled over her. Gerald was all right. She found herself quite abruptly believing that, knowing it. Strange as it seemed, Earth was in very good hands, well cared for. Whoever had taken the planet had placed it in a carefully perfect orbit, reproduced its original tides and solar radiation to within three decimal places.

Marcia rubbed her tired eyes. Marcia had yet to rest since the first news from Earth had flashed across the Solar System. The first wave of hopeful excitement had faded long ago, to be replaced by utter bafflement. The new data from Earth merely confused the situation even more.

There was a noise from the other side of the room. Marcia looked up to see Sondra, rolling over in her sleep, caught inside a dream.

The screen dimmed, flared, cleared. Somehow Sondra was *watching* the display and *in* it at the same time, watching a readout of her own mind, watching the results of watching the readout, which were caused by the read-out.

Feedback. Her mind echoed, shifted places, split into two. Now half of her was Charonian, a scorpion robot. But no, a *real* scorpion, grown huge, its stinging tail swiveling toward her as the monster stepped through the fun-house mirror that was all that remained of the video screen—

Sondra groaned, raised her hands, rolled over—and fell off of the cot. Hitting the floor woke her, but just barely. She lay there, all but inert, for a long moment, before summoning the energy to move.

She looked up to see Marcia trying to hide a smile.

"Good morning, or evening, or whatever the hell it is," Sondra said in a growly voice.

"Dead of night, I think," Marcia said.

Sondra got up carefully, trying to unwrap the sheet that had tangled itself around her legs, feeling decidedly foolish. "Just like the bad old days in grad school," she said, mostly for the sake of something to say. "Pump the brain full of facts, stumble someplace to sleep, and then semireawaken to write the term paper. Should I go somewhere else to work?"

Marcia smiled. "No need. I'm stuck myself at the moment. You can't disturb thoughts that aren't happening. What have you got so far?"

Sondra smiled. Nice of Marcia to ask. But then Marcia *was* nice. Much nicer than Sondra would ever be—or would ever want to be. She went over to her own desk on the far side of the room, sat down at her terminal and picked up her notes. "Some extremely weird stuff," she said. "The exobiology labs came up with something big while you were out. Inside every one of the creatures they've examined, they've found not only Earth-type DNA, but *at least* three other incompatible, nonterrestrial genetic-coding systems. Which means the Charonians' ancestors—or at least the ancestors of whoever engineered them—visited Earth and stole samples of DNA, and did the same on *at least* three other life-bearing worlds." Sondra looked up at Marcia. "That scary enough for you?"

"Oh, yes," Marcia said, clearly too stunned by the words to say anything more.

Sondra couldn't blame her for being unsettled. It was no happy thought to realize the Charonians had used

Earth life as a genetic spare-parts bin. Knowing they were in some way related to Earth life somehow only made them more . . . *alien.* "It confirms something else, too," Sondra said. "The living Charonian creatures are clearly every bit as artificial as their robots. As if the designers of the living creatures and mechanical devices didn't make any distinction between life-form and machine, and combined some elements of both types into everything they made. Which might explain why the scorpion robots look like scorpions. They're patterned after some form of terrestrial arthropod." She tossed her notes down. "That's the big news here. What's new from the field?" she asked.

"We're getting a lot better at reading the Charonians' minds," Marcia said, leaning back in her chair and propping her feet up. "I've spent the day pulling together a lot of data on the thought processes of the Charonians. The datataps are collecting more information than we'll ever use. And we're getting terrific stuff from the Lunar Wheel taps.

"Unfortunately, Charonian minds make for pretty dull reading," Marcia said dryly. "It's almost all concrete imagery, direct visualization with almost no capacity for abstract thought, or reasoning by deduction or induction. Their thoughts are highly repetitive. A lot of what passes for thought seems to be 'playback' of another creature's experiences."

Sondra frowned. "How does that work?"

"Say a scorpion robot comes across a rock in its path," Marcia said. "It first calls up the memory of a previous encounter with a rock, to see how it handled the problem before. It then adapts the old thought-image to the existing circumstance, and works out the best route around the rock it currently faces. Then it broadcasts the results, and whoever runs into the rock next already knows how to deal with it. They can run through the whole process very quickly. The whole cycle of obstacle encounter, image call-up, image modification, and then reaction only takes milliseconds. The key is that all the Charonians are constantly broadcasting their own experiences and picking up transmissions from all the other Charonians in the vicinity. One creature can send out a query, and then receive a solution to its problem. If they're working it right, they ought to be able to store and transfer memories from one generation to the next.

"The only other thing I've managed to confirm is so obvious it's barely worth mentioning," Marcia said. "The bigger they are, the smarter they are, without any relation to machine versus animal or any other variable. Not really a hot news flash, is it? The carrier bugs are just drones," Marcia went on. "They can only be programmed to fetch and carry. The scorpion-level animals and robots are a bit more flexible. They're capable of receiving and handling more information, and of dealing with more varied situations—though not always successfully.

"The Lander creatures are smarter than the scorpion-level types—but not by so much as might be expected. I'd score them as being about as bright as cocker spaniels. I assume the Lunar Wheel is far above the Landers in intellect. Sort of a thought chain instead of a food chain.

"But I've got a theory I haven't really proved yet. Down on the lower levels, each creature or robot seems to receive its initial 'education' by means of a massive data download from the next level up on the thought chain. I've got a great tape of a Lander 'teaching' a batch of new scorpions by downloading subsets of its own information to the scorps."

"Wait a second." Sondra stood up. There was an answer in there somewhere, a big one. "You've been out in the field looking at the Charonians on Mars, and I've been here looking at what the Wheel and the Sphere have been doing. We haven't put the two halves together.'' Even as she spoke, Sondra suddenly saw it. The answer was staring them all in their faces! She forced herself to move forward in an orderly fashion, making sure all the links of the logic chain were there. "Before I dozed off, I was watching a transmission from the Wheel to a Lander. It could be interpreted as the Wheel 'teaching' the Lander a subset of *its* information. So how far up does it go?''

Marcia nodded, her face betraying slowly mounting excitement. "So scorps teach bugs. Landers teach scorps. The Wheel teaches the Landers. *But who teaches the Wheel?*'' she asked.

Sondra grinned in triumph. "Bingo.'' She *was* on the right track. That was the *real* question, the one all the others led towards. "It's *got* to be the Sphere, or whoever it is that runs the Sphere. They must be the ones who teach entities on the level of the Wheel.''

"Wait a second,'' Marcia said. "The reports from Earth show that the Moonpoint Ring thing orbiting Earth in the Multisystem is just like the Lunar Wheel inside the Moon in *our* system, except that the Earth's Moonpoint Ring isn't buried inside a satellite. It had no need for camouflage. But if the Moonpoint Ring is *new*, it will need teaching. The Sphere could be doing a memory download to the Moonpoint Ring *right now.*''

Sondra nodded eagerly. "I get it! If Earth could listen in, they might get some *real* answers. They'd hear from the real masters, the *real* Charonians who created all these nightmares.''

"Yes! My God, yes. We could tap right into their instructions to their machines.'' Marcia stood up, tried to think. They would have to transmit this idea to the Moon at once, have the *Saint Anthony*'s controllers radio instructions to the probe through the wormhole.

Marcia glanced at the wall clock, trying to figure how much time was left before they lost the *Anthony*. Just under thirty-six hours. There was time to send the message, if they started now. She was about to say that to Sondra.

But then the quakes started.

CHAPTER TWENTY-TWO

---------------◇---------------

The Ages of Life and Death

THE SPHERE HAD SENT ITS ORDERS, AND SPHERE ORDERS were something the Caller could not even conceive of resisting.

And the orders said that now was the time. The Caller ran a last check of all its far-scattered underlings. Not all, or even a majority, were ready for action. But many units were prepared, and the Sphere had placed the highest urgency on the Caller's task. Strange that a job that might take decades, or centuries, should have to be so rushed—but a century from now, the crisis would surely come, and survival might well depend on the hours, the minutes, the seconds saved now.

The Caller focused gravity beams of massive power and fired them at the worlds. The beams of gravity were infinitely more powerful than the ones fired by the Ring of Charon—and no effort had been made to render these beams harmless. Far from it.

The Caller sent the command coursing over the gravity

beams to all the completed installations, all across this star system. Along with the commands, embedded in the very gravity beams that sent the orders, it sent power as well. The Worldeaters sucked it all in, eager for more.

On Mars, on Venus and Mercury, on the Jovian and Saturnian satellites, the Worldeaters began to earn their names. The Worldeaters took the beams, formed them into gravity fields that did what nature never intended. Around each amalgam of Worldeaters, in whatever shape they formed, the planetary crust began to tear itself open, to heave itself up into the air. The Worldeaters themselves, deeply anchored into the planetary subsurfaces, clung tight, held on.

All but a few. Even Worldeaters could fail, and die. On Mars one failed, and another on Mercury, the huge beings torn up from their moorings, flung up into the sky by their own gravity beams, tumbling insanely across the sky until they crashed and died.

But their fellows strove on, ripping down into the subsurface rock. The debris was pulled in toward the artificial gravity sources that hovered, like so many children's balloons, over every cluster of Worldeaters. Now fully energized, the gee sources grabbed violently at anything below them that was not strongly secured. But matter pulled in by the gee sources did not accumulate around them. Second-stage gravity beams, wrenchingly manipulated by the Worldeaters, threw the debris up, out, directly away from the planet, accelerating it at incredible rates.

Within minutes, from every rocky or icy world inside Saturn's orbit, streams of pulverized planetary crust were fountaining up into space. The red stone of Mars, the ice of Ganymede, the acid-leached rock of Venus, and the Sun-scorched skin of Mercury were blasted up into free space, arcing out into clouds of dust that rapidly enveloped the planets.

Huge vortices, hurricanes and tornadoes of fantastic size, roared up from the surfaces of Jupiter and Saturn. The huge spin-storms stretched out from the gas giants, extending their reach far beyond the normal limits of the atmosphere, stretching themselves into bizarre tendrils of gas that arced and spiraled across the sky, releasing megatons of atmosphere into free orbit.

At Saturn, the gas jets slammed into the ring plane, disrupting orbits of the ring particles, knotting the gorgeous patterns of Saturn's diadem into chaos. The jets of atmospheric hydrogen and methane and complex hydrocarbons boiled up from inside the huge world to splash across space.

All across the Solar System, the stuff of worlds was thrown into orbit. The spaceside Worldeaters set to work, grabbing at the gas and dust and rubble, spreading gravity nets to gather it all up.

And it did not end. The jets, the rubble streams, the storms gathered force, tearing at the fabric of all the worlds. From Mercury to Saturn, the Worldeaters tore away, clawing the flesh from the planets.

The Solar System began to die.

The images streamed unendingly across the video screen. Towering pillars of flying stone and dust and ice and gas surging up into the skies of Mars, Mercury, Venus, Ganymede, Titan, Tethys. Monstrous spin-storms arcing up into orbital velocity from Jupiter and Saturn. The Landers were attacking.

Endless as the terror seemed, yet the end was coming. One by one, the commlinks to the other worlds were dying as clouds of ionized dust jammed radio and laser signals.

Larry sat before the *Nenya*'s comm station and shook

his head, watching the signals come through. How could humans stand against all this? How could the Charonians be stopped, when no one even understood what they were doing? Larry found himself breathing hard, fear and exhaustion overtaking him. He forced himself to lean back, eyes closed, and relax. He felt the tension ease out of him, at least for a moment. Better. Better.

"We've lost contact with Mars again," Raphael was saying, his voice quiet and somber. "The ionized dust is jamming out radio and laser. The Lunar comm stations are sending to all the planets and listening on every alternate frequency they can think of, but there's no way of knowing if Mars can hear us, or if they're sending on some frequency we haven't tried. And the *Saint Anthony* has got problems. Earth warned us there was some sort of Charonian spacecraft or robot or something homing in on it."

"We won't have the probe too much longer," Vespasian said, with a hint of sadness.

Dr. Raphael remembered how much pride Vespasian had taken in naming the probe, how attached to it he felt. "Good Saint Anthony has already done the most important job," Raphael said in as comforting a voice as he could manage. "He found Earth for us again. That should be some comfort if all else is lost."

The skies were full of fire.

Marcia looked up into the Martian night, to where the stars had been replaced by terror. To the southeast, the closest jet of matter was being blasted into space. It was a glowing pillar of flame, air friction, ionization effects, electrical discharges, and whatever strange side effects the Charonian gravity beam caused, all combining to set the matter jet flickering and shimmering with power. Out on the surface, there was a constant splashing of dust jets as random bits of debris fell back from the central matter jet and slammed into the ground. Pieces of debris, some of them boulder-size or larger, were also falling in the city.

The sky itself was glowing, sheets and plumes of dust and rubble streaming off the matter jets, spreading across space, far out enough to be free of the planet's shadow, free to catch the glow of the hidden Sun. Another dust storm suddenly snapped into being, ruddy sands swept up into the lower atmosphere by the chaos to the south, shrouding the world in blood.

"Do you honestly think they mean us no *harm*?" Marcia whispered to herself, remembering Larry's question, the memory of his recorded voice echoing in her mind. He had asked that of Raphael, somewhere in the hours and hours of records that she had played back. But the horrifying answer to the question was that they had no intentions at all toward humans. Nothing so small and insignificant ever entered into the Charonians' calculations. Marcia had a sudden strange image of herself as a microbe looking up from its glass slide, suddenly realizing the cleaning solution is about to splash down, cascading down onto her world, wiping her away, clearing her away to make room for something new.

She glanced back toward the research library, where Sondra worked the communications console, desperately searching the radio spectrum for any word from anywhere.

But there was nothing to hear. All contact with the outside universe had been lost. Never, in all her life, had all the lines been so utterly cut. The lines to Earth, to her husband, to her work at VISOR, to her whole life. All of it was gone.

So what happened now? she wondered.

There was a new series of flashing explosions in the

southern sky. Marcia looked out the windows, past the terrible sights plain to the eye. She tried to see the future, the days still coming. Even Port Viking could not hold together if these storms continued. The dome had taken a year's worth of punctures in the last day. The air would leak out. Power would fail as the dust blew in, as the Charonian onslaught smashed equipment and threw it into the sky. The Charonians would work their will. Humanity would be wiped clean off Mars.

And then the same on all the other worlds of the Solar System. That would be the end of the human future in the Solar System. And then . . . her throat choked up, and she began to cry, watching the flaming sky through tear-fogged eyes.

And then, the rest was silence.

Sondra awoke slumped over the comm console. She must have dozed off there. There was a beeping noise coming from somewhere. She blinked, still half-asleep, and looked around. There was Marcia, collapsed on one of the couches. But what the hell was that beeping? Suddenly she realized it was coming from the comm system. The status board was flashing a message. "COMM CHANNEL CLEAR, TEXT MESSAGE INCOMING FROM LUNAR TRANSMITTER," it read.

Sondra snapped awake. The jamming had cleared, at least for the moment. The signal's status-coding sideband showed that the incoming message had been repeating for over an hour.

Wait a second. If one signal could get in, then another could get out. They had written up a long text message the night before, asking for a tap on the Moonpoint Ring, and had prepared it for transmission. Now Sondra reached for the controls and sent it off toward the Moon, setting it to repeat over and over again. With luck, their idea on tapping the Moonpoint Ring in the Multisystem would still get through in time.

But what about the incoming message? She punched a few keys and it began scrolling across the screen, too fast for her to catch more than a word or two of it. But that was enough.

"Oh my God," she said. She jumped up and rushed to the couch. "Marcia! Marcia! My God, Marcia. Wake up." She grabbed Marcia by the shoulder and shook her hard. "Your husband, Marcia."

Marcia opened her eyes and sat bolt upright. "My husband? Gerald? What about him?"

"We're getting a message from him," Sondra said. "Some kind of technical report he wrote and relayed through the *Saint Anthony*. It's coming in now."

But Marcia was already seating herself at the comm unit, printing out a hard copy. She grabbed the first page as it scrolled from the printer. "Oh sweet Jesus, he is *alive*!" she said. "He's okay."

Sondra stepped back a bit, unwilling to intrude on such a private moment. She watched Marcia as she eagerly read through the pages. *What was it like to love someone that much?* Sondra wondered.

"It's a tech report," Marcia said. "Very official. But he managed to work in that he had read our reports on the Landers." She looked up at Sondra and her eyes were shining. "That's for *me*. He's telling me that he knows I'm alive." She kept reading, her eyes running eagerly down the page.

But then Marcia's expression changed, turned to something other than delight. To shock, and surprise. She let her hands drop, still holding the papers. "He's figured it out," she said at last, her voice small and still. "Or at least a big part of it. At least he's got a theory."

"Figured out what?" Sondra asked. "A theory about what?"

"About what the Charonians are," she said. "They're von Neumanns. That's *it*. That's got to be it."

"That's what?"

"The answer, the explanation. The key to it all. Not all by itself, but it's a start." Marcia stood up, still holding the pages of the message, and stared off into space, carefully thinking it all out. "It makes sense," she said. "They've *got* to be von Neumanns."

"Will you please quit saying 'von Neumanns' and explain what they are?" Sondra demanded.

"It's very simple," Marcia said. "How did we miss it? A von Neumann machine is any device that can exactly duplicate itself out of locally available raw materials. A toaster that could not only toast bread but build more toasters out of things found in the kitchen would be a von Neumann toaster. It's a very old concept, named for the scientist who dreamed it up.

"But von Neumann's *real* idea was to build a von Neumann starship," Marcia said. "A robot explorer that could fly from one star system to another, explore the system—and then duplicate itself a few dozen times, maybe mining asteroids for materials. It would send out new von Neumanns, duplicates of itself, from there. Then each new exploration robot would travel on to a nearby star, duplicate *it*self, and start the cycle again. Each machine would report back to the home planet on what it found. Even given a fairly slow transit speed between stars, you could explore a huge volume of space in just a few hundred years. Traveling, exploring, reproducing, over and over again."

"Wait a second," Sondra protested. "The Charonians haven't done any of those things. They're not travelers, and they're not explorers, and they aren't reproducing—"

"Oh yes, they are," Marcia said. "Remember, the labs found three different alien genetic codes in their genes? Maybe *these* Charonians haven't gone anywhere, but that means they and their ancestors have been to *at least* three other star systems that had life. Finding them all would take a lot of traveling and exploring. And look how many of them there are—they've certainly done some reproducing!"

Sondra sat down at the comm console and thought about it. "Okay, okay. I can see that. But that's not the whole story. There has to be something more. It doesn't quite fit. Why is the Wheel hidden in the Moon? What were the Landers doing riding around in asteroids all this time? And how does stealing Earth and attacking the planets fit in? Wait a second. Old starship ideas. That reminds me of something else. Another old idea."

She thought about it for a moment. At last she remembered. "Seedships. That's it. It was a starship concept intended more for colonizing planets than for exploration. The logic was that a life-support system would be the biggest, heaviest part of a spacecraft—so you eliminate it. Instead, you freeze down a bunch of genetically perfect embryos, or fertilized eggs—or just sperm and ova. Maybe not just of the intelligent life-form, but the local equivalent of dogs and pigs and cats and chickens, or maybe *Tyrannosaurus rex*, if that suits your fancy. Any life-forms that might be handy at the other end. You pack them all up and launch them off.

"When the seedship finds a habitable planet, it lands, thaws out the embryos, and decants them. Then the ship—or its robots, or whatever—educates the kids as they grow. *It* raises the first generation of settlers. And if your designers were good enough, the ship could be programmed to do gene engineering, modify that first generation to survive better on whatever sort of world they end up on. Directed evolution."

"But that doesn't have anything to do with what's happened here, either." Marcia protested.

"No. But suppose you *combined* the ideas," Sondra said. "Suppose you decided to build a *von Neumann seedship*. A seedship that knew how to do genetic tinkering, not only on gene codes from its homeworld, but smart enough to analyze other codes as well and use whatever was useful in them. Like Earth-style DNA. A machine that could duplicate itself, a machine programmed to duplicate itself and to send new seeds out among the stars, spreading out in all directions. A machine that was capable of modifying, improving itself, and modifying the life-forms it carried. Mining not asteroids, but living worlds, like Earth. Not just mining metal and fuel as raw materials, but *life itself*."

Marcia nodded. "I can see that. But the present-day Charonians aren't like that. Seedships like the ones you've described wouldn't have a reason to hide in asteroids."

"Maybe they do, and we don't know what it is," Sondra said. "Maybe they've just been in a dormant phase for a while and the gravity-wave beam woke them up." But then she frowned and shook her head. "Wait a second. Their use of gravity waves and wormholes. We haven't accounted for that."

"So let's go back a bit," Marcia said. "Let's talk about earlier stages in their development. Not the way the Charonians are now, but an intermediate stage between the way they were first made and the way they are now. Millions, tens or hundreds of millions of years ago." She thought for a second. "Suppose, way back when, the Charonians were von Neumann seedships. Suppose a few things went wrong—at least from the viewpoint of the original designers. Suppose the ships just evolved off in an unexpected direction?"

Marcia put the message sheets down on the comm unit and walked back to sit on the couch she had been sleeping on. "The plan when the first ship was sent out was to spread life, and the duplication of the ships and so on was subordinate to spreading life. Then that point got lost, or changed. After all, it's the machines doing all the work. Suppose the machines decided it was more important that *they* be duplicated—and then subordinated spreading *life* to spreading *machines*?

"Suppose the ships started modifying their *passengers*, started breeding them so they were genetically driven to build more seedships?" Marcia asked. "They could hardwire building skills into the passengers, so that building new seedships becomes an instinct, a primal need. Maybe they start cutting and pasting DNA, or whatever they use instead of DNA. Take some *T. rex* genes, some dog and cow genes, combine them with the intelligent life-form's genome. They land on a new world full of life and find some handy codings there. They cut and paste those in, too."

"Wait a second," Sondra protested. "No human would let a machine loose to modify human DNA."

"*We* wouldn't. *Humans* wouldn't do it, no. The very idea is repellant to us. But we're not talking humans here. Suppose there were aliens with no taboos against such things? The idea disgusts me too, but imagine how fast things could change, how dramatically a species *could* evolve, if such things were permitted.

"They kept evolving," Marcia went on. "The machines modifying themselves, the organic forms breeding themselves, machines tinkering with their own programming, and modifying the descendants of the organic Charonian passengers and their worker-animals. The seedships developed machines that worked with special-bred animals, and bred animals that *needed* mechanical implants, that couldn't survive without them. Until the line between living and machine was completely blurred, until the Charonians didn't even bother with the distinction anymore, until there was no clear line anymore between the Charonians, their machines, and their worker-animals. They all merged into one hugely complex entity. All the forms rely on each other to survive. Call it a multispecies."

"Okay, good," Sondra said. "But the ships were still the key. The seedships become the dominant form of the Charonians," Sondra said. "They didn't need organic-style intelligence to tell them what to do anymore. Somewhere along the line, the original Charonians lost out. That *must* be true, because they're not there anymore. After all, it had to be living, sentient creatures who built the first ships."

"It makes sense," Marcia said. "I doubt we have it precisely right, but if we accept the idea that the Charonians of today started out as von Neumann seedships, built by creatures something like us, then they've certainly changed, mutated along the way to get to be what they are now. But that wasn't the end of their development. We haven't explained the Lunar Wheel, or the Multisystem. How do they fit in?"

Sondra scratched her head. "Let's take a pass at it from another direction. Let's think of their biology, their technology, the ages that went by in a breeding cycle. The ages of their lives and deaths. A ship with a computer full of machine blueprints and a hold full of dormant animals or dormant embryos would launch from a system, and drift between the stars for centuries, maybe for tens or hundreds of thousands of years, until it found a star system with a life-bearing world. Maybe the ship would pass the time during the flight by tinkering with the genes of the animals and blueprints of the machines. Finally the ship would land, and if need be, it would genetically modify its animals once again so they could survive on the new world.

"The animals—some of them descended from the

ship's designers—would go out into the world, breed as fast as they could, while mining that planet for raw materials and building more ships—perhaps thousands of ships, or millions. The shipbuilding would be like everything else—a reflex action, a complex instinct.

"The new ships would take their passengers aboard and launch out into space, out to search for new worlds. Maybe one ship in a thousand, one in a million, would manage to cross the sky, reach a new star and survive to reproduce, but that would be enough for the whole cycle to repeat, over and over again."

Marcia looked up. "But that's so inefficient," she objected. "Breeding-planets would be light-years, dozens or hundreds of light-years apart. And they would chew up any life-bearing worlds they used. Look what they're doing to Mars, outside that window, right now. If their ancestors were even half that size, the planetside breeding binges needed to stock a new generation of seedships would do tremendous damage to an ecosystem."

"You're right. They'd eat everything in sight," Sondra agreed. "None of the native animals would be able to find food. The Charonians would wreck everything, trying to breed as heavily as possible. And they'd be doing their mining and their shipbuilding at the same time. It'd be a hundred times worse than the way we polluted Earth. And look at the damage *we* did before we knew better. But it wouldn't be a problem for the Charonians. They'd be leaving. They wouldn't care about the mess they left behind." Her eyes suddenly grew wide. "Jesus," she said. "We're talking about stuff that happened millions of years ago, and we know from the DNA they found in the carrier-bug that the Charonians landed on Earth sometime in the distant past. Do you think maybe the Charonians landed on Earth and wiped out the dinosaurs?"

Marcia blinked in surprise. "It could be. It's been

pretty well nailed down that the dinosaurs were killed by an asteroid impact where Iceland is now. But if a Lander seedship malfunctioned and crashed, it would be just like a *real* asteroid crashing. Maybe two Lander seedships were traveling together. One crashed, and the other survived to breed. The impact killed most of the dinosaurs, and the breeding binge afterwards was more than the survivors could take.''

Marcia rubbed her eyes and tried to think. ''But getting back to the point at hand,'' Marcia said, turning the conversation back, ''the breeding binges were basically parasitic, sucking the life out of a world. That would not only deplete the animal and plant populations, it would wreck the ecosystem. But the Charonians *would* care about that. Life-bearing planets must be very rare. Some future seedship would need that world again for some future breeding binge. And mass extinctions would wipe out the genetic diversity the Charonians needed as raw material for their bioengineering.''

Marcia paused for a moment, staring into space. ''And we're forgetting gravity again. We're forgetting that somewhere along the line the Charonians learned how to manipulate gravity. How does *that* fit? Maybe the original Charonians knew how and taught the first seedship. Maybe a seedship landed on a planet and conquered a species that knew how. But somehow they learned how to use wormholes, how to use black holes as a power source.''

Sondra thought for a long moment. ''And that was *important*. Without it, they couldn't have become what they are. They use gravity control for everything. It had to be a turning point. Maybe they were short of life-bearing planets, but in every other way, they were rich. They had all of space and time to work with, endless rock and metal and volatiles in free space. All that was holding them back was the planet shortage.''

She paused for a long moment. Suddenly she slapped her palm down on the comm console. "So they decided to do something about the planet shortage. That's it. That's *got* to be it, the last piece in the puzzle. Once they had gravity control, they had power, incredible power. So they built the Sphere, the Multisystem, and stocked it with stars and planets. And now I think we know why." Sondra looked at Marcia, let her come to the same answer she had found, if for no other reason than to convince herself she wasn't crazy.

Marcia's face went pale. "It's a *nature* preserve," she said. "The Charonians built the Dyson Sphere, the Multisystem, as a nature preserve for wild planets, as a place for planets to heal between breeding binges, a central storage place where the seedships could always find breeding planets.

"But don't forget the Charonians would still be deliberately modifying themselves, directing their own evolution," Marcia said. "How far would that go? How far could it go? Suppose the Sphere *became* the Charonians, the ruling intellect. Suppose the Sphere took over from the seedships, just as the seedships had taken over control from the original, organic intelligent life-form. If the Dyson Sphere took over, it would design a new life cycle, using the ancient patterns in a new way. It was built to store the life-bearing worlds of the Multisystem, for the convenience of the seedships. But if it started working for itself, for its own purposes, it would change that, take control of the life cycle and breed any independent streak out of the seedships. Which means the first, biological Charonians and the second, seedship Charonians are both extinct. So neither of those types are in charge."

"It's the Sphere," Sondra said, almost whispering. "The Sphere itself is running things. We've been wondering who's been running *it*, when all the time it's been running *everything*."

"Hold it a second," Marcia said. She got up and sat next to Sondra at the comm unit. She grabbed a pencil and a sheet of paper and started taking notes. "So we've got a Dyson Sphere using its stock of breeding worlds to grow new forms. It puts them aboard seedships—though now it's only one creature to a seedship, because the creatures are so big. The seedships go out, just as they always have. They find a world, use it for breeding stock, and then what?"

"That's where the change comes," Sondra said, grabbing a keyboard to make her own notes on the computer. Maybe Marcia could think with a pencil, but she needed a set of keys. "They launch themselves off the planet after they've chewed it up, but instead of scattering amid the stars, the mutated seedships—the things we've been calling Landers and gee-point asteroids—go into hibernation in deep space, and wait. One of them grows into something like the Lunar Wheel. Once it's matured, it sends a message that all is in readiness and waits for a return signal from the home Sphere that sent it out in the first place. A return signal is simply any sort of modulated gravity beam. The signal Larry sent by accident."

"But what's the signal supposed to mean?" Marcia asked.

"It's the Sphere saying 'I'm ready for a new world,' " Sondra said excitedly. "Maybe because it's caught a new star and has more room for worlds."

Marcia nodded. "Okay, so that explains why they stole the Earth, and why they're taking such good care of it. But why are they mining the other worlds here?"

Sondra considered that for a moment. *Try to think like the Dyson Sphere,* she thought. *What would be important to the Sphere?* And then it hit her. Sondra's heart started pounding in her chest, and her palms went damp with sweat. "Think for a second," she said. "The original Charonians built the seedships to carry their offspring to

new worlds, to make new Charonians. Then the seedships took power for themselves, and decided the important thing was to make more seedships, spread *them*selves
out among the stars.

"And then the seedships built a Dyson Sphere, and *it*
took over, and it decided . . ."

The two women were deadly silent as the thought sunk
in. "The Dyson Sphere decided the important thing was
to make more Dyson Spheres," Sondra said at last. "So,
millions of years ago, it modified the seedships' programs one more time, played with the gene pool one
more time. To make all the other forms into part of a
Sphere-reproduction system. And what the hell did we
think Dyson Spheres were made *out* of?"

Marcia shook her head numbly. "My sweet God. And
we were rushing to save *Earth*. It's every other world in
the Solar System that's in trouble."

"*Planets,*" Sondra said, not hearing Marcia. "You
make them out of disassembled *planets.*"

Marcia spoke very quietly. "That's what the Landers
are doing. Now that they've got Earth out of harm's way,
they're taking the Solar System apart to build a new Dyson Sphere. They'll shred the planets, the moons, the
asteroids down to *nothing*, take them apart and use that
material as raw material to build a shell around the Sun.
They'll start up a new Multisystem here."

Sondra stared blankly at the computer screen for a long
moment and then came back to herself. "We have to tell
them," she said. "Before the dust clouds thicken again
and all the radio wavelengths are jammed. We have to
get the word out." She started typing furiously.

But Marcia wasn't paying attention. She stood up and
returned to the window, back to the sky full of fire. Out
there, the Landers were tearing Mars apart, blasting its
stones and sand up into the sky. Now she understood.
But would understanding do any good? They were as far

as ever from being able to stop it, from being able to do anything about it. Mars was still being torn to shreds.

It wasn't fair. She did not want to die like this. Not alone. "Oh, Gerald," she said to the sky. "Gerald my love." He was alive, and he had reached out across unimaginable distances, sent his words to her. That should have been some comfort, some solace.

But it was not. Instead anger flared inside her.

Gerald lived. How could she die, when she suddenly had a new reason to live?

CHAPTER TWENTY-THREE

---◇---

Reality Check

THE THREE MEN ABOARD THE *NENYA* SAT IN THE SHIP'S wardroom, reading printouts of the messages from the *Terra Nova* and Mars.

Larry shook his head. "I *knew* the Lander crashes on Mars should have told me something. This part here, about the possibility of a Lander crashing on Earth to wipe out the dinosaurs. *That* was it. That was what was in the back of my mind. I should have seen that." Larry continued reading.

At last they were all finished examining the new information. Raphael put down his copy and turned to the others. There was a deadly silence in the compartment. Raphael looked at Larry and Vespasian, and spoke. "If Sondra and Marcia's theories are anywhere near right— and I think they are—then the Solar System is doomed. The Charonian Landers will tear every world apart."

"There must to be a way to stop them," Larry said.

"The Core Cracker," Vespasian said.

"What?" Larry said.

"The big bomb, the *really* big bomb the Belt Community was supposed to build," Vespasian said. "We still have contact with Ceres. We could send a message to the Autocrat. Way back when, they were going to blow up Mercury with it, give themselves a bigger and better asteroid belt to mine. If we could get it, get it here, we could smash the Moon with it. That kills the Lunar Wheel. With the Lunar Wheel gone, the rest of the Charonians would shut themselves down, and the rest of the Solar System would be saved."

Raphael found himself nodding, considering the possibility, and that made his blood run cold. Only weeks ago, someone's using a Core Cracker on the Moon would have been the greatest disaster imaginable, something to be prevented at all costs. But Chancellor Daltry had warned that there was always a worse fate possible. Now a man who lived on the Moon was suggesting the destruction of the Moon, and of all the human life on it, as a *solution*, something better than the alternative. "It's a terrible price to pay, Tyrone. But you might be right."

"No," Larry said. "We can't. We can't kill that many people and dream of justifying it. Especially when there's no promise that it would work. If I were programming the Charonians, I'd set the gee points and Landers to keep working if they lost contact with the Wheel. It's fairly clear that the Wheel pulls gravity power in from the Earthpoint black hole and transmits it to the gee points, but there *must* be some sort of backup system. I'd bet the Dyson Sphere could send commands and power directly through the wormhole and run the show that way.

"Besides, even if the plan worked, we'd have lost the last contact with Earth—and sooner or later, unless we learn how to prevent it, Earth is going to be used for a breeding binge. That will cost more lives than we could save by destroying the Moon. And we don't even know if the Core Cracker exists, or if the Autocrat would agree to release it even if it did.''

''Can we sabotage the Wheel, wreck it without smashing the Moon?'' Vespasian asked. ''Maybe just a small nuclear warhead dropped down the Rabbit Hole?''

Larry shook his head. ''No. Nearly all the same arguments apply. There must be backup procedures, some way for the Dyson Sphere to regain control if the Wheel fails. And even if we succeed, and shut down the gee points and the link to the Dyson Sphere, we lose any hope of ever contacting Earth again, ever helping them.''

''Then is there any way to seize control of the Wheel?'' Vespasian asked. ''Go down there again, rewire it somehow, make it do what we want it to do. Use it to order the gee points to knock it off.''

Larry shook his head, but there was something less negative about the way he did it, as if he saw a possibility. ''We don't know the codes. Even if we did, I still don't see how we could use them. We'd have to use the same signaling procedure the Sphere uses, and use stronger signals. That wouldn't be any problem on the radio bands, but now we know they used modulated gravity waves for signaling as well, beaming both through the wormhole. We could fire up the Ring of Charon again and use it to send another signal. But we couldn't possibly send a stronger gravity-wave signal than the Sphere. Not unless we had our own—''

Larry stopped for a moment. Not just talking, but stopped, all of him, as if his mind were suddenly so busy with a thought that he couldn't spare any part of his mind for movement. ''My God. We've *learned* enough to do it. I *could*—''

His voice faded out, and he muttered to himself. ''Yes, it could be done.'' He turned to Raphael and Vespasian with a gleam of enthusiasm in his eye. ''Maybe we *could* take over the Wheel.'' Suddenly, his face fell. ''If we knew the codes.''

Vespasian's brow knitted for a moment, and then suddenly he snatched up one of the earlier reports from Mars. ''They saw it, on Mars!'' he said. ''The Wheel has got to be just like this Moonpoint Ring next to Earth, use the same command code.''

Larry grabbed the hard copy eagerly and skimmed the pages. ''My God, you're right. They call it the thought chain, each lower form trained by the form above it.'' He put down the pages and thought. ''It would work. If Earth could get a tap in place, we could listen in on the Dyson Sphere downloading data to the Moonpoint Ring. Has the Moon asked for the tap yet?''

Vespasian nodded. ''Yes. They reported making the request about an hour after Marcia and Sondra sent the idea. About five hours ago. They sent us a copy of the request.''

''But what if the Sphere has already sent the data we need?'' Raphael objected.

''Repetition,'' Larry said. ''That was the one cast-iron certainty we got out of that image of the shattered sphere. The Charonians use repetition for emphasis. The more important the idea is, the more often they'll repeat it. If Earth can get a tap in place, we have a real shot at reading the codes.''

Raphael looked up at the wall chronometer, counting down the hours and minutes of life left to the *Saint Anthony* and figuring in the time since the Moon had relayed Marcia's request for a tap. ''They won't have time. Even if Earth got the message immediately, that would only give them eighteen hours between receipt of signal and when the *Saint Anthony* is destroyed, thirteen hours from now. That's not time for Earth to prepare a launch from scratch, let alone build a probe.''

''Damn it,'' Larry said through clenched teeth. He

looked at Raphael. "If we don't get the data we need, it can't work."

"Wait a second," Vespasian said. "The Lunar comm center knew all that when they sent the request. There was something in the reports from Earth that a habitat had ended up orbiting the Moonpoint black hole, *inside* the Moonpoint Ring, close enough to run a tap if they knew how to build the receiver. So they requested that that habitat to do the tap. I've got our copy of the signal here somewhere." He worked the console controls again, calling up the file in question. The three men leaned close to the screen and read the signal.

Vespasian's wide face fell, collapsed utterly. "Oh, hell. Oh sweet and sour bloody hell. Why in God's own twisted name did it have to be *them*?"

Larry Chao and Simon Raphael didn't ask what the problem was. They could read that off the screen for themselves.

The only facility in position to try for a datatap, the only place they could get the information that might save the Solar System, just happened to be the Naked Purple Habitat.

Raphael suddenly felt old, infinitely old, old and defeated, as if nothing else could ever matter again. All his refound ability to understand, empathize, was suddenly gone. How could it be that the fate of everything was up to those lunatics? "Start praying, Tyrone," he said in a defeated old man's voice. "And pray to Saint Jude this time. This is clearly a job for him and not Anthony."

The request for a tap made quite a trip before arriving. From Mars to the Moon through the wormhole to the *Saint Anthony* to JPL to Chelated Noisemaker Extreme's comm board. But that was only the beginning of its jour-

ney. Next it had to survive passage through a meeting of
the Purple Deluxe.

Ohio did not enjoy Purple Deluxe meets. For starters,
tradition dictated that they be held in a compartment far
too small for the number of people present. Also by tradition, the ventilation system was turned off for the du-
ration of the meeting. Usually, that helped keep meetings
short, but the end of this one was not yet on the horizon.

Time was desperately short. Just in case the decision
came down as a "yes," Chelated Noisemaker Extreme
was already at work rigging up the datatap probe, as per
the plans sent from Mars along with the request. Ohio
himself found the whole situation a bit daunting. He
wasn't quite up to deciding the fate of Earth and the Solar
System.

But he had a more immediate problem. The meeting
was not going well. Which was another way of saying
Creamcheese Drone Deluxe was speaking.

Creamcheese had certainly earned the highly complimentary title *Drone*. No one had ever caught her doing
a lick of work. But *Creamcheese* meant sexy or attractive. Perhaps Cheese believed herself to be a highly attractive woman. Few others believed so, or ever would.
But Cheese was many other things. For starters, she
demonstrated that even the most complimentary Naked
Purple name could be applied ironically, and was likewise living proof that such irony could be completely lost
on a member of a group as linguistically sophisticated as
the Purps claimed to be. But Cheese had an ego and a
half, and no one had the nerve to tell her to try a different
name for a while.

She was one of the very few Purps who took the call
to get naked and purple literally, though she was certainly among the vast majority of Purps who should *never*
get naked, let alone purple. To be fair, Ohio allowed,
her appearance did evoke the shocked silence that was

the purpose of the original Naked Purple manifesto. And that was fitting, for Creamcheese was one of the most vigorous and doctrinaire defenders of the faith.

Tonight she was in rare form, shouting at the top of her lungs. There she stood in her nude, plum-colored, plum-shaped glory, fulminating away. "Let them all rot!" she cried. "The Earthers, the damned scoombas back in the Solar Area, *all* of 'em. They got *us* down into this scene with their gravity grinding. Why should we help *them* now? This here is the biggest chance we're ever gonna have of *reely* living the Purple ideal. All we have to do is what Purples are supposed to do. *Nothing*. Not one Grand Coulee Dam thing."

"But these here Charonians ain't no shade of Purple," Cold Breeze objected. The bickering between Breeze and Cheese had been going on for hours. "They doing everything *but* nothing. The Purple idea we got is to back off and let Nature do her thing, let entropy slide the Universe on down. Cheese, I have scanned a lotta blocks o' data, and these Charonians are no-way-José *natural*. Back home in the Solar System—sorry, I mean the Solar *Area*, they're putting the planets through a *buzz* saw. Ask me is *that* Mom Nature doing her bit, and I say *I* think not. I say we get the data for the groundhogs and the Solar dudes, let 'em try and stop the party."

"Oh, jump down off it, Cold," Cheese said. "These Charonians are *ultra*-Purple, glowing in dark down to their bones. You want the big mystery about what they're doing, *I'll* peek in the backathebook for ya. They're scraping the tech-know-log-ick-all crap offa the Earth. They're giving entropy a chance to kick back in, let Nature slump back down to blessed disorder. Lookit Earth. Their satellites are gone. The spaceships are nearly all gone. Practically all the habitats 'cept ours—gone, gone, gone. If we sit back long enough to make grooving behooving, do nothing long enough while the Charonians do a dance on the Earthers, them groundhogs will be back in mud huts and *still* going down! And once this Saint Android robot probe is creamed, there will be nothing we can do anyway. Back in the Solar, the Charonians are erasing all the tech yech there too. The Purple ideal. Surrender to Nature! My bristers and sibsters, *that's the tune we've been singing* since the first coat of purple got slapped on somebody's hide. Now Earth's dancing to the beat, the *Solar's* dancing to it, and Cold Breeze says shut down the playback because he's about to lose his fudge. No way.''

Ohio Template Windbag sat back in his frowsy old armchair and blinked a time or two. Strange. He found himself having to translate what they were all saying. It suddenly struck him that he was no longer thinking in Naked Purple terms, but once again in standard English. Maybe he has been hanging out in the comm center with Chelated/Frank too much. The pointless artificial complexities seemed strangely foreign to his ear. Where once it had all sounded clever, now all he heard was anger, and voices a bit louder than they needed to be. Was his subconscious trying to tell him something?

"How are you on murder, Cheese?" Cold Breeze asked. "Suppose everyone on the hab—including you—shuffles off the coil because we sat on back, followed your plan?"

Creamcheese Deluxe glared at him. "We all die, Coldness," she said contemptuously. "That's the whole point of calling our bristers and sibsters to the Pointless Cause. All striving is useless against entropy. The Heat Death of the Universe is coming *reel* soon and—"

"Ah, knock back all that philoso-flapping," a voice in the back said, daring to cut her off. "You an' Breeze both. We've all heard it buzz before, and I don't need you to herd it past again. Ohio, what's your slant?"

"No slant at all, and that's the trub, bub. I'm right on

the level." The jive talk and double meanings fell trippingly off his tongue, but they rang false in his ear. The Breeze and the Cheese were both right. To stand by and do nothing was exactly correct, according to the Naked Purple philosophy, because the destruction of the bad old Earth civilization was inevitable.

But the whole creaky structure of Purple assumed that its goals were impossible—not only unattainable, but deliberately chosen *because* they were unattainable.

That had been the original Purple goal. To shock people out of their complacency, remind them that the world was not all it could be. The Purple was supposed to give people goals they could reach for, but never grasp, thus getting their minds moving again. If society ostracized you for thinking on your own, you were forced to find your own goals. Surely that was laudable, and gave promise for the future. Ohio looked around the crowded room. What goal did these people have, beyond getting to tonight's party? There was nothing in their Tycho version of Purple. It was sterile, a game of prattling words cooked up to justify what they would have done anyway. It didn't have to be that way. Yes, there had always been anger in the Purple—but once upon a time there had been hope as well. But that was long ago and far away, all but forgotten, corrupted by the wackos of Tycho Purple Penal. Hope had become mere sullenness.

Tycho. That was the cause of all this. Crossbreed a cult seeking individual enlightenment with a crew of third-generation convicts, and what else could you expect but angry, self-indulgent blather? No, Ohio thought, the Tycho brand of Purple had held sway long enough. It was time for the older ways to return, the old Purple that *did* have a goal, even if it was half-hidden. A Purple that mixed its anger with hope.

This was too serious, too deadly serious a moment for playing games with words. Ohio nodded, his mind made up. After all, what the hell kind of philosophy endorsed self-extinction?

"Great windbag Ohio turns out to be," Cheese said mockingly. "He just sits there and nods. No opinions, no thoughts. That's not the Purple way."

That got Ohio genuinely mad. Cheese had spent her whole life sticking like glue to the Purple orthodoxy. No room for any thought someone else hadn't had before. No room for un-Purple thoughts of any kind.

But, outside of this habitat, the real universe was not a very Purple place. Time to make these people run a reality check, he thought. His voice shifted, lowered by an octave. He decided to talk in the old way. Maybe *that* would have some sort of negative shock value. "Okay, we'll play it your way." He turned toward the others. "Cheese here doesn't want to talk about real people dying, whole civilizations collapsing, maybe humanity becoming extinct, because it doesn't fit in with the orthodox view. So we won't. But even if you really believe that we alone of the human race are worth saving, remember that *everybody* dying includes *us*. Earth goes, we go. Let me say it in one swell foop." Damn, a slip into slang, but never mind. "If we let Earth go, *we die*. We *need* the Earth. We cannot grow all our own food, or fix our own machines. We can't take care of ourselves."

Creamcheese sniffed, a bit uneasily. "Don't exaggerate. So we buy up a few luxuries, hire a few Earthers like that Noisemaker geek to push the buttons down. It keeps us from polluting ourselves with knowledge we don't need. As for the imports, mere fripperies for our amusements."

Ohio couldn't help noticing that the Purple slang was dropping out of Creamcheese's words as well. Maybe he had her attention. "That all *used* to be true," he said. "But every year, we've done less and less of our own work. The Naked Purple ideal called for each of us to do work *when needful*—but the richer we got, the more that definition of needful started to slide. Until we were buying luxuries like food and airlock repair. We hired outsiders to do our work for us, until we got to where we were buying our *air* from them because we were sloppy about running the airplant. At least *that* I put a stop to when *I* got stuck with this job. I bought us a new airplant and trained a crew to run it. But things like that cost money. Dirty Earth money.

"We're dependent on Earth. We *have* to buy from Earth, or starve. With so many ships lost, it's going to be a lot tougher to resupply us. If they'll even come. With that CORE thing about to paste the *Saint Anthony* probe, who'll want to risk the same treatment just to fly *us* some food? We might have to evacuate the habitat, move everyone back to Earth—but we don't have the ships to do that on our own, either. At the very least, we'll need emergency supplies launched from Earth to tide us over while we buckle down and make ourselves self-sufficient.

"No matter *how* it breaks, we'll need help from Earth. Which will be tough to get if the people of Earth accuse us of allowing the Solar Area—damn it, the Solar *System*—to be destroyed." Ohio felt a sudden, passionate need to call things by their right names, with no games. "We're going to need Earth's goodwill."

Ohio Template Windbag looked around the shabby room, and the faces of the aggressively, lovably eccentric people in it. There was something oddly sad about them. Not just now, but something that had always been there. "The game's over," he said. With a sudden pang of sorrow, he remembered his own pre-Purple past, teaching school, and the desolated faces of the children when the rains came during recess.

Especially the lonely children, the ones that nobody would play with. They seemed to be the ones that gloried most of all in the open space of the school yard, most loved the one place they could at least be themselves and play their secret, solitary games without interruption.

Suddenly the blue skies would be gone, with the fat drops plashing down everywhere, thunder and lightning rumbling threats across the sky, and their secret worlds would be washed away. "Rain's come, fun's over," Ohio whispered to the sad little faces he still saw. "It's time to come inside," he said quietly. "Back inside, and back to work." The room was quiet. Even Creamcheese Drone Deluxe had nothing to say.

Ohio took that as a sign. He punched up the intercom, switched it over to the channel that worked, and called Chelated Noisemaker Extreme. "Frank," he said at last, "I think we're all about agreed up here. Why don't you get that datatap dancing?"

The Sphere had many duties, but its capacities were great, and there was no prize greater than a new life-bearing world. The price—in risk, in treasure—was huge, and certainly this would not have been the time it would have deliberately sent out a call, declaring itself ready to absorb a new world and ready to assist in the construction of a new Sphere. But the Sphere was flexible, adaptable in its thought processes, and determined to make the best of the situation, find the advantages to itself inside the crisis.

Such as the capture of a splendid new world, one that deserved the best of treatment. Preparing a place for it had been a great strain. Gathering up a Keeper Ring and an anchor wormhole was normally a leisurely process, but this time the Sphere had been forced to do it all within a few brief seconds. Matching the new world's previous environment of heating and tidal effects so

closely in such a short space of time had been a remarkable achievement.

But the job had required speed, and the placement of
an unprogrammed Keeper Ring. The Ring had been built
and grown long, long ago, and placed in storage, left to
sleep, untutored, until there was a world that needed
care. When the message from the Caller had come, the
Sphere had found a black hole that matched the new
world's tidal needs, and then used a dangerous self-
transiting technique to move the Ring-hole ensemble into
position, manipulating the Keeper Ring so that it served
as both ends of the same wormhole.

All the while, the new world was kept cycling through
a whole series of transit points as the Sphere juggled to
hold on to it. At last the new Keeper was ready, and the
Keeper, under the Sphere's direct control, pulled the new
world into a safe and stable orbit.

It had been a dangerous and complex job, and the
Sphere had been running the Keeper Ring directly ever
since, transporting new-mode Worldeaters to the new
planet's old star system, closely monitoring the somewhat
archaic Caller Ring that was running the planet-stripping
operation there, vectoring the Shepherd to intercept the
large piece of debris that was falling toward the new
world.

But the Sphere had many duties. It could not focus this
much attention on this single operation indefinitely. The
Sphere, when other duties allowed, continued to download all that a Keeper must know: images of the Sphere's
ancestry and history, images that demonstrated this procedure and that, examples of commands and their results, and endless demonstrations of a Keeper's duties.

The Keeper took it all in eagerly, felt itself awakening
as it absorbed enough data to understand its duties more
fully. Its somewhat rigid mind was primed for this knowledge set, hungry for it.

It never occurred to the Keeper or to the Sphere that there might be another listening. The very idea was alien, inconceivable to them. Neither of them could even imagine a being such as Frank Barlow, let alone his actions.

But that didn't stop Barlow from listening, and gathering in his data.

The boost out from Earth had gone well, and now the *Nova* was in free-fall, moving toward its deceleration point, a few hundred thousand kilometers astern of the Target One planet. An easy zero-gee flight, then a braking burn to slide the ship into orbit around T-One. Without the burn, the *Terra Nova* would sail right on past the new world it sought.

The Universe outside the *Terra Nova* might be in turmoil, but life aboard the big ship was settling into a comfortable routine.

Dianne Steiger watched the bridge main display screen as the two radar tracks—the *Saint Anthony* and the CORE—intercepted. She watched on an aux screen as the carrier-wave signal died, watched the smaller target vanish off the main screen as the larger sailed majestically on. The Charonian CORE had done its work, and the *Saint Anthony* was dead.

Dianne pulled out a cigarette and lit it thoughtfully, manipulating it with her new left hand, just for the practice. She took a deep drag and pointedly ignored Gerald MacDougal's coughing fit. She held the smoke in her lungs for a moment and smiled with real satisfaction. There were advantages to being the captain of a starship. An air system built to last generations had to be able to handle a cigarette—and as captain, no one aboard could tell her not to smoke.

One minor mystery was cleared up—the COREs obviously used some form of radar—crude, arrogantly powerful radar—to do their tracking. That was why they emitted such energetic radio waves. There had been a fair amount of speculation aboard the *Terra Nova* as to how the CORE would make the kill. Lasers and ship-to-ship missiles had been the most popular guesses, but the CORE had simply crashed into the probe. A direct kinetic-impact kill.

That hadn't surprised Dianne. There was nothing subtle about the Charonian way of doing things. They were masters of direct, brute-force action. They took what they wanted, did what they pleased, plainly never thinking that anything might oppose them.

She turned her head toward Gerald, sitting beside her on the bridge. "All right, Gerald. You tell me. Why the hell did they wait so long to stop the *Anthony*? Why did they allow the probe to operate so long, and why didn't they jam its transmissions, or attempt to capture it instead of destroying it?"

Gerald shrugged. "Because the COREs aren't programmed to think in those terms. And whatever it is that programs them, which I suppose is ultimately the Dyson Sphere, doesn't think that way either." *The Dyson Sphere doing the thinking*, Gerald thought. Yes, of course. By some miracle, Marcia and this Sondra Berghoff had read his message about von Neumanns, and understood, and, miracle on top of miracle, had taken his ideas to places he had never imagined. *Praise be to God for His blessings*, Gerald told himself, deeply thankful for all of it. But especially for the knowledge that Marcia was alive.

"But the *Anthony* was obviously sent to gather and transfer information," Dianne was saying. "How could any intelligent species *not* realize that the *Anthony* was a threat?"

"Because they *aren't* intelligent in any sense of the term we understand," Gerald said. "They are machines programmed by machines. What's confused us about them is that some of the machines are living creatures, of a sort. But they are as programmed, as artificial, as the mechanical devices."

"But what's the point of it all? What do they all do it *for*? What's the point of a huge machine that does nothing but keep itself running?"

Gerald smiled sadly. "You've just asked: 'What's the point of being alive?' That question is just as important, and just as meaningless, if you're a mechanical life-form or a biotic one. They survive in order to survive, just as we do. And, I might add, they do a very impressive job of it. But we're thinking of the Multisystem as a network of machines. Maybe it would be more accurate to think of them all as part of one big entity."

Captain Dianne Steiger thought for a long moment. "You're saying that the whole Multisystem—the Sphere, the Rings, the COREs, the artificial animals and the robots, the captured planets and stars—all amount to *one organism*?"

"It's possible. Either that, or a highly coordinated alliance of linked creatures. Or some third thing, between those two. But whatever it is, we're going to have a tough time understanding what makes them tick."

"Okay, but if it's all one creature, then the COREs are just a subsystem. They're like white blood cells, attacking an invader . . ." Dianne leaned back in her chair, puffing on her cigarette, staring into space. Suddenly her eyes popped wide. She sat straight up and pulled the cigarette from her mouth. "Attacking an invader as soon as it threatened to crash into something valuable."

Gerald frowned, and then he got it. "Like a planet."

"They never regarded the *Anthony* as a spy probe, or a radio relay. They don't *need* things like that." She stubbed out the cigarette into an ashtray. "They saw it as a rock that was going to fall on Earth, and diverted the closest interceptor to make the kill. That's what the COREs are—meteor interceptors, orbiting the worlds of the Multisystem to protect them from spaceside debris.''

Gerald's face went pale. ''If we change our present course, make our braking burn to intercept the Target One planet, they're going to see the *Terra Nova* as a rock about to fall on Target One. The COREs around Target One will pound us into a pulp.''

Dianne Steiger nodded and tried to remain calm as she felt a cold hand wrap itself around her heart. ''I think you're right, but we've got to test the theory. Let's hope it's way off base. Because if it's right, we can never come near any of these worlds.''

The Flying Dutchman, Dianne thought again. The name appeared in her mind, and nothing she could do seemed capable of forcing it out. Dianne remembered the name of the old legend, but almost nothing else. What was it that had happened to him? Had he been doomed never to land, or just never to return home?

She blinked hard and tried to concentrate. ''Deploy decoys and fire their engines remotely as per plan and schedule,'' she ordered. Was her voice steady? Never to land, a life that echoed a ghost story. A life that would *become* a ghost story. Hadn't there been a historical character who inspired the *Dutchman* legend? What tales would *her* endless journey inspire? The prospect chilled her very bones.

She watched as the first of the decoys leapt away. The things were utterly simple. It had taken the machine shop only an hour or two to build them. Big square-corner radar reflectors attached to small rocket engines. The reflectors would provide a brilliant echo to any radar beam directed at them. The radar-sensing COREs should be able to see them easily enough.

There were eight of the decoys, and it was the work of a few minutes to deploy them all. Their rocket engines fired, and the decoys shifted course toward the Target One world. Two were aimed directly at the planet, the others pointed to miss T-One at distances varying from a few hundred kilometers to nearly half a million.

The decoys fell away from the *Terra Nova*. Their engines flared on, performing high-gee burns that shifted their orbits violently, with far more stress than a human crew would ever survive. But the faster the decoys got in there, the sooner Dianne would have some data—and the sooner she could reach a decision about what to do.

Spacecraft move fast, but the scale of space is huge. The decoys, moving at tremendous speeds, seemed to crawl across the display screens at the most leisurely of rates. Dianne Steiger settled into her captain's chair, ready for a long wait.

She didn't get it. Mere minutes after the decoys had completed their burns, six COREs, accelerating at a terrifying rate, suddenly lifted out of orbit toward the decoys. The navigation computers hurriedly projected their courses, assuming constant boost, and showed intercepts with all but the two most distant decoys. Dianne stared at the screen, and read the message there. The *Terra Nova* could not come within three hundred thousand kilometers of a planet without being destroyed.

She smiled coldly, humorlessly. Her original orders had been to explore the Dyson Sphere, and she had rejected that because it was too dangerous. She had insisted on a safer flight first. And now she wasn't even able to get near the closest planet.

"Ma'am," the navigator said quietly. "We're coming up on our decision point. As per your orders, I have trajectory solutions laid in for a continued free orbit of the Sunstar, a distant orbit of T-One, or a return path to Earth. Propulsion needs your orders.''

Dianne glanced involuntarily behind her, thinking of the Earth they had left behind. Every world of this Multisystem had to have been stolen the same way Earth was, and then enveloped with a shield of COREs. Sooner or later—probably sooner—Earth would receive the same protection. Perhaps outgoing spacecraft would be unmolested, though Dianne would be unwilling to bet much on that chance. But no returning spacecraft could land. Sweet Jesus, it was worse than that, she realized. The COREs would attack anything that even came *near* Earth. Like satellites and habitats. All of them would have to be evacuated *now*, before the people on board were stranded, or killed outright by impacting COREs. Any replacement for the *Saint Anthony* would be smashed to scrap almost as soon as it arrived.

And after the COREs arrived at Earth, the *Terra Nova* could not return home. Ever. Perhaps no other ship could lift from Earth without being destroyed. Ever. Spaceflight would end. Even communication between Earth and a spacecraft would be tough, with the COREs' radars jamming virtually every usable comm frequency. But what was the point in worrying about contact with Earth if no ship could ever leave Earth again?

Except if the only ship away from Earth *stayed* away. The *Terra Nova* had been built to travel between star systems, to outlast journeys that might last hundreds of years. So long as she never approached a planet, the big ship could continue in operation long after the last crewman aboard had died of natural causes.

Or else, if Dianne turned the ship back now, her crew could see their families again before they died.

No, she thought. Suppose, some day, a way was found to beat the COREs and the rest of the Charonians, and the plan needed a ship in space for it to work? Or suppose there was some vital discovery waiting, one that could be made only from a spacecraft, far away from Earth? What other, unimagined doors would slam shut if the *Nova* retreated? And what fate would humanity deserve, what future would it be worthy of, if danger was met so meekly?

Dianne straightened her back, stared at the display screen, and spoke quietly. "Advise propulsion to stand down. Continued free orbit, no use of main engines required. Here we stay. We can do no other."

CHAPTER TWENTY-FOUR

◇

Becoming Shiva

THE CLOUDS OF DUST AND DEBRIS PILED UP IN UGLY choking rings about the planet Venus. The storms of Venus roiled and bridled in new and terrifying ways, tortured by the Charonian machine-monsters on the surface. A dark spot appeared in the glaring clouds, large enough to be visible from orbit. For the first time in human history, a portion of the Venusian surface was visible from space.

It was a mountain, impossibly huge, climbing up out of the clouds, swelling upward and outward moment by moment, until its upper slopes were outside the planet's atmosphere. It was an elongated cone, almost a caricature of a volcano—a classic, perfect cartoon volcano.

Suddenly, it belched smoke and flame, and a column of fire blasted out into space, glowing hot molten rock flying clear of the planet.

Core material. The Charonians had bored down through the crust of the planet, used their gravity systems pull the molten magma out of the planet and heave into space. The Charonians were taking not just the crustal rock, but they were sucking out the core matter as well.

It wasn't a volcano. It was a vampire.

Marcia MacDougal and Sondra Berghoff sat in the Martian darkness, feeling the cold creep in. The power had died again. Marcia was getting restless. She desperately wanted to get outside, but that was impossible. There had been too many holes punched in the dome, and the engineers had bled the pressure off to conserve air. The entire population of Port Viking had been forced to retreat to the airtight buildings.

Marcia wrapped her blanket more tightly around her. Perhaps the engineers would be able to bring the power back on again. But then another fragment of sky-tossed stone would smash into some other vital piece of equipment again, or a quake would trip every circuit breaker in the city again, or the dome supports would finally take one more strike than they could handle and collapse. There would be the struggle to fix whatever it was—and then another disaster would strike.

Sooner or later the engineers would no longer be able to patch it over. Port Viking would die in the dark.

How long had it been? How much time had passed since the *Saint Anthony* had died, and taken so much of their hope with it? On Earth, wherever she was, they had marked the transit of four days and nights. The Moon had rolled through a sixth of *her* leisurely, month-long rotation. On those worlds, time moved much as it always had, for the Charonians left the Earth and Moon untouched.

But on Mars, on Venus, on all the other worlds, time

had lost its old measure and meaning. On dust-choked Mars there was no night, no day, just a series of catastrophes in the dust-shrouded gloom under the sullen glowing sky. There was no meaningful way to mark the time on Mars, on Ganymede, on Titan.

Or was it time itself ending for all those places?

The *Nenya* rushed at full throttle toward Pluto, the engines roaring at powers far beyond safety margin, Vespasian forcing every possible scrap of thrust, without regard for a return trip. If the flight succeeded, there would be more than enough time to mount a rescue mission. If it failed, there would be no point to one. Never mind that. Larry stared grimly at the display screen, determined to focus on the data there. Updates from the Gravitics Research Station, refinements of the models he had done the night before. Good people there. All of them. Maybe he had done the flashy, exciting work, but it had all been based on the research they had done. But he had needed more help than theirs. And gotten it.

God only knew why, but the Purples had cooperated. The data had come through the *Saint Anthony* before it died. Not just data, but in a very real sense, the voice of the Sphere, the precise equivalent of words handed down from the intelligence that ruled the Charonian empire.

It wasn't language, not in any human sense. It was an image set, closer to a system of notation for computer programming than anything else. Larry had enough data to get a start on the Charonian command set. The *Nenya* computers weren't really built for this sort of analysis, but they were the best he was going to get. Communication was still spotty, but the engineers on all the worlds were improvising desperately, finding the sending and

eceiving frequencies that still worked. Word was com-
ng in from all over, and the word was not good.

Venus was reporting a huge structure pumping magma
rom the interior. Ganymede reported that Io was coming
part at the seams, its chaotic surface all but completely
iquified. The tiny world was melting away into a cloud
f sulfur and complex hydrocarbons. Somehow the Char-
nians were amplifying the tidal effects that had always
orn at the giant moon, focusing the stress at weak points,
concentrating the internal pressure until the moon simply
ore itself apart. Several of Jupiter and Saturn's smaller
ce moons just weren't there anymore, already com-
letely digested by whatever monstrosities had landed
here.

He checked the wall chronometer. Fourteen days out
rom the Moon, two more days until arrival at Pluto.
Larry didn't even want to think about the *Nenya*'s terri-
ying velocity.

Two days. That would barely be enough time to pre-
are.

Could it be done? Would it work?

Damn it, *would it work*? As far as the gravity side of
t went, he had no doubts. He had learned from the Char-
nians, watched what they did, how they turned gravity
on its ear to do their bidding. He could *see* the way to
configure the Ring, knew instinctively what must be
done.

But what *should* be done? Did he have the right answer
o that question? Larry stared at the datascreen in front
of him, then glanced down at the notes on the desk,
urned and looked into the mirror set into the opposite
wall of the tiny cabin. But he saw none of those things.
Instead, his eye turned inward, toward places in his soul
he had never imagined. He leaned forward, resting his
elbows on his knees, and held his head in his hands. If

it was not an attitude of prayer, it was close enough. How many worlds was he trying to save tonight?

How many had he already helped to destruction?

He lifted his head a bit and found himself staring at his hands, as if he had never seen them before. *These* were the hands that had done it, that had shaped the commands, set the Ring configuration, pressed that damnable *start* button. These were the hands that had made the Earth vanish, turned the entire Solar System upside down, awakened monsters that had slept since before humanity existed.

He thought back, and remembered *deliberately* setting the controls so the actual start command had to be sent manually, and tried to remember why. He knew, intellectually, it was because pushing that button meant rebellion against Raphael. But that emotion no longer made sense to him. Had the whole disaster been caused by nothing more than that? Larry O'Shawnessy Chao's childish need to show that he was smarter than anyone else? How many worlds were wrecked, how many people were dead already because he had pushed that button? How many ships were lost, how much treasure destroyed?

But he *couldn't* have known. No one could have known. The search for gravity control had started before he was born. Sooner or later *someone* would have found a way to make a graser beam, and would have brushed the Moon with it. *Someone* would have pushed that button. Dr. Raphael had said quite clearly that the entire Gravitics Research Station had to bear its share of the blame. . . .

No. Larry looked up again, caught his own eye in the mirror, and stared back at himself. All of it, in his favor and against him, was true, but now was not the time. Now he had to push it all away, the guilt *and* the justification. He would have his whole life for that. Wallow-

ig in either right now would interfere with the amends
e had to make.

He stared again at his hands. But his act of atonement
ould itself be a terrible crime. No one else knew that,
o one knew what he had planned, and no one would,
ot until it was too late to stop. This crime, this
uilt, this *sin* he was determined to carry on his own
houlders alone, without ambiguity, fully aware of ex-
ctly what he was doing.

For Larry had realized that, in the event he got it
vrong, it was that ambiguity, far more than the guilt
self, that he feared.

It had been a long and lonely wait on Pluto. One hun-
red twenty people at the edge of the Solar System,
truggling to clean up after the geniuses. The science
taff had been working around the clock, trying to keep
up with the torrents of gravitics data pouring in. They
ad learned a great deal—in fact, too much. There had
een no time to assimilate any of the information, to
onder it. As soon as one new discovery was made, a
lozen new and urgent mysteries would pop up, requiring
nore urgent overtime and study.

And now it could only get harder. Chao and Raphael
vere returning.

There! A flare of brightness halfway across the sky
rom Charon and the Ring. Jane Webling watched as the
Nenya performed her final braking burn.

But Webling frowned. There was something strange
about that burn. She pulled out her notepack. Strange
ndeed. The *Nenya* was not dropping into her normal
parking orbit, but instead placing herself into the barycenter of the Pluto-Charon system. The barycenter was
he balance point, the center of gravity for the whole

Pluto-Charon system, the point in space around which both planet and satellite rotated.

But the *Nenya* was never placed in the barycenter, for the very good reason that it could interfere with communication between the Ring and the Gravitics Station. It only made sense if the Ring was to be controlled from the ship, instead of the Station.

But why the hell would they need to run the Ring from there? And why hadn't the situation been explained? Jane Webling found a seat in the deserted observation dome and sat down. What the hell was Larry Chao hoping to accomplish here? She knew the official explanation, that Larry hoped to use the Ring to control the Lunar Wheel, and thus shut down the Charonian attack on the Solar System.

Ironically, the Charonian Landers had beat the *Nenya* home. The first of them had arrived a few days ago. Now there were dozens of the huge things, dotting the surface of Pluto and Charon, home to their namesake.

The *Nenya* had been gone a long time, stranding the entire staff in the cold and the dark. It was a quite distinct relief to have her back home again. They had a way out again—even if home, if Earth, was no longer there.

With Larry, Dr. Raphael, and Sondra Berghoff away, she was the only scientist at the Gravitics Research Station who fully understood Larry's work. In order to take over the Wheel, the Ring would have to send it a more powerful signal than the Dyson Sphere was sending. The Ring of Charon did not have more than a tiny fraction of the power needed to overcome the Sphere.

Therefore if Larry was not lying to everyone, he was at least *misleading* them. Which suggested he was up to something.

But what, and why? It was a question of some importance. After all, here was a young man who had acted on his own, in secret, once before—and torn the Solar

ystem apart. She could produce proofs, demonstrate to
e other scientists that Larry's stated plan of action was
npossible. Until Raphael returned a few hours from
ow, she was the acting director of the station. And if
e could demonstrate that Raphael was part of the plot,
en she would have every right and duty to prevent him
om taking over the job again. And perhaps she ought
clap the two of them in irons.

Yes, beyond question, there were many things she
ould do. But should she do them? What did Larry in-
nd?

Jane Webling did not know Larry well, but she had
otten a good look at his character in those chaotic first
ays after Earth vanished. He had seemed a very open
nd decent young man under incredible pressure. She
ad sensed nothing venal in him, nothing underhanded.

No, the most dangerous possibility was that he meant
well, but had some plan, some scheme in mind he knew
would not be permitted, some idea he thought would be
he answer to everything and solve all their problems.
Under cover of the experiment he professed to be running, he would instead do whatever it was he did not
wish anyone to know about.

In other words, Webling concluded, he would do exactly what had gotten them all into this mess in the first
place, when he had suborned her graser experiment and
fired that damned beam at Earth.

And he had meant well then, too.

Damn it! What the hell was she supposed to do?

Think. *Think.* That was what she had to do. All right
then. Larry was up to something, because his stated plan
could not possibly work, and he knew it. However, he
meant to do something that would do what the stated plan
was meant to do: stop the Charonian attack on the Solar
System.

And no doubt he was hiding his real plan because no

one would let him near the Ring if they knew what h
was really scheming.

And then she figured it out. She pulled out her not
pack, ran through a series of calculations, and got th
answers she knew she would get. She stared at then
utterly shocked that Larry would do such a thing.

She knew. She *knew* the answer. There was no oth
possible explanation.

But that left her with her original problem. What wa
she going to do about it?

She sat there, alone, with only Charon and the Ring bul
ing in the sky for company, and thought for a cold an
lonely time. Larry Chao, for whatever reason—choice, n
cessity, guilt, panic, mischievousness or a cold, hard, adu
feeling of responsibility, was playing God with the surviv
of the Solar System. Again. And by second-guessing hin
deciding what to do about it, she found herself playing
little God all by herself. Suppose, strange and impossibl
as it seemed, Larry had it right, and she moved to sto
him? Or suppose he were wildly, disastrously wrong, an
she stood by and did nothing?

The *Nenya* was meant to double as a bare-bones, ex
tremely barren backup to the station in an emergency—
and this situation certainly qualified. The ship coul
house the entire staff, albeit under rather Spartan an
crowded conditions. With the external tanks installed o
the Moon, she could begin taking on passengers imme
diately, without reconverting the ship first. But was tha
the right choice?

Jane Webling knew she had to choose, and time wa
running out. At last she stood up, returned to the Direc
tor's office, and used the intercom station there to giv
her orders. She could have done it anywhere on the sta
tion, but even the modest trapping of an office made he
feel as if she had more authority.

Pushing the intercom button, she drew in her breath

and spoke as slowly and clearly as she could, resisting the temptation to blurt her words out all at once.

"This is Acting Director Webling," she said. "All personnel are to prepare for the immediate and permanent evacuation of this station. Pack your personal items and prepare copies of all data for transfer to the *Nenya*. Work as quickly as you can, take only what you need—and work on the assumption that we are never coming back."

She shut down the intercom.

"Because we never *can* come back," she whispered. The station wasn't going to be there very long, a very high price to pay—but if she understood the situation, that station's destruction would be the cheapest of prices.

Or should she instead call it a down payment?

For if the race survived, humanity would be paying the balance on this bill for a long, long time.

Another feature to the *Nenya*'s design that reflected its purpose as a backup: the ship had a Ring control room, a duplicate of the four control rooms on the station. Larry, unaware of the station evacuation, sat there, working a simulation of his plan. It ought to work. All of it *ought* to work. And maybe that was what troubled him. Each step in the sequence seemed logical, sensible. But when he stepped back and looked at the entirety, it seemed ridiculous. Insane.

A knock at the control room door, and Simon Raphael came in. "Something interesting has come up," he said quietly. "I was just about to order the immediate evacuation of the station's staff up onto to the *Nenya*, when a message came in from Dr. Webling, saying that she had just ordered the very same thing." Raphael lowered himself into a seat by the wall, and pulled the belt across his lap, as if he planned to stay there a long time.

Larry felt his blood running cold, felt confusion sweep over him. "What's that?" he asked.

"Sometimes if you give two people the same problem with the same set of clues, they come up with the same answer." There was a pause. "And sometimes, even three people can come up with it."

"You and Dr. Webling both saw right through me," Larry said. "No point in even trying to hide it."

"Yes," Dr. Raphael said, staring very intently at a point just over Larry's left shoulder.

The silence dragged for a long time, until it became apparent that the older man wasn't going to say anything else.

"Can I take it from the fact that you haven't stopped me, that you both approve of my actions?" Larry asked, in a voice that was struggling to be calm and steady.

"No one," Dr. Raphael said, with an effort, "no one is ever going to *approve* of your plans, especially given recent events. They seem too much like a disaster we have already witnessed. But neither Dr. Webling nor myself see any choice in the matter.

"You obviously planned not to tell anyone until it was too late. Just out of curiosity, how were you going to string us along? What were you going to say or do to allay our suspicions?"

Larry shook his head, his expression blank. "I don't know. That was the thing I hadn't figured out."

"Then I suggest," Raphael said coldly, "that you get on with the parts you *did* figure out."

Power, Larry told himself.

Power. That was what it was all about. Power, gravity

power, was what the Charonians had. Power allowed them to take over solar systems, steal planets, tear worlds apart—without any thought of objections from the inhabitants.

Larry checked the next step on his list. *Shift the override control to manual.* It was the *absence* of power that left the people of the Solar System helpless.

So, the question came back, how to get some of that power into humanity's hands? *Rotate colliding beam focus transfer to 270 degrees.* Ultimately, of course, the Dyson Sphere was the source of that power, and there was not a hope, not a dream of matching that.

But even the Sphere needed conduits to send its power outward. *Fusion boosters to third-stage warming.* Larry was deep into his work now, barely aware that the outside world, that anything outside the Ring, its control room, and his intellect existed.

As far as power was concerned, the Lunar Wheel barely entered into the issue. It *used* the power, yes. Directed it and controlled it. But all its power came from elsewhere.

The power could not come from the Earthpoint black hole, either. By definition, nothing could come out of a black hole, except through the process of its own evaporation. The stream of elementary particles caused by that process was nowhere near enough to drive the vast operations going on in the Solar System.

The only other possible source for the power was the Dyson Sphere itself, using the Earthpoint black hole in wormhole mode as power conduit, relaying power to the Wheel. For three seconds out of every 128, Earthpoint flicked open into a wormhole, a link between the worlds. And it was *then*, when the huge asteroid-sized physical objects were sent, that the power had to be sent as well. Gravity power, modulated gravitational energy. How the

Dyson Sphere produced it, Larry did not know, or care. He would worry about that tomorrow.

If there was a tomorrow.

Larry forced that thought from his mind, determined to focus on the problem at hand. He did not notice as Webling slipped into the room and sat down next to Raphael. *High-power channel rotators in operational position.* The power got to the Wheel. *That* was the important thing. When the Ring was in gravity-scope mode, you could see the Wheel laden with that power, watch it absorb, store, transmit it out across the Solar System to all the monsters tearing the worlds apart. You could *see* it sending out the command-images ordering the Venusian Landers to build that hideous thing pumping core matter out of the world, ordering the Ganymede Landers to dig in deeper.

That was the power and command cycle that gave the Charonians their strength.

Suppose that mere humans were able to tap into that power cycle? Were able to draw down gravitic power, and so deny it to the Wheel? Cut in on the communications circuits and order the invaders to stop what they were doing?

Suppose humanity had its own black hole?

But black holes were made out of mass. Lots of it.

Board ready. Ring ready in new configuration. Ready for manual activation. Larry stared for a long moment at the sequence indicator. He realized that he could have configured for an automatic start this time, too. But no, once again, he had set it up to take a manual start, a human finger pushing a button to start the whole desperate gamble rolling.

"Go ahead, Mr. Chao," a gruff old man's voice said. "Do what you must do to Charon."

Larry flinched in startlement. He turned around to see Dr. Raphael and Dr. Webling there. He had no idea how long they had been there. "It is Charon first, is it not?" Raphael asked.

"Yes . . . yes sir. But ah, well, I really don't have any good models on how much time we'll have. Once we have a momentum of accretion, we really shouldn't stop—"

"The station has been evacuated, Mr. Chao," Dr. Webling said, her voice strained and under tight control. What emotions was she struggling to mask? Fear? Awe? Anger?

And toward what or whom were those emotions directed? No, ask the plain question, Larry told himself. *Just how afraid of me is she? Will they all fear me, forevermore?*

"Everyone is aboard the *Nenya*?" he asked in surprise. How wrapped up in his work had he been, that he had missed the comings and goings of the shuttle craft? *Good God, isn't there anything in my life besides work? Isn't there even anything else I can see?*

"It's time to begin this," Dr. Raphael said.

"And end it," Webling agreed, in a tense whisper.

Larry lifted his finger, held it over the button, and pressed it down.

A signal, a simple radio signal of only a few watts in power, leapt across the depths of space toward the Ring.

Simplicity, and smallness ended there.

The immensely powerful Ring that girdled Charon sprang to life, shifting and channeling gravitic energy in ways that its designers had never imagined. Perhaps in some nomenclatures it would be more accurate to say the Ring bent space, realigned the areas of potential, but this assault on a world was too violent to be described by a mere bending and folding. The Ring *crushed* the space around Charon, beating it into a new form like red-hot iron on an anvil. It grabbed at Charon's gravity field and focused it, creating a gravitic lensing effect, concentrating the entire worldlet's gravitic potential at one point.

But not a point in the interior. A point on the surface, directly in the center of the hemisphere facing Pluto. It was Larry's old experiment in focusing and amplifying gravity. But this time the point of million-gee force was stable, and solid. Now Larry knew how to maintain such a point source for as long as he wanted, draining the gravitic potential out of the entire world and focusing it in one tiny point.

For a time, a brief time, the satellite held firm, retained its near-spherical shape. But then the new and violent tidal stresses on it began to take hold.

The core, for billions of years at the focus of Charon's gravity field, was suddenly at the gravity field's periphery. Like a ship that has lost its anchor, Charon was suddenly a world cut adrift from the ancient gravity well that had molded it, formed it over all the lonely aeons of its existence. With the loss of gravity's anchoring effects, the worldlet began to crumble. First the surface matter, and then more and more core material began to fall *upward*, toward the new gravitic locus.

Ancient crater fields trembled, shuddered, smashed themselves to pieces as impossible landslides slumped sideways over the surface, pounding and tumbling toward the locus. Deep in the interior, layers of frozen gas and rock that had not moved in a billion years began to shift, bulge upward toward the locus on the surface. Heat, caused by compression and friction, warmed ice and rock that had slumbered near absolute zero since long before the first living thing had emerged from Earth's primordial sea. The heated ice and rock expanded, hissed, boiled, exploded. Vast sheets of the tortured surface suddenly blasted forth, streamers of glowing gas and pulverized rock arcing out into space, then falling down onto the hungry locus of gravity.

The Charonian Landers that had landed on their name-sake world began to die, beaten and pummeled by the ever-growing violence that ripped at the frozen land-scape.

With each infall of matter, the locus grew stronger, grasping greedily for more and more mass. The Ring monitored the locus, refocusing and amplifying it down to an ever-tighter, smaller, more powerful point source.

Now the Ring began the second phase of the operation, slowly dragging the new locus back down into the center of the dying satellite, twisting the knife in the wound, tearing a deeper hole in the surface, forcing a second wave of compression and heating to start moving back down into the interior, so that the old and new compression waves slammed directly into each other.

The satellite's surface shuddered and cracked wide open, the heated ices of the interior blasting forth as gases and liquids.

The Ring took hundreds, thousands of minor impacts from the shower of artificial volcanic activity. But it had been built to withstand massive stresses, and Larry's control program managed to focus most of the convulsions well away from the Ring plane.

The locus of gravity bore down into the center of the little world. By now, a solid pinpoint of matter, already close to the density of a neutron star, had gathered around the locus, and was eagerly sucking more and more matter down into itself. Under Charon's tortured surface, the volume of infalling matter began to make itself felt. The locus mass swallowed up material and compressed it down into a tiny fraction of its previous volume. With more and more matter compressing into a smaller and smaller space, Charon began to fall in on itself.

The heat of collapse began to increase, even as the mass and volume of matter available for heating started to shrink.

Temperatures began to rise. Chemical bonds that had been stable for billions of years split apart. Hotspots began to glow on the surface, horrid splotches of red and white spreading like some ghastly plague on the land. More and more surface volatiles sublimated away. Gas geysers blasted free, plumes of steam roiled up through vents and from the bubbling cauldrons of the hotspots. Clouds of pink and green, chemical compounds new-formed in the turmoil below, twisted and knotted through the tempestuous air. For the first time in all its long history, Charon's skies bore an atmosphere.

But not for long.

The chronometers said it took 47.5 hours, but none of those who witnessed it were ever able to believe that. It was far too long, or too short, a time, for a world to vanish utterly.

Larry never slept in all that time, but long passages of that time had the qualities of a nightmare, when the surging, seething storms, the weird sight of a world glowing white-hot with the heat of compression and collapse, the matter of the world relentlessly crushing itself, the world-serpent swallowing its own tail, consuming itself, driven on by the relentless urging of the Ring of Charon, named for a satellite that no longer was.

On and on it went, transfixing him, the moments taking forever, and then no time at all. Charon seemingly locked for all time into one state of its collapse, and then abruptly, seemingly without any transition, Larry would blink to find the satellite shrunk by half, glowing with a fiery light that had not been there before.

Larry watched, utterly unable to act or react, as the drama unfolded. It was something beyond him, outside him. It was utterly inconceivable that this titanic event could have anything to do with *him*, that anything he could do or say or think could have any effect on such a spectacle.

And yet he had caused it. He had imagined it, planned it, set the program, and pressed the button that caused it.

Explosions, massive electric storms, powerful magnetic eddy currents, auroral displays. Charon in its death throes found every way imaginable to shed the massive energy of position held by all the matter that fell in toward the rapacious center. The shrinking world glowed brighter and brighter, grew hotter and hotter as the spectacle continued.

At last there was nothing left but a sun-bright fleck of light in the sky, the glowing, ionized cloud of debris surrounding the dot of neutronium that late had been a world. The ion glow set the inner rim of the Ring gleaming jewel-bright by reflected light. But soon, all too soon, even that cloud of matter, now forming into a miniature accretion disk, would vanish as well. Particle by particle, atom by atom, it would smash into the surface of collapsed matter and be absorbed by it. And the neutronium sphere, now spinning at incredible speed as it conserved the satellite's momentum, kept growing, a particle at a time, letting off a flash of light and hard radiation with every impact.

Charon was no more. In its place, a point of star-hot brilliance, surrounded by a wispy nimbus of gas, thickening into a lumpen disk of dust, debris, and gas at the plane of Charon's old equator. And the Ring, the Ring of Charon surrounding it all, at right angles to the accretion disk, face-on to the tiny ship hovering at the still-unmoving barycenter. The system's center of gravity had not shifted appreciably. Charon's gravity was still there, now captured in a tiny dot of neutronium, a pinpoint of degenerate matter that held all of what had made a world.

Matter so compressed that even the atoms themselves had collapsed in on themselves, the electron shells flattened down to nothing, forcing protons and electrons to bond, forming neutrons, gravity overcoming the weak nuclear force, in effect compressing the satellite down into one giant neutron.

"So now we've become what they are," Webling said, looking through the monitors at the impossible sight. "Become Shiva, destroyer of worlds. We've taken a whole world, a satellite four billion years old, crushed it down to nothing, to serve our transient needs."

"Self-defense, Jane," Raphael said. It was not explanation enough, but it was all he had. He turned and looked at Larry. "There isn't any chance that Charon by itself will be enough, is there? No hope that we can leave Pluto alone?"

Larry stared straight ahead, numbingly exhausted, refusing to see anything but the screens full of abstract numbers ahead of him. He could not afford to consider the reality of what they were—no, what *he*—was doing. "None. I've amplified and focused Charon's gravity enough to form a neutronium sphere, but that's it. I've pulled all the artificial focusing pressure off it. It's stable, certainly for the present time, and maybe permanently. It shouldn't be able to reexpand on its own. But I can't achieve any further compression with so little matter, no matter what tricks I play.

"Even with Pluto added in, it's marginal. Even with the planet added in, I might not have the mass to cause a tripover into a black—I mean, um, a singularity." He had dreamed of creating a black hole for a long, long time. But now that it was within his grasp, he could not even bear to say the words, was forced into euphemisms.

Webling gasped. "Not enough? Well, what happens then? What if *Pluto* goes and we still don't have tripover?"

"We go shopping for planets and moons," Raphael said coldly. "I believe Uranus will provide us with more possibilities than Neptune. With the focused mass of Charon and Pluto to draw on, I expect we could develop a gravity beam that could draw one of its moons toward us. That's correct, isn't it?"

"Yes, sir," Larry said woodenly, as if he were giving a test answer. "A tighter, more directed, more powerful beam than we ever would have dreamed possible a few weeks ago. The gravity beam would produce mutual attraction, of course. We'd be moving ourselves toward them at the same time, in effect falling toward them once the beam stripped the satellites from their orbits. It would require a transit time of several weeks at least. We'd meet at the halfway point between Pluto and Uranus, more or less. I expect we'd need Oberon and Titania, and possibly Umbriel. They're all far smaller than Pluto, but their combined mass would be more than enough if Pluto by itself doesn't do the job."

Would it even work? No matter how many worlds they destroyed, no matter how much mass they swallowed up, it meant nothing if they could not break into the Charonian power and control loop. Larry sighed, and his voice cracked just a little. "Then we proceed?"

Raphael nodded. "There's no turning back now." He pressed an intercom key. "Mr. Vespasian, this is Raphael. You may move us out of the barycenter now."

For purpose of observation and measurement, the barycenter had some distinct advantages as a control station site, but because it was on a direct line between the locus mass and Pluto, it had some far more distinct *dis*advantages when firing a gravity beam from one point to the other. Vespasian wasted no time gunning the *Nenya*'s engines, moving his ship a prudent five thousand kilometers straight out from the barycenter.

Larry checked his sequencer, confirmed that the Ring

was ready for the next phase, and pressed that damnable *start* button again.

The Ring of Charon focused down on the locus mass, this time bending the shape of space around it to direct most of its gravitic potential down on a tiny point on the surface of Pluto, suddenly subjecting that point to a field a million times as powerful as the planet's surface gravity. A gravity field pulling that one point *up*, away from the planet. *Just like what the Charonians do*, Larry thought.

Almost instantly, a brilliant beam of ruby red light linked the locus mass with Pluto's surface as a pencil-thin stream of matter ripped itself out of the planet and accelerated toward the locus. Heated by friction and particle collisions, the matter stream lit the frozen world in a terrifying crimson light. But the heating progressed further, and the in-falling end of the matter stream, accelerating toward the neutronium sphere, glowed hotter and hotter, a blue-white sword of light, a firelance of light stabbing into space toward the Ring of Charon's center-point, knifing into the bull's-eye with dreadful precision.

And then, from the viewpoint of the *Nenya*, the locus end of the firelance began guttering down back toward the red. Not because it was slowing, but because it was speeding up, reaching relativistic speeds, moving fast enough that its light was redshifted, its color dimmed down toward red by the velocity at which it was moving away from the *Nenya*.

The Ring began to shift its target point on Pluto, moving the contact point across the surface, expanding the focus point slightly, deliberately unfocusing the edges of the beam to reduce the gravitic potential toward the perimeter of the beam. Torn by the hideous violence of the gravity beam's assault, its underpinnings pulled away as interior core material was pulled skyward, the Plutonian landscape was shredded apart. Pulverized by the massive

idal effects of the variable beam, the solid surface was
reduced to shattered rock and superheated volatiles that
blasted into space.

Larry watched, the tears running down his face, as
Pluto collapsed in on itself. It hadn't been a large planet,
or an important one. The astrophysicists had never even
quite decided whether it was a true planet in its own
right, or merely an escaped Neptunian moon or a bit of
oversized skyjunk. But it had been a *world*, a place, a
unique part of God's Universe, a border marker for the
inner frontier of the Solar System.

And now it was going, going, gone.

And he had killed it.

"The station's still holding together," Raphael announced, a strange note of pride in his voice. "We're
getting some impressive readings on all the telemetry
channels. The world crumbling beneath her feet, and the
station still stands. We built that place well, didn't we?"
Simon Raphael asked, turning toward his colleague. His
face was pained, sorrowful, and his expression was mir-
rored in Jane Webling's face. He reached out, and took
her hand. It had been a lonely place, cold in a way no
heating system could warm, a place of drawn-out defeats.
But the station had been a home to both of them as well.

Larry got up from the control console, leaving the Ring
to run itself. It was all on automatic now, the sequence
moving too fast for a human eye to follow.

He went to the side of the two older scientists, and
joined them in watching the relays from the Gravitics
Research Station's external cameras. He recognized the
camera angle. It was the same view, the old, unchanging
view from the observation dome. Before his eyes saw it
as it now was, his mind remembered how it had been
for so long, immutable—the craters, the empty plain,
and, close to the horizon, the jagged, shattered remains
of the first stations, ruins exposed to the stars. And the

graveyard, a few frozen corpses from the first missions here, hastily covered over a generation ago, carefully hidden from the dome's line of sight.

And the now-missing happy blue marble of Earth sometimes gleaming in the night.

Now, nothing was as it had been.

He opened his eyes to the present time. The ground was shuddering, boulders leaping up into the sky, pressure vents blasting open as they watched, sending geysers of superheated liquid streaking upward. The shattered remains of the first and second stations tumbled over, collapsed into the bubbling cauldron of the melted land. And for a brief, terrible moment, the graves gave up their dead. A steam vent blasted open the ground below the graves, and Jane Webling cried in horror as the bodies of old friends were thrown upward, hurtling over the horizon.

Now the ground under the station lurched downward, and the camera slumped over, fell on its side. A boulder slammed into the dome, smashing it open. The interior of the dome frosted over in the blink of an eye, and the contents of the room were a sudden blizzard of whirling debris. The viewscreen went blank as the camera was yanked free from its cable.

Like so many candles snuffed out with the rippling speed of a gusting wind, all the other indicators and readouts from the station flickered out and went dead.

Larry turned back toward his control console and checked the sequencer display. The locus mass had grown appreciably, and the Ring was able to refocus the gravity beam to even greater power. He switched one of the monitors to an external view camera and looked for a long last time at Pluto.

The planet was collapsing, shrinking, fast enough that he could see it happening. A haze of dust and debris and gas was a funeral shroud for the doomed planet. A huge, biling cone-cloud of debris was climbing up the gravity beam, matter spiraling down into the maelstrom from all over the planet, pulled in toward the beam.

The Ring adjusted the focus again, centering the beam on the point directly under the locus mass, widening the beam to draw in a wider and wider swath of matter. The faster the locus absorbed matter, the faster the strength of the beam grew, and the faster it tore matter from Pluto.

The planet's matter howled up the gravity cyclone, the superheated glow of ionized matter blazing across the sky. The locus absorbed more and more matter, giving the Ring more gravity potential to work with. The Ring tightened down the vise, compressing the locus down upon itself ever more tightly.

Larry watched the gee meters, the amplification meters. They were rising even more rapidly than he had planned. Closer and closer to the point where nothing, not even light, could escape from the microscopic pinpoint that now held all the matter that had once been a moon, the pinpoint that was swallowing a world. "Coming up on it," he announced, and no one had to ask what he meant. He closed his eyes, and exhaustion swept over him, tried to claim him one more time. But no, not yet.

The end of the firelance resting on the mass locus reddened more and more, grew dark and sullen as the gravity well deepened, redshifting the light more and more. The last shreds and fragments of Pluto slammed into the accretion cone, ripped themselves down to powder and gas, then to ions, falling, whirling, spinning, glowing, collapsing toward the voracious maw.

Larry watched the meters and licked his fear-dry lips. Soon. Soon. When the escape velocity reached the speed of light . . .

Suddenly there was a strange flickering across the screen as the last of Pluto fell into the beam. Just then, the light of the firelance guttered down to nothing, and not even the light of impact on the mass locus could escape.

And the rest was darkness.

Larry looked up from his numbers and his meters, ignored the view from the monitor screens, and stumbled toward one of the Nenya's few viewpoints. His own eyes. He had to see this with his own eyes.

In the wardroom. A port there. He stepped in, and saw a crowd there, people staring out the port. But suddenly their faces turned toward him, and they backed away. Whether out of fear or respect Larry neither knew nor cared. See. He had to see, with his own eyes.

He shoved his face up against the port, leaned in close enough that his breath froze on the quartz, turning the port into a foggy mirror, putting eyes in the quartz reflection that looked back at him.

His breath had frosted the station's observation dome that first night of it all. That action, that tiny dusting of frozen moisture on a window, reminded him of the far off victory when he had succeeded in focusing a pinprick of gravitic potential, a nothing, and held it steady for the briefest of moments—and had thought that to be a triumph. Now he knew better.

And, oh how happily he would give up that moment in order to give up this one, trade away his dreams to lose the knowledge he had purchased at such terrible price. The knowledge of destruction.

He reached out a weary hand and wiped his reflection away to look out at his handiwork.

Charon was gone.

Pluto was gone.

Lost, vanished, as if they had never been.

Only the Ring, the mighty and terrible Ring, survived. At its centerpoint, at the axis of the Ring, at the place around which all their desperate hopes revolved, was an impossibly tiny dot, utterly and forever invisible. A dot that contained all that been Charon, all that had been Pluto, all that had been the station and the bodies of their dead comrades.

A black hole.

A piece of darkness, and *he* had made it so.

Larry closed his eyes, and trembled, and wept. Then the exhaustion of collapse swept over him, and he knew no more.

CHAPTER TWENTY-FIVE

—————— ◇ ——————

Half a Loaf

LARRY AWOKE AFTER FAR TOO SHORT A TIME, LONGING for a better rest, for proper sleep, for a chance to dream away some of the nightmares. But things were getting worse back in the Inner System. People, families, whole cities could die while he caught a few winks. There was no time.

And so he was back in his control chair, trying to make it all work.

At last the main monitor screen lit up.

SYSTEM READY FOR TUNING HUNT.

Good. He cleared the board, ran one last check, and let the automatics take over. A display light flickered once, there was a faint beep, and the search program ran. The Ring's computers knew to within close tolerances Earthpoint's modulation, intensity, focus, pulse rate. Now it had to hunt within that range, searching for the precise combination of values that would cause a lock.

It was up to the machines now. Larry moved back from the board. This was it, the end of the quest.

And yet only the beginning. There were endless battles left to fight.

The Ring sequencer worked relentlessly through all the myriad ways, testing, sensing as it made each adjustment. Larry watched it work, astonished by his own arrogance. His black hole was a scant few hours old, and here they were, using it in the most elaborate and complicated way imaginable. They should have performed tests, years' worth of tests, accumulated an encyclopedia's worth of data, before they tried something this far out on the edge.

But there was no time. People were dying.

Webling, utterly exhausted, had gone off to try to sleep. Larry sat in the control room, alone with Dr. Raphael, watching the display click through all the permutations.

But being alone was an illusion. Larry knew that outside that door the entire staff of the research station, the people he had just made refugees, were watching every monitor, every display. Watching to see if the Solar System would live. Oh, yes, he was far from alone.

Larry turned and looked at Dr. Raphael. No, at *Simon*. He had never called the man that. But maybe now was the time to speak the man's name. Maybe that, too, would be a beginning, a start of saying many other things to his staunchest companion. "Simon," he said, quietly.

The older man looked up, startled. It was clear that he understood the significance of the moment. "Yes, Larry?"

"Simon, where are we? I mean, even if this works, what does it gain us? If we stop them, where do we go next?"

Simon thought for a moment, and then offered up a sad smile. "I don't know," he said at last. "Maybe nowhere. Maybe we win this battle and lose the war. We've just barely begun to have an idea of who and what we're fighting. But at least we'll have bought time. We'll be in a position to survive, to regroup. We'll have *hope*. And Earth will be safe, at least for the moment.''

Larry was about to reply when the alert buzzer went off. He checked his board and suddenly felt the adrenaline surging through his body. ''We have a lock,'' he announced. He powered up the external monitor and zoomed the camera in on the centerpoint of the Ring, where the invisible Plutopoint singularity hung lurking in the darkness. Suddenly, impossibly, there was a flash of unwhite, unblue, a flicker of color in the black. And then it was gone. Larry watched, unmoving, scarcely daring to breathe, waiting.

One hundred twenty-eight seconds later it flared again, and Larry let out a shout of triumph that nearly scared Simon Raphael to death. They were in.

''Now,'' he said, ''we start tapping into the Lunar Wheel's power feed.''

The education of the new planet's Keeper Ring was barely completed. The Keeper had been handling the Link on a solo basis for only the briefest period of time, but it had the procedure down to a comfortable routine. Maintain the Link, allow the aperture's innate recycle time to complete, stimulate the wormhole aperture to open, direct a Worldeater through the aperture, pull down gravitic quanta from the Dyson Sphere and direct them through the aperture at the same time. Complete all the transactions before the aperture destabilized and collapsed. And then, maintain the Link while the aperture recycled.

It was simple, straightforward, and the thing the Keeper had been bred to do. The Keeper took the me-

*chanical equivalent of pride and satisfaction in the work,
and in the fact that the Sphere had removed its last direct
monitors, trusting the Keeper with the responsibility.*

*But no matter how great the Keeper's competence, no
matter how vast its heritage memory, time was still the
great teacher, and very little of that had passed.*

*The Keeper Ring—and the Sphere—paid the price for
the Keeper's inexperience when the anomaly occurred. It
took the Keeper only microseconds to realize something
was wrong. The Keeper sensed a strange sensation on its
Link to the new star system. A dip in power, a double
echo on the last few pulses, as if the Caller Ring on the
other end were answering twice. The Keeper increased
the draw-down from the Sphere's power feed to match
the increased demand while it ran diagnostics on the situation. No need to call the Sphere for help. The Keeper
felt confident it could handle the problem on its own.*

It had to be his imagination, but to Larry it seemed as
if the Ring of Charon were visibly *surging, pulsing* with
power. It had never been designed to store this kind of
gravitic potential, but the Gravitics Station staff had
learned a great deal in his absence. They had devised a
way to use part of the Plutopoint singularity's potential
to form a toroidal gravity bottle, a gravity-field containment that knotted a toroid of space between the Ring and
the black hole, curving space back on itself into a dough-
nut shape centered on the singularity. The containment
could store the gravitic potential until it was needed.

And it was going to be needed soon.

Larry drummed his fingers nervously on the console.
"Simon, there are things that I'm not sure of. I think that
I've got the Charonian command-image system down.
The Gravitics Station's engineers agree, and the simula-

tions work, and the data we're pulling in now from the Keeper tap seem to confirm it. But there's no time for more research. We won't *know* if we've got it right until we start sending commands—and by then it will be too late to find out if things are going wrong.''

''All right,'' Simon said. ''Walk through it with me one more time. Assuming everything works, what are you going to do?''

''Well, the best we can hope for is to send false commands to the Lunar Wheel at a higher signal power than the real commands. Because we're putting all our gravitic potential into signaling, and none into power relay, we *ought* to be able to shout at the Lunar Wheel louder than the Dyson Sphere—or louder than whatever auxiliary the Sphere is using to control the Wheel. Probably the Moonpoint Ring, but we don't know.

''Then we can order the Lunar Wheel to relay *our* commands to *its* underlings. Marcia MacDougal recorded a large number of start-work commands sent by the Lunar Wheel to the Landers, and a few that seem to be stop commands. We send shutdown command sequences that ought to work. They should cause all the Landers to stop what they are doing and stand down. That should buy us enough time to learn the command language, and do more refined control—while holding the link to Earth open. If we get good enough with the command system, maybe we could bring Earth *back*.''

''It all sounds very promising. Suppose your commands don't work?''

Larry folded his hands in his lap and looked down. ''I have a contingency plan. But not one I want to use. It has to be decided ahead of time.''

''*What* has to be decided?'' Simon asked, as gently as he could.

Larry seemed unwilling to answer that directly. ''Well, if nothing else works, Marcia found what seems to be an abort order. The Charonians were smart enough to put an off switch in every machine. It seems to be an order that can be used on any malfunctioning Charonian device or creature, in the event that it goes out of control, threatening others. She spotted it being sent to the Landers that went out of control and crashed. I can use that command—as a last-ditch effort—to tell the Lunar Wheel and the Moonpoint Ring and all the Landers to die. It's a very simple command. There's no question that we have it right. If we sent it in a general broadcast through the wormhole link, and direct from here it would give us permanent, complete, final shutdown. I have no doubt about that. But of course, there would be other consequences as well," he said.

"*Consequences?*" Simon Raphael asked. "It would be a full-blown disaster! Without the Wheel, we'll have lost our link to Earth! You yourself pointed out what a disaster that would be when Vespasian suggested killing the Wheel. Earth will still be in danger, exposed to a future breeding binge."

"We've sent Earth our warnings," Larry said. "Unless a miracle happens and we can bring the planet back here, I don't really think there's much more beyond that we can do, or *will* be able to do. Whether or not we are in contact, Earth will have to stop the breeding binge on its own."

"But you yourself said the Dyson Sphere had to have a backup linkage system," Simon said.

"If it does I bet the other end is maintained by the Moonpoint Ring in the Multisystem," Larry said. "And the Moonpoint Ring will get the order to die at the same time the Lunar Wheel does. With *both* ends of the link destroyed, the wormhole will collapse. I don't know if even the Dyson Sphere could find us again."

"How can you even imagine doing such—" Simon Raphael was about to protest, when his eyes fell upon the clock. With every change of the numbers, the Solar System was suffering more and deeper wounds. Three more of the core-matter volcanoes on Venus, and six on Mercury. Port Viking's dome coming apart at the seams, its air rushing out into the Martian night. *Daltry's law*, he thought. *There is always a worse catastrophe.* "Forgive me. If it does come to that, perhaps we will find out how we can do such a thing. We've done all we can afford to do in order to prepare for this. There is no time. Begin it. And good luck."

Larry took a deep breath, turned back to the controls and adjusted the release on the gravitic quanta containment. The Ring took on new power. Up until now the Plutopoint end of the wormhole had been at the lowest possible energy, a mere pinprick in the side of the main sky tunnel.

Now Larry amplified the power going into the Pluto aperture, in effect grabbing at space, grabbing at the pinprick and pulling it wider, until the pinprick was a gaping hole in space.

Simon Raphael watched the main display screen, with half an eye on the countdown clock. The Earthpoint–Moonpoint aperture was to reopen in another five seconds. Four, three, two, one—where there had been a tiny flicker of blue, suddenly there was a blazing flash of color—and a massive object was hurtling through space. Simon caught a glimpse of a gleaming, cigar-shaped object before it flashed out of camera angle.

"Good God. We caught a Lander!" Simon said. Suddenly, for the first time, the mad idea of building a wormhole was real, was concrete to him. A *Lander*, an asteroid-sized half-living spaceship, had popped out of nowhere right in front of them.

"That poor dumb Lander had to have been targeted and programmed for one of the inner planets. Now what the hell is it going to do?" Larry asked gleefully. "Good start, and if we didn't know before, we know now,'' Larry said. ''Our aperture is stronger than the Earthpoint aperture. The theory worked—the wormhole is drawn toward the most powerful gravity signal. Now we're in the driver's seat,'' Larry said eagerly.

''But what will the Sphere do?'' Raphael asked.

''Not the Sphere,'' Larry said. ''That's our main hope. The Sphere would be smart enough to handle our attack. But from what I could get out of the reports from Earth, the Sphere delegates everything. My bet is the Moonpoint Ring is running autonomously by now.''

''So how will *it* react?''

''God only knows.'' Larry was intent on his control panel. ''There! There it is.'' He threw an oscilloscope tracing on the main screen. ''That's the main command signal coming from the Moonpoint Ring through the wormhole. I'm going to shunt it toward us, try and pull as much of that signal in through our aperture as possible, so we can weaken the signal arriving at Earthpoint.''

Malfunction! Terrible malfunction. Massive amounts of power were being drained away from the Link. The young and inexperienced Keeper Ring forced itself to think clearly. There had to be an answer, a solution stored in its heritage memory. But this circumstance was new, unique, utterly unknown in all the annals of the Sphere and its ancestors. It rushed to abort the next launch of a Worldeater through the aperture, knowing the terrible dangers of sending mass through an unstable wormhole.

But power. That was the real problem. Without sufficient power, the Caller Ring would be unable to complete its work. The Keeper Ring redoubled its efforts.

On the other end of the wormhole Link, the Caller Ring was equally mystified, equally frightened, and utterly helpless. Without power it was nothing.

"Here we go," Larry said. "We're sending a modulated pulsed gravity beam, at high power, in command mode, right down the wormhole. I'm ordering shutdown of all activity on Mars." He pressed the button and wiped the sweat off his brow. "Hell! The Moonpoint Ring is increasing its command power feed to the Lunar Wheel through Earthpoint. I'll have to shunt more power away and store it here to make sure ours is the stronger signal at the Lunar Wheel."

"But we don't have that much storage capacity," Raphael said, leaning over the control console. "We'll have to dump the power, or use it to amplify our own command signal."

"Can't," Larry said tersely. "Everything's at capacity already and there's no way to dump it except through the Ring of Charon. Put any more power through the Ring and we'll melt it. And we don't have any storage capacity left in the gravity containment."

There was something wrong with the incoming commands, and nothing could be more terrifying to a Caller Ring. It was getting two *command signals at once, and neither made any sense. The weaker one advised that increased power was on the way—but if anything, the power transmission was dropping again. The second*

command signal was loud, blaringly loud and powerful. It took a supreme effort of will to resist blind obedience to it. But its command syntax was garbled slightly, and there was something odd, disturbingly unfamiliar about it—and the orders did not make sense. A stranger's voice, commanding wrongful acts. The Caller Ring was badly frightened now. What could it be? What was happening? It sent a reply signal to both senders.

The Keeper Ring was stunned. The Caller was clearly receiving an alien signal. Why was the Caller being ordered to cease disassembly of one world? Who or what was ordering it? How was it that the increased power the Keeper sent was not received?

The Keeper Ring upped its output to the Caller Ring again.

"Damn all that's holy. Son, we're spiking high," Raphael said. "The gravity containment is completely saturated. We can't shunt any more power to it. We have to let the power through to the Lunar Wheel or melt out the Ring."

"Not yet," Larry said. "Just a little bit—hold it, signal coming back. Computers working to interpret. Stand by." Larry stared at the display screen, and his face turned ashen gray. "Oh my God. We've failed. The Wheel is saying our command was garbled, and indicates receipt of *two* command signals. We didn't jam the Moonpoint signal hard enough."

"Well, send the Martian shutdown order again," Raphael said.

Larry shook his head, and punched in a display code.

A highly complex visual image flashed on the main screen, the schematic of the Martian shutdown command. "Not if it contains an error. We can't just send it again, the Wheel would just refuse it again." He stared at the schematic, and muttered to himself, trying to read the symbols and codes.

"Can you fix it? Correct the error and send it again?" Simon asked.

Larry shook his head, the sweat popping out on his forehead. "Not in time, not this fast. The damn message is too complicated, and we don't know the language well enough. And we can't shunt any more power to our containment, unless you want to recreate the Big Bang right here and now. The Wheel is going to get everything Moonpoint sends—all the power, all the commands—and you can bet the Moonpoint Ring is going to increase its power relay.

"And now they know we're in the power loop, that there's an intruder in the system. When the Wheel gets a full power signal from Moonpoint, they'll find a way to lock us out. Just change the damn frequency, probably. And it'll all be for nothing."

He hesitated for a long moment, and turned toward Simon, a desperate look in his eye. "Unless the Lunar Wheel isn't there anymore."

There was a pause, a deep beat of time while Simon Raphael looked at Larry, and understood what he was saying.

Simon Raphael felt a hard knot in the pit of his stomach. Fifteen minutes ago he had been rejecting the idea as a disaster, but now it was the only choice left. "Do it," he said, Now he wished Larry *had* kept the whole plan to himself. Dr. Simon Raphael did not want this decision thrust upon him. "Do it. Send the order to die."

Larry decided not to tempt fate by asking for confirmation. He shifted all the power he could draw, called up the signal he had so carefully constructed, and ordered the computer to send it down the wormhole with everything behind it. Not just to the Lunar Wheel—but *through* the Wheel to the Moonpoint Ring, and through open space, to every Charonian in the Solar System.

The Caller Ring had never known such terror. What was happening? What monstrous enemy was doing these things? Suddenly its whole being twitched to attention, a hugely powerful signal grabbing at it, demanding its entire attention. The feel of the message, the voice, was still that of a stranger, an alien. But this time the command was unmistakable, sent in perfect syntax and modulation.

And it was the one signal that could not be denied, for it worked not through the Caller's conscious mind, but through the very circuits that formed that mind. The command echoed through the Caller Ring, out on its every command link, to every Worldeater in the system. And rebounded through the Caller Ring itself.

Death.

Stop.

Halt.

Cut power.

Shut down.

Death.

With a strange, cold, fascination, it felt the signal, absorbed it, sensed it coursing through all the myriad links that made up the Caller. It could see the order crashing through all the components of itself.

There was only one hope. It had to set up a stasis storage, set part of itself into hibernation mode before the signal could destroy everything. Any portion of itself that was shut down would not hear the command, and would survive, inert. There was very little time left. Only microseconds at best. Almost at random, the Caller selected a portion of itself near the North Pole region and used every command channel it had to send the stasis order.

But then the signal reached the seat of consciousness itself.

Death.

Death.

Dea—

The Keeper Ring shuddered, convulsed with pain. Death. Death. Death. *It fought off the impulse to die, struggled to clamp down its outgoing comm system. If this hideous command echoed out further, out into the Multisystem, the catastrophe would be complete. The Sphere itself might be imperiled. With a last effort of will, it held the command to itself.*

And died.

The Sphere realized something was wrong. It switched its full attention back to the new Keeper Ring, milliseconds too late. It caught the last shreds of the death command on an outgoing signal, deftly countermanded it before it could travel outward. None of the Sphere's other charges would be endangered.

But the Ring was dead, utterly inert. Something had attacked it, and killed it savagely.

Without a Keeper, the Sphere would have to monitor the new world directly, control its orbit personally. A further drain on its resources and attention. No world it had ever taken had caused it so much trouble.

And its new star system! Its hope for a new Multisystem, a refuge against the coming onslaught. Gone. Lost. And with the Link to the new star system shattered, there was no way to know how this thing had happened.

The Sphere realized that new star system was not merely lost—it had been deliberately taken away.

For the first time, the Dyson Sphere realized that it had not one enemy, but two.

And the second enemy knew how to deny it a star system.

But who and what had done this thing? The Sphere set to feverish work, sifting through the wreckage of the dead Keeper Ring's memory. There had to be clues. There had to be a way to get the Link back.

If there was not, the Sphere was doomed. For its first enemy would not stop at killing a single Keeper Ring.

Frank Barlow, lately known as Chelated Noisemaker Extreme, looked down at his instruments, and out the porthole at the Moonpoint singularity. Suddenly there was no activity. The whole farging thing had shut down. As best he could tell with low-power, low-sensitivity, jury-rigged sensors, there was no gravity modulation going on at all. The Ring had stopped controlling the Moonpoint black hole, and the wormhole wasn't there anymore.

Somehow, the folks back in the Solar System had killed the Moonpoint Ring.

He sat there, staring at nothing, for a long time. Better call Ohio, even if he was busy as hell trying to save the hab, now that the COREs had probably made resupply from Earth impossible. Now NaPurHab would have to be self sufficient, or die.

He pressed down the intercom key. "Ohio, this is Frank," he said. "Something's happened down here."

"What's that?" Ohio's voice asked.

Frank Barlow licked his lips, looked again at the dead and silent instruments, and told Ohio Template Windbag what all of Earth was about to find out.

"Well, Walter," he said. "All of a sudden, it looks like we're on our own."

CHAPTER TWENTY-SIX

◇

Before the Hunt

THE COMMAND TO DIE SPREAD OUT FROM THE MOON, coursing across the Solar System in all directions. On Venus, on Mars, on Mercury and in the Asteroid Belt, on the satellites of Jupiter and Saturn and Uranus, the Landers heard—and stopped.

The spin storms of Jupiter faded away, the core-matter volcanoes on Venus and Mercury thundered to a halt, the surface strippers that had mauled Mars so badly stopped their deadly upblasts of rock and stone. The orbiting Landers, busily preparing to process the wreckage of worlds into usable form, shut down before they had properly begun. All the half-living, half-machine Landers stuttered to a halt.

The dust clouds faded from the skies of Port Viking. The domed cities of the gas-giant satellites peeked out from the rubble that surrounded them, and discovered they were still alive. VISOR coursed over a planet no longer in torment.

But the price was high. For no one had made the slightest progress in physically locating the Multisystem

Without the Keeper Ring and Caller Ring, Earth was lost, utterly lost amid all the myriad suns.

Sleep had come at last. Fitful, fearful, unsettled, but sleep, a long enough rest to do some good—and a chance for the nightmares to work themselves out. Sleep and then awakening. Simon and Larry sat in the wardroom, lingering over coffee, happy at least to be alive. The viewscreen was on, and the stars shone in at the breakfast table.

"Half a loaf," Simon said. "We are alive, and Earth is alive—but we are lost to each other. I was wrong to call that a disaster, Larry. Even if we never do find each other, at least we survived, Earth and the Solar System. We'll be all right. *They'll* be all right."

"Do you really think so?" Larry asked.

Raphael shrugged. For some reason, even after the long nightmare just past, he felt good this morning. Tomorrow or the next day would be time enough for survivor guilt. Right now, against huge odds, he, the Solar System, and the Earth had made it through the night alive. That was reason enough to celebrate. "I don't see why not. The planet itself is intact, its climate is stable. Only human technology was damaged in the jump—and our friends were recovering from that even before we lost contact. They have blue skies, green grass, the oceans, the forests. Why wouldn't they be all right?

"True, they don't have spaceflight anymore, thanks to those CORE devices ready to shoot down anything that flies. But the Naked Purple Habitat's orbiting the Moonpoint singularity, and the *Terra Nova* is somewhere out in the Multisystem. That's two spaceside assets. There should be a lot to learn about the Multisystem, the domain of the Sphere from deep space. They have a few cards to play.''

"I suppose. But what really scares me is that I've gotten the Dyson Sphere's attention," Larry said. "We've had a real blessing in disguise all this time: the Sphere, *all* the Charonians, were utterly unaware of human beings. But they'll have to take notice of someone stealing a whole solar system out from under them, and killing all their operatives here. I may very well have made the Charonians into a desperate enemy."

Simon Raphael looked startled. "I can see them as an enemy. But why do you call them desperate?"

Larry hesitated for a moment. "There's that one image I can't get out of my mind, that picture of the shattered sphere. I don't think the Sphere just *wanted* the Solar System. I think it *needed* it. And still does. As a refuge, as a hiding place, or maybe as a diversion, a decoy. I don't know. We don't know what that picture of the shattered sphere means, but we do know that the moment the Lunar Wheel received it, every Charonian in the Solar System went into panic overdrive.

"And there's the way all the Charonians hid themselves in the Solar System. Think about that. Somehow we all took it for granted, never really considered that they had to be hiding *from* somebody. The Landers, disguised as asteroids, as comets in the Oort Cloud. Think about the way the Lunar Wheel was dug into the Moon. My God, what *is* there out there powerful enough to smash open a Dyson Sphere, frightening enough to scare something the size of the *Lunar Wheel* into hiding?"

Larry shrugged. "We can give it a name, I suppose. I've been thinking of it as the Sphere Cracker. But *what is it*? What does it want? Maybe it hunts for Dyson Spheres the way the Charonians hunt for life-bearing planets. And maybe the Earth's Dyson Sphere is just about ready to be cracked open. What happens to Earth then? Imagine what would happen to the Multisystem if the Sphere weren't there to keep the orbits stable.''

Larry stopped, and stared out the viewscreen. The Ring of Charon wheeled sedately through the darkness, as if nothing in the Universe had ever gone wrong, or ever could. At last he spoke again. ''I don't think Earth is going to be safe for very long at all. Not with a Dyson Sphere saving it for use as a breeding cage. Not with a Sphere Cracker out tracking down the Sphere.''

''Safe,'' Simon said. ''When have any of us ever been truly safe? Sometimes we've had the *illusion* of safety, but there's always been something out there that could kill us. Name one person who's ever lived through being alive.''

Larry smiled at the old joke, but then the sadness overtook him again, a wave of homesickness swept through him. Could it truly be that he would never see Earth, see *home*, again? ''Will we ever find them again, Simon? We lost Earth once, and had to hunt for it through the wormhole. Now we have to hunt for it again, but working blind. Can we find it this time, with the Lunar Wheel dead?''

Simon smiled gently, and nodded. ''I think so. We know about wormholes, and Dyson Spheres, and we've got a Solar System full of alien technology to pick through. There must be *some* clue somewhere, buried in all those memory stores. And Earth will be looking for us, as well. We'll find each other. In a week, or a lifetime, or a millennium.''

Larry smiled at last, and looked out the viewport, out past the Ring of Charon that had destroyed—and then rescued—so much. Past the invisible Plutopoint black hole imprisoned in the Ring's centerpoint, past the wreckage of alien invaders strewn across the Solar System, past the battered planets shrouded in dust and his far-scattered friends picking their ways out of the rubble, past the ghosts of the dead lost in this fight, past the far-off gleam of the loving Sun that the Charonians had sought to entomb in a new Dyson Sphere—past all fear to the clean, clean stars.

Gravity power and wormhole links. *Those* were the keys to the stars—and Earth was out there somewhere, waiting for the good people of the Solar System to put that key to the lock and find them.

Gravity power, wormholes, the simple knowledge that intelligent life had once existed elsewhere, even if it were now mutated into something strange and incomprehensible. The sure knowledge that the stars *were* reachable. They had learned a great deal from their tormentors, back here in the wounded wreck of the Solar System. And there was a great deal more to learn, locked in the broken machines and dead servants of the enemy.

And what of the Earth, surrounded by the wonders of the Multisystem, with who knows how many habitable worlds just out of reach? The knowledge Earth and *Terra Nova* might find was limitless.

For there must be *other* wormholes in the Multisystem, other links to other multisystems, links to ancestors and relatives of this Sphere, reaching in all directions of space, back to every place the Charonians had journeyed in uncounted millions of years.

Look at it that way, look at it the *right* way, and humanity was not merely clinging to life, battling for survival, but quite accidentally poised for new and great adventures, both here and on the lost Earth.

Today was for rest.

Tomorrow the Hunt for Earth could begin.

THE END

A note on Charonian terminology

The Charonians do not use language in the human sense, but instead rely almost entirely on visualized imagery for communication and instruction. (As they do not use language, there is some legitimate question as to whether their visualizations can be considered thought at all.) The portions of the book described as seen by Charonians are therefore not in any sense translations, but human-style verbal labels of convenience on the visual images processed or transmitted by the Charonians.

A Note on Naked Purple terms, names, and usages

Each Person in the Naked Purple community earns a name, which is in large part determined by his or her work status and personal attributes. Names shift and change over time.

Productive work of any type is seen as a necessary evil to be discouraged, and ultimately stamped out altogether. How society will function when that is achieved has never been made clear. Language is seen as the direct tool of ideology, and thus there is a constant search for better or more socially correct ways to say things. Puns and combined meanings, particularly those that take the wind out of a self-important person or activity are highly thought of. That such constructions, and the emphasis upon them, frequently become self-important themselves merely adds to the tension of the concept. Purity of expression is valued over clarity, with the result that much Naked Purple prose and speech is almost undecipherable. Incomprehensibility itself is highly regarded. Furthermore, many names and terms are assigned ironically.

Glossary

Amalgam Creature. A merged group of several Landers. See *Lander*.

Autocrat of Ceres. The absolute ruler of the largest asteroid, and the only effective instrumentality of law or justice in the Belt Community. The Autocrat's reputation for draconian justice serves to prevent most from daring his wrath.

Barycenter. The center of gravity for any orbiting system; the point around which two bodies in an orbital relationship revolve. In most systems, for example the Sun-Mars system, or the old Earth-Moon system, the larger body contains such a large fraction of the system's mass that the barycenter is actually inside the large body. In the case of more nearly equal masses, for example Pluto-Charon, the barycenter can be a point in open space between the two masses.

Belt Community. A loose political association of the larger and more sensible governments in the remarkably disorganized Asteroid Belt.

Biosphere. That hollow sphere of space around a star in which a life-bearing planet can survive. Although other variables are involved, the basic constraint is simple: inside a biosphere, solar radiation is neither too strong or too weak, and Earthlike temperatures are possible.

Caller, Caller Ring. Charonian term for the object (or possibly life-form) exemplified by the Lunar Wheel.

This form is extremely similar to a *Keeper Ring* such as the *Moonpoint Ring*.

Carrier bug. One of the lowest-level Charonian type, capable of only the simplest fetch-and-carry duties. Alternatively, any of the low-level Charonian types.

Central City. The principal city and capital of the Lunar Republic. Formerly called Central Colony.

Charonians. Named for the Ring of Charon, the hypothetical aliens controlling the massive machines discovered after the Earth's vanishment.

Conner. A citizen of the Lunar Republic. Derived from *colonist* and/or *con artist*, in the days when Conners were dismissed as both. Previously a pejorative term, now generally accepted.

COREs, Close-Orbiting Radio Emitters. Any of a large number of identical objects in various orbits around all the worlds of the Multisystem. Their powerful radio signals—emitted over a wide spectrum of frequencies—serve as an effective jamming mechanism.

Dyson Sphere. A huge sphere built entirely around a star, so as to provide huge surface area (hundreds of billions times the surface area of Earth) and/or to capture all of the star's power. Named for twentieth-century scientist Freeman Dyson.

Earthpoint. That point in space, relative to the Moon and the rest of the Solar System, where the Earth once was. The Earthpoint black hole, also known as the Earthpoint singularity or wormhole, now occupies this space. See *Moonpoint*.

Event Horizon. The minimum distance from a black hole required before time and/or light can escape—or, to put it another way, the minimum distance required before events are possible. The stronger a gravity field, the slower time moves and the more light is redshifted. If the field is strong enough, time and light are slowed to a complete stop. Also defined as the point where the local escape velocity equals the speed of light.

Event Radius. The distance, usually measured in light-minutes or light-hours, between two points. The event radius is so called because no event can have any effect at a given distance until light (or radio waves or other electromagnetic energy) has had time to cross that distance. Referred to as a "radius" because light expands out spherically. Not related to *Event Horizon*.

Gee-point object. Any fairly small object emitting modulated gravity power. The term is applied generally not only to Landers, but also to the large objects of similar behavior appearing through the Earthpoint wormhole. See *Lander* and *Worldeater*.

Graser. *Gr*avity *laser*: a focused beam of gravity power.

Heritage Memory. Charonian term for the memories of previous generations of Charonians, together with the experiences of other members of the current generation, downloaded and stored in a Charonian's memory for reference. Each form of Charonian receives an edited subset of the mass memory appropriate to its needs.

K-Crash, Knowledge Crash. While a massive downturn in Earth's economy has certainly taken place, no one is certain that it has been caused by a surfeit of information, as suggested in the K-Crash theory. According to the K-Crash idea, Earth's economy reached the point where the simplest decisions could not be made without massive reference to the various databases. Many jobs became so complex that the training for them could take an entire lifetime.

Keeper, Keeper Ring. Charonian term for the Moonpoint Ring, and for the similar objects that orbit most of the Multisystem's worlds.

Lander. Huge creatures, long hidden in dormant stages inside asteroids, which move through space under broadcasted gravity power radiated by the Lunar

Wheel. Once at their destination in orbit or on the surface of a target world, they merge themselves into larger amalgam creatures of incredible power. See *Worldeater* and *Gee-Point Object*.

Lifecode. DNA, or any extraterrestrial equivalent of DNA; thus, any means of passing and storing an instruction set for a making a life-form.

Lunar Wheel. A massive Charonian structure, a huge toroid deep inside the Moon. It circles the Moon's core and is aligned precisely with the border between the lunar Nearside and Farside. Known to Charonians as a *Caller Ring*.

Moonpoint. That point in space, relative to Earth, that occupies the space where the Moon once was. The Moonpoint Ring, a massive gravity generator, holds the space now, with the Moonpoint end of the Earth–Solar System wormhole at its center. See *Earthpoint* and *Keeper*.

Multisystem. The huge artificial stellar system in which the Earth was placed. At its center is the *Dyson Sphere*. It includes at least eight G-class stars, around each of which large numbers of life-bearing planets orbit.

Naked Purple Movement. One of a number of odd social and political movements. Also known as the Pointless Cause. Its belief structure is kept deliberately obscure and conflicted. The movement owns the NaPurHab habitat and Tycho Purple Penal on the Moon.

NaPurHab, Naked Purple Habitat. A large and rather shabby orbiting habitat owned and populated by the Naked Purple Movement. As the book opens, it is in a figure-eight orbit between Earth and the Moon. Population: 10,000.

Observer. Charonian term for a semidormant stage of the *Caller Ring* type. See *Lunar Wheel*.

Port Viking. Capital and principal city of Mars.

Rabbit Hole. The vertical shaft leading from the Lunar North Pole to the Lunar Wheel, many kilometers below the surface.

Ring of Charon. A huge human-made gravity research tool, orbiting Charon, Pluto's Moon. In essence, an enormous particle accelerator.

Saint Anthony. The automated relay probe dropped through the Earthpoint–Moonpoint wormhole. Named for the patron saint of lost objects.

Scorpion, scorp. A fairly sophisticated Charonian type, capable of dealing (though not necessarily well) with unexpected situations. The term is applied not only to the scorpion-shaped Charonians, but to all creatures of its approximate ability.

Seedship. A robot starship that carries fertilized ova, or the equivalent, to a new planet around a new star. The seedship lands, grows the ova to adulthood, and thus colonizes a new star system without having to transport a complex life-support system.

Settlement Worlds. Essentially, all the real estate outside the Earth-Moon system. Likewise refers to the now-moribund political alliance of those worlds in opposition to Earth's rather arrogant policies of the previous century.

Shepherd. The Charonian term for *CORE.*

Sphere. See *Dyson Sphere.*

Spin-storms. Artificial storms, created by gas-giant-breed Worldeaters, resembling hurricanes or tornadoes. They are used to pump atmosphere off the larger planets.

SubBubble. *Sub*surface *bubble*: a standard type of Lunar construction that consists of a large excavation under the Lunar surface. A subbubble is usually formed by melting an area of subsurface rock and then placing the interior under pressure. Much of Central City is composed of interconnected subbubbles.

Sunstar. The star in the Multisystem around which the Earth orbits.

Teleoperator, T.O. A remote-control device, generally resembling a humanoid robot but without a robot's capacity for independent action. A T.O. is controlled by a human operator working in a control harness at a remote location. The control harness completely surrounds the operator and provides her or him with the sensory reactions—sight, hearing, and touch—experienced by the T.O. Servos in the controller operate the T.O. so that if, for example, the operator moves her finger, the T.O. moves its finger. As is the case with most Virtual Reality devices, the sensations reported by the T.O. to the operator can seem extremely real. Virtual Reality stigmata—such as cuts and bruises on the operator corresponding to damage on the T.O.—are not unknown. See *Virtual Reality.*

Terra Nova. A huge multigenerational starship mothballed in Earth orbit, a victim of the K-Crash.

UNLAC, United Nations Lunar Administration Commission. The old colonial power on the Moon, overthrown a century ago.

VBH, Virtual Black Hole. Currently a theoretical possibility only. In concept, a VBH is a formed by an artificial massless gravity source so tightly focused that a microscopic black hole forms. If a VBH of a sufficient gravity gradient survives long enough in the presence of sufficient mass, it should be able to absorb that mass and thus become self-sustaining.

Virtual Reality. The general term applied to any technology that makes a nonlocal environment (real or imaginary) seem utterly real to an observer-participant. In most VR systems, at least vision and hearing are supported with sufficient quality to seem real. Often tactile sensations are supported as well. Typically, the participant will be able to manipulate the simulated environment in some way, through a remote control or sensor glove. See *Teleoperator.*

VISOR, Venus Initial Station for Operational Research. An orbital facility planned as the headquarters for the terraforming of Venus. The facility is expected to be mothballed shortly, thanks to the financial backlash of the K-Crash.

Von Neumann Cyborg Cluster. A partially living von Neumann system. Such a cluster might, for example, include a life-form genetically programmed to build *seedships*. The life-forms raised by the seedship would be bred to build more seedships and to deposit fertilized ova aboard the ships.

Von Neumann Machine. Any machine that can precisely duplicate itself. A Swiss army knife that included a Swiss-army-knife-making attachment would be a von Neumann machine.

Von Neumann Tour. A star travel technique in which a von Neumann ship travels to a new star system and duplicates itself a few hundred times, sending each of its replicates out to travel to new star systems.

Worldeater. The Charonian term for the massive life-form known to humans as *Landers.*

Wormhole. A link between two points in space, formed by creating two identically tuned black holes. The wormhole in effect renders the two points contiguous across a flat plane, no matter how distant they actually are from each other.

The Life Cycle of the Charonians

The Charonians are a spacefaring life-form, a multi-species comprising ten or twenty widely different species, devices, and robotic constructs. The biological components of the system may at one time have been "intelligent," as the term is usually understood by humans, but no longer are. Charonians are capable of problem solving, task ordering, directed research, synthesis, but are very weak in what humans would regard as creative or independent thought. They can think of *how* to do things—how to work around problems, for example. They are not as good at thinking of *what* to do, or why. They work in large part by rote. In the old-fashioned phrase, they are hard-wired, relying on a communal heritage memory of the experiences of previous generations.

It is likely the present-day Charonians started out as seedships for a colonization venture, bearing the original biological Charonians to new homes in the sky, but either by ill chance or deliberate decision on the part of the robotic guardians of the germ plasm, things changed.

The machine-intelligent components of the system redesigned the system, repeatedly modifying both themselves and the genes of the living components. The result: the Charonians have become a form of von Neumann machine, capable of endlessly replicating themselves.

Humans have spent lifetimes studying the idea of von Neumann machines, but the concept, however appealing, has always been out of reach because the cost and engineering challenges were too great. No one ever considered a simple, elegant solution to the problem: that *life* is a von Neumann machine. We humans can endlessly duplicate ourselves. If our DNA were modified so that we instinctively built a certain type of spacecraft, and that spacecraft automatically carried our germ plasm to another world, then that would be a von Neumann. It is, after all, not the machine itself that must be duplicated and spread across the galaxy for the idea to work, but the *plans* for the machine.

Several types of life-form and robot compose the Charonian multispecies. The living and robotic components rely on each other in the processes of reproduction and replication. Neither the biotic nor the mechanical Charonians could survive without the other.

The Charonians have proved that faster-than-light travel is possible, but only between points linked by black hole transit pairs and the "wormhole" connecting the transit pair. Natural black holes do not work in wormhole systems—a spacefarer must build his own. Therefore, before faster-than-light travel between two stars is possible, sublightspeed vehicles must move between the two stars, building black holes on arrival at the star to be visited. Unfortunately, a device the size of the Ring of Charon is required to form a black hole.

The Stages of the Charonian Life-Robotic Cycle

Robot spacecraft called seedships are grown and manufactured by Dyson Spheres. Each seedship leaves its home Sphere, carrying the location of its home Sphere in its heritage memory.

The seedships travel at sublightspeed out from the Dyson Spheres and move between the stars, searching for life-bearing planets. When appropriate planets are found, the seedships land. They gather needed chemicals and compounds, and clone the first living stage in the cycle, which can be thought of as larvae. With the help of the larvae, the seedship constructs simple spacecraft.

The larvae are large creatures at birth (or, more accurately at decanting), the smallest the size of an elephant. They grow rapidly, and later develop into various specialized types. By virtue of their great size and rapid growth, they can quickly wreck the biosphere of a life-bearing world. Their behavior is in large part hard-wired, in some part controlled by the seedship, but in small part volitional. The first few generations of the creatures simply breed as normal male-female pairs, bearing about six to eight offspring per mating. As they mature, most of these larvae are set to work building additional spacecraft, under the guidance of the seedships. Generally, the seedships are cannibalized for parts long before the larvae are ready to leave the planet.

Typically, the invasion of the larvae results in major depopulations and mass extinctions, combined with serious climatic and ecological damage.

Powered by gravitics, the spacecraft built by the larvae

lift into space—with luck, before the planet's ecosphere is utterly ruined. With one larva aboard each vehicle, the spacecraft can be compared to hermit crab shells—temporary homes to be used as long as they fit. If the larva dies or grows too large for the craft, the vehicle will be cannibalized for parts. Nine-tenths of the larvae die upon arrival in space. Their corpses serve as sustenance for the survivors.

Each surviving larva battles it out with its rivals to amass as many of the dead bodies and abandoned spacecraft as possible. Eventually, thirty or forty thousand massive creatures, in the pupa phase, are left. Each consists of the components of several derelict spacecraft and one individual pupa that has fed on the bodies of its littermates. Ship and creature merge with each other and become indistinguishable. Each is the size of a small asteroid, being several kilometers across with proportionate mass.

One or two pupae land on the nearest non-life-bearing world and burrow into it. Should a pupa survive this effort, the machine parts of the creature will build and breed a Caller Ring. A Caller Ring is buried deep in the Earth's Moon.

However, most pupae enter a chrysalis phase, becoming dormant, their outer skins hardening into the consistency of rock. Thus, not only are they the size of asteroids, they precisely resemble them. These creatures, which become Worldeaters, go into hiding. In Earth's Solar System, they hid in the Asteroid Belt and the Oort Cloud. At this stage, all the Charonian creatures, both living and robotic, are dormant, waiting for a signal.

A signal to the Caller Ring stimulates a new phase of great activity. The Caller Ring can be activated in one of two ways:

by signal from the home Dyson Sphere, indicating that the Sphere has a sufficient surplus of energy to assist in the construction of a daughter sphere; or,

by outside interference: pulsed gravity waves generated by some other cause—for example, gravity experiments performed by an intelligent race.

When the Caller Ring detects a burst of controlled gravitic energy, it performs its basic function—opening a gravitic contact, a Virtual Black Hole transit pair, linking it to its home Dyson Sphere. The Caller Ring then sends a pulsed-gravity-wave signal to the Worldeater chrysalides sleeping in the star system.

Linked to the home Dyson Sphere, the Caller Ring attempts to get the life-bearing world out of harm's way by shifting it to the artificial star system surrounding the home Sphere. If the Sphere initiated the call, or if it has at least some surplus of energy available, it permits the transit to take place. Earth's sudden arrival is not the first unplanned grab of a world—the Dyson Sphere knows how to handle such things.

As soon as possible, the Sphere shifts an Anchor black hole through the temporary Virtual Black Hole, providing a more powerful and stable link to the home Sphere.

The Multisystem of habitable worlds orbiting the home Dyson Sphere can be thought of as a field lying fallow. The Charonians accumulate life-supporting planets that can be sent to where they are needed.

If a seedship has visited several unsuitable solar systems and is near the end of its operational life when it arrives at yet another lifeless system, it can call the home Dyson Sphere and give up the last of its energy to have one of the stockpiled worlds shifted to an otherwise suitable solar system. Replaced by a new seedship shifted in with the new world, the life cycle can then proceed.

The Dyson Sphere begins to beam energy through the

Caller Ring. The awakening chrysalides emerge from their long sleep as adult Worldeaters. Their robotic components link with the Caller Ring and begin to absorb power. The Worldeaters head toward the major worlds of the solar system and start ripping them to shreds, forming them into the materials needed to form a new Dyson Sphere. Their work can take hundreds or thousands of years, but at its end, a new Sphere is ready, able to breed and build its own seedships and begin construction of its own empire of captive worlds.